18 Thoughts

Jamie Ayres

A Division of **Whampa, LLC**
P.O. Box 2160
Reston, VA 20195
Tel/Fax: 800-998-2509
http://curiosityquills.com

© 2015 **Jamie Ayres**
http://jamieayres.com

ISBN 978-1-62007-832-7 (ebook)
ISBN 978-1-62007-833-4 (paperback)
ISBN 978-1-62007-834-1 (hardcover)

To Dan, Kaylee, and Ashley, because I saved the best for last.

Thank you for my continuing education of Star Wars.

I wouldn't trade you for all the Starbucks frappuccinos and cake pops in the world.

xoxo

TABLE OF CONTENTS

BEFORE

Riel looked at the three of us. "Now that we've said our goodbyes, it's time to get going. I have an appointment at the Throne after this."

Conner turned to Nate, a struggle to remain civil clear on his face. "I'd say it was nice to meet you, but—"

"Oh, save it." Riel scowled at him. "Your paths will cross again soon."

Nate nodded. "And FYI, I'm not giving up. May the best man win."

And right then, I knew I had problems. My best friend was in love with me and counted my boyfriend as his enemy. Sam would still be on the loose somewhere on Earth, and I had a feeling he'd move close to Grand Haven so he could torture me for getting him kicked out of the Underworld. Plus, Nate would have some sort of side effect that made even Riel chuckle with delight.

Problems for sure. If being a spirit guide didn't almost kill me, the drama that lay ahead for my senior year of high school just might. But the thought that I even had a senior year of high school to look forward to made any possible drama seem so beyond *worth it*.

Riel gathered us in his arms and prayed in a tongue I didn't recognize.

I decided I should end my journey the same way I started, with a prayer. Except this time, I wasn't ready to die. I was ready to live.

PROLOGUE

"Every heart sings a song incomplete,
until another heart whispers back."

—Plato

Nate

It took one glance away from the road, one look at the guy racing me, one second of distraction… I tried to brake. Braking too late, braking too hard as I groped for the wheel to redirect my path. The front driver's side of my car collided with his passenger's side, metal crunching against metal. My door crushed inward, and jagged steel punctured my leg. Blood sprayed upward and to the side, coating the crumpled door in new paint. Like a bucking horse, the rear of my car lifted high off the ground.

I lurched upward with the swaying of the vehicle's weight.

My body off the seat.

Feet ripped from my tightly laced Converse sneakers.

Knees pressed against the underbelly of the dashboard.

Chest above the steering column, the back of my head hitting the sun visor.

Then I came back down with the vehicle, the front of my head slamming against the steering wheel.

Blood trickling down my forehead as if this moment were in slow motion when all I wanted was for it to be over.

Suddenly, the airbag deployed and punched me in the face, and I thought I'd slip into unconsciousness, a welcome relief. But the sun glared off the hood off the car, awakening me. My eyes bulged, refusing to blink; my dry throat hitched with an inability to scream.

And I couldn't breathe, couldn't breathe, couldn't breathe.

The brake pedal sheared off the floorboard.

Definitely too late to brake now.

The car, still moving forward with a force more powerful than gravity, veered off the side of the road.

For one split second, the feeling of freedom bewitched me, the weight of the world disappearing as my car and I took flight. I'd always dreamed of flying, but not like this. I blinked. Then I wanted to cover my face, to place my fists over my eyes so I wouldn't see green streaks through the glass, trees waving to me in my peripheral vision as I tumbled and spun with the car. But I couldn't. Because my fear-frozen hands were occupied, bending the plastic and steel frame of the steering wheel under my terrified death grip as I held on with everything I had. If I let go, I was a goner for sure. I wondered if I was a goner regardless. Would my life flash before my eyes any second now? A primal scream escaped my lips, my uncontrollable paralysis disappearing, but then I froze at the thought of being shocked into silence again. Because I needed to do something, do something, do something. Then the car

made a touchdown,

spiking in celebration,

tearing hinges,

slamming on its side,

flipping,

soaring,

(How was this happening? Was my car really as light as a football?)

BAM!

And the doors sprung open, the car screaming that it was done.

But I wasn't.

In one last convulsion, the seat rammed forward with the force of the landing, ejecting me from my seat. I smashed into the windshield, headfirst. A shattering of glass pierced my whole body in the process, and for the second time today, I was flying, all on my own. As I sailed through the air, I felt like vomiting, but blood leaped from my mouth instead. I spied the car still rolling, and then I squeezed my eyes shut. Shock froze my heart, made it stop and go to sleep.

Then the asphalt slapped me awake.

I imagined this was what jumping to your death from a tall building felt like. I tumbled across the pavement and landed facedown in a heap of mud, grass, weeds, rocks. I opened my eyes timidly and stared down at the blood surrounding me. My stomach turned, and I quickly averted my gaze. I needed to focus my mind on anything besides the sight of my blood. I inhaled deeply, hoping to center myself. The field where I landed smelled of smoke, metal, hay, and if I didn't know any better, freshly turned graves. I sighed. If anything, the scents made my panic worse. I glanced around anxiously, searching for something, for anything that could help me.

Then I saw it: a shiny black spider hung upside down from her carefully crafted web, and she had a red hourglass mark on the underneath of her abdomen. I knew that sign. My time was up. For a brief moment, I wanted to laugh at how an hourglass is filled with sand and how my body felt full of sand, weighted down. My head spilled grains of fear. Time was running out. A small leg of the spider touched my hand, not threateningly, but reminding me to move. Do something.

But I couldn't move, couldn't scream. So I shifted my gaze instead, forcing myself to take in the scene. A mistake. My blood oozed out of my body faster than a waterfall. The thought made me think of when I visited Ruby Falls in Tennessee one summer. The 145-foot high waterfall was 1120 feet underground, and on our tour, the guide said they still didn't know where the source of water came from. The memory seemed odd at a time like this, but I didn't know the source of where all my blood came from, either. Water slipped down my cheeks, completing the metaphor.

I blinked away the tears and peered toward the smoke. Dad's car looked like one giant, crushed soda can, the wheels still spinning. Suddenly, the vehicle burst into flames. My ejection was a blessing and a curse.

Do I still want to live? If I survived, I doubted my life would ever be the same.

My thoughts turned to Bo, the kid racing me.

Where is he, where is he, where is he? Please, God, let him be okay.

I prayed he wore his seat belt.

I hadn't meant to forget that safety feature when I decided to drag race another student home from school today. Suffice it to say, I wasn't in the right frame of mind for making wise decisions. Being forced to move to a small town three hours away the summer before my senior year sucked, but this? A gazillion times worse. If I didn't die, my parents just might kill me.

I tried getting up to look for him but winced instead. The shock of the accident receded, and panic set in with the pain, rifling through me now. Every part of me hurt. *My nose must be broken. Bones must be broken, lots of them.* I cried out as if my heart had broken, too.

How long will it be until I bleed to death? I looked at my skin, now a red bodysuit, patches of it missing, ripped off by the pavement. Blood covered every single inch of my arms, the scrapes visible through my tattered shirt. I couldn't get a good view of my legs, but I sensed more blood oozing out there, gaining speed like the car had before I wrecked. I could *feel* that my body was shattered, *feel* wetness on my stomach. Laughed at the absurdity of it all. I spilled my guts to Lindsey, my girlfriend, while we ate ice cream last night, our last date. Now I *literally* spilled my guts. *God, I'm such an idiot!*

I cried, wanting to scream for anyone to help, but no sound came. No one came. We were on a deserted highway. No cars rushed past; no screeching sirens heralded our rescue. Instead, wild sunflowers towered like angels, their heads nodding like a cheerful welcoming committee to the afterlife. My heart thudded dully in my aching chest. Only wheezing breaths now. Head spinning. A sour taste in my mouth. Tears behind my closing eyelids. A painful lump in my throat around my bobbing Adam's apple.

Then a sharp intake of breath.

Fear didn't grip me. Fear moved me.

Told me to *do something.*

Using all my strength, I slid my hand into my jeans pocket, praying my cell phone hadn't fallen out or broken into a million pieces. Trembling, I dialed 9-1-1. When the operator asked what my emergency was, I opened my mouth to speak but gagged on the words instead. I couldn't remember who I was, or why I called, or anything.

Frozen, I focused on the fluffy clouds dotting the perfect blue sky, one looking eerily like an angel stretching his hands toward me. A light radiating from the strange cloud blinded me. I squinted and gritted my teeth, fighting a wave of dizziness. Warm blades of grass surrounding my pounding head pressed against my face. Time slowed, and darkness closed in on me like the heavy curtains signaling the end of a performance. I pulled in a fragile breath, praying it wouldn't be my last but thinking maybe it'd be easier if it was.

A TV played quietly in the corner of my hospital room… not that it mattered, since I couldn't *see* the screen. Doc said an optic nerve slammed against my brain in the car accident, resulting in some serious damage. The doctors thought my loss of vision to be temporary, but after five full days of total darkness, I was losing hope fast.

Despite all my injuries, I'd taken a three-hour ambulance ride to Grand Haven today because Dad had to start work at his new job here. Apparently, I couldn't screw up anything else for him.

Day one of being stuck in North Ottawa Community Hospital, and time slowed to a crawl. My drag racing earned me a total of twenty-four stitches across my left leg and abdomen, staples in the top of my head, a broken nose and left arm, temporary blindness—*fingers crossed*—a major blood transfusion, internal injuries that included a battered liver and spleen, eight broken ribs, and deep bruises and cuts covering the entire length of my body.

On top of all that, they'd set me up in a room with some kid who'd been in a coma for two months, so I had nothing to watch and nobody to talk to. Mom did her best to keep me company, but the way I constantly felt her swarming my bed made me nervous. Claiming fatigue, I encouraged her to go set up our new house while I rested. Now, I shoveled the last bite of bland chicken and stale bread into my mouth, trying not to vomit. This was my first taste of real food, if you could call it that, in five days. Up until now, all I had had were ice chips following my emergency surgery, and my IV of course. Already I'd lost eleven pounds. I hated to think of how much weight I'd lose in muscle while wasting away in this hospital room for the next month or so. Inhaling deeply, I hoped to calm myself, but the combo of disinfectant in the air and the way my stitches pulled along my abdomen with the breath almost caused me to vomit all over again.

I heard the door swoosh open.

"Checking in on me already? I think my fever's gone down a bit now."

Someone yelped in a high-pitched voice. "Oh, sorry. I didn't realize Conner had a new roommate." A girl.

Oh my gosh. New roomie is h-o-t, even with his broken nose all bandaged up.

Hot? "Are you talking about me?"

"Huh? Yes, you're Conner's new roommate, I guess?" *Hot? What am I even thinking? My best friend is in a coma! Who cares about Mr. Hottie? He's probably gay anyway. The good-looking ones always are. Ugh, what's wrong with me these days? I like Conner.*

Sounds like somebody needed a Valium. "Whoa, take it easy. You okay?"

She cleared her throat. "Um, yeah."

I forced myself to smile, groping for the button on the side of my bed to sit all the way up, in case I needed to make a run for it. "Sorry, I thought you were my mom coming in. I'm Nate, new in town. They transferred me to this hospital today."

Nate, that has a nice ring to it. "Nice to meet you. I'm Olga."

She sounded about my age. I wondered if she was as pretty as she sounded. "Olga has a nice ring to it, too. I'd shake your hand, but obviously, I can't see a thing with these bandages. I've got this temporary blindness thing going on right now."

And that would be why he's still talking to me. Oh well, bonus! I can stare at him all day, and he won't even know I'm a creeper! I hope he can't hear my heart pounding. Gah! Shut up, Olga. You love Conner, remember? "Wow, that… stinks."

Okay, this girl was kind of… different.

"Pretty much sums up the situation. I drag raced another kid on my way home from the last day of school. I'm the one who wasn't wearing a seat belt and flew through my windshield, but the other kid is the one who died. Can you believe that twist of fate?"

I stared into the darkness, trying not to be swallowed by it. If I hid behind my reckless attitude about Bo's death, then maybe I wouldn't feel like I died, too.

And I thought I had problems. "I'm sorry to hear that. Sounds like you're lucky to be alive."

"Am I?"

"Um, yes, I think so," she said, and I heard her scuff her shoes on the linoleum.

Everyone ignores me on a daily basis, but the one day, one day, I want to be left alone, the nurses give Conner Mr. Talkative as a roomie.

I laughed at the girl's honesty. "Sorry. My mom says I suffer from verbal diarrhea. But Helen Keller said character cannot be developed in ease and quiet. Only through experience of trial and suffering can the soul be strengthened, ambition inspired, and success achieved. Anyway, you probably want to visit with your friend. I'll shut up now."

"Um, yeah, thanks." *Who do you think you are anyway, the town troubadour?*

I let out another laugh. "Ha! That's a good one. Most people don't even know what that word means. You must've rocked the Verbal on your SAT."

Now she laughed, nervously.

"Huh? What word? Thanks?" *As if I don't get enough mocking at school already.*

"No, troubadour. Is Grand Haven looking for one of those? Because I had this street performing thing with a guy back home, something we liked to do for fun on the side."

The room dissolved into silence for a minute.

"I didn't *say* anything about a troubadour."

She said the words slowly, cautiously.

"Yes, you did. I heard you loud and clear, even if I can't see a thing. You're not one of those people who treat blind people like they're deaf, too, are you?"

I heard her drag a chair to her friend's bedside. I felt her looking at me even though I couldn't see her.

"Sorry, I didn't realize I said that out loud. That sailboat boom must've hit my head harder than I thought. I've been in such a daze these past two months; I can't tell if it's sadness over Conner's coma, or if I've suffered permanent damage myself." *Just shut up, Olga! Or Mr. Hottie will suggest a nice padded room for you the next time the nurse walks in.*

Adrenaline pumped through my veins as she referred to me as Mr. Hottie again, and I decided to call her out on my new nickname, even though I knew I should keep my lips sealed. "You think I'm hot?"

"What? No!"

My body tensed. "So I'm ugly?"

"Uh." She cleared her throat. "I think I'm gonna read to Conner." I heard her fumbling through a bag.

"What did you bring to read?" For some reason, I couldn't stop talking to her.

"It's a novel by Timothy Zahn called *Dark Force Rising*. It's the second volume of a Star Wars trilogy he wrote. I finished reading volume one to Conner last week."

"Hmm, Star Wars, eh? I don't know why, but I pictured something completely different, like some bodice-ripping cover."

She snorted. "Oh great. So your first impression of me is I'm some bimbo incapable of stringing more than three words together without giggling?"

Although I have to admit, I'd pick up a bodice-ripping novel if this guy was half-naked on the cover. Oh my gosh, why did I think that? What's wrong with me? Conner's not even out of the woods yet, and I'm crushing on the new kid in town?

I expertly felt around for my glass of water and took a sip, trying to figure out this chick. "Why do you keep talking about me, to me, in the third person?"

"Huh?"

"You said you're crushing on the new kid in town, and I know I can't see and all, but the only new kid in here is me, right?"

She sucked in a breath. "What? Are you high on hospital meds or something? Is this some kind of twisted joke?"

Olga sounded as confused as I was.

I took a deep breath. "Possibly, and no."

"Look, I don't know why you're messing with me, but you're starting to freak me out."

Freaking her out? What did *I* do? Goose bumps broke out all over my body.

I angled my face in her direction and tried to sound sincere because it was clear to me now I dealt with one huge batch of crazysauce. "Sorry. I'll really shut up now."

Yeah, you do that, and don't forget to take your dose of Ritalin tonight! Oh great. I need to pee. But if I walk down the hall, there's the chance of running into Toe-touch Tammy visiting her dad, and I already had enough of her at school today. Thank God it was the last day of actual classes. Ugh, I should not have drunk that second cup of coffee from the hospital cafeteria on the way in. I really do need to get a grip on my caffeine addiction.

I shook my head in frustration. "Look, Olga. I'm all for shutting up, but that's gonna have to work both ways, all right?"

"What are you talking about? I haven't said a word." Her voice was quiet.

Why is it that if there are freaks within a mile radius, they find me? Maybe I should call a nurse to check on him. Maybe he needs a nice sponge bath to calm down. Baths always relax me. I could offer to help. Ugh! Seriously. What's wrong with me? Yes, he's hot, but he's also a freak. You're at the top of the class, Olga. Doesn't take a genius to figure out you should stay away from him. Read to Conner, and forget about Nate. Or maybe I should get another coffee first. I must be suffering from sugar withdrawal. That's why I'm having all these thoughts. Or maybe I need therapy like Mom suggested.

I placed my hands over my ears, longing for the hours of quiet boredom I had all day. The walls closed in on me, the room getting smaller by the second. "Go to therapy, visit Conner, drink some coffee, or go to the bathroom. Whatever you do, try to shut up for like two seconds. I can't believe I apologized to you for talking too much."

"Excuse me?" She sucked in a deep breath but hesitated before saying anything else for a few seconds, and I basked in the silence. "Do you need me to get a doctor for you? Or some pills?"

I crossed my arms over my chest, my stance of defiance, and winced from the pain instantly shooting up my ribs. "You're the one who needs pills! You never shut up!"

"I barely said a word." *I better get out of here.*

Was this girl sniffing too much glue or something? The sound of a chair scraping against the floor alerted me to the fact that she was getting ready to leave. I wished I could see her. "Oh, really? I suppose some other silly girl who sounds exactly like you rambled on about giving me a sponge bath?"

On second thought, maybe he needs an exorcist. Can he read my mind or something?

I couldn't believe what I was hearing! I laughed, bitterly, and winced in pain again. "Read your mind? Are you messing with me? Because I'll have you know teasing a blind man like that has got to be on a top-ten list somewhere for how you know you're a douche bag."

"I'm not messing with you! I didn't *say* anything about a sponge bath." *I thought it. I swear, this guy must be the devil or something. Get me out of here now! But is it safe for me to leave Conner unattended with this guy in the room? Maybe I should press the nurse call button. But what would I say? Maybe I am the one who's crazy. Maybe I'm imagining things. I'll call Mom when I'm done here, tell her I need to see that shrink after all.*

I didn't know if she spoke out loud and was still messing with me, or if I really could read her mind somehow. She sounded frightened, sincere, even if she was crazy. Before I could offer a reply, I heard the door swish open again.

"Ready to get those bandages off your eyes?" the doctor asked.

I sat up straighter in bed, too fast, and dizziness washed over me.

"Are you kidding? I've been counting the seconds."

And honestly, I couldn't wait to look this Olga chick in the eyes the next time we crossed paths and see if she really was as crazy as she sounded.

"Hello, Olga. How are you today?" my new doc asked, gently guiding my body into a wheelchair.

"Oh, you know, the usual. How's the fam doing? Did your wife like the book you bought for her birthday?" Her voice jumped, her words quick and high pitched.

I felt movement, and I only hoped the motion was taking me far away from the weird girl in my room.

"Yes, she loved it! Already read the whole thing, though, so I'll have to stop by the Bookman again soon for another recommendation."

"Any time, Joe. Take care."

Her words echoed off the walls, and I could tell we were passing right by her. I tried to ignore the goose bumps appearing all over my body, the feel of my heartbeat speeding up. Weird. Suddenly, I didn't want to leave

16

her anymore. The desire to reach out and touch her hit me harder than the impact of Bo's car, but I swallowed the urge.

"You, too. See you soon," Dr. Joe answered.

After I heard the door shut behind us, I asked, "What happened to that girl in there? She said something about a sailboat boom knocking her in the head."

I kept my voice calm, uninterested, even though I desperately wanted to know more about her.

"I don't know if that's any of your business."

I held up my hands in surrender. "Fine, but whatever happened, you might want to do a brain scan. She was acting really strange."

"Well, if I had to give a brain scan for every person who acted strangely, I'd be a very rich man."

"Aren't you?"

He chuckled. "Well, I guess that depends on what you define as rich."

"I define rich by counting all the things I have that money can't buy."

The doctor snorted. "That's a deep thought, kid."

I shrugged. "That's just how I roll."

I'd always been a thinker. Confucius, Plato, Aristotle… those were my heroes. One day, I hoped to join the ranks of the greatest philosophers of all time.

I heard doctors and nurses scurrying down the hall, probably with a crash cart, racing again to bring back someone from the dead. My last thought before Dr. Joe ushered me into a new room was I'm lucky to be alive, but I didn't quite believe those words yet.

PART ONE

"Love is not love
Which alters when it alteration finds,
Or bends with the remover to remove.
O no, it is an ever-fixed mark
That looks on tempests and is never shaken;
It is the star to every wand'ring bark,
Whose worth's unknown, although his height be taken."

Sonnet 116
from William Shakespeare, Shakespeare's Sonnets

CHAPTER ONE

*"The people you care about most in life
are taken from you too soon."*

—Nate's Thoughts

Olga

I sunk down into the chair after Dr. Joe and Nate left, sliding my glasses to my forehead so I could rub my eyes. *Pull yourself together.* When I looked at Conner, not thinking back to two months ago proved impossible. The image of ambulance doors swooshing open into chaos, the sound of my own moaning filling my ears until I spotted Conner, still unconscious, being unloaded from the ambulance behind me, made me shudder. Nurses in scrubs had hurried toward us, and I screamed for the ER doctors to take care of Conner first. Wet, burned clothing clung to his pale skin, and the fear I'd never get to touch him again beat against my mind like the violent thunderstorm that landed us in the hospital.

I picked up his hand now and held it between mine. Fifty-two days, that's how long he'd been in a coma. His team of doctors agreed he'd have a difficult time making a full recovery at this point. I couldn't even begin to imagine what his medical bills must look like, but luckily, the decision to keep him on the ventilator and feeding tube after the first month was an easy one for Conner's parents. Just like me, they weren't giving up. In fact, nobody was. Balloons, cards, flowers, and other gifts littered his hospital room. Conner's Care Page had over ten thousand messages—prayers and get well wishes from everyone in our community and then some.

My stomach rumbled. I knew I should eat something. The only substance I inhaled on a regular basis was caffeine. I'd even started eating my Peanut Butter Captain Crunch cereal with black coffee instead of milk for breakfast, willing myself to stay up 24-7 and keep a vigil by Conner's bedside. Of course, this new habit caused my huge blowout with Mom this morning. She kept telling me to go out with my other friends, that I exhibited unhealthy behaviors. But even though Nicole, Sean, and Kyle, our other friends, loved Conner as much as I did and visited often, they didn't quite understand what I was going through. I alone dived into the freezing water and tried to save our friend, and I worried every day that I'd failed, that I hadn't acted quickly enough.

A slew of swear words rose in my throat, another new habit, fighting to get out every single time Mom yelled at me to "go out and have some fun." This morning she even mentioned something about making me go to counseling.

"Like that would help," I'd told her.

Usually, I went along with whatever my parents suggested. I wasn't sure what made me so bold these days. All I knew is that while Conner slept, I became more awake, more desperate to live on the edge.

Sighing, I swiveled my gaze around the hospital room as I stroked Conner's hand. New guy had one giant, gray suitcase shoved in the corner. Temptation to rummage through his belongings overwhelmed me. I knew I should resist the urge. Thanks to Mom's discipline, I conquered willpower a long time ago. But the need to find out more about him made me tiptoe across the scuffed linoleum. I glanced over at the door, considering a nurse or Conner's parents or worst of all, Nate, interrupting my spy work. The fear almost sent me back to my chair, but tired of being scared all the time, I hefted Nate's suitcase in from of me and quickly unzipped it.

Nothing particular should've stuck out at me. There were faded jeans, a few pairs of corduroy pants, some pop culture tees, an olive-green hoodie, a blue Michigan sweatshirt, some song books, a watch, a massive pile of CDs, a book on philosophy, and a DVD of *Citizen Kane*. Yet, for whatever reason, there was a flash of recognition at seeing every single one of these items. If I had my doubts about déjà vu before, I certainly couldn't ignore them now. Like a creep, I picked up his hoodie and inhaled, the scent of vanilla and musk washing over me.

After putting it back, I zipped up his suitcase, cramming his belongings back into the corner where they belonged. I put my palms to my eyes, agitated at the wetness there, and tried to hold back my tears. I'd had enough to cry about these past two months, and I didn't even know *why* I cried now. Ashamed, I rushed back to my chair.

I decided to read to Conner until Nate returned. Finding my bookmarked page, I smiled. I'd just finished reading the entire Lord of the Rings trilogy to him, and Star Wars novels wouldn't be my first pick for our next read aloud, but Conner obsessed over the franchise. He even nicknamed our group of five friends the Jedi Order. We had done everything together until two months ago, when lightning struck Conner on our first spring sail. The bolt of electricity flung him off our boat, and I jumped into Lake Michigan to save him. The verdict was still out on whether I succeeded or not.

Just as we were learning about a new Dark Jedi consumed by bitterness and scheming to corrupt Luke Skywalker to the Dark Side, a new urge overtook me.

I picked up Conner's hand again. "Look, they say you can hear me. Now that you have this new roommate, there's something I need to say real quick before he gets back. We came pretty close to dying, and in case that happens again anytime soon, I don't want to wait to tell you this. It's kinda a big something that I pictured involving flowers and candles and music, but it's too late for that. So I'm just gonna spit out the words. I love you. I mean, I've always loved you, since the first day of kindergarten. But I'm also in love with you. A lot. I'm not entirely sure when my love turned all romantic or whatever, but I think it was in the sixth grade. Remember when Josh snapped my bra? And you told him that you really didn't want to commit homicide at such a young age, so he better not touch me ever again? Yeah, I think that was the day. So anyway, you don't have to say anything back, when you wake up. You can pretend like you never even heard me say this if you don't feel the same way. But if you do feel the same way? Well, I'm ready to get married whenever you are."

I paused, hoping the shock of my statement might cause him to wake up, since we were only seventeen, but nothing.

Before I could assure Conner I was only kidding, the door opened.

"You're still here, huh?"

Oh great, Mr. I-Belong-In-An-Insane-Asylum is back. Time to go! "Yeah, I was just leaving."

Nate maneuvered his wheelchair to his bed, then climbed in while sporting a big grin on his face. He also sported new clothes. Instead of a hospital gown, he wore flannel pajama pants and a Tony Hawk T-shirt. I guessed now that he could see again, he wanted to wear something other than an oversize dress that tied in the back.

"You're gorgeous."

His comment made me stop, because hot boys didn't usually tell me things like that. "Excuse me?"

"I got my sight back." He pointed to the eyes that were covered with bandages just an hour ago. Eyes that were my favorite shade of blue, the color of the ocean. The ocean that had nearly claimed Conner's life.

"I see."

"Earlier, I wanted to kick the crazy girl out of my room, but now I desperately want her to stay."

I smiled. "You think *I'm* the crazy one?"

He scoffed, which turned into a coughing fit that lasted a good thirty seconds. After taking a swig of water, he said, "Look, we've obviously both been through some traumatic experiences. From what I can gather, we've both hit our heads pretty hard. Let's chalk up our first meeting to all the pain meds they have me on. Deal?"

I nervously tugged at Conner's covers and decided to test his theory. "Deal."

But only because you're crazy hot.

"I prefer Mr. Crazy Hot from you."

I gasped. *If you can hear this, repeat after me. I'm an idiot.*

"That's true, I am."

I want coffee.

"Cream and sugar?"

"Oh my gosh! Crap, crap, crap!"

"So I take it I was only hearing your thoughts earlier? You didn't really say all of that stuff out loud?"

I shook my head. "How is this happening?"

"Maybe it's life imitating fiction. You've been reading aloud from that Star Wars novel every day, desperately wishing for some mysterious magic like the Force to come and heal Conner. And you got me instead." A big, goofy, and hot grin appeared on his face.

"This isn't the time for jokes!" He really was a weirdo if he thought this was funny.

"Whoa, chill."

"I can't chill. And how can you be so cool about this? We have to figure this out. Can you hear everyone's thoughts?"

He lay in his bed. "Yours are the first I've eavesdropped on."

Inhaling a deep breath, I tried to calm down. *Oh, who am I kidding? There's no way I'm going to be cool about this.* "What do you think this means?"

"I'm the luckiest guy on Earth." He grinned again. "But hey, did you really think I was gay earlier? The Zac Effron look overkill?"

Rolling my eyes, I told him, "I'm not sure if anything could ever be overkill when it comes to Zac Effron."

He smirked at me. "See, that's what I figured."

I nodded, then looked down at Conner and wished I could see his eyes.

"So, what's your story?" Nate gestured from me to Conner.

"Um, we were out sailing two months ago and—"

"No, I mean, how do you know each other?"

"Oh, we've been best friends"—and my secret crush—"since kindergarten."

"Ah, I'm about to be a senior. You?"

"Same." I was about to say more when I remembered he could hear every freakin' thought in my brain. "I've gotta go. See ya around."

He said something else, but with a grunt, I bolted from the room, hoping my thoughts were safe for now.

CHAPTER TWO

"People who don't even know you can change your life in a matter of seconds."

—Nate's Thoughts

I made the one-mile trek from the hospital to the Bookman for my work shift. As I passed the park, I watched a couple enjoying a picnic, a group of boys tossing around a football, wheezing joggers stumbling around the nature trail, an old man tossing some birdseed to greedy sparrows at his feet... all everyday things. I wished I could exit this Crazy Train and join normal again.

Strolling through the door, I squinted against the fluorescent lights of the bookstore and greeted Nic with a nod. As my best friend since the fourth grade, she secured me this job the day I turned sixteen. Her parents owned the bookstore.

"Tough afternoon at the hospital?" she asked as I clocked in at the computer.

"That's an understatement." I took a sip of the large coffee I'd bought at the hospital before leaving, wishing for bed and a good book instead of work. But no matter what magical properties coffee possessed, it couldn't grant my wishes.

"Something new develop with Conner?"

I slowly shook my head. "No, but I met this guy named Nate, Conner's new roomie. And you're not going to believe this, but he can read my thoughts."

Saying the words aloud convinced me I must've gone mad. Surely, Nate must've tricked me somehow. I felt like puking at the thought of it being a cruel hoax and at the thought of it all being real.

Nicole ushered me over to the wooden bench in the reading nook, and I wished I could disappear as she leaned against the YA bookshelf to my right. "What? How can he read your thoughts? He's, like, a legit mind reader?"

I loved how easily Nicole accepted this as fact; she even bounced from foot to foot in front of me like the idea excited her. A headache formed from my brain working overtime, and I tried to shut out the upbeat, jingly tune coming from the music kiosk machine in the back of the store. First, final exam week at school and now this. I wanted to Google Nate, but I never got his last name. Tomorrow I'd have to investigate, but how could I be sneaky about spying when he could read my thoughts?

"I don't know, Nic. He said I'm the first person he's ever 'heard' before. I have no idea what that means."

Thank God business was slow tonight. Apart from a typical summer tourist browsing the shelves, the store remained empty aside from Nic and me. Her parents had the night off. I could only trust Nic with this new information that potentially labeled me certifiably insane.

"Maybe he's lying to you."

Trying to calm my nerves, I inhaled and exhaled deeply. The papery scent of new books waiting to be discovered had me wishing I could rewrite my own story. "Maybe, but he did read my mind perfectly. He could repeat everything I thought."

"Maybe he's lying about not reading other minds then."

Taking a long sip of my coffee, I nudged my foot into hers. "Why would he do that?"

She shrugged as our sole customer approached the counter with a book on the history of West Michigan.

I looked at the clock. Only twenty minutes into my four-hour shift, and I already wished the night was over. With the little coffee I had left in hand, I decided to make good use of my time. I meandered over to the Religion and Spirituality section and perused the books there, hoping to conduct some research on mind reading. I hadn't spent much time in this section of the store. Leeriness settled in the pit of my stomach. As a Catholic, Mom had always taught me "mystical" topics such as psychics and ghosts should be avoided. No lack of books about psychics and ghosts here, though, along with angels and a number of other spiritual topics like dealing with grief, whether or not dead people watched over us, listening to our intuition, and out-of-body experiences. The list went on and on.

But nothing quite matched what happened between Nate and me. There was a book on igniting our sixth sense that seemed like the closest thing to what I experienced, but I didn't know if I wanted to devote an entire night flipping through it. Maybe I'd go home and watch the movie on Netflix instead. I'd never seen *The Sixth Sense*, but I heard the surprise ending was intense.

Just as I placed the book back on the shelf and turned around, Nic jumped out of nowhere and made me spill my coffee all over my Harry Potter shirt. One of the perks of the job, besides working with my best friend, was we could wear T-shirts to work, as long as they were book related.

"What did you do that for?" I shrieked.

She gave a maniacal laugh. "Because I wanted to scare you. Duh! Sorry about your shirt, though."

I moved around her in search of some paper towels we kept hidden underneath the front counter. "The only reason you were able to scare me is because I was already looking at those freaky books."

"Find any answers?"

"Nope. But I have a question for you. Why aren't you questioning the state of my sanity with this new information?"

She glanced at the door as a new customer walked in, and before answering my question, she took the time to greet him. "I don't know. I guess I don't want to stress you out more than you already are."

"So your backup plan is to support me no matter what, no matter how crazy I sound?"

Leaning against the counter, she scrutinized her manicure. "You've been crazy for years. You're acting like it's a new thing."

I threw my coffee-stained paper towels at her. "Just keep on with the jokes. I should be having my mental breakdown any minute now, and then you can really have some fun."

Nic threw the paper towels away and grimaced as she straightened the piles of miscellaneous junk underneath the counter. "Sorry. So, can this new, creepy guy hear your thoughts even when he's not in the room? How far does this ESP trick extend?"

I took the hair tie off my wrist and tied my funky mess of red curls into a tight bun. "That's a very good question. Oh, and by the way, did I mention creepy guy is also super hot?"

"Excuse me, but can you help me locate a book?" the customer I'd forgotten about asked.

Nic swung her head up from below the counter and effectively slapped her black ponytail in my face. "Sure thing, one second." She turned to me and winked. "No, but it looks like you have an excuse to see Mr. Hottie again. If I were you, I'd want to know if he can hear me right now."

Oh crap. Why hadn't I thought of that? I poured myself a free cup of coffee, an employee benefit of working at the Bookman, although it was a benefit to our customers, too. If I was going to stay up all night Googling mind reading, I needed more caffeine.

As I sat, sandwiched between Nate's and Conner's hospital beds, my gaze hopped between each of their beautiful faces, a welcome distraction to the sterile, bland walls. After surviving thirty minutes of awkward small talk between Nate, Conner's parents, and me, we were finally alone. Well, Conner still lay in his bed with no change in his condition today. I hated how the white hospital linens matched the color of his skin.

I'd had my fair share of paranoia over the past seventeen years, but nothing topped being in Nate's presence. To make matters worse, my Internet searches on the subject were little to no help at all.

"I'm sorry I make you uncomfortable. Believe me, that's the last thing I want."

I leaned toward Nate, my two long braids falling over my shoulder in the process.

"I like your hair today," he said.

I noticed the way his eyes, clear as glass, lit up when he looked at me.

Then I reminded myself I had to stop *thinking.* "About the whole mind reading thing, you can still only hear *my* thoughts?"

He leaned back on his pillows. "Yep, thank God."

"What's that supposed to mean?" I leveled him with my eyes and twirled one of my braids.

"Can you stop doing that? I can't focus on answering your questions when you flirt so beautifully."

My cheeks flushed red. "Oh, sorry. I wasn't trying to flirt."

"That's what makes you so cute." He traced a finger across the staples on the top of his head. "People are so negative these days. I'd hate to listen to all that noise all the time."

I chewed the inside of my lip, wondering how annoying I must sound to him. "In my defense, I'm going through the toughest time in my life right now. I'm not usually such a Debbie Downer."

"You're doing remarkably well for everything that's happened."

"So, could you still hear my thoughts last night after I left the room?" I asked coolly, but secretly dying to know the answer. Which I guess was futile. Ugh!

He nodded. "Tell Nic the creepy, hot guy says hi."

I stood and slapped his unbroken arm. "What? No! How long did you listen?"

Rubbing his arm, he said, "Right up until you decided you were going to stay up all night Googling mind reading. I didn't want to stress you out any further. Then I figured I'd have to come clean on listening in, and you probably wouldn't be too happy about that, so I should stop."

My eye twitched in anger. "Ya think? If you can turn it on and off, then out of respect for me, you shouldn't ever listen to my thoughts again."

Nate's face turned an adorable shade of red. He smiled wide, displaying all of his perfect teeth, and I remembered again how he heard my every thought. "When you're in the same room as me, not listening is a darn hard thing to do. Even far away, tuning you out proved difficult."

"Listen, even if I find you good looking or whatever, I'm still pissed. That was a rotten thing to do. You need to learn how to exercise some control if we're ever going to be friends."

He looked down, suddenly occupied with the bandage on his hand. "I know. I wanted to stop, but curiosity got the better of me. How far is the Bookman from here anyway?"

"About a mile."

"Hmm, where are you going from here?"

"Just back home, but that's less than a mile from here. I have to study for my last final tomorrow. Last day of school and all."

He lifted an eyebrow. "Oh, really? My school ended last week. Why don't you go somewhere two miles away, and then call me to see if I can still hear your thoughts?"

I gave him a faux salute. "Yes, sir!"

He smiled. "Sorry, I didn't mean it as an order, just a suggestion."

Swatting away his apology, I said, "I know. It's just I don't drive, so I'll need to call Nic first and see if she can pick me up, or this experiment of ours will take a while."

I turned my back to him as I dialed Nic's number and stared down at Conner, wondering if he heard all this. "Hey, Nic. Do you think you could pick me up from the hospital? Yeah. Okay, thanks. See you soon." I spun around to face Nate again and noticed him checking me out. I cleared my throat. "She'll be here in five."

"Perfect."

I tilted my head to the ceiling. "I can't believe we're creating an experiment to see how far away you can hear my thoughts."

Nate stretched his arms above his head, and the hem of his shirt lifted up a few inches, revealing a nice set of rock-hard abs, although the perfection was scarred with a few noticeable scrapes. I tried unsuccessfully not to stare.

He batted his lashes at me. His ocean-colored eyes were so heartbreakingly beautiful. "You can touch them if you want."

My whole body stiffened. "You know, with all those cuts and bruises, I'd think your arrogance would've died a little in that accident." For the first time, I saw a long black shadow pass over his features.

"Well, I'm not the one who died. Bo did. And if I don't keep up my arrogant attitude, then I'll be forced to think about everything and I... I..."

I didn't need to read his thoughts to realize he needed some comforting. "Look, I've wept more tears of guilt than anyone these last two months. I've been sad for so long I don't even think I remember what happiness feels like. Each day Conner doesn't wake up, I come a little more undone." Fidgeting with the strings of my hoodie, I couldn't believe I unloaded all this on someone who was practically a stranger, but I figured he could hear it all anyway. "There's no use in dwelling on what we can't change." At least that's what Mom and Dad kept telling me. "Maybe an angel is watching over us and sent us to each other, to help us face whatever is coming. Grief has a way of bringing lost souls together, right?"

His eyes were enormous as they stared back at me, the most soulful eyes I'd ever seen. "Happy is the man, and happy he alone, He, who can call today his own; He, who secure within, can say, Tomorrow do their worst, for I have lived today."

He fumbled with the button on the side of his bed with shaking hands, reclining it a little, and I figured I should let him rest.

"Who said that?"

He pulled the hospital linen up to his neck. "John Dryden."

I closed my eyes, searching through the pages of my near-photographic memory. "Mmm. The English poet from the seventeenth century?"

"Someone knows her literature."

A squeaking cart rolled through the door, and a nurse carrying a disposable medi cup walked in. "Time to take your pills, Nate."

I reached out and held Conner's hands as I watched Nate and the nurse. She asked him some questions, but his answers were lost on me. The squeaking cart brought a flashback of Conner's first night at the hospital, the whoosh of life-saving machines being brought down the hallway as the doctor shouted directions to the nurses in the ER. Tracing figure eights on Conner's hand, I tried to keep my mind here, tried to forget that horrible night.

The nurse left. I hadn't noticed her exit until Nate's voice broke through my memory, his tone soothing.

"Funny how one little thing can derail us, sending us on a downward spiral. But like you said, maybe we can face this together now. You want to watch a movie with me? My mom brought all my favorites from home. You can invite Nic to come up so I can meet her."

He motioned toward the stack of DVDs on the side table and flipped his hair out of his face. The familiarity of his gestures made me speechless. I looked at him, intoxicated by my sense of knowing him when I didn't know him at all. How all of this fit together with his ability to read my mind, I didn't have a clue, but I needed to find out.

After squeezing Conner's hand one more time, I walked over to Nate. "Not today. I need to get going. Here's my phone. Type in your number so we can conduct our little science experiment."

He handed me his cell. "Wow, so we're going with the forward route. All right, give me your number, too."

I looked down at him, my eyes narrowing. "You're really enjoying this, aren't you?"

Giving a studious nod, he said, "I can't deny I am. I know I shouldn't, but you're my one ray of sunshine in this storm. I like you."

We exchanged phones again, our fingers lightly touching, and I tried to hide a smile as I slid my fingers into my pocket. "Okay, I'll call at a mile and a half, too, to see if you can still hear me."

"I'll be listening."

"Oh my gosh, can you get any more creepy?"

With that, I was out the door, the sound of his laughter the only thing *I* could hear.

Normally, I liked to think I'd be more upset about a guy hearing my thoughts. But for some strange reason, the conversation we had just had held this familiarity that brought a sense of peace to me.

My phone buzzed in my pocket, alerting me to his text: Got that déjà vu feels around U 2

I shook my head and sent him a text back. Although I'm getting used 2 U listening 2 my thoughts, it doesn't mean I like it. U don't have 2 remind me of your power so much

Nic pulled up a minute later, her eyes alive with excitement. "So, how'd it go?"

"He heard our entire conversation at the Bookman last night." I banged the door shut.

"He eavesdropped on us?" She slammed on the gas, lurching me forward, and yelled, "Jerkface!" back toward the hospital.

I laughed. "Nic, it's not like he has some bionic ear with super hearing. He can just hear *my* thoughts."

She huffed. "Fine, then think jerkface for me."

I did, and a second later, my phone buzzed again. "Nate says to tell you he's sorry."

She paused a moment, flicking her blinker on to leave the parking lot. "Tell him he's not forgiven. Where am I taking you? Home?"

I nodded, typing in her response to Nate. "Yeah, but drive a little farther up to Mancino's. I have to travel at least two miles for my and Nate's experiment. Oh, can you clock the distance, too?"

She hit the button on her odometer. "Cool. You can treat me to a slice of pizza while we're there."

I rummaged through my purse to make sure I had some cash. Surprisingly, I had a twenty-dollar bill in my wallet. Dad must've snuck it in there. He always took care of me in quiet ways like that. "Okay," I told Nic. "We can even spring for some cheesy breadsticks. Tell me when we hit a mile and a half, okay?"

"Sure thing. So, was there any flirting action between you and Mr. Hottie today?"

Pressing my finger to my lips, I signaled to her I didn't want to talk about flirting with him "listening" in, then changed the subject. "Are you ready for your last finals tomorrow?"

She winced. "Kind of."

"Nic, they're our last finals before we apply for early college admission."

She nodded. "I know, but kissing Sean is so much more fun than studying."

Sean and Nic went to the prom together last month. Their relationship began that night. Watching their romance unfold over the last six weeks had felt weird. They were the happiest I'd ever seen them, but one of our best friends still fought for his life while they continually sucked face. My phone buzzed in my pocket just as Nic announced the mile and a half mark. It was another text from Nate: *U have 2 find happiness whenever U can. B happy 4 ur friends*

I rolled my eyes.

"What'd jerkface say this time?"

Deciding I needed some fresh air, I pressed the down arrow on my window. "Nothing I didn't already know. I just don't like to feel judged."

Another text: *Not judgin—gently remindin*

Another minute later, Nic announced the two-mile mark.

I thought the words: *Can you hear me now?*

Incoming text: U promised 2 call

I hit the voice button on my phone.

"Olga?"

"Geez, how'd you know it was me?"

"Because you programmed your number into my cell phone, silly."

"Oh, right."

"And just so you know, it's your fault I'm craving pizza now."

"What? The mystery meat, frozen carrots, and the green Jell-o isn't cutting it for your taste buds anymore?"

"Not quite. You want to swing by on your way back and drop me off a slice? I'd love the opportunity to meet this Nicole and prove I'm not the jerkface she thinks I am."

"Maybe another time. We need to study tonight, remember?"

"Two-point-five miles," Nic yelled into the phone.

"Quick, think fast," Nate told me.

J-E-L-L-O, was all I could think at the moment.

"Hello? Are you thinking something?"

I shot a triumphant fist in the air. "Woohoo! Nate can't hear my thoughts anymore."

Nic smiled. "So all you need to do is stay over two miles away from jerkface at all times."

"I am not a jerkface!" Nate argued.

"Maybe not, but we're pulling into the pizza place and I'm hungry."

I hung up without another word, so I wasn't surprised when my phone alerted me to another one of his texts: UR only safe 4 a little while—dont 4get we promised 2 help each other ☺

This thought should've creeped me out, but it didn't, and that's what scared me most of all.

CHAPTER THREE

*"It isn't always enough to be forgiven by others;
sometimes you have to learn to forgive yourself."*

—Nate's Thoughts

The next four weeks flew by in a blur. Nothing new happened. School ended, my finals aced. The usual summer tourists flocked to the Bookman, so my work schedule increased from twenty to forty hours a week. I checked in on Conner, and Nate, every day. But there still hadn't been any change in Conner's condition, and his parents or Nate's parents were always there when I visited, so Nate and I didn't talk much. I figured that didn't matter, since he knew all my thoughts anyway. He tried calling and texting me a few times, but I hadn't answered. The whole idea of wanting to flirt with him confused me, and I didn't need any more complications in my life right now.

So when I finished vacuuming the store at quarter till closing time on Wednesday night and felt a tap on my shoulder, I then yelped in surprise when I saw Nate staring back at me.

"What are you doing here?"

"Med Team Nate said I was finally free to go home, so, naturally, I came straight to you."

I looked him over from head to toe. He wore jeans sporting holes in the knees and a Batman T-shirt fraying at the hem. Aside from a bandage on the left top corner of his forehead and a cast on his left arm, he looked completely fine.

"Thanks. So how's it going?" he asked with more enthusiasm than a normal guy who barely knew me should. No doubt he heard my thought about him looking fine, thanks to the supernatural ability God seemed to have gifted him with. And I did think he looked fine, in more ways than one.

I scoffed. "Like you don't know!"

"So I have a gift, eh?"

A smile crept across my face, despite my efforts to keep the gesture hidden.

Mrs. Moreno, Nic's mom, cleared her throat as she dusted the shelves nearby.

"Um, listen, we're kind of trying to close up the store. So unless you intend to buy something, do you mind waiting for me outside?"

"As a matter of fact, I did come here for something." He leaned in and gave me a quick peck on the cheek, then headed toward the children's literature section with a crooked gait.

Both his kiss and his walk were awkward, but at least the latter had a reason for it. I couldn't think of a good one for why he kissed me.

"Because I wanted to," he called across the store.

Wrapping the cord around the handle of the vacuum, I blushed as I passed Nic washing the windows.

She eyed me suspiciously and whispered, "You're totally crushing on jerkface!"

"What? I am not. I love Conner."

"That doesn't mean you can't like somebody else."

"Will you please shut up? He can hear my thoughts!"

I rushed back to the storage room and thought about hiding out until eight o'clock, but I didn't want to get on Mrs. Moreno's bad side. Instead, I headed to the front desk and waited for Nate so I could close out the cash register. A minute later, he limped toward me with an armful of picture books.

Cringing at the sight of him straining to carry all the books under one arm, I rushed over to help. "What have we got here?"

"Pop-ups are my favorite, but you're running low on those, so I had to compromise."

I laughed while I started ringing up the books. "I'll make a mental note to order more now that you live here. Not what I pictured you reading, though."

"What did you picture?"

"Oh, I don't know, perhaps something from our romance department with a bodice-ripping cover."

He snorted. "Oh great. So your first impression of me is I'm some bimbo not capable of understanding a complex sentence or being able to string more than three words together without giggling?"

I faux laughed. "Looks like you have a perfect memory, too. Seriously, who are these books for? Oh, and your total is seventy-four dollars and twenty-three cents."

He took a wad of four twenties out of his pocket. "I thought I'd buy some books to keep at the hospital for the kids."

Aww, he's buying books for sick kids? That's pretty sweet.

Nate shrugged. "I noticed some of the books in the playroom were outdated. These looked good. You guys definitely need to stock up on your pop-ups and comic books, though."

"Duly noted." I smiled at him despite the nervousness that came from being around him.

He smiled back, looking happy and also like he had smiled at me from the other side of this counter many times before. Again, I couldn't say why.

"Olga, you can take off a few minutes early to go out with your new friend if you want," Mrs. Moreno said from behind me.

Oh, great job, Mrs. M. Throw me to the wolf like a piece of meat!

But Nate's smile was as big as the state of Texas. I couldn't deny him anything with a grin like that, especially after buying all those books for sick kids.

"Okay, thanks." I turned back to Nate. "Just let me grab my purse from the back room."

The floors creaked behind me, part of the store's charm in my opinion, and I knew Nic was following me.

"Do you need me to come with you as backup, or do you trust this guy?" she asked as I retrieved my bag from an empty drawer in a filing cabinet and slipped on my hoodie.

"Naw, I'm good."

"Okay, just call or text me as soon as you're home to fill me in on all the juicy details."

"This isn't a date. I'll probably just hang out at the boardwalk with him for an hour, and that'll be the end of it, so don't get your hopes up."

She narrowed her honey-brown eyes at me. "Whatever you say. Just call me."

I waited while Nate finished some small talk with Mrs. Moreno about the area beaches, restaurants, and such. Nic followed us to the front door to lock up, and as she did, she grabbed my arm just before I stepped out.

"Don't do anything I wouldn't do," she whispered in my ear.

What's wrong with her? We were not going on a date.

Then she peered around me. "Nice meeting you, jerkface. Treat my girl right."

"Oh, you don't have to worry about that, Nicole." He put his arm around my waist as she shut the door with a wink. "So, where are you taking me for our first official date?"

I smiled. "Not a date. But if you're okay to walk a little bit, we can catch the world's largest musical fountain show at the boardwalk. It's about a half mile's walk from here, or did you drive?"

"I had my parents drop me off. They can pick us up when we're done, too."

"The way you drop money on books, I figured you'd have a sweet ride of your own."

"Well, my dad let me use his car until I totaled it last month. I lost my license for a year because of the accident, too. Hang on a sec; they're waiting in my mom's car. I'll give them these books and tell them to pick us up in two hours. That's all the time they'll give me."

Slowly, he made his way over to a BMW. *Yep, rich.* He rested the weight of his body against the vehicle as he spoke to his parents, the passenger side door open. His mom handed him a pill and water, and he took a few swigs from the bottle before handing it back to her. I watched as his mom made him put on a black sweater over his T-shirt. After a minute, he checked his reflection in the window and limped back to me, his parents beeping once as they drove away.

I bit my lip as we started our walk. "Are you sure you're up for this type of exercise?"

"Olga, I've been cooped up in the hospital for a month. The fresh air is nice, as long as you don't mind walking very slowly with me."

"Don't mind at all. Will give me a chance to get to know you better, since you already know so much more about me with your unfair mind-reading advantage."

"Sorry, but life isn't fair, right?"

Every hair on my body stood on end with the truth of his statement. "I'm sorry about my flippant remark earlier. I should've thought about the whole driving thing before I asked." The electricity from being so close to him reminded me of the charge I felt before lightning struck Conner, and I tried to shake it off. "Do you want to talk about it?"

Nate shook his head. "Why? Talking about it won't change the fact that Bo died."

"I know, but I thought God brought us together for that purpose, remember? So we don't feel so alone all the time." Although, I'd done a crappy job of being there for him the past month.

Neither one of us said a word for a few moments.

"I guess," he said finally.

"In case nobody has told you this yet," I said quietly, trying to sound reassuring, "what happened was an accident. That means it wasn't your fault. You couldn't drag race by yourself."

He looked over at me, his watery eyes meeting mine. "That's just it, though. He never would've drag raced if I didn't start the whole stupid thing. Bo should've been the one who got to live, not me."

"Maybe you're right. But the bottom line is you're here. That must mean something." I picked a piece of lint off my hoodie.

Sighing, he scrubbed a hand over his face. "What does it mean exactly?"

"That the universe isn't through with you yet. Maybe God has a bigger plan for your life than he did for Bo's."

He looked down, kicking a rock off the sidewalk with his good leg. "I know. But I keep thinking about Bo's parents, his siblings, his friends, his girlfriend. How much they miss him. I barely knew him, and I miss him. Then I feel even guiltier because now I'm glad I'm not there, in the same town, where they'd all be looking at me with their sad faces."

"You think they blame you for the accident?"

"I don't know. I never saw them. Only the police visited me in the hospital during their investigation, issued me some hefty tickets. They held his funeral on my last day in town, but my doctor there wouldn't release me for it. Again, I felt guilty for having the excuse. But it doesn't matter if they blame me or not; I do enough blaming for all of us. My guilt is the one thing I have left to hold on to in this world."

Placing my hand in his, I said, "Not anymore."

He gave me a small smile. "Thanks."

"So, what's next? I mean, you're out of the hospital and that's good, but I imagine you're still hurting pretty badly."

"Yeah, I'll need physical and occupational therapy for the rest of the summer. A lady will come to my house for that part."

I tilted my head to the side, trying to offer some words of sympathy. "I guess you're lucky to have the summer off to heal at least. When do you get the cast off your arm?"

He shrugged. "Not sure. Could be another three weeks or a total of three months. There will be plenty of doctor appointments and specialists to visit as we figure out stuff. Plus, my mom is forcing me into counseling with some lady named Dr. Judy at the hospital, since I refuse to talk to my parents about the accident."

My mouth fell open. "You're kidding? My mom has been trying to get me to see her for months now."

"You haven't gone, though?"

I rubbed my eyes, then adjusted my glasses. "No thank you. I don't feel like rehashing the details of the worst day of my life."

He nodded. "Right? My parents and I will already be dragged through months of lawyers, courts, and mediation meetings, going over every single detail of the accident repeatedly. I've been holed up in the hospital for a month already, ready to climb the walls. My mom says I'm suffering from emotionally regressive behavior, though, so she won't take no for an answer with the counseling thing."

"What does regressive behavior mean?"

He let go of my hand and wiped a bead of sweat from his forehead. "You saw how neat I kept my side of the room at the hospital. I'm just fixated with controlling every little thing. I guess because I can only control the *little* things at this point. I'm trying not to be a jerk to my parents, but I can't stop myself from snapping at them constantly. Doesn't help that I can't sleep unless I take some pills. And even then I wake up screaming."

Before I knew what I was doing, I wrapped my hand in his again. I could see in his eyes all that he'd been carrying around. For the first time since Conner's accident, I felt more sorry for someone else than I did for myself.

"Do you ever feel like you're losing your mind?" he asked, our gazes meeting.

"You know I do."

"Oh yeah, you've lost your mind to me." He smiled at that, his entire face settling with affection and understanding.

I let out a shaky laugh because, once again, the notion didn't seem too terrible. Relaxing a little, I changed the subject to other things. One, because I didn't want to focus on my feelings too much around him. Two, because I was very eager to learn more about this mystery guy.

"At the hospital, the other day, I heard you mention to the nurse something about being in an indie rock band in your hometown."

Music and the smell of hot dogs and roasted peanuts wafted through the air, signaling we were close to Waterfront Stadium now.

He glanced at a rusty shop sign swinging in the wind. "Yeah, I was lead vocalist and guitarist. We called ourselves the Sidewalk Poets."

This similarity between him and Conner jarred me. "Conner does the singing for an indie band here with his friends Sean and Kyle. Plays guitar, too."

"Yeah?" He tripped on an uneven part of the sidewalk, and I quickly caught him. He slid an arm around my shoulders, smiling. "For support," he told me. "Well, this sucks. I was kind of hoping to play my musician card to make you fall in love with me instead."

I shuddered from the wind whooshing off a passing car. At least I told myself the tremble was from the car, and nothing to do with Nate's comment at all.

"What's the name of their band?"

"Cantankerous Monkey Squad."

He barked out a laugh. "How'd they come up with that?"

My gaze traveled to the brick buildings lining the street. "He saw one of those cymbal-clanging monkeys in a shop here one day. He thought of

Angry Chimps first, but after some brainstorming, the guys decided on the name they have now. I gave them the cantankerous part. What's the origin of your band's name?"

"Well, from about the time I turned ten, I wrote poetry. Even though most of my poems were complete junk, as I got older, I figured I could make them sound better by turning them into songs, so I did. The first time we played, the band consisted of me and one other guy, and we set up on Main Street and left my guitar case open. We made sixty dollars. We thought we were cool walking home with thirty dollars in our pockets for playing pretty terrible stuff. So we came up with a name for ourselves and started playing on the street most Friday nights."

"You must be very well read. I mean, you quoted Helen Keller and a poet the other day, and you write poetry. No offense, but you don't seem like the type who'd sit long enough to read much."

"Well, what's much? I don't read typical stuff, though. I study philosophy books written about the great thinkers like Confucius, Plato, and Aristotle. They're my own personal heroes." He paused, sucking in a few deep breaths. "What about you? You have a hero?"

Inhaling a deep breath of my own, I noticed how the air smelled cleaner, and I wondered if the difference had anything to do with Nate embracing my world. He seemed to have such a pure spirit, so full of life, even if he had gotten the wind knocked out of him recently. "Jesus. Mother Theresa. People who live simple lives but do extraordinary things. Most people would probably find that ridiculous."

"I don't think it's ridiculous."

Someone honked in the distance, making me jump. "So what do you like to do when you're not playing music?"

He shrugged. "Play video games or watch movies."

"But you're an adrenaline junkie, too."

Sweat trickled down his temple. "The drag racing gave me away, eh? Yeah, my idea of exercise isn't pumping iron at the gym. I'm always skateboarding, kneeboarding, snowboarding. Depends on the season. I guess, once my legs are better, I'll have lots of opportunity to hone my boarding skills, since I can't drive anywhere."

I smiled. "You've found your silver lining. Are you going out for any sports when we start school in the fall?"

"Nah, I never got into team sports. Tried baseball and soccer for a season, but I don't like being told what to do by the man." He said the last two words using air quotes.

Finally, we reached the boardwalk. Our small town had made its annual metamorphosis into a tourist trap. The boardwalk was crowded, the surrounding green and Waterfront Stadium even more so. Big bands occupied the summer months in Grand Haven with dances scheduled every Wednesday evening at the stadium. Tonight, a national jazz artist drew lots of dancing. Suddenly, I become an epileptic at a light show concert, my vision reduced to stuttering bursts that sent me grabbing onto Nate.

"Hey, you okay?"

"Just feeling light-headed." I closed my eyes, thinking of how I'd been here with Nate before. I was sure I knew him from somewhere but felt equally sure that knowing him was impossible. Forgetting things, especially people like him, wasn't in my character.

I felt Nate's hand move from my shoulder to my head, smoothing down my hair. His black sweater was soft on my face and smelled like fresh laundry.

"In a strange way, it makes sense we'd know each other," Nate whispered. "I can read your mind, which should be impossible. That kind of opens up all kinds of possibilities, doesn't it?"

When I felt his lips gently brush the top of my head, I got dizzy again but for a whole 'nother reason. "You're right. The quickest way to figuring this all out may just be to hang out with each other."

"Good. So is this all free?" Nate asked me.

I'd barely opened my mouth to tell him that was one of the best things about Grand Haven when a girl wearing a sundress shoved a piece of paper in my face.

"Don't forget the sand sculpting contest at Grand Haven City Beach this Friday night!" she sang, moving onto the next person.

I was about to chuck the paper into the trash when Nate grabbed it from me. "Now this looks like a great event for our real first date."

Raising my eyebrows, I said, "I'm not ready to date yet."

"Then will you at least dance with me?"

"In case you haven't noticed, I'm not the dancing ty—"

The word died on my lips when he suddenly pulled me into the throng of dancers. I was surprised to see his moves were decent for someone dealing with a bum leg and broken arm. As we crossed right, stepped side left, stepped side right, then stepped together to complete a jazz square, he lifted his good arm to the side to end with jazz hands.

I threw my head back in laughter. "Wow, you're rocking some old-school skills, huh?"

He tried to cover his wincing, but I heard a small whimper escape his lips. "Oh, please, girl, you ain't seen nothing yet!"

I laughed again. "I think you should take it easy for now."

Nate brushed a hand through my hair again. Both gestures, my laugh and his physical affection, felt odd, different, but in a good way.

"Hey," he said.

"Hey." Suddenly, I felt the urge to brush a hand through his hair, too, but it was damp with sweat, so I resisted.

"I'm glad you aren't avoiding me tonight." He took my hand in his and held it to his cheek, brushing the side of his hair.

Sighing, I said, "I should be."

"Why?"

"Because you just heard my thought about wanting to touch your hair, didn't you?"

"So, we're back to the issue of me reading your thoughts again?"

"I guess so."

He shook his head, then pulled me over to the side of the bleachers. "Relax. It's summer, and I intend to enjoy the beautiful sunset with a beautiful girl tonight."

Feeling myself blush, I decided I needed something cold, and fast. "Do you want to get an ice cream cone? Dairy Treat is just across the way. I'll buy."

He took a step forward and held out his hand. "Only if you let me pay. This is our first date. I don't want to set a precedent for our entire relationship."

Shaking my head, I let my hand fall into his, and we started walking. "Not a date, so how about we each just pay for our own?"

"Nope. I pay for both of us, or I'm not going."

I looked away, fighting a smile. "Fine, be a gentleman." *He is kinda perfect.*

Nate dropped my hand and wrapped an arm around my waist, pulling me toward him. I realized he probably had the boldness to do so because he could hear my thoughts. There was no guessing game involved. He knew how attracted I was to him.

"Olga?"

"Yeah?"

"I wish you could hear my thoughts right now, wish I could put into words how strongly I feel about you."

"Um, okay, how though? We barely know each other. And didn't you think I was completely insane just a few weeks ago?"

He gave me a long look, and then we crossed the street with the crowd. "I'm sucked into your thoughts a good deal of my time, so I know you a lot better than you know me. But I'm hoping to change that."

"Can't you stop? I don't want you listening in! It's infuriating."

"Not really. I'm too curious. It's like trying to shut off my own thoughts."

"But you're sure this is a recent thing? I mean, could you have heard other people's thoughts all along and just thought they were yours?"

"Yes, no, and no."

I rubbed my temples, a headache coming on.

He massaged my shoulders. "Relax. Ice cream makes everything better." Stepping up to the window, he placed the order. "A Rockpile shake for me, and a chocolate-dipped cone with a double scoop of banana ice cream for the little lady here."

"Are you poking fun at my five-foot-two status?"

Slipping a ten out of his wallet and handing the crisp bill through the window, he said, "I swear I'm not. I just say awkward things when I'm nervous."

My heart gave a little jump. "And why would you be nervous?"

He accepted his change, then handed me my ice cream cone. "Because I think I could fall in love with you really fast."

I licked the ice cream off my cone, grateful for something to do, even though the act felt too sensual in the moment. "How'd you know what I wanted anyway?"

Catching me by surprise, he traced the outline of my forehead, then my cheekbone, all the way down to my chin. "How do you *think* I knew?"

I closed my eyes and cringed, suddenly feeling shy again. "Oh, right, duh. We should start a magic show or something. I could use the extra money for college."

He nodded, taking a sip of his shake. "I'm game. You want to attend the University of Michigan, right?"

"Ever since I was five when we visited my cousin there. I have the grades, if I can hold myself together for senior year. I just hope Conner is awake by then. It's his eighteenth birthday next week, too."

He seemed to twinge at my words, pressing his lips flat and shoving some hair out of his eyes.

We crossed the street again and remained silent for a few minutes while we ate our ice cream, both of us seemingly lost in thought. Or maybe he was lost in my thoughts.

When we reached the bleachers, we hiked all the way to the top and squeezed ourselves into a spot meant for one to get maximum viewing for the sunset behind the dunes, then the musical fountain show.

Nate sat back, slinking an arm around my shoulder and shaking his head. "So is this show as hokey as it sounds?"

I took a bite of my cone. "Pretty much. I mean, they've done a lot of cool updates over the course of the last few years, so it's more modernized and stuff, but it's no Las Vegas."

He looked up at me with a sly smile. "No dancing girls in bikinis coming by on water skis then?"

Taking another bite, I said, "Only the drunken tourists."

"I'd rather see you in a bikini. What do you say to a beach date on Friday, and then we can go to that sand castle contest? We can enter if you want."

"Mmm." Another bite. "I suppose I could go after work at three. I can't stay out too late, though, because I have to visit Conner."

"You know." He paused, giving me a sidelong glance. From the softness of his voice, I could tell I wasn't going to like the next thing that came out of his mouth. "I understand why you feel the need to visit Conner every day, but how can you blame yourself for his accident? You can't fight nature. It was a random lightning strike."

It was the decisive way he said the words that shook me to my core, like I'd been beating a dead horse and now I needed to put the stick down. And then Nate was there, wrapping his arms around me, knowing I needed to cry even before I did. These weren't sad or happy tears, just ones that needed to be shed. I'd never been more scared these past two months, every day getting out of bed not knowing if Conner would still be alive. I didn't know why, but Nate's arms around me told me everything would turn out okay. The Grand River slapped against the harbor, making watery noises and drowning out the sound of my sobs. It felt so good to cry, so good to be held.

I glanced at my watch and noted the time was ten o'clock on the dot. Just like magic, the musical fountain show started, the lights and Beatles music a welcome distraction.

Nate leaned against the side of the railing and kept his arm around me. His embrace wasn't too little or too much; it was just what I needed.

After the twenty-minute show, he shuffled down the bleachers with the rest of the crowd before turning toward me and helping me off the last step.

I smiled. "Thanks. And hey, maybe I can visit Conner Friday morning so we can stay out later."

Nate blinked rapidly, like a Morse code for *really?*

"Olga!"

I turned, and there were Kyle and Sean with Nic. *Nosy*, I thought toward my best friend, throwing her a look she didn't return. She looked like she desperately needed to tell me something. When Sean was about an arm's length away, he launched himself at me, throwing his arms around my waist and swinging me around.

I ruffled his afro, because that's what the Jedi Order always did when we saw him.

"I've been trying to call you. Don't you check your phone, girl?"

I pulled my cell out of my purse and cursed mentally. I'd forgotten to turn off the silent mode after my work shift ended. Five missed calls. How could I have been so careless? No doubt, all of these calls could only mean one thing.

"Conner?"

I met Kyle's eyes and he nodded, hugging me tight.

"He's awake," he whispered in my ear as a wave of applause and cheers came from the crowd when the band starting to play again.

I glanced at Nate. He'd been so nice to me all night long, and I felt bad leaving him, but after eighty days, Conner was finally awake. Words escaped me, but of course Nate knew.

He nodded toward the street and gave a slight smile. "Go."

Taking long, measured breaths, I wiped the tears from my eyes as I rushed down the hospital corridor. I couldn't believe he was awake and apparently talking. He remembered everything and didn't seem to have many side effects. Doctors were running tests but already declared his dramatic recovery a miracle, if you believed in that sort of thing, which I did.

Mr. and Mrs. Anderson, Conner's parents, were standing outside his hospital room when I arrived, talking to his main doctor.

"May I go in?" I bounced from foot to foot, and I'm sure it looked like I needed a potty break pretty bad.

His mom nodded. "Yes, of course. But just a heads up… Conner is a little… off."

"Off? But the gang said he was completely fine."

Nic, Sean, and Kyle were parking the car. They'd dropped me off at the front entrance, giving me the opportunity to see him first, and alone.

"It seems like he is, but his personality is different. I'm sure we'll have the old Conner back soon, but I want you to be prepared."

"Okay," I said, drawing out the word while pushing his door open.

My shoes clacked across the tile, and I studied him sitting in his bed in a relaxed position. His blond hair disheveled, he looked sexier than ever.

"Took you long enough." His husky voice echoed across the room, sounding… flirtatious?

"I know! I'm so sorry! Phone was off." I rushed to his bedside and gently wrapped my arms around his neck.

"You can squeeze me harder, Olga. I'm not going to break."

I laughed, giving him a little squeeze, still afraid this was all a dream, then carefully sat next to him on the bed.

He cupped my face in his hand. The passion that rose in his eyes—unexpected and almost dark—caused me to suck in a breath of surprise. He caught my hair in a painful grasp and pulled me toward him with a fierce longing. I went numb as he attacked my lips with his, too confused to move. When he shoved his tongue in my mouth, I put my arms against his chest and shoved him backward.

Blackness seemed to have swallowed up his pupils. His gaze on me was still and small, like a cat observing its prey. "What's wrong, baby? I thought this is what you wanted."

Baby? "I do. But, Conner, you just woke up, and I don't know. It just isn't how I imagined my first kiss."

"Your *first* kiss? Well, that explains why you were so bad at it."

My cheeks flushed red as he laughed. My chest rose and fell with rapid breaths. Mrs. Anderson was correct, this wasn't the Conner we knew. But I had to try to get through to him.

"So, could you hear everything we've said to you? I mean, while you were in your coma."

He shook his head, confusion spreading across his features as he batted his long lashes at me. "Some of it. What are you hoping I heard? Let me guess, the part when you told me you loved me?"

I bit the inside of my lip as I nodded, wondering why he'd taunted me. If I could've crawled inside him, I would have, so desperate to understand his puzzling actions, his unusual gruffness.

"I get it. The good little Catholic girl inside you thinks there's a lesson to learn here. But you're wrong. This didn't happen so we can finally fall madly in love with each other and start living the lives we were meant to live. From now on, I'll do what I want, when I want, and that includes not being tied down by some heavy relationship."

Nodding numbly, I bit back my retort. Although shocked by his outburst, I was certain his behavior resulted from a side effect that would go away with time. We sat there in silence for a moment, me thinking of something to say, and him scrolling through the numbers on his phone. I didn't know what else to do. My lips felt full and rubbed raw from his aggressive kiss, and my heart felt sick. Suddenly, a familiar, annoying voice pierced the silence.

"Ohmigawd! Conner!" Tammy squealed, walking in wearing jeans that gave a new definition to skinny. "You're up!"

"Hey, girl. How you doin'?"

She squeezed into the space in front of me and perched on the side of his bed, forcing me to stand. "I'm a helluva lot better now that you're awake. I was so worried about you!"

He pushed a stray piece of hair out of his face. "Is that so?"

Blinking, I glanced around the room, searching for our friends, anyone to help. "What are you doing here anyway?"

She looked up at me, nose high in the air. "None of your business."

Not feeling an ounce of patience for her, I pulled her off the bed and reclaimed my spot. "Look, you should go. Conner needs his rest."

She rolled her eyes and turned back to him. "She's such a party pooper. You've been in a coma for almost three months. Do you really want *me* to leave?"

I didn't miss her stress on the word "me." But Conner wouldn't pick her over me, no way.

"No, Tammy, I don't want *you* to leave." Conner grabbed my hand. "Olga, I'll catch up with you later."

All I could do is gape, wanting to say something, but remaining speechless.

Tammy tossed her perfect blonde hair over her shoulder and waved goodbye.

I stood, staggering a bit. My legs felt like they were made of spaghetti, and I fought the urge to cry. Bursting into tears in front of my nemesis wouldn't do any good. Yelling at Conner after all he'd been through didn't seem right, either. I thought about being bold enough to yell at Tammy, but looking at her, I realized she wasn't worth the effort. Hopefully, that still counted as boldness, knowing when to walk away.

Just as I was leaving, Nic finally showed up with Sean and Kyle.

"Where are you going?" she asked me.

"Conner doesn't want to see me right now." I rubbed the back of my neck.

"What do you mean?"

"You'll see. He's not himself. Or maybe he blames me for being in a coma. I don't know. I'm gonna go home. Call me when you're finished visiting, okay?"

She nodded, frowning.

Down the hall, I ran into Nate, literally. You'd think a guy who could read my thoughts would sense me coming.

"Unless you're thinking of your exact location while rounding the corner, how would I know that?"

I shoved past him. "Whatever."

He chased after me, but I could hear him struggling, his shoe scrapping the floor as if he had to drag his leg behind him. "So that visit with Conner didn't go very well."

"Nope." I didn't know why I was being so mean. Conner's behavior wasn't his fault.

Nate stepped in front of me, blocking my path, and wrapped me in a hug. "He's been in a coma for a long time. I'm sure he's not mad at you about the accident. It just might be a few days before he's back to his old self."

"How do you know? Can you read his mind too?" I mumbled into his sweater.

He leaned back slightly and brushed a piece of hair off my forehead. "Still just yours. Thank goodness. Your thoughts are enough to keep me more than occupied."

I knew he was only trying to keep things light, but his comment annoyed me.

A girl who looked about our age walked by us in the hallway, ogling him.

"Hey, you!" I called, and she turned. "He thinks you're hot."

I whirled away from Nate and thought, *You can bother someone else for a change.* Then I raced down the corridor toward the exit, finally letting my tears fall, along with my hopes that anything would ever be normal again.

CHAPTER FOUR

*"No matter how bad your heart is broken,
the world doesn't stop for your grief."*

—Nate's Thoughts

A week and a half later, on Conner's eighteenth birthday, I stood off to the side of the stage, my eyes wide with shock. The Cantankerous Monkey Squad had just finished opening for another local band at Snug Harbor restaurant for a Rock & Roll Fund-raiser event benefiting the arts. I thought it was too soon for Conner to do concerts with Sean and Kyle. Conner should've needed months of all sorts of therapy for what he'd been through. But the doctors labeled him a miracle, and his parents thought the more he immersed himself in old habits, the quicker we'd get the "old" Conner back. Right now, the "new" Conner had a beer in one hand and another hand all over some groupie wearing barely there jean shorts and a see-through floral lace tank revealing her hot pink bra, their lips locked together in a passionate kiss.

Dizziness washed over me as I watched their major display of PDA, unable to tear my gaze away no matter how badly I wanted to. Finally, I started to back away but stumbled into something. Turning around, I discovered a *someone*.

"What a douche bag." Tammy. At first, I thought she was talking about me bumping into her, but her gaze was locked on Conner. "I can't believe this crap. I thought he was one of the good ones."

I swallowed, my throat tight. "What does it matter to you if he's hooking up with some random tourist?"

She sucked in a breath. "Because *we* just hooked up *last night.*"

"You hooked up with—" I stopped because I realized I'd shouted. And I was about to say my boyfriend, but he wasn't, never was. I'd just wished he was for most of my life.

"I guess neither of us matters to him anymore. What a douche bag."

"Yes, you said that already." I rubbed a hand over my face, wishing I could erase this whole night from my memory.

"I know. It makes me feel better each time I say it. Douche bag, douche bag, douche bag—"

"Please stop." I glanced at Conner again; I couldn't help myself. Then I wished with everything I had that I hadn't looked, because he was totally copping a feel in front of everyone, and instead of slapping him in the face like she should, the girl copped one right back. "I think I'm gonna puke."

Tammy slid her hand down my arm, and she wrapped her fingers around mine. "Come on, let's get out of here."

"Where?" I whimpered, allowing her to lead me through the crowd and toward the exit.

Once outside, Tammy immediately fished her cigarettes out of her purse and lit one up. After an inhale, she pulled the paper from her lips and blew rings of smoke into the air like a distress signal.

"Why did you bring me out here?" I asked, swatting the smoke away with one hand and slipping off my glasses with the other. The hot air made the lenses fog up, and I used the hem of my shirt to clean them.

"Because we were just torturing ourselves back there, and we're better than that. At least, I am."

"Says the girl who hooked up with him last night like it was no big deal. Do you even realize how much I love him?" I laughed at my own question. "Of course you don't. That'd require you to actually understand what love is."

"How can I understand something when it's never been given to me? Not all of us are as lucky as you, princess."

Her comment made me drop my proud shoulders. She had a point. When her father was rushed to the hospital for alcohol poisoning last month, I heard two nurses gossiping about Tammy. It was then I learned the truth about her. Her mom had died during childbirth, and her dad had been drinking ever since. Tammy was the one who supported him with her modeling jobs around the state.

"I'm sorry." I didn't know what else to say.

"It's okay." She took another puff of her cigarette before flicking some embers to the ground. "Anyway, I guess I did you a solid."

"How do you figure?"

"Oh, come on, everyone knows you were saving yourself for him. Now that you know he's not doing the same courtesy for you anymore, you can move on. It's time to let go, don't you think?"

I took a breath, then coughed on the secondhand smoke and pulled out my asthma inhaler. "Easier said than done. And did you even like him?"

Taking two puffs, I waited for her answer.

"Of course I did. I liked him a lot. I dare you to name ten girls in our class off the top of your head who didn't have a crush on Conner sometime during the last three years. My point is, that's not our Conner in there. He might not ever be the same again. In my experience, it's best to cut your losses before you end up emotionally bankrupt."

I looked at her for a moment, wondering if all her hardship had made her wise. Before tonight, I just thought it'd made her another mean girl ruling the school. "Why are you even talking to me?"

She stomped out her cigarette and kept her gaze there a moment longer, the small fire sizzling on the sidewalk. When she looked at me, I swear I saw a flicker of hope in her eyes. "Because I think it's also time to let bygones be bygones."

Maybe in the world of mean girls who ruled the high school social class, this was as close as you got to an apology. She'd been the bane of my existence during our junior year, ever since she decided I was the only obstacle in her way of snatching Conner for herself. She'd even tricked him into not asking me to the prom and taking her instead, but then we had the freak accident a week before the dance anyway.

But when I looked at her now, I saw beyond our differences and recognized something we had in common. We both needed a friend who understood the disappointment of love without even saying a word. And in some weird way, maybe she did do me a favor. My love for Conner always overshadowed everything else, and for the first time ever, I realized maybe those feelings weren't necessarily a good thing. Now I knew. I couldn't go back and do anything differently, but I could move forward and focus on other things for once. Better to live on the edge than maintain the status quo and forget to live at all.

Still, forgetting Conner would take some time. I wasn't usually the forgetting type.

After an entire summer of avoiding awkward run-ins with Conner and his various out-of-towner hookups, the time to start our senior year finally arrived. Over the past ten weeks, I'd pretty much managed to successfully dodge Nate, too. He still stopped by the Bookman occasionally. We'd make small talk about what each of us was up to, and then he'd sit by the window and peruse the magazine or book he just bought while drinking his free cup of coffee. He looked good sipping that coffee, too. He'd gained some weight, got a tan, had his cast and bandages taken off. Hanging out with him, showing him around our small town, keeping our beach date, would've been the polite thing to do.

But it was just too humiliating to remember over and over again that he could hear my every thought. Because what I thought about most was how much Conner broke my heart. I thought him waking up from his coma would be our second chance, but the truth was, we never even got our first chance. Maybe I could've forgotten him if he'd woken up his old self and we had that chance and it just didn't work out. Although some part of me felt like we must have tried at one point and discovered the truth I feared all along: There's nothing like a romance to destroy a friendship. Especially a romance born out of desperation. So I needed to get over Conner. The problem? I didn't know who I was without him by my side. And I definitely didn't want Nate around while I figured that out.

Instead, most of my summer nights were spent hanging out with the girls, Nic and Tammy. Nic thought me befriending Tammy was strange at first, but it wasn't long before the two of them were squealing and giggling together even when I wasn't around. Somehow, both of them had convinced me to try out for the cheerleading squad at the beginning of August. Nobody was more surprised than me when I actually made the team. And even though my mom thought about cheerleading being a dumb sport for bimbos, I won her over by reminding her how good the activity would look on my college applications. Plus, Tammy's dedication as team captain and "go get 'em" attitude was contagious, and I loved being part of the squad. Something told me Tammy was probably the reason I made the team in the first place.

Soon I'd have my own captain duties to tend to for the sailing team. We'd have our first meeting this week. I always loved being part of the sailing team, too, because it was the only co-ed sport. Conner was usually my partner, but that wouldn't be happening this year. Even if he was back to his old self, I didn't know if he'd actually be eager to get back on the water given everything that'd happened. I wasn't, but I needed to face my fears.

Closing my eyes, I knew sleep would remain out of reach with too many thoughts about seeing Conner at school tomorrow. The handful of times I had seen him over the summer, it seemed like he delighted in making a mockery of my feelings. I couldn't make heads or tails of it, only accepted the accident had fundamentally changed him.

My bedroom door creaked, and a shadow appeared in the moonlit glow of the room. I sat upright, ready to scream for my dad, when I heard a familiar voice.

"Olga, it's okay. It's me, Conner."

He managed to noiselessly close the door and make his way slowly to my bed, where he sat on the edge. How could he be sitting on my bed? Of course, he had sat there many times, but that was before, when he had been Conner. But this wasn't Conner anymore, was it?

I thought of telling him that, or asking, but as soon as I opened my mouth, all words left me. I was in that annoying haze of searching my mind for what I wanted to say and then failing to recall what I searched for in the first place. Suddenly, I felt self-conscious and pulled the covers around me, cringing at the thought of how my crazy curls must be standing up with static at this hour. Things like boys showing up in my bedroom unannounced in the middle of the night didn't usually happen to me. Maybe to other people, but not me.

"I woke up, and I needed to talk to you. I knew I should wait, but I didn't know if I'd be myself again the next time I saw you." A beat. "I'm glad your parents still leave their apartment door unlocked." Another beat. "Olga?"

Dad said the moment he felt like he had to lock our front door would be the moment he moved to a smaller town.

"What are you doing here?" I instantly regretted how bitter I sounded. Obviously, Conner was distraught and needed my help.

And just like that, he was crying. "I don't know. It's like ever since I woke up from that coma, I've been sleepwalking. I can remember all the terrible things I've done, but it's like I have no control over myself. Then I woke up in my bed tonight, and I felt like the old me again. I know that doesn't make sense, but—"

"Is this some sort of twisted prank?"

More tears came, spilling over his cheeks. I'd only seen him cry one other time, and that was back in kindergarten when he got the chicken pox and had to miss our class field trip to the fire station.

"I swear it's not. Something is haunting me; I don't know how to explain it. I'm sorry. I know I've been incredibly rude to you this summer, but you're the only one I wanted to see when I woke up tonight."

Shame slithered up my insides, reminding me this was Conner, and I owed it to both of us to help him. I sat up straighter and handed him a tissue off my nightstand. "What happened tonight?"

"My parents staged an intervention."

My hands flew to my chest and felt the fast beating of my heart. "Without me?"

I didn't know why I was hurt by the exclusion, but I was nonetheless.

"It was only with them and this therapist from the hospital, Dr. Judy."

"Oh."

"Yeah."

"So, her intervention worked?"

He ran a hand through his blond hair. "Not exactly. I could feel something in my spirit responding to her, like I was scared, but I didn't know why. Then, when I woke up in the middle of the night, I felt something leaving me."

"And then you were back to your old self again?"

He nodded. "Olga, I know how insane I sound." His voice was barely a whisper. "I won't blame you for not believing me, for not forgiving me for all the things I've done since I woke up from that coma."

For a moment, we just sat there, neither of us saying anything. Finally I said, "I don't know if I forgive you yet for all the things you've done, but you'll probably be surprised by how easily I accept your explanation."

"Really?" His voice cracked.

I cleared my throat. "You're not the only one who has had supernatural things happen to them this summer."

"All right. What does that mean? Your friendship with Tammy?"

I threw my pillow at him, and we laughed quietly. The gesture felt familiar, good. "No. You know that new guy in town?"

He nodded. "Nate."

"Well, he can hear my thoughts."

Doubt flickered in his gaze. "Hear your thoughts? How? Does he hear everyone's thoughts?"

I closed my eyes, suddenly feeling tired. "I don't know. And, no, just mine."

He leaned back on his hands. "Do you think the two of us are connected?"

Stifling a yawn, I asked, "What do you mean?"

"Don't you think it's weird this creepy dude who ends up being my hospital roommate can only read your mind, the only girl I've ever loved, and then I miraculously wake up, but I'm not myself? And then—"

I held a finger to his lips, afraid to breathe. Afraid to think. "Conner." Taking a deep breath, I forced myself to continue. "You said I'm the only girl you've ever loved."

"Yes, that's correct."

I couldn't believe how easily he said those words! I'd been stumbling over telling him how I really felt for the past five years and could never get the right words out. And I'd never heard him sound more sincere, either. Was he finally manning up? Ready to be more than my friend? My heart pounded, and I swallowed, trying to think of what to say. I sat in the darkness, stunned but feeling like I finally found some light.

"I'm sorry; I wish I was doing this better. Telling you I love you with flowers, candles, romantic music, and stuff. But I'm just scared I won't be myself again tomorrow, so I had to tell you now. Please don't give up on me, no matter what I do, okay?"

No matter what I do. Suddenly, those words gave way to fury. His whole life, I'd been accepting, I'd been forgiving, I'd been hopeful, I'd been denied, I'd been depressed, I'd been lonely… but now I was just angry. I couldn't help the feeling. It rose up from the pit of my stomach and couldn't be stopped, like I rotated through the seven stages of grief in reverse order.

Before, I would've set him on my pedestal and did as he asked, because I loved him. But was that really love? Is that what I wanted? Bitterly, I thought of everything he'd done this summer. The images were almost intolerable. So he wasn't himself when he did all those things. If the lightning strike had fundamentally changed him somehow, it'd done the same to me. Maybe I was still in love with him. Maybe I'd always be. But right now, that didn't matter, because he had *destroyed* me this summer, the me that could get past whatever he did.

"You should go home." I held the covers tightly to my chest.

He looked at me, his eyes widening, like he needed to do a double take to make sure it was really me telling him to leave. "I'm sorry."

I wanted him to explain himself, but of course, he didn't. "Sorry for what exactly? Sorry for all the time I spent at the hospital only to be cast aside the moment you woke up? Sorry for shoving your tongue down my throat and then ridiculing my feelings for you? Sorry for sleeping with Tammy and only God knows who else? Sorry for realizing too late that you love me? Sorry for coming here at all, for thinking I'd forgive you like it was nothing? Well, I'm sorry. It doesn't seem like I'm the same person you thought I was, the person you fell in love with. And you know, you're the one to blame for that."

A sudden stiffening took over his posture as he stood, his muscles rigid. "Olga, I'm sorry for all that, and so much more. I understand why you're hurt. It was wrong of me to come here tonight expecting anything. I just hoped—"

"The least you could've hoped for was I wouldn't punch you in the face. Get. Out. Now."

A part of me, the old part of me, wanted him to stay. Instead, he strode away with another whispered sorry. Holding my breath, I listened for the click of my bedroom door, expecting a sigh of relief to come. Saying what was really on your mind brought freedom, right?

I lay back down, shaking under the sheet. Soon, morning would come and bring with it the first day of our senior year. Who knew what the months ahead held for us? Every school year brought a wave of new surprises, but between Nate's mind-reading trick, my new friendship with the most popular girl in school, and Conner apparently suffering from a major bipolar disorder, I had a feeling this year would have more twists and turns than a roller coaster.

Twisting and turning was all I did for the rest of the night, and when dawn broke, I realized that feeling of freedom never did come.

CHAPTER FIVE

"Sometimes we have the right to be mad,
but that doesn't give us the right to be cruel."

—Nate's Thoughts

When I arrived at school, the anger from the night before turned to worry. Conner wasn't at school. Given his recent behavior, our friends seemed unconcerned, figuring it was more of the "new" Conner they had come to know. I wanted to explain about his frantic visit to my room in the middle of the night, but shame kept my mouth shut. I did, however, text Conner as I walked to my second period, imagining all kinds of worst-case scenarios. Despite the prospect of a lunch detention, I left my phone on during class in case he contacted me. He did neither. I sent him another text on my way to third period and decided if I hadn't heard from him by lunch, I'd leave campus in search of him. What I'd say to him if I found him I wasn't sure of yet. The good girl inside me told me to say sorry, but the part of me that had grown a backbone didn't think an apology was in order. So what should I do?

As it turned out, no search party was needed. He showed up to the cafeteria wearing sunglasses, and one of Tammy's old cronies on his arm. Make that two cronies, one for each arm. I thought they were both named Amanda, ironically, because their answer to almost every question sounded like the end of their name: duh.

On all accounts, it looked like the "new" Conner had returned. I seriously needed to research bipolar disorders when I got home this afternoon. In the meantime, I waved in relief at the sight of him, and the gesture was all it took for him to saunter over with his new groupies, the whole cafeteria watching him as he did, snickering while looking at their cells. *Weird.*

"What's up?" he greeted.

I noticed right away he was newly inked on his left forearm, a fresh tattoo of a naked lady's backside sitting on the beach, a dark moon shining behind her.

"When did you have time to get this? After you left my house last night?"

A wave of confusion rippled across his face. "What are your talking about?"

My mind raced. I leaned forward, staring into his eyes. "Conner, are you in there?"

He threw his head back in laughter. "The Conner you once knew is dead. It's time you got over him."

A weight dropped in the pit of my stomach. "In case you forgot, I am. Or are you just going to act like last night never happened between us?"

I blanched, realizing what others around us in the lunchroom would assume happened with a comment like that. Too late to take it back now, though.

He made a *tsk*-ing sound. "Oh, Olga, I'll always be your *special friend.* We can do the friends with benefits thing if you want."

I slapped him in the face. "The only benefit I'd get from sleeping with you at this point is an STD. What's happening to you? I thought Dr. Judy's intervention worked. I thought you were sorry for everything."

Shrugging, he said, "Relax. I've devised a way for you to get over me. See?"

He pulled his cell out of his pocket and held the phone under my nose. A dating website with my picture displayed on the screen. Specifically, a picture of me wearing my Princess Leia Star Wars costume from last Halloween.

"What's this about?"

"It's my little thank you for saving my life. Tammy suggested it back in June when we hooked up, but I only just now got around to actually posting your profile. And look, you've already gotten two dozen hits, which isn't that great considering I already e-mailed it to all my contacts. But still money well spent, I'd say."

"I hope you're joking."

"Oh, no, it's totally legit. You want to hear your profile?" He scrolled through the screen and read. "Young virgin woman available, funny and quick, which honestly, would be like having sex with me! As my class valedictorian, I'm kind of a big deal. I love Jesus, but he can't take me out on dates, so give me a call. I think that pretty much sums it up. Jazz hands."

"Jazz hands?"

"Always end with jazz hands. Isn't that what your boy Nate says?"

"How about ending this conversation with me punching you in the face?" Nate suddenly stood behind me.

"Oh, hey. We were just talking about you. I can tell what you see in my girl here." He held up the picture of me on his phone. "I bet you'd like to tap that, huh, Han Solo? Is that why you hung out at the bookstore all summer? You were hoping for a little role play action, weren't you, son?"

Nate pushed him in lieu of an answer. Conner pushed back, and then it was on.

I'd always been a fan of knights in shining armor, rushing in to save the damsel in distress. There's always that scene where good guy faces undeserving guy in order to win the affections of the fair lady, the camera zooming in on the action as the villain falls to the floor. I felt like I was in a movie, watching Nate's fist connect with Conner's nose. The only difference being I'd never seen Conner as the bad guy until now, but his eyes, dark and darting, suggested he was. He hopped to his feet, vengeance on the agenda, swinging his fist toward Nate's face. But Nate ducked, then slammed into Conner, driving him to the ground where they engaged in a wrestling match, Conner pinned underneath Nate.

Gauging certain thoughts while in a state of disbelief proved difficult. Everything about this situation felt wrong—Conner wasn't a villain. But one small detail filtered through: the lunchroom swarmed toward our table, screaming at Nate, because to everyone else he was the bad guy here. And with that in mind, distressed as I was, I stood up on the table and shouted at the masses to, "*Stop!*"

My plan worked. It also left me standing stupidly with nothing else to say, so I hopped down, grabbed my backpack, then grabbed Nate's arm and left the cafeteria with both in tow.

"You're dead!" Conner called from behind us, but I kept dragging Nate away from the scene of the crime.

What a douche bag.

"You can say that again."

"I didn't say anything."

Nate smiled. "I know."

"You were listening to my conversation with Conner?"

"Yeah, and good thing, too. FYI, that guy you call your best friend is a monster."

The tears leaked onto my cheeks.

"Hey, I'm sorry. Are you okay?"

"Am I okay? I should be asking you that question." *He sure looks okay, better than okay.*

A huge grin spread across his face because, of course, he heard everything. "Maybe we should go somewhere so you can inspect me for injuries."

"If you don't wipe that ridiculous smirk off your face, you'll be going back to the hospital sooner than you'd like."

"Right." He took a deep breath. "Well, we can't go back to the cafeteria. I'm guessing you don't want to skip school. So where do you suggest we hide out for the remainder of lunch?"

"The journalism room should be safe. The dean will find you eventually, wanting to know what happened back there. But we can hide out in my office until then."

"You have an office?"

"Perks of being the *Bucs' Blade* editor-in-chief. Technically, the office doesn't belong to me. It's just a small, closed-off space in the back of the journalism room."

He stopped and gripped my shoulders, turning me toward him. "I want to ask you something."

I peeled off his hands and continued walking. "Go ahead. I'm sure you'll know the answer before I even open my mouth."

"Will you go out on a date with me this weekend?"

"This weekend?" My traitorous heart wouldn't stop pounding.

"Yeah, ya know, Friday or Saturday night… whichever works best for you."

I rubbed the back of my neck. "Why would you want to go out with me? I'm a freak. There's something wrong with me."

He adjusted his book bag on his back. "I'm the one who can read your mind, and you think you're the one who's a freak?"

"Ha! Didn't Edward say that in *Twilight*?"

"I don't know what you're talking about. I don't read romance books about sparkly vampires or watch those movies. I'm too manly for that."

"Hmm, that's too bad. Because finding a guy who is manly enough to admit he reads books like *Twilight* would be a total turn-on."

"In that case, I loved all four books."

I took the stairs two at a time, staring at the steps as I did because if I looked at Nate, I knew I'd blush. "An-y-way, being a freak comes naturally. I've been the freaky genius girl since kindergarten."

He snorted. "Freak meets geek. A match made in heaven."

"You aren't a geek, far from it."

"I thought I'd just made it clear I was the freak, though."

"So now you're calling me a geek?" I sneaked a look at him, and I couldn't help admiring his beauty, inside and out. Maybe he didn't appear *hot* to every girl like Conner did, but he was undeniably adorable to me.

His face flushed. "Only in the best sense of the word."

"Which means what exactly?"

Skimming his fingertips along his perfect jawline, he said, "Someone who's unusually intelligent and therefore doesn't care what others think, which is why you shouldn't mind going out with a freak this weekend."

I snorted. "I think outside school, a safe distance of two miles should be kept between us at all times. There's too many complications that could happen if we spend time together."

My feet slipped on the last step before reaching the top. Nate rescued me with his quick movements, hugging me. There was no reason for me to keep holding on to him, but I did anyway. His arms were so warm as he clutched the back of my shirt, and his heart pounded against my chest like a drum. My heart fluttered in response. I let go immediately, refusing to make things more complicated between us. Robotically, I led him toward my office.

"Like what?"

"I can't name any off the top of my head, but I'm sure there are a million."

"Well, I'd say it has a million advantages."

"Like what?"

"Exhibit number one, the lunchroom just now. I'll always know when you're in trouble and need my help."

"I don't know. Nothing feels right anymore." I looked down at my watch, calculating the minutes until school ended. "Obviously, I don't have any delusions about dating Conner. I don't even want to talk to him ever again."

"You want some advice?"

"No."

"Yeah, I figured. And if I knew what was good for me, I'd keep my mouth shut because him acting like a jerk brings the odds in my favor. But from what I can gather from your thoughts, it sounds as if he's been a really good friend of yours for over a decade. Maybe you owe it to him to not give up on your friendship so easily."

I sighed. "You're right. Just this morning, I resolved not to be angry with him. But now I just hope I can keep myself from killing him and his latest bimbo."

"Jealous much?"

"You know, you have your moments where you rate a ten on the jerk meter, too."

"Touché." He closed the distance between us. "But I find your feisty side sexy."

Groaning, I quickly opened the door to the empty journalism room, then made my way to the back office.

"So you seriously do have your own office?"

I chuckled morosely because I doubted his surprise. "I share the space with Nic. We both write for the paper. We were going to share the coveted titles of business managers for our student publication this year because it's a really big job getting enough ad space to pay for all we want to do, but when Conner got struck by lightning on April first… it just made me think, go big or go home. So I told Mrs. Cleveland I wanted to run for editor-in-chief, and we didn't even have to vote. Everyone on the paper thought it should be me."

He leaned forward, studying an article I'd written about prom styles through the ages pinned to the bulletin board. "This was from April's issue. I'm guessing it's the last article you wrote?"

"You'd be correct."

Shuddering, he said, "You didn't go to prom."

It wasn't a question. Slumping down in the desk chair, I put my head in my hands and sobbed.

After a painful few seconds, Nate slipped his arm around my shaking shoulders. "Olga, I'm so sorry for everything that's happened to you. Nobody should be under this much stress."

"You should leave. I'll be fine."

He leaned down and whispered in my ear. "I don't want to leave. Maybe I can help you figure things out. Just last night, Conner was himself and wanted you to promise to not give up on him. The Olga I know, the one full of faith and hope, wouldn't throw in the towel so quickly."

I stared at him. "You didn't listen in last night, did you? What do you do, stand outside my window so you can hear my thoughts or something?"

He leaned back. "What? No! But the scenario has been on instant replay in your mind all day. Kind of hard to ignore."

"Oh, right. Sorry." My voice came out hoarse. "But how could you help me figure things out?"

With his jaw set in thought, he answered after a minute. "We should probably start with Googling the side effects of coma patients."

He flipped open the laptop, then asked me for my password. Embarrassed, I told him Conner99.

"Why the 99?"

Bringing up Google, I typed in my search. "It's the year we met."

There was a lot to sift through during the twenty minutes we had left for lunch. The sites mentioned a variety of personality changes we'd seen in Conner—everything from disinhibition, impulsiveness, childish behavior, lack of initiative, and inappropriate sexual activity. The last one seemed especially accurate. What I wanted to know was when this side effect would switch off so I could have my best friend back. But, of course, there were no real answers for timelines. Some stated a few weeks, while others seemed to think two years, and some stated the side effects could be irreversible. The advice was to be patient with the person, not make a big deal out of their behavior, and direct them toward the appropriate doctors for help. Overall, there was little reason to hope. Frustrated, I snapped the computer shut as the bell rang.

"Are Conner's parents taking him to the doctor for help? Maybe they could prescribe some meds to get his behaviors in check. I mean, he's basically destroying himself. They have to see that, right? No matter how happy they are to have him back."

I slung my book bag over one shoulder. "When he visited me last night, he said they had staged an intervention with a therapist. But what I don't get is why he'd be himself last night, then back to jerkface Conner today."

Nate nodded. "Dr. Judy. I see the same therapist."

My mouth fell open. "Is she like the only therapist in this town or something? My mom has been trying to get me to her office for months."

He shrugged. "I don't know. But whatever is going on with Conner can't be fixed with therapy alone. Maybe he has a bipolar disorder, or maybe schizophrenia, or maybe something we haven't thought of yet. I can eat lunch with you in here every day if you want to avoid Conner and do some research."

Opening the door, I was taken off guard by a group of five guys huddling together in the hall, all laughing at my dating profile. Nate whispered something to a nearby teacher standing in her doorway, and then she yelled at the boys to put their phones away.

"Thanks," I mumbled. We walked in silence to fifth period. His mind seemed distracted, his gaze anywhere but on me. Maybe he was looking for other guys with their phones out so he could bust them, too. I hoped he wasn't looking for Conner so he could punch him again.

When I arrived at my Multivariable Calculus class, Nate followed me in.

"What are you doing? You're not in this class, are you?"

He hit his forehead with the heel on his hand. "Oh, right!" The bell tolled five times, the sound of a ship, reminding us Grand Haven was the Coast Guard capital of the good ole USA. "Well, if you need me, all you need to do is think it, and I'll be there as fast as I can."

"Okay, thanks." As I took my standard spot in the front row, I couldn't help but grin as he waved at me through the small window of the door before taking off for his own class.

Mr. Propert wasted no time in calling me up to the Smart Board to work out a problem we had for summer math homework. I breathed a sigh of relief when he declared my answer correct. A calculus theorem I could figure out and prove with no problems or worries. After all, I was captain of the math team, too. But trying to decipher Conner's new behavior or my feelings for Nate... I didn't have a clue.

Nate joined me in my journalism office every day the first week of school, even opted for after school detention for the fight instead of serving his sentence at lunch so he could help me. On Friday, we snarfed down greasy cafeteria stuffed-crust pepperoni pizza and sweet potato waffle fries while hovering over Google searches on the laptop together. Today, we even shared a caramel-flavored iced latte. As I ate with abandon, my mind whirled over the endless possibilities.

Throwing his napkin down, Nate belched. "Excuse me."

"Nice, Barca." For some reason, I'd started referring to him by his last name sometime during the week. I think it made me feel more like a journalist researching a story, rather than a heartbroken, distraught friend trying desperately to find answers.

"Thank you. So, only ten minutes left on our lunch hour research. What do you conclude?"

I looked around at my desk scattered with notes. "I conclude I know nothing. Maybe the way Conner is acting isn't so abnormal after all. Maybe it's just a normal response to a traumatizing event. He may not be someone I want for my best friend anymore, but at least he's alive, and he seems happy. His parents have him visiting a doctor, that therapist, and the school counselor. I think the best thing I can do right now is wait and..."

"Meditate?"

"I was going to say pray."

"Oh. Why did you hesitate to say that word?"

I tossed my glasses on the desk and rubbed the sleep from my eyes. "I don't know. I guess I don't know if you have any type of spiritual life, and I didn't want to spook you."

He took another sip from the latte, then offered me the last of it.

"Don't I seem like someone who has faith? I accepted the reading your mind trick fairly easily."

Running a hand through my frizzy hair, I decided to wrap my curls into a bun and secure it with a pencil. "True. So you go to church?"

Nate caught a strand of my red hair between his fingers and tucked the piece behind my ear. What startled me wasn't the intimate gesture but how natural the touch of his hands on my skin felt. "Olga, I find that, sadly, attending church and having faith seldom go hand in hand."

"Is that your passive-aggressive way of stating you're too good for church?"

He frowned. "Not at all. I'm just saying there are plenty of people at my last church who I'd be surprised to find in heaven, and there's a lot of people I know who've never stepped foot in a church that I'd be shocked if they went to hell."

Slipping my glasses back on, I said, "I'm sure you're right. Still, maybe you want to start joining me for Youth Alive? It's a prayer group I lead on campus. We meet every morning in the library before school starts."

Nate shrugged. "Maybe. Have you ever tried meditation, though?"

"No, have you?"

"Absolutely. I've read a lot of psychology and philosophy books that speak about meditating. Actually, the ability to intentionally *not* think about anything for a little while is something I've practiced more and more since meeting you. I know you don't like the weird little brain hack trick I can do, so I'm trying not to. Would you like me to teach you how to meditate?"

"Now?"

"Why not? It decreases stress, and no offense, but you've been suffering from a major anxiety problem ever since we met."

I stretched my head to see out of the office window into the journalism room. Nobody seemed to be spying on us, but I still asked, "Here?"

"Sure."

I curled up in the desk chair and watched him for a moment. "Okay. What do I do?"

"The first step is making your mind completely blank and empty."

"How do I do that exactly?"

Nate's eyes were wide and earnest. "First, I release all my worries from the day. Then, I recite a short, positive message over and over again until my mind grabs ahold of it, and then I get rid of all my thoughts and emotions."

"I'm having a hard time picturing this working."

"Look, let's just start. Practice makes perfect. Start with taking long, deep breaths. Relax and feel any pure energy coming to you until your mind is a blank slate."

I twisted the Morticia Addams ring on my finger, the one Conner gave me on my sixteenth birthday, while Nate pulled out his phone and played some soft instrumental music.

"To help create an environment of relaxation," he explained. Putting one open palm on my knee, he said, "Let's begin then."

He closed his eyes, and I did the same, placing my hand on top of his. Hearing his deep breaths, I matched his inhales, holding for a count of three, then exhaled. I confessed all my sins to get rid of my worries like Nate suggested, then recited the words of St. Francis because they spoke to me in the moment: "Lord, make me an instrument of your peace." I imagined all my thoughts drifting away in a little cloud high into the sky until it disappeared.

And then.

I'm sitting on the couch in Kyle's living room. Music throbs in my ears and shakes the halls as Nate belts out the lyrics that Conner wrote for the Cantankerous Monkey Squad song, "Return." I glance at the people gathered for the first house party of the school year. Mostly the stoner nonconformists clique litters the green carpet, moshing as Nate hits all the right notes. I notice a cheerleader named Brittany sitting on a Detroit Lions inflatable chair in the corner, practically foaming at the mouth while she watches Nate sing. Tammy passes around a plate of cookies in the kitchen off to the left. Dave, a guy from my Driver's Ed class this semester, offers me a beer, and I turn him down. Several people on the back porch play a drinking game called Quarters by the Keg.

Nate walks toward me after he sets down the microphone, his eyes pleading. "Olga, I always see you."

He extends his hand, and I take it, letting him lead me toward a bright light.

The vision left abruptly, and Nate and I opened our eyes, gasping.

"What the heck was that?" I shrieked.

"No clue."

"So you saw that, too?"

"The party scene? Yep."

"Well, of course you did. You read my mind."

He shook his head. "It wasn't like that. *I* saw it for myself."

"But you didn't manipulate that creepy vision, make me see what you wanted?"

He looked at me, his face free from expression, his eyes full of hurt. "How?"

Zipping up my sweater, I said, "I don't know, with that freaky mind connection."

"No, that was my first time ever having a vision. Usually meditating clears my mind. It does not conjure up weird little daydreams on its own accord."

I kept my gaze on his, watched for any trace of a lie, and found nothing. "But that didn't feel like a vision necessarily. It felt like a…"

"Memory."

"Yeah, did you think that, too, or did you just read my thoughts?"

The bell rang, and he jumped to his feet. "No, I thought the same thing. It felt like a distant, hazy memory from another lifetime or something."

"What do you think it means?" I gathered my things and stuffed them into my bag.

"I don't know. Some people believe meditation can help you retain memories, even recall lost ones. Maybe we're just both insane?"

I laughed aloud, even though it wasn't funny, because that's what crazy people do.

CHAPTER SIX

*"Two people can look at the exact same thing
and see something totally different."*

—Nate's Thoughts

The final bell rang at 2:37 p.m. Not that I'd heard a word any of my teachers said after the vision with Nate.

"So, Olga, I hear you're going out with the new hottie in school. How'd you make that happen?" Brittany asked, the same Brittany who drooled over Nate in our shared vision.

I slammed my locker. "Who says we're going out?"

"Tammy."

"Yeah, well, Tammy wouldn't recognize the truth if it bit her in her perfect little a—" The loud speaker came on, announcing the cancellation of some club meeting after school and effectively saving my tooshie. Swearing was out of character for me, but the frustration of the last few months slowly corrupted me. "Gotta go. See ya."

"If you're not going out with Nate, do you think can you put in a good word for me?" she called down the hall.

Yes, I *think* I can.

Walking quickly toward the parking lot to catch a ride with Nic, I stopped Tammy on the way.

"Hey, what's with the rumor you're starting about me going out with Nate?"

Her gaze bounced around to every passing classmate. "You already heard that one?"

"Explain."

Tammy ran a hand through her short, blonde hair. "You know how I have last period with Conner. Well, he was talking smack about sleeping with four girls this summer, and how it could've been five, but he didn't go through with one because he'd known her since she was five, and he felt bad the girl was actually in love with him."

My stomach twisted into knots. "What?"

Tammy's face fell, and to her credit she looked like she was going to be sick over his behavior, too. "So, I couldn't help myself. I wanted to see if there was one last shred of humanity left in him. I turned around and told him he was a liar, that the girl he referred to had way more class than to ever think about sleeping with him and had already moved onto bigger and better things with the new hottie in town."

Tears welled up in the corners of my eyes. "What'd he say to that?"

Tammy shook her head slowly. "He said I was right, that Olga Gay Worontzoff was too classy to sleep with him, but I wasn't."

Squeezing Tammy's shoulder, I said, "You're too classy for all the guys at this school, even most of the girls. I hope you didn't put up with his bullcrap."

A flush crept across her cheeks. "I slapped him in the face."

I laughed. "He's getting a lot of that action these days, but he deserves it. What'd the teacher do?"

She shrugged. "She told Conner he had it coming, then moved his seat to the other side of the room away from everyone and told all of us to sit down, shut our mouths, and get our work done."

"Well, I agree with her. He did have it coming."

My phone dinged, a text from Nic popping up: *u comin?*

"I gotta go. Nic is waiting for me."

Tammy nodded. "Why don't I drive you home? We've barely had time to hang out this week."

"We've seen each other every day at cheerleading practice."

"Yeah, but that's all work and no play. I need a good girl talk."

"You and me both." I sent Nic a text and walked with Tammy toward the parking lot.

"Are you excited to cheer in your first football game of the season tonight?"

"I guess, but it kind of sucks because I really need to get a head start on studying and write the weekly blog on the school's website for the *Bucs' Blade*."

"Jesus, Olga, you sure are boring."

"Hey!"

She unlocked her Lexus with the remote on her keychain. "Sorry, but sometimes the truth hurts. You need to come to Kyle's party tomorrow, though."

I froze, my fingers on the door handle, my mind flashing to the vision I shared with Nate. "I wasn't invited." I'd never been the sensitive type, but I felt a little hurt. My good buddy didn't invite me to his party.

"Yes, you are. Get in. I'll tell you all about it."

I obeyed, then waited a few minutes as Tammy got situated.

Finally, when she turned onto the road, she explained, "Kyle just found out this morning his parents are going out of town for the weekend. When we chatted at lunch, I told him it was the perfect opportunity to throw the first big house party of the school year, and he agreed. Something you would've already known if you actually ever joined us in the cafeteria."

Squinting at the sun pouring in through the windshield, I nodded. "Sorry. Nate and I have been doing some research up in the journalism room, though."

"Right. Does this research include investigating his mouth?"

Gah! "No! We did meditate together, though."

She laughed. "Hot. When?"

"Today, but it was weird."

"Good weird or bad weird?"

"Both." I told her how the meditation started out relaxing, but then turned weird, including every detail I remembered about the vision of me at Kyle's house party. Even though I spent most of my summer hanging out with her and Nic, I'd only told Nic about Nate reading my thoughts. So, I took the opportunity I had now to clue Tammy in on that little tidbit as well.

She nearly bounced off her driver's seat in irritation. "I can't believe you kept this from me!"

Raising my eyebrows, I said, "Do you really blame me? This whole situation is crazy!"

"Okay, but you have to tell me everything. Now."

"I already did."

Her shoulders slumped. "So you guys haven't figured anything out yet?"

Flashing a bitter smile, I said, "Concerning Nate and his reading my mind or our research about Conner during lunch?"

"Either."

"Your guess is as good as mine on both accounts."

"Maybe that vision you guys shared today means you can see the future when your souls connect in a deep way or something. I think you should both come to Kyle's party tomorrow night and try to recreate the scene as much as possible. See what happens. I'll even make cookies."

I fidgeted nervously with the zipper on my sweater. "You know, that's actually a good idea." But I didn't see how Nate would be playing with the Cantankerous Monkey Squad.

Tammy smiled wide. "Don't sound so surprised. I do get those from time to time."

There were people everywhere, shooting hoops in Kyle's driveway, playing Quarters by the beer keg set up on his back porch, gathered around the island in his kitchen and munching on snacks. Plastic red Solo cups littered every countertop. The Cantankerous Monkey Squad's self-titled song blared from the living room, and a group of stoner nonconformists were moshing on the green carpet in front of the band while Nate sang all the right notes, Sean nailed the rhythms on his bass, and Kyle whaled on the drums. *Wait, Nate?*

"What's Nate doing singing with the band? Where's Conner?" I shouted to Nic over the loud music.

"Oh, yeah. I was so busy at the store today I never got a chance to tell you. The Cantankerous Monkey Squad came to blows last night after playing at Music Walk downtown."

"What happened?"

"Well, Sean and Kyle are tired of Conner hooking up with all the girls, ranging anywhere from thirteen to twenty. And you know he's messing

75

around with drugs and alcohol, too, don't you?"

I shook my head. "I'd heard he was the Beer Pong champ this summer, but I hadn't heard anything about drugs."

"Yeah, he likes to smoke a joint before they play a show now. Says it relaxes him."

Shuddering, I thought of how my meditation with Nate was supposed to relax me but only ended up making me freak out even more. "Hmm, so they just finally had enough and kicked him out of the band last night?"

"Pretty much. We all went to Jumpin' Java for a cup of coffee afterward, and Nate was sitting at a table by himself, so we invited him to hang with us. Then the boys got to talking about music, and Kyle asked if he'd fill in for Conner tonight at the party. They practiced all day together."

I raised one eyebrow, thinking again of the vision as I followed Nic into the kitchen. It was weird, all the details coming together like magic. I felt entranced, destined to follow a certain path.

Already coolness filled the air with all the windows and doors open in the house, even though it was only the first week of September, summer barely over. Most of the girls were wearing sweaters or coats, but I'd forgotten mine. The weather wasn't the only thing giving me the chills, though. All the details of Kyle's house party were the same ones I had seen earlier in my vision with Nate. Tammy leaned against the hardwood island in the kitchen, offering up the brownies and cookies she made for the party. Her outfit wasn't weather appropriate either: a Victoria's Secret Pink tank top with Billabong black cutoffs. A perfect high ponytail shimmered with gold gel among her blonde highlights.

She seemed to have noticed my nervousness because she grabbed on to my hand tightly and led me to the back porch, where she approached the keg and poured two cups full, then handed me one.

"Here's to new friendships and finding out answers tonight! Bottoms up!" She clashed her cup against mine, then took a big drink, practically finishing her beer in one gulp.

I'd never drank a sip of alcohol before, unless you counted the drop of Sacramental wine I tasted after the priest dipped the broken bread in during Communion. Something told me Tammy wouldn't count that, and I knew she'd hound me until I had the full party experience. So I tilted the plastic cup to my lips and drank it all. When I finished, I couldn't help burping and making a face.

Tammy laughed. "If I were to guess, I'd say that was your first beer. How'd you like it?"

I knew I should lie, make myself look cool. "Disgusting."

Something told me the truth was better.

Tammy nodded, taking my cup from me before pouring two more beers. "Beer is an acquired taste. Cheers."

This time, I shooed the cup away. "No, thanks. I think I'm a one-drink type of girl."

As in that one beer is the only one I'll ever drink in my whole life! Yuck!

Nic swooped in from behind and snatched the cup, taking a sip.

"Ugh, how can you drink that stuff?" I asked her.

She froze, sniffing near my mouth. "Oh my gosh! Did you drink your first beer without me?"

I shrugged. "Oh, right. Sorry. I didn't mean to, and I definitely didn't like it."

"Well, too bad. You'll have to have another one, with me this time."

Shaking my head, I said, "No way. I'll puke."

Tammy giggled, already refilling her cup a third time. I was surprised she seemed so eager to drink considering all the problems alcohol caused with her dad. Maybe she inherited his alcoholism gene and couldn't help herself. "You're such a girl. Here, try one of these. I bet you'll love it." She reached into the cooler and pulled out a grape-flavored beverage.

"Hold up," Nic hollered. "Olga's first night of partying. I have to get a shot of this." She grabbed her cell phone from the back pocket of her skinny jeans and snapped a picture. "I'm texting you the picture now."

"Send it to me, too," Tammy told her. "I want as many pictures of us together during our senior year as possible. Time to make some memories!"

I smiled, then guzzled about half of the bottle, liking the taste more than the beer at least.

"There, happy?" I asked Nic, then let out a burp. I probably should've eaten something today.

She yanked the bottle from my hands and drained the rest. "Now I am! Come on, let's dance, girls!"

We followed her into the living room. As we swayed to "Haunted," another original by the band, I felt all kinds of spooked out. My balance was off, I was already woozy, and I kept stumbling as I honed in on the lyrics. *But in this haunted house there's danger in every direction/ I pray to God he would give me some protection/ And in this haunted house we're not the same people/ But you, my friends, are my sanctuary, my steeple/ I hope if I die young ,I'll find my way back home/ So you'll feel me and know you're not alone/ In this haunted house.*

For the past five years, I heard Conner play guitar and sing every week. He had such raw talent, and I knew it'd be tough to replace him. But as I listened to them playing, I couldn't deny Nate had skills, too.

Conner. He walked in with a group of guys, slamming the door behind him. I recognized one boy with him, Dave, from my Driver's Ed class, and I remembered he had been in my vision, too. I thought the lack of Conner in my vision was a bit weird, though. The group headed to the porch toward the keg, but they already seemed drunk. Brittany pressed against Conner like a kitten as he poured his beer. The walls closed in on me, the floor swimming, as I tried not to think about Conner hooking up with yet another cheerleader.

"I think I need a break," I shouted to Nic and Tammy over the music.

They flashed me a thumbs-up and kept dancing while I awkwardly hobbled to the couch. As I sank down on the cool leather, the song ended and Nate addressed the crowd of twenty-something people gathered in the living room. His words barely registered as I watched Conner, the way he wiped his hand on his jeans when he spilled his beer, the way he cocked his head to hear what Brittany said, the sound of his laugh more musical than any instrument. All these gestures were so familiar to me, but the boy he had turned into since the accident was a total stranger.

When Nate belted out the lyrics to "Return," Conner suddenly shifted his focus to his former band. He stepped into the living room, away from Brittany and the crowd he'd come in with. Dave followed, but Conner ignored him. Shrugging, Dave made his way to the couch and plopped down next to me.

"Hey, Olga. You want one?" He shoved a Solo cup in my face, filled to the top with beer, effectively sloshing it down my—correction—Nic's white laced top. "Oh, my bad. It's such a nice shirt, too."

He proceeded to wipe the beer off my breasts. Yeah, I pretended that's what he was trying to do. Not cop a feel at all.

Shoving his hand away, I said, "Dude, it's fine."

Absentmindedly, I touched the top of my sprayed hair. Tammy had styled my locks into a Mohawk by giving me three small French braids on each side of my head, then combing the Mohawk section in the middle until it reached her desired height. I was skeptical at first, but I had to admit I looked pretty tough, like someone who shouldn't be messed with.

"Nice hair, too. You trying to impress somebody tonight?"

My head automatically snapped to Conner; I couldn't help myself. And, boy, did he ever look like he needed a Xanax or Valium or whatever he probably took these days. His hands were fisted at his sides, and his whole body twitched, like he planned to launch himself at the "stage" any moment now. But he also looked like he fought the impulse.

Was "my" Conner in there somewhere tonight? As soon as I thought the question, his gaze shifted to me. He stared intently, like his eyes pleaded for help. Grasping on to the side table for balance, I stood and left Dave hanging midsentence, not that I knew what he had said anyway. I walked slowly, making sure my legs would work properly, still feeling a buzzed effect. All the while, Conner's blue gaze drilled into me. I longed for X-ray vision, a chance to see past his bruised skin and into his soul to find the answers I needed. I wanted him to reach out to me, to tell me he was himself again and this would all be over now.

"Conner." My heart pounded, and my legs shook just from being this close to him. "Are you okay?"

"Olga," he said on a sigh. "Your hair." He reached up, like he was going to brush a stray piece of hair away from my face the way he used to. But just before contact, he stopped himself. His whole countenance changed, and then his hand brushed the front of Nic's blouse, A.K.A. my boobs, making me shiver. "You're all wet. Was someone doing shots off your chest? And if so, can I be next?"

Ugh! Why does he keep acting like this?

His hand still cupped my ta-tas; he traced his fingers over the slope of my breasts.

For some reason, I just stood there, frozen. Then I heard Nate's voice over the microphone. "Hey, get your hands off her!"

Nate jumped in front of Conner, guitar still strapped over his shoulder while Kyle and Sean kept playing. Conner shoved Nate backward, almost making him fall.

"What the hell is your problem, man?" Nate yelled.

Kyle and Sean finally took that as the cue to stop playing and got behind Nate in a heartbeat.

"My problem is you're here, playing my songs with my band."

"It's not my fault your actions caused your friends to drop you."

Conner gave a low growl, foaming at the mouth. *Wait, foaming? What? Is he puking up his beer or something? Wouldn't surprise me. That awful taste is still in my mouth.*

Then, without warning, Conner threw a punch, clipping Nate's jaw. Nate stumbled to the side, but Kyle and Sean caught him before he went down. Kyle stepped in front of Nate, waving his drumsticks in front of Conner's face.

"Get out of my house!"

Panting, Conner circled me. "Fine, but I'm taking her with me. You took something that belonged to me. Only fair I return the favor."

He grabbed a fistful of my Mohawk and yanked me backward against his sweaty body. *What the heck? This goes beyond douche bag behavior now. This is full-out psycho!*

Nate grabbed one of my arms, effectively engaging me in a game of human tug-of-war.

"Like hell you are," Kyle yelled. "Now, are you gonna let go, or are you gonna make all three of us beat some sense back into you? Literally."

"Conner," I called, my head aching. "Please. You have to get a grip on yourself. You have to stop all this nonsense. Please."

He stilled, dropping my hair and closing his eyes for a few seconds. A passive expression spread across his face as he reached for the car keys in his pocket. "Whatever. This party is lame anyway."

He backed out of the room, staring everyone down. Even in the dark, I caught the sight of his eyes flashing black when he turned to walk out the door.

What the heck?

Nate pulled me into his arms. "Are you okay?"

His guitar whacked my stomach, and I cringed.

"Oops, sorry about that." He set the instrument on the carpet, leaning it against the wall.

I shook my head. "I'm so glad you saw what was happening and stopped it. That was... intense."

He chewed on his lip for a few seconds. "I always see you."

"And hear me."

He extended his hand, and I took it. "Come on, let's get some fresh air."

Nic and Tammy ran over to see if I was all right, but I batted their concerns away and let Nate lead me to the backyard where our fellow classmates gathered around the flames of a bonfire, roasting marshmallows, completely unaware of what just happened inside. Nate handed me a water bottle.

"Thanks." I took a sip, grateful for the pure taste, no trace of alcohol whatsoever.

Nate's concerned gaze raked all over me. "I think it's best you stay far away from Conner from now on. We can still investigate if you want, but that guy is toxic."

I swallowed the lump in my throat.

He leaned toward me. "So is it me, or was that vision we shared pretty close to what we experienced tonight?"

I nodded. "Yeah, but do you think the vision we had somehow influenced how we acted, like our subconscious sought to fulfill it?"

Shaking his head, he looked down at me through the thick shield of his lashes. "You seriously think that's all there is to it?"

No. "Yes. I don't know." *That's all I wish there was to it.*

"Why do you wish that?"

Darn it! "Because my life is already too messed up to add another complication right now."

He moved his hand through his coffee-colored hair. "There's only one solution. We need to meditate together again."

"How will that solve anything?"

A pause followed. "You have to admit the vision might be our best chance at figuring out this thing between us. Maybe it'll even help us solve Conner's mystery. I can't shake this feeling that all this weird stuff is connected somehow."

He moved toward me, determination written on his face.

I placed my hand on his chest to stop him, but the feel of his hard body underneath his thin shirt caused me to rethink. His grin grew wider, and I knew he heard my thoughts. "Ugh! I can't do this here."

"Then where?"

Pulling my cell out of my pocket, I noted how early the hour was. Plenty of time before curfew to go somewhere else. "I don't know. You want to go for a walk or something?"

Since neither of us had a license, it seemed like the most logical thing to do. I only wished I would've brought my jacket. By the fire, I was warm. Looking Nate up and down in his jeans and T-shirt, I realized how hot he looked. Hmm, maybe he could keep the cold away.

"No problem." He smiled at me, taking my hand in his again, pulling me up.

Our bodies collided, and we both laughed.

"Hi," I whispered, placing my free hand on his shoulder to steady myself.

"Hi." He bent down and brushed his lips across my fingers.

Someone whistled across the bonfire at us, then shouted, "Get a room!"

The others laughed and snickered.

"Let's go." I dropped his hand and stomped into the house, hoping he followed me.

As I stalked past the kitchen, Tammy threw her arms around me. "Where have you been? It's time to party!"

Cheers rang out from the crowd.

Untangling myself from her, I said, "Relax. I'll be right back."

Tammy sighed, long and loud. "But you're supposed to be my date tonight!" She spied Nate behind me. "Is *he* the reason you're sneaking out of here? Oh, did you guys figure out the vision thing?"

She squealed and clapped her hands together.

"You told her?" Nate eyed me with a stern expression.

"Relax, she's so wasted she won't remember any of it tomorrow." *No need to tell him I informed her before she started drinking.*

He smirked. "Yep, no need to *tell* me anything."

Eek! I turned back around, only to bump directly into Kyle. "Do me a favor and take care of Tammy while I'm gone, okay?"

"No problem."

Nate opened the front door for me, then stopped at Sean's truck and retrieved a Darth Vader hoodie from the backseat. "Here you go. I *heard* you were cold."

"Thanks." I slipped on the black hooded sweatshirt.

"Which way are we heading?"

When we reached the end of the driveway, I pointed left.

"Right."

"No, left."

He laughed. "I know. I was just agreeing with you."

"Oh." I zipped up his hoodie. "So you're a Star Wars fan, too?"

"As creepy as this may sound, a lot of things about you have rubbed off on me since we met. I watched all six movies over the summer, even read a few of those novels."

"Cool. I don't think that's creepy at all. Hey, there's a lawyer's office in that old Victorian house." I pointed across the street. "Since they're closed now, we could sit on their porch swing and try the meditation thing."

"Works for me."

We sat down together and joined hands.

"You remember my directions from before?" he asked.

Nodding, I closed my eyes and relaxed. The cool, crisp air brushed my cheeks. Frogs croaked happily; the smell of wood smoke from the bonfire at Kyle's house lingered in the air. This time I recited a Psalm that Mom had crocheted onto a pillow at home: "Cast your burden on the Lord, and He will sustain you."

And just like before, after a few minutes, a vision appeared.

We're at Jumpin' Java Coffee House off Washington Street. Nate's standing next to me at the entrance, looking sexy in a tight blue T-shirt and a pair of baggy corduroy pants. His hair is crammed under a wool cap, a few brown strands peeking out onto his forehead. He gently places his hand on the small of my back. "I'll get you something." He pulls out a wallet attached to a chain from his back pocket.

I tug at my shirt collar. "Barca, you are a gift from the gods. Truly."

He leans toward me. "A gift from God, I am. Unwrap me, you will."

I give him a playful nudge.

Tammy appears next to us, smiling mischievously. "You two are so cute."

Nate hands me an espresso.

The vision disappeared like smoke in the wind. Both of us jumped apart.

"I'm beginning to think these visions happened already. They feel too real to be premonitions."

Nate shuffled his feet on the porch. "Then why can't we remember? Do you think we've been reincarnated and we're remembering a different life or something?"

"I don't know." As I said the words, I realized I felt old, like I had lived a lot longer than I remembered. I could almost hear my former self from a vast distance telling me to not waste a minute of life, to take nothing for granted, to love myself, believe in myself, fight for myself. Maybe I just couldn't handle my alcohol very well.

Nate gazed at me, all the pent-up energy radiating from his body, and I knew what he wanted. "So, what do you think we should do now?"

"Maybe forget about the whole thing and head back inside. I'm not ready for this much weird," I muttered, standing and then pausing by the porch steps.

"I think we should make plans to go to that coffee house next weekend with Tammy. We'll see if the vision comes true again."

Nodding, I said, "With all the other freaky things happening to me, I'm sure it will."

After we trudged back across the street in silence, he caught my wrist. "You act like these visions are a bad thing."

"Aren't they?"

He took my hand and tugged me closer to him. "They're weird, yeah, but they're things *I* would like to happen."

I scrubbed my free hand over my face. "Do you think if we purposely avoid doing the things the visions show us, then we can stop them from happening?"

Nate sighed. "Is that what *you'd* like to happen?"

Scraping my shoe against the concrete wall of the house, I released his hand. "I don't know what I want."

"Well, let me know when you figure it out."

"I won't have to!" I shouted.

Without a backward glance, he stomped away from me.

The hinges of the front door groaned as Nate disappeared inside, and I couldn't help but notice that my body responded in the same way every time he left me.

CHAPTER SEVEN

*"Thoughts, like water, will stay on course
if we make a place for them to go."*

—Boyd K. Packer

I glanced at the clock and remembered the day: Sunday. My eyes burned with exhaustion, but tired or not, I knew I needed to attend Mass. As I stood under the scalding hot water in the only bathroom in our two-bedroom apartment, ominous questions plagued my mind as I remembered the strange dream I had had last night.

Conner, Nate, and I stood in this lobby full of labeled doors with an angel. I knew he was an angel because his wings were popped out, practically blinding me with his great beauty. He spoke to us about the meaning of our names. He told me Olga means holy and that God consecrated me for a purpose and was giving me a new beginning. He addressed Nate as Nathan and said his name meant to give and because he had given freely to me and some girl named Grace, he'd been given a second chance at life. Then the angel told Conner his name means strong willed and that God would test him to see if he really wanted God's help.

What did it all mean? Just like the visions I shared with Nate, the dream felt like a memory. My mind whirled with tired thoughts. Maybe I wasn't meant to figure everything out. Trying to control things hadn't gotten me very far, had it? I was so tired and down all the time, even if I managed a good night's sleep. Holding on too hard to stuff I needed to let go of wasn't working for me. And too much worrying about the future was removing me from the present. No matter what secrets lay in my past or what things awaited my future, the present was the only existence I had. I had to do what was necessary right now. Nothing more, nothing less.

A knock on the door disrupted my swirling thoughts. "Olga? You have a visitor."

The thought of it being Conner or Nate made goose bumps break out all over my body. "Okay, I'll be right out."

After dressing in my denim skirt and my silver top with the sequined heart in the middle, I headed out to the kitchen, following the heavenly scent of fresh coffee and the sound of my parents talking to someone, but not a boy. To my surprise, Tammy sat at the glass table with them. Same model-tan legs, stylish blonde hair, sparkling blue eyes, despite the fact she must be hung over. She was dressed in a long gray tunic, a bulky belt around her waist, paired with black leggings and boots.

"What are you doing here?"

"Jeez, don't sound too excited to see me."

"Sorry. I just meant it's early." I glanced at the clock. Nine thirty a.m., a half hour until service.

"I've decided to start the list we talked about. Remember, the one about eighteen things I missed during my nonexistent childhood?"

I remembered the conversation we had last night after I went back inside Kyle's house, effectively avoiding Nate the rest of the party. Tammy's dad had been a complete drunk, and since her mom died during childbirth, Tammy spent her childhood taking care of him. She became a model at the age of thirteen just to pay the bills at home. Several of our talks this past summer revolved around her childhood of misery. So at the party, I told her she had some making up to do, and that I'd help her get in touch with her inner child during our senior year. The idea just popped into my head, and I wasn't sure where it came from, but I thought the whole quest sounded brilliant. Not to mention it'd keep my mind away from You-Know-Who number one and You-Know-Who number two. Yep, wasn't gonna think about them at all anymore. Just me and my girls from now on.

I knew I should eat something even though I wasn't hungry, so I walked toward the kitchen counter to grab a bagel and spread on some cream cheese while I pondered what to do for Tammy today. "Sure thing, but your list will have to wait until after Mass."

"Silly, coming to church is the first thing on my list. I've never been."

With my bagel wrapped in a napkin in one hand, I turned around and smiled. "Well, what are we waiting for then? Let's go."

"We'll follow you out," Dad said, grabbing his car keys from the hook on the kitchen wall before shutting off the lights.

A minute later, a rush of affection took over as I rode with Tammy in her Lexus, listening to her sing along to the Cantankerous Monkey Squad songs on her iPod. Here was this stereotypical cheerleader who I discovered had so much more in her than meets the eye, a girl who would befriend an unpopular girl like me in *her* time of grief. Conner screwed her worse than me, literally. And her dad had been a hot mess these past few months. I stifled a muffled sob from thinking about all the stuff Tammy had told me about her life during our girl talks this past summer, but she still heard me.

She turned the volume down. "What's wrong? Did you and Nate get into a fight when you stepped outside for a while last night?"

I shook my head. "No. Well, maybe. I'm not sure what it was. Not a fight, but I don't think we ended our talk on good terms, either."

Suddenly, I felt a million years old again; the weight of everything that happened in the last twenty-four hours made my shoulders droop. But I knew I had to play my tears like they were good ones. I couldn't drag her down with me. Besides, what good were tears anyway? They only served as reminders of how weak I'd become. Today I refused to wallow in self-pity. Today I would do something to contribute to the greater good. I would make today about Tammy, not about my stupid problems. "I'm just laughing so hard I'm crying. You know, remembering the band's parody of "Time of Your Life" by Green Day."

When Conner was in his coma, Sean and Kyle had retrieved his songbook from his room so they could play the stuff he'd been writing in the hospital room, hoping the gesture would help wake Conner up somehow. One of them was titled "Ode to a Septic Tank," a song about him convincing me to jump into a pile of poop on Halloween night, also my sixth birthday. Nic and I rolled on the ground in laughter for a good ten minutes when the boys played it for us. Then, Nic made them play the song again so she could film it with her iPhone and post the video online. At that point, a good month into Conner's coma, I never thought I'd laugh again. The song saved me in a way, showing me that life could go on, no matter what happened, even if I felt like the world should stop.

Tammy steered the car into Saint Patrick's Community Church parking lot with one hand and held up her other hand for a high five. "I just watched the video again on YouTube the other night. Hands down, "Ode to a Septic Tank" is the funniest piece of crap I've ever heard."

She laughed at her own joke, and I joined her. As we got out of the car, I thought of how that was the best thing about Tammy. Even though she didn't truly laugh often enough, her giggle was infectious and made me want to say funny things just to hear her cackle.

"Tammy?"

"Yeah?"

"I know I haven't been dealing with everything very well. But I just want to thank you for making me become friends with you. It's been the best distraction I could've hoped for."

She nodded. "Well, we all have our role to play in life. Reigning Queen of Distraction and Denial is mine."

"Mmm-hmm. But don't sell yourself short. I think your role is so much bigger than that."

Scrunching her brows, she pointed to the front entrance of the church. "Let's hope so. Maybe God will throw me a bone today and let me in on his purpose for my life."

Wrapping my arm around her skinny shoulders, I said, "Absolutely. And remember, whatever doesn't kill us makes us stronger. Those bad things made you who you are, even more so than the good things."

Did I believe those things about myself, too? This morning I decided I needed to give up control. I still couldn't see how any good could come out of my situation with Conner, but I needed to grab hold of childlike faith as things unfolded, knowing God would only give me what I could handle and trusting there was a higher reason to everything I faced.

"Whatcha got going on after Mass?" I asked casually. Having "childlike" faith spawned another bucket list idea for Tammy.

Tammy tilted her head and fluffed her hair. "I'm not sure. I think I'll go home and make lunch for my dad. I'm feeling Christian today. But then I'm free. What were you thinking?"

As the sun streamed through the stained glass windows, dappling us in golden light when we stepped inside the church, it felt like a personal blessing from God. But I couldn't let Tammy in on my surprise yet. "Oh, the usual. Hanging out with the Jedi Order. Are Kyle's parents still out of town?"

"He said they will be until late tonight. Why?"

"Just wondering. I have some volunteer hours to fulfill here for NHS—"

"What's NHS?"

"National Honor Society."

"Oh, you mean a club for smart people. That's why it doesn't ring a bell. You're probably like the president or something."

I shrugged. "Maybe."

She rolled her eyes.

"Anyway, I'm gonna hook up with Nate afterward, and then I'll text you later, okay?"

"Okay, I didn't realize you were at the *hooking up* stage yet, though," Tammy said with her usual sarcasm, giving me a quick hug.

"Your connotations for hooking up are not the same as mine."

"Oh, really? Are you sure about that?" She pinched my side.

I put my hand over her mouth. "Again, shh! We're in a house of worship, for Pete's sake!"

Nate actually answered my texts, and he wasn't upset with me anymore.

So a few hours later, he helped me set up little card tables all around Kyle's basement with old toys as the centerpieces. After texting Nate, I'd called Kyle to enlist his help with giving Tammy another piece of her childhood back: birthday parties. She never had one, and even though it may not have been her actual birthday, there was no reason we couldn't celebrate. Cabbage Patch and Barbie dolls, My Little Pony and Strawberry

Shortcake figurines, Superman and Batman action heroes, and best of all: Star Wars bobblehead characters were dispersed throughout the room.

"What do you think?" I asked Nic as she entered the room.

She wore cutoff jeans and a plain white T-shirt, a pink bandana tied into her straight black hair like a headband. Nic wasn't a fashion diva measured against Tammy's standards by any means, but she always looked adorable. "Wow."

"Pretty retro, eh? Nate and I searched our attics for old toys, and this is what we pulled together."

"Awesome!" Sean walked in behind Nic and held out his hand for a fist bump. "Darth Vader is coming with me to college for sure."

I rubbed his afro. "Yeah, okay," I told him, trying to keep my voice steady, tears threatening to fall, knowing the Jedi Order would have to be apart for the first time all too soon.

Nic popped open a soda and took a sip. "Anything for you, baby." She stretched on her tiptoes and planted a passionate kiss on his lips before turning back to me.

His gorgeous black skin couldn't hide his blush. "Everything looks great, but what exactly is the theme here?" Sean asked.

Running my fingers through my hair, trying to tame the frizz, I explained, "The theme is every birthday party she's ever missed. That's why I hung up a piñata and Pin the Tail on the Monkey—"

"I thought it was a donkey?" Nic interrupted.

"It is, but since we have the Cantankerous Monkey Squad, I thought we could mix it up a little." My lower lip trembled at the name of the band, and I wished Conner were a part of this. Old Conner would've loved helping us do something for Tammy.

"Slip'N Slide is ready to go!" Kyle shouted when he opened the French doors leading to the backyard.

I clapped him on the shoulder as he walked past me to grab a pop. "Fantastic. Let's head out to the driveway to wait for Tammy. She should be here in five."

"Did you hear from Conner at all today?" Nate rubbed the back of my neck as we lumbered around to the front of the house.

"Nope, and I don't expect to." I shoved a piece of gum in my mouth so I wouldn't cry.

A few minutes later, Tammy honked her horn as she parked her Lexus in Kyle's driveway, and we all launched into a chorus of "For She's A Jolly Good Fellow." She pretended to faint, fanning herself with her perfect, manicured hands.

When we finished singing, Tammy let loose a small squeal. "Thank you! But what is this all about?"

I placed my hands on her shoulders, steering her toward the backyard. "Part of your life list. Missing out on your childhood meant you didn't have birthday parties, so we thought it was time to fix that."

"But it's not my birthday."

Shrugging, I said, "Why should we let that stop us from celebrating you?"

"All right, who wants hamburgers?" Kyle shouted, and everyone shot their hands in the air.

After we ate more food than our share of a Thanksgiving feast, I played the ever overly cautious mother type, telling my friends to wait thirty minutes before we ventured outside.

"Doesn't that rule only apply to swimming? We can just do the Slip'N Slide," Kyle said, sweeping his blond hair away from his eyes.

"Yeah, but I still think it's wise to let our food settle before diving headfirst down a slippery hill into a pool," I argued, drumming my fingers against my full stomach. The truth was, I just didn't want to change into my bathing suit while feeling so bloated.

Sean emerged with a six-pack. "Fine, then we'll kill time with a drink. The last ones leftover from the best party ever!"

"Oh no, not more beer." I groaned.

"Oh, stop your gnashing of teeth. This is my party, and I'll make you drink beer if I want to," Tammy said with a stomp of her foot.

Sean moved down our line of friends, handing the cans off one by one. I diverted the attention away from drinking, or lack thereof, by handing Tammy a gift basket full of classic kid toys: a Slinky, Play-Doh, a Star Wars coloring book with some crayons, a Barrel of Monkeys, and even a cymbal-banging monkey in a red hat, just like the one Cantankerous Monkey Squad was named after.

As she squealed with delight, I slid a piece of paper out of my pocket and cleared my throat. "I wrote you a little ditty to go with the gift. This basket contains items I picked to help you let loose. They're yours for your fake birthday, so put them to use! I hope you know you're now in the Jedi Order for life, and I hope you never attack any of us with a knife. But even if you do, I'll love you the same, and I'm sorry that, unlike you, this poem's pretty lame.' Cheers to Tammy!"

Everyone raised their can to the middle of our circle and clinked, then chugged, except me. I only swallowed a mouthful before deciding again I absolutely hated beer.

Kyle lifted his can in another toast. "Here's to great memories and new experiences our senior year. And speaking of new experiences, Tammy, would you like to go on a date with me?"

Tammy blushed, actually blushed. I didn't think anything could make her embarrassed. "Aww. Sure I would."

I'd seen the way Kyle watched Tammy these past two months, so his question didn't surprise me. Nor did the way he asked, so casual. That was Kyle's calling card, no nonsense. But I wasn't sure Tammy should rush into a relationship right now. It seemed she always had a boyfriend, and I wondered if it stemmed from a need to focus on someone else so she didn't have to deal with other areas that were much more difficult.

"Here, here." Nate chugged the rest of his beer before crushing his can and then shooting it into the nearby garbage can.

"Let's get this party started!" Nic grabbed Tammy's hands and mine. "Pool time!"

"Hell, yeah!" Nate could hardly seem to contain his excitement. "I hope all you ladies remembered your bikinis!" And no doubt, there was the reason why. "Last one out is a rotten egg!"

Sean shoved him out of the way. "Your breath is a rotten egg!"

Everyone hurried off to change, but Tammy just stood there, adjusting her bra. "Well, what am I supposed to do? Go in my birthday suit?"

I laughed, not doubting she would, but then Kyle stuck his head out of the bathroom door. "You left your suit here to dry after we went in the hot tub last night, remember?"

Kyle had an appreciative look on his face as he tossed the leopard-print bikini to her, and I rolled my eyes.

When we all reconvened in the same spot, I couldn't help noticing all the boys staring at Tammy's halter top, which barely covered her massive boobs. I also couldn't help trying to adjust the top part of my red lifeguard style one-piece suit. *So not sexy.*

"Always the party pooper, aren't you, Olga?" a familiar voice behind us rasped. "You've had that suit since freshman year. When are you finally gonna ditch the damn thing and buy yourself a bikini that shows off that hot bod?"

Conner. I wanted to tell him to scram, to stay away from me, but no matter how badly he'd hurt me, I believed there was still some trace of my best friend within him somewhere.

My eyes softened behind my glasses at the thought. "How'd you know where we were?"

He shrugged. "Lucky guess."

The Jedi Order formed a line of scrimmage, blocking Conner from coming any closer. We stared him down for a moment, and I swear I saw his eyes flash before Kyle took a step forward. "Did I stutter last night? I thought I made it clear you weren't welcome here anymore. What you did, what you've been doing, it isn't cool, man."

"I know." His pleading eyes stared at me again. "What I don't know is why I keep doing what I'm doing. But I want to stop."

Conner?

I expected him to say more, to explain, but he didn't. Instead, a bewildered expression washed over his face. His eyes shifted around our circle of friends, like he was noticing us for the first time.

"What's up?"

Kyle shook his head at him. "We've built a mammoth Slip'N Slide, that's what's up."

Conner blinked slowly, like he couldn't comprehend the words.

"Are you going to apologize? I'm assuming that's why you came," Sean's voice barked, unusually sharp.

"Of course. I'm sorry. Can I stay and hang out with you guys?"

Nate bolted forward. "Hell no!"

I knew Nate's answer was warranted. Conner had been acting like the biggest jerkwad on the planet. Still, I had an overwhelming impulse to keep him near.

Stepping forward and turning my head, I caught a glimpse of the dazed expressions of my friends. They were just as confused over

Conner's behavior as I was. After a moment of silence, I finally spoke up.

"Maybe we should give Conner one more chance?"

"Are you frickin' serious?" Nic chided.

"Um, yes? If it's okay with you all." I narrowed my eyes at Conner. "But if you screw up again, we're done. You can't keep doing what you've been doing. We won't let you."

He glanced at Nate, then brought his attention back to me. "Deal."

"Come on, bro." Kyle grabbed his arm good-naturedly. "I'll race ya down the slide. If you win, I have to forgive you. If I win, you have to give me that Ewok Village LEGO set. I've had my eye on that since sixth grade." Kyle turned around and winked at us.

I watched numbly as they opened up the slider, then crossed the backyard.

Nate cleared his throat. "Any theories for what's going on with him yet?"

"Yeah. I think we've got a live case of Dr. Jekyll and Mr. Hyde on our hands. Come on. Let's see how this plays out."

I approached the Slip'N Slide with caution, because this was a forty-foot homemade creation, with spraying tubes on both ends and concluding in the most massive inflatable pool we could find at the bottom of the slope in Kyle's yard. Kyle liked my and Nate's creation so much he bought two more Slip'N Slides to connect as one, placing them at an angle down the slope so both sides met together at the pool. Kyle and Conner stood as kings of their own mountains, the rest of us counting down, "On your mark, get set, go!"

Kyle pushed off with great speed, but unfortunately, Conner had the bright idea to stride several steps backward before taking off in a run, then launching himself down the slide. The pool at the bottom was unable to stop his momentum. He skimmed over the top of the surface before bumping into a tree so hard that a fountain of blood squirted out from the top of his head.

"Oh my gosh!" I screamed. "Conner!"

I sprinted to the bottom to discover he wasn't responding to my voice.

Oh crap! How much abuse can one body take? "Go call 9-1-1, now!" I shouted to Nate. "We need an ambulance!"

I dropped to my knees and in desperation tried to wake him up by shaking him before realizing that could do more harm than good. Sean handed me his T-shirt to put on Conner's head to stop the bleeding.

Finally, he came to with a goofy grin on his face. "What up? Why is everyone staring at me?"

"You don't remember what just happened?"

"I think I must've bumped heads with Mr. Tree. Is he okay?"

I glanced around and discovered everyone stood over us. Nic gnawed her lip in worry, Tammy pulled at her hair, Kyle bounced from foot to foot, Sean rubbed his face. All telltale signs that this was as bad as it looked.

"There should definitely be a G.I. Joe public service announcement about Slip'N Slides. Wait, did I just pass out?"

I nodded. "Yeah, and there's blood coming out of your head." *A lot of blood.* "But stay calm, an ambulance is on its way."

The mother of all sirens rang down the street a minute later, a blessing and a curse.

"Remember when we read *The Odyssey* for English last year?" Conner asked me. "The sirens were creatures whose songs led sailors to death." He blinked rapidly. "Did you hear them when they came for me… that day we went sailing? I know you blame yourself for my freak accident, but it's not your fault. I'm just a freak who attracts freakiness."

I gently brushed his cheek, trying to stay calm. "Well, take comfort in the fact that you're not the only one."

He closed his eyes.

"Conner, don't you leave me! Don't you dare leave me!" I yelled, overcome by emotion.

Someone touched me on the shoulder, and I turned around to see Nate, looking genuinely distraught. He squatted, hand still on my shoulder, and whispered, "The paramedics are here. You have to get out of the way."

Standing next to Nate as I watched the paramedics load Conner onto a stretcher, I had this sense of déjà vu, which was strange since I'd never seen Conner being loaded into an ambulance; I was knocked unconscious by the sailboat boom. Plus, I hadn't known Nate then, either. But I couldn't shake the feeling of familiarity.

"Do you get the sense that we've done this before?" I asked Nate reluctantly.

He nodded. "Should we meditate?"

"I don't think this is the time or place."

"I figured, but I don't know what else to do." He tugged on the strap of my bathing suit, giving me goose bumps. "What about hypnosis?"

"What about it?"

"I don't know. I've been thinking maybe it's something we should try to get some answers. Couldn't hurt, right?" His gaze traveled over the little scene in the backyard. Nate had the air of someone who always knew exactly what to do. He would make a good boyfriend. He squeezed my hand.

Ahh, stop thinking!

I swallowed hard and looked toward Sean and the rest of our friends, thinking of history repeating itself. We were all headed to the hospital to visit an injured Conner once again. I gathered all my courage and strength and muttered one line with childlike faith. "Please help, God."

For a moment, the whole world disappeared and I stood in a classroom of sorts. Gasping, I pressed a hand to my chest. The angel from my dream grabbed my other hand.

"Congratulations. You passed."

He patted me on the back and gave me one last glance before popping his wings out. Then he was too beautiful to behold, so I looked away.

The vision dissolved as Tammy called to me from the door, telling me to hurry up and change. In that moment, I knew my intuition was right. These things had happened; they were real memories. For better or worse, I couldn't remember everything, but going forward, I knew I'd be a different person now. These past six months, life had a way of darkening my vision until all I could see was the rainy cloud of my problems. Somehow I'd forgotten a chunk of my life, but I still sensed the wonderful lessons that I'd learned to help me grow as a person buried inside me but fighting to rise up to the surface. If I changed my focus to becoming that stronger and more peaceful version of myself, then maybe the cloud would disappear and I could become again the person I once was.

CHAPTER EIGHT

*"Just because someone doesn't love you the way you want them to,
doesn't mean they don't love you."*

—Nate's Thoughts

I didn't see Conner again until the next afternoon. The ER was a hot mess with the full moon and all, so getting all the tests the doctor ordered took forever. By that time, visiting hours were over; the hospital staff kicked us out. Then of course, he didn't come to school. Nic had to work, Tammy had cheerleading but as the captain excused me from practice, and Kyle went home sick, so I bummed a ride with Sean to visit Conner, unsure what version of him we'd be visiting.

"How you doing, man?" Sean asked as we walked into his room.

"Hey, Sean." Conner held out his hand for a fist bump. His eyelids fluttered, and then his gaze met mine. "Olga, how are you?"

Frozen in my spot, I regarded his expression and tone for a moment. This was definitely *my* Conner. I struggled with my thoughts, wondering what I should do or say, before deciding I should just enjoy him while it lasted. "I'm good. So, you're really okay?"

He winced. "My head hurts. Had to get staples."

Sean frowned. "Well, maybe the accident knocked some sense into that noggin of yours. You seem like your old self again. We've missed you, dude."

Conner drew back and sank into his pillows. "You noticed something different about me?"

"I'd have to be blind not to." Sean picked up the remote and flipped through the channels.

"You told him about my visit," Conner whispered to me.

I shook my head, tears burning the back of my eyes.

Conner cleared his throat. "Sean, I'm really sorry for the way I've been acting."

Sean shrugged, his eyes locked on the TV.

"I promise I'll find a way to make it up to you, to the Jedi Order."

Finally, Sean looked at him. "Well, you better. You're my boy and all, but you need to stop acting like a whack-job. Think you can handle that?"

Conner's eyes filled with sadness, and he rubbed his face with the back of his hand. "I sure hope so. I need you guys. I can't lose you. I don't know what I'd do if I did."

I released a huge sigh of relief.

Conner glanced at me. "Sean, do you mind running down to the cafeteria to get me a root beer? The nurses won't bring me any pop."

Sean set the remote down on the side table. "Sure thing. You want anything, Olga?"

Nervous, I adjusted my glasses. "Nah, I'm good."

We watched him leave the room before turning toward each other.

"Conner."

"Olga, I'm so, so, so, so sorry."

I fought back a wave of nausea. Why was my heart racing so fast? Hadn't my heart decided to not care just a week ago? No, not my heart, my mind, and my heart rarely went along with what I thought. Some feelings I just couldn't seem to get rid of, no matter how much I tried.

"You remember everything you did to me? To everyone?"

He patted the extra space beside him on the bed, signaling for me to sit. "Not really. Some of it, yes, but it's not like the last time I came to. I'm losing track of time. I'm really scared."

The air tightened around me. "Did you say anything about it to your parents or the doctor?"

He reached out and tentatively tucked a long piece of hair behind my ear. "I'm too scared they'll lock me up in a white, padded cell. I have no idea what I should do, or what's going on with me. You?"

I picked up his hand and squeezed his palm. "I've been doing some research. The best theory I've come up with so far is maybe the trauma of your accident is causing a bipolar disorder. I think we should tell a doctor. Maybe there's a drug you can take to help you get through this."

Conner glanced around the room, looking more terrified than ever. "I don't know. I don't want to rely on some drug all the time to be myself. There has to be another way."

Feeling a little lost for words, I nodded once. "Look, maybe there is, but until we find it, what does it matter if you have to take a few pills a day if it helps you?"

"Yeah, because drugs have helped me so much these last few months."

I knew his sarcasm was the indirect expression of his truth. "Conner, don't be an idiot. You obviously need serious help, and who knows how long you'll stay good again before you destroy yourself?"

He closed his eyes and let out a breath before glancing at me again. "When did you get so tough?"

"The night you slept with Tammy." My voice broke.

"Ouch."

"Whatever, Conner. After everything that's happened, you're lucky the Jedi Order isn't telling you to get lost. The least you can do is man up and get help."

I choked on the reprimand. Honestly, being so hard on Conner after all he'd been through killed me, but sometimes people needed tough love.

"Ugh. I know. But unless you can dig up Freud himself to do a case study on me, then I don't know what will help."

Placing my hands over his, I said, "Maybe that's what you need, a psychiatrist. A visit from Dr. Judy temporarily helped you before. If you keep up regular visits with her, maybe a few times a week, then maybe you'd be okay."

He hugged me close. "You know you're a genius, right? But I can't do this without you by my side. My parents will be here soon to take me home, and I want you to come with me. Can you call your parents and ask them if you can spend the night?"

My mouth went dry at the thought. "I haven't spent the night at your house since I was nine."

He leaned forward and kissed my forehead. "The age your parents deemed coed was inappropriate, I know. I was so disappointed. But I know you can convince them. Play on their sympathy. Please, Olga. I need you."

"Okay, but only if you speak to the doctor about what's going on with you. Maybe they can do something besides medicating you. Maybe they can't. Whatever the case, you can't go on like this."

Sean came back in with the can of pop, and I took the opportunity to step into the hallway to call Dad. I knew he was my best bet. Sighing, I slid my phone out of my pocket.

"What?" Dad barked on the other line after I asked the question.

I explained the situation, minus the part about Conner's split personality.

"I don't know," Dad answered. "For one, it's a school night. Two, your mom won't like it. I don't like it, either."

My guilt over placing my dad between a rock and a hard place caused me to hesitate, but my concern for Conner won out in the end. "I know, Dad. But Mom will listen to you if you insist."

Silence for one Mississippi, two Mississippi, three Mississippi, then, "It's really that important to you?"

Heart pounding. "Yes. I'm worried about him. And his parents will be hovering over him the whole time, but he said he needs me. Please. He's been through so much these past few months."

"Okay," he said quietly. My parents knew Conner well, and I felt guilty for playing on Dad's sympathy.

"Thank you, Dad. Thank you so much. I owe you big time."

He chuckled over the line. "Oh, don't you worry. You'll pay up soon. Are you coming home for a change of clothes?"

"Yeah, but I'll just stop by for a sec before you and Mom get home from the marina. Sean can drive me."

"Okay, then. I'll see you tomorrow. That is if your mom doesn't kill me before then."

"Dad," I said more sharply than I meant to. After all, he was letting me go. I still couldn't believe I had the nerve to ask.

"Just make sure you come straight home after school tomorrow, all right?"

"Yes, sir."

I put my phone back in my pocket, then headed down the hall to tell Conner some good news for once.

Conner sat down at the card table in his basement, swinging himself around the chair to face me over the back. "So, guess what happened at the hospital when you and Sean left?"

We'd just finished dinner, a five-course meal when it came to Erin, his mom. His parents were delighted I was spending the night, weird as that sounded. They trusted me, and they hoped my presence was a good sign things were finally going back to normal. At least, that's what Erin whispered to me as we cleared the table together.

"They made you take some drugs?"

"Nope, they used electroshock therapy on me." He made the announcement unflinchingly, like announcing he was taking the dog for a walk.

"What?" The only thing I knew about shock therapy came from reading *One Flew Over the Cuckoo's Nest* and watching the subsequent film in English class last year. Hollywood's portrayal didn't exactly paint a pretty picture.

"Turns out I wasn't too far off with my idea of getting struck by lightning again to reverse the effects."

I winced. "Well, I hope it was less dramatic than that."

"It was. The doctor gave me a muscle relaxant first and put me under general anesthesia. Then they placed electrodes on my scalp, and the current caused a brief seizure. Doc said ECT is one of the fastest ways to relieve symptoms in people who suffer from mania like me. It's used when mood or psychotic symptoms are so severe that it may be unsafe to wait until drugs can take effect or when the patient doesn't want to take drugs. Both reasons applied to me. I'll go back Wednesday and Friday for another session."

I took my glasses off and polished them on the corner of my shirt so hard I thought for a moment I might break them. "You think the shock therapy helped then? Because it still sounds barbaric to me."

"Here's the thing: while I was having my seizure, I also had a vision. Only it didn't feel like a vision, but rather a—"

"Memory." I slid my lenses back on, willing my hands not to shake.

With a fixed stare, he studied me. "Yeah, how'd you know?"

"I'll explain later. Go on."

"Okay. Well, I sat in a prison cell, naked, with fierce cuts across my back like I'd been whipped. And you were there with some girl named Grace. I've never seen her before."

My eyes went wide at the mention of her name. "And that's it? Nothing else happened in your vision?"

He shook his head. "No, Nate was there, too. He shot you in the neck with a tranquillizer gun, and then everything went dark. Told you I thought he was connected to all this. Then I woke up, and when I did, I had that same sensation of something leaving me like the night before school started."

I just stared at him.

Hands clasped behind his head, he finally asked, "Well, what do you think?"

"It's possible," I said slowly, spinning the Morticia Addams ring on my finger, "that we are on the edge of glancing into an alternative universe. In a sense, we may be time traveling."

"Huh?"

This wasn't the response he expected, and I knew how strange I sounded, but what else could be happening? It took a while to explain my two visions with Nate, in addition to my weird dream that also mentioned Grace and the memory I had of the angel earlier today in Kyle's backyard.

"I think you're on to something," Conner said when I finished.

"You do?"

Giving a shrug, he laughed. "I don't have any better explanations, and you're much smarter than I am. What do you think we should do about it?"

Now it was my turn to shrug. "We surrender ourselves to the process. I expect things will be revealed to us in due time. Until then, we focus on everything that truly matters. We won't give up, but we'll trust that whatever is meant to happen will happen, and that we'll have the strength to deal with anything that comes our way."

Conner half closed his eyes. "Sounds easier said than done, but I'll try to follow your lead." Then he added a bit sheepishly, "Did you know I got tattoos?"

"Yeah, I saw it that one day at lunch, the day after you came to my house."

He nodded and smiled. "Right. But I used the plural form."

My eyes widened. "How many do you have now?"

"Six."

"Six! Where?"

Standing, he ditched his shirt, dropping the material to the floor. I'd seen him shirtless countless times, but never like this. Just the two of us. Alone. In his basement/bedroom, his parents upstairs.

His abs were still ripped with muscle, but now he had two black wings inked along each side of his ribs. Conner pointed, counting, "One, two." He trailed a finger across his bronzed chest, where two red stars hung just above his nipples that were... pierced with two gold rings.

Oh, good Lord.

"Three, four. You already know about this one." He turned his left forearm toward me, squinting at the naked lady. "You ready for the grand finale?"

No.

He turned around; an enormous Grim Reaper took up the back of his right shoulder. "Six. What do you think?"

He still had his back to me. I stepped forward to outline the ink with my finger, his body trembling under my touch. After a few seconds, I trailed my hand down his arm and squeezed his bicep. "I think you look like a rock star."

He bent down, picked up his discarded shirt, then slid the material over his head before walking to his dresser. "Those aren't the only disturbing new things I've found." He pulled out a contraband of *PlayBoy* magazines, a six-pack of beer, a box of cigars, and a bag of weed.

I went to him, only needing to look in his eyes for a second to know it was safe to hug him. This was *my* Conner. Dropping his head to my shoulder, he cried. Now I could count two other times I'd actually seen him cry, even though he frequently fell off bikes, skateboards, and skis while growing up.

I half pulled, half drug him over to his bed to sit down. "Conner, whatever is going on with you isn't your fault. I'm sorry I yelled at you last week when you tried to talk to me."

His face twisted in anguish. "I deserved to be yelled at. I was acting like a turdnugget."

I laughed.

"I'm not joking," he said, no trace of a smile.

"I know. It's just, you said turdnugget."

He shook his head, but he smiled, too. "You're so ridiculous sometimes."

Raising my eyebrows, I said, "This coming from the guy who jumped off Sean's roof in eighth grade and broke his leg."

"Hey, Sean and Kyle jumped, too, and they were fine! I'm a magnet for freak accidents, remember? I'm the King Super Freak."

I toyed with a loose thread on his black jeans. "Yeah, I'm sure it had nothing to do with them jumping off the lowest point of the roof and you jumping from the highest."

"That's because I was trying to impress you."

Turning my face up to his, I told him, "You don't ever have to *try* to impress me."

His blue eyes went wide. "Maybe with other girls I don't have to try. But with you I do, and I always will." He reached over and flipped a switch off and another one on. His lamp went dark, but the wall lit up with "I love you" spelled out in Christmas lights.

"When did you do this?"

"While I waited for you to get here."

As he moved closer to me, his arm and leg grazed mine, making my breath hitch.

Then a knock at his sliding glass door startled us. We turned. Sucking in a quick breath, I realized Nate stood just outside, a scowl on his face.

"What is he doing here?" Conner asked, flipping the light back on.

"No idea."

Carefully, I rose from Conner's bed and strode across the room to answer the door. Nate's face was hard, and I tensed for a confrontation as I opened the slider. "Hey. What are you doing here?"

I counted to thirty in my head before he finally answered. "I should ask you the same question."

My eyes narrowed. "How'd you even know I was here?"

He tapped his forehead.

"Nate, that's not fair. You can't stalk me like this."

"It's not knowledge I'll ignore when I find out you're alone in a room with this monster."

Conner leaped off his bed and joined us. I was hoping he'd extend his hand like a gentleman and formally introduce himself, since Nate had never met *my* Conner before.

"If I'm a monster, you're a freak."

Nate's eyes widened, clearly surprised that Conner apparently knew about his mind reading ability. I'd half forgotten I told him about the phenomenon the night he sneaked into my room.

"And you're crazy if you think she needs your protection. I'd get out of here if you know what's good for you."

Nate shrugged. "Guess I don't know what's good for me then."

He stepped around us, walked over to the couch, then proceeded to turn on the television.

"Is this guy for real?" Conner asked me.

Ignoring his question, I went and stood in front of the television. "Conner wants me to stay the night because he's scared of what might happen to him. This doesn't involve you."

"Yeah, you should go," Conner echoed, coming over to stand beside me.

"Sorry, but his well-being isn't really a priority for me. You are. So I'm staying." Nate leaned back on the couch, propping his feet on the coffee table.

Conner knocked his feet down. "What's your problem, man?"

Nate jumped up, getting in Conner's face. "My problem is you only think about yourself. So you're scared of what might happen to you? What about Olga? If you claim you have no control over your actions, then what's stopping your monster from making an appearance later tonight and hurting her?"

The muscles in Conner's jaw were tight as he reached into his pants for his wallet, then held out a twenty dollar bill. "Look, dude. You've been a loyal bodyguard and all, but Olga doesn't need to be protected from me. I'm fine now. Your duties are done here."

Nate took the bill from Conner and ripped it in half before letting the pieces float to the ground. "I'm gonna mess you up so bad, you freakin' piece of sh—"

I slapped my hand over his mouth before he could finish. "You'll do no such thing. His well-being is linked to my well-being, so you're going to put up with him if you still want to spend time with me."

"I'm not going to let you put yourself in danger."

"Nate, listen. I'm thankful I have you around to protect me, and I love the way you try to keep everything calm and normal for me, but you can't shelter me, and you need to trust my judgment."

"I do," Nate said, standing in front of the couch. "You don't think like a rational, normal person when it comes to him."

"Please, like you've brought a whole plate of normal to the table." Conner's words came out rushed, like he'd been waiting to say them all night.

I swallowed, hard. "Look, guys, I think we know normal isn't in the cards for us this year. Can we at least agree on that?"

Nate tugged at his shirt collar. "Yep."

"True. But I still think he's to blame. Everything got all cuckoo when he came to town." Conner ran a hand over his hair, studying Nate.

"So now I'm to blame for your bad behavior?" Nate pursed his lips, his eyes wide.

"Yes, you are! I was in a coma for months, and then I get you for a roomie, and as soon as you leave the hospital, I wake up. Except it's not me who wakes up but this monster living inside me. And you can somehow read Olga's thoughts, and now you're trying to hook up with her and take my spot in the band?"

"I'm not trying to hook up with her. Only guys like you do that."

"Only guys like you do that," Conner repeated in a high voice before applauding in deliberate false fashion. "Wow, good job. That one really hurt."

Nate shook his head. "Don't mock me."

"Don't mock me." Conner twisted his mouth in an ugly smirk.

"Go to hell."

"Right back at ya. Or just go… anywhere."

I threw my hands in the air. "I've had enough of this crap, so I'll be the one going. Conner, why don't you start working on all that homework you haven't kept up with. I'll be back in a half hour."

Conner jutted out his chin. "Where are you going?"

Crossing my arms over my chest, I said, "For a walk. Nate, let's go."

"Aww, he's going, too? But I was hoping we could have a pillow fight later and maybe braid each other's hair."

"Conner, do your homework." I yanked Nate outside and then slid the door closed.

Following me around the side of the house, Nate let out a huff as if he were the one annoyed. "Olga—"

"Don't even. You're gonna shut up and listen to me yelling at you inside my head while I walk you home. Understand?"

"Yes, ma'am. I mean, no. I should be walking you home."

I turned on my heel, which enabled me to make direct eye contact so there'd be no misunderstanding. "I am spending the night at Conner's house, not with Conner. Do you understand the difference?"

His nostrils flared. "I understand he's on the road to nowhere good and he's bent on taking you with him. Why do you still feel like you have to fix him?"

"Because I'm the one who broke him!" I shouted, which made the neighbors flick their porch light on. My muscles quivered; my whole body tensed.

Nate gathered me in his arms and smoothed my hair. "Hey, this isn't the antique store downtown," he whispered. "It's not a if you break it, you buy it situation. I get that you feel like you were responsible for his coma. I hear your thoughts. You were the one who invited him sailing to make Tammy jealous. You didn't make him wear a life jacket. You should've administered CPR earlier. Should've called 9-1-1 sooner. But you know what? You shouldn't have had to make Tammy jealous. You shouldn't have had to act like his mommy so he'd be responsible. And you dived into the freezing water to save him, risking your own life. How long are you going to live with this mantra on repeat in your head?"

I sniffled. "I'm trying not to think that way. Actually, I've prided myself on making strides toward that goal in the past week. You should've heard my thoughts right after the accident. At the time, it was hard imagining ever feeling not responsible."

He sighed disapprovingly. "You're lucky I came into your life when I did."

"Why is that?"

Tilting my chin toward his face, he said, "Because you don't need to be alone anymore, trapped in your head with your loud, critical thoughts. You needed someone to remind you of how perfect you are." He cupped my face in his hands, and the night dissolved into silence.

Time slowed as he bent his face to mine, his lips just centimeters away from my mouth. "Nate, stop. I can't handle this right now. You should go. This has nothing to do with you."

He took a step back. "This has everything to do with me."

"How do you figure?"

"Do you see how I look at you?" His eyes widened, brows furrowed. "Like you're my whole world? The problem is, I look at you like you look at him." He made a sweeping gesture toward Conner's house. "And I don't like that you're willing to give him a million second chances, but you won't even give me one."

Adrenaline pumped through my veins, making my heart wake up. "What do you mean?"

A building smile spread across his whole face. "Go out with me this Saturday. Let me take you on our first official date."

The wind blew a stray piece of hair into my blinking eyes. "Barca, I don't think that's a good idea."

"Why not?"

"A million reasons."

"Come on, Olga. Just one date. That's not too much to ask for, right? And we owe it to ourselves to explore this connection we have." He looked slightly sheepish, making me feel sorry for him.

I sighed. "Will you leave me alone tonight if I say yes?"

"If that's what you want." His voice was softer than a whisper. "But I'll still be listening, for your safety, and maybe for my own sanity."

"I can live with that. Yes."

"Yes?"

Wrinkling my nose, I said, "Yes, if you can stop gloating."

"I'm not gloating."

I pushed up my glasses. "Not with your words, but you're gloating with your facial expression."

He smirked. "Sorry. How's that saying go? Let him without sin cast the first stone."

Bending down, I searched the grass.

"Did you lose something?"

"Oh no, I'm just looking for a rock."

He shoved me gently. "Now who's gloating?"

I grinned. "You sound surprised. Weren't you the one telling me a minute ago I was perfect? Now don't worry. I'll pick out a smooth one. No jagged edges to mess up your pretty face."

Pulling me up, he drew me against his body. I closed my eyes, imagining his lips on mine before I remembered Conner.

"Oh, come on, his thirty minutes aren't up yet."

Pushing back, I let my hands remain on his chest. "Whatever. I shouldn't hang out with either one of you after the way you both acted back there. But anyway, we can't be trusted alone together."

"I must halt your line of reasoning. You can't employ a double negative."

Staring back at him, it was hard to ignore the heat between us. "So you're the grammar police now?"

He slid my arms around his neck. "Yep, and I'm gonna have to take you as my prisoner. Come with me, ma'am."

I laughed. "You promised you'd leave if I agreed to a date this weekend, remember?"

"I remember every word you've ever said."

With all the visions we were having, I seriously doubted that.

Lacing his fingers through mine, he said, "Until tomorrow."

As I walked around the side of the house on the fading green grass, the wind picked up, blowing fallen leaves across our path. Usually I looked forward to fall, an opportunity for more fun times with my friends during another school year. Now all the signs of my favorite season only reminded me that change was coming, and I hated change.

As I opened Conner's slider door, I noticed he'd dimmed the lights. The Christmas lights were back on, and a lit candle glowed on the coffee table next to a small vase of wild flowers. Conner sat on the couch, watching me come in.

"Hey, I thought you were gonna work on some homework."

"I had more important things to do" He kept a steady gaze on me, unblinking.

"Really?"

He pressed a button on his iPod, then stood and wrapped me in his arms, swaying us to Adele's cover of Bob Dylan's song, "Make You Feel My Love."

I bit my bottom lip. "What is all this? What are you doing?"

He leaned his head back, studying me. "Setting the room for romance. I remember when I was in a coma and you told me you loved me. You said you always pictured saying those words with candles, flowers, and music. And I wished the same thing when I first told you the night before school started. So now I'm trying to do things right. I just hope you believe in second chances as much as I do."

I nodded. "I do, Conner, but a lot has happened since then. And to be honest, this is getting to be too much for me to handle right now."

"Just let me get this off my chest." He reached out and touched my cheek with the back of his hand. "I know words are pathetically insufficient, and a relationship between us can't work right now, when I have so far to go in straightening my life out, but the plain and simple truth is I love you more than anything. And I hope you hold on to that truth no matter what happens."

Tears leaked from my eyes.

"Are those tears of happiness or tears of sadness because you like Nate now?"

Behind his neck, I twisted my Morticia Addams ring, a nervous habit. "Do you think you can have feelings for two people at once?"

I felt dizzy waiting for his answer, not just from being spun in slow circles around his room.

Abruptly, he said, "I guess. I've certainly had my fair share of girlfriends. But are we talking about love feelings? Because maybe some people fall in and out of love all the time, but for me, there's only ever been you."

He pulled me toward him and kissed me hard, his unshaven skin stubbly and rough, but I didn't care. I kissed him back like I was the one drowning this time and only he could save me. For a moment it was only us who existed, and then thoughts of Nate crept in my mind, how he would probably know what was happening and might even come back. Then suddenly, in my mind, I was kissing Nate, like *really* kissing him.

"How did you know how to find me by the wormhole?" I asked him.

I pulled away and looked at Conner, feeling like I'd just seen a ghost.

Conner's pupils were huge and confused as he looked back at me. "You're thinking about him, aren't you?"

I stared at him in silent horror, worried I'd lose both of them and end up alone in the end. Maybe that would be best for all of us. "I told him I'd go on a date with him this weekend. That's how I got him to leave."

Telling Conner about the date was easier than telling him about my vision. I picked the lesser of two evils.

He swept his arms around the room. "Well, you should tell him tomorrow you're canceling, don't ya think? How are we going to work things out between *us* if you're going on dates with him?"

I hesitated, unsure of what to do or say. "I promised him."

Shoving his hands in his hair, he yanked on the strands. "Olga! For once in your life, can you just think with your heart instead of your head? Think about the future. Who do you want to end up with?"

You, my heart screamed. But the words wouldn't come out. Somewhere deep inside me, I knew we'd been down this road before and it didn't end well. And it made me not trust my feelings now.

"Then go." Conner turned around and blew out the candle. When I didn't move, he repeated the words and shuffled to his bed to lie down.

For a moment, I froze, listening to the sound of the wind picking up outside and to Adele singing about the winds of change blowing, but I wasn't ready to be set free. The old Olga would've obeyed Conner's wishes and left. But not anymore. I walked over to his bed and lay next to him. Flipping on my side, I faced his back, waiting for him to say something or fall asleep.

"I'm sorry," he said quietly. "I know I have no right to tell you what to do."

I opened my mouth to speak, but before I could, he continued, "He's probably a lot better at this stuff than I am. Probably will bring you two dozen roses instead of picking some lame ones from his mom's garden out back. Probably quotes poetry to you and stuff." Turning over, he faced me. "I wish I were better with using my words, wish that I wasn't so quick to lose my temper, especially these days."

"It's okay," was all I could think to say.

"No, it's not. I know I don't deserve it, but will you still stay the night with me?"

I nodded. Lying against him, I felt so warm on the inside I thought I could never feel cold again.

"I wish we could stay like this forever," Conner whispered, closing his eyes.

"Me too." But I was smart enough to know that in this life we seldom got what we wished for. Life was too complicated for such things.

CHAPTER NINE

"Why, sometimes I've believed as many as six impossible things before breakfast."

—Lewis Carroll, *Alice in Wonderland*

S o," Dr. Judy began, "tell me why you're here today, Olga."

It was Friday, early afternoon, before my shift at the Bookman began. As soon as school ended, I had Nic drop me off at the hospital. I hadn't been able to sleep ever since I spent the night at Conner's on Monday, especially with the excitement and dread building inside me at the prospect of my first proper date. Excited because a guy as perfect as Nate wanted me, and I couldn't deny I liked him back. But also dread because my first date wouldn't be with Conner, and to make matters worse, he was still being *my* Conner. Of course, this should fall under the "Yay" category instead of "Nay," but now my date with Nate felt like cheating. The night outside Conner's house when I said yes to Nate, I honestly figured Conner would be acting like a jerk again by morning. Even without Mom's constant encouragement to see a therapist since everything fell apart in April, I knew I had reached my breaking point. So yesterday morning, I finally caved and called the number she'd placed on my computer desk months ago. Certainly, the fact that Conner, Nate, and now I all had the same therapist was no coinkydink. Maybe somehow Dr. Judy held all the answers to our questions.

"Well," I said, taking another sip of coffee from my travel mug. "My life has turned into something out of *The Twilight Zone*."

She cleared her throat. "Many people probably feel the same way about their own lives, but can you give me some specifics on your situation?"

"Where to start? My best friend was struck by lightning in April during our first spring sailing trip and then lapsed into a coma for eighty days, and after he woke up, it's like he's this completely different person most of the time. Then I met this other guy at the hospital, Conner's roommate for a while, and he can hear my thoughts. But only mine, so, of course, I tried staying clear of him, but I just can't figure out how he's doing this mind trick and—"

"Okay, slow down." Her face held a solemn expression. "Take a deep breath and try to relax."

I inhaled like she told me, which only caused me to yawn. "I know I sound crazy, but I don't care about looking crazy anymore. I need help. That's why I'm here."

Dr. Judy nodded. "I'm sure almost losing your best friend was a very traumatizing experience."

I nodded. "So you agree I am crazy?"

She leaned back in her chair. "I'd have to spend a few more sessions with you to formulate any type of diagnosis, if there even is one at all. It's probably more likely you're suffering from Post-Traumatic Stress Syndrome."

"What's that?" I fingered the cross on my necklace, praying for some answers.

"It's an overwhelming emotional shock presented after a deeply distressing ordeal. Usually, while people are dealing with the crisis at hand, instinct kicks in and survival mode takes over. However, sometimes after weeks or even months have gone by, the reality of everything that's happened begins to sink in and affects our day-to-day activities. The symptoms can manifest themselves in many ways, but one way is hearing or seeing things that aren't there."

I swallowed, then glanced toward the door, hoping nobody in the waiting room down the hall could hear our conversation. Then I worried I was being a paranoid freak and swallowed again. "So you think Nate's mind hack is a figment of my imagination?"

"No. I'm merely trying to help you figure things out. If you can't logically accept that this boy is reading your mind, then do *you* think you're imagining this part of your relationship?"

"Not really. I mean, even though logic tells me this can't be happening, I guess faith in the supernatural tells me he can and is."

My mind flashed to Conner, a picture of him drinking backstage during the summer and making out with that tramp. A part of me didn't want to ask Dr. Judy about him, my logical side telling me I should focus on one mental breakdown at a time. But then again, I'd spent most of my life putting his needs above my own. Old habits die hard. Besides, putting others before yourself was what friendship was all about, right? "Hey, can post-trauma stress cause destructive behavior, too, like drinking too much and stuff?"

"Absolutely." She gave me an understanding nod. "Are you drinking?"

I shook my head. "No, not me."

Her mouth tightened. "Olga, your parents did the right thing by referring you to me. We all want to help you. Even if you don't feel like you can trust me yet, trust that."

I stared at the framed picture of Grand Haven Pier hanging behind her desk. "You think I'm lying."

"Are you?" She pursed her lips, waiting for my response.

"No. Another patient of yours is drinking. Conner Anderson."

My focus on the picture dissolved, a memory floating in the peripheral of my vision. In it, I stared at the same picture in a trancelike state, Dr. Judy asking me if I'd visited a gravesite yet.

Attention shifted to the present, and I looked at the woman in front of me accusingly. "But you knew that already."

"I cannot discuss any of my patients with you." Her voice softened. "We're here to talk about your problems. How are you sleeping? Are you eating a healthy diet?"

I snorted. "Well, coffee is a natural diuretic, but it probably doesn't help me in the sleep department. Look, I know you can't discuss Conner, but you can listen to me talk about him, right?"

Whatever memory I had of Dr. Judy, she probably didn't share it with me. It was already frightening, stepping around in this darkness, not knowing what the danger was but sensing something lurking. If I told my therapist everything, she'd probably lock me up and I'd never see the light of day again. For now, all I could do was elaborate on the facts I'd already eluded to.

Dr. Judy's lips twitched as if she were holding back a smile. "If that's what you want to talk about."

Sagging against the chair, I closed my eyes. "I just think you need to know the whole story if you have any chance of helping me."

For the next forty-five minutes, I talked mainly about Conner and a little bit about Nate, and Dr. Judy listened. Really listened. And even made some light jokes. She felt like the mom I always wanted. Even though I love my mom, I always felt like she was too self-absorbed and serious to ever take the time to really understand me.

By the time I finished, Dr. Judy's eyes glittered with what looked liked amusement. "Let's say for argument's sake I believe you and don't think you and your friends are insane at all. Why do you think this stuff is happening to the three of you?"

"No clue. If I had answers, I wouldn't be here in the first place."

Her gaze traveled around the office, seemingly watching something I couldn't see. Maybe *she* was the crazy one. "Olga, humor me."

Pressing my palms against my cheeks, I sighed. "God's angry with us?"

"Why God?"

"I don't know. Everyone's always suggesting he's trigger happy with lightning strikes when he's upset with people."

"But do *you* believe that about God?"

Shrugging, I admitted, "Not in the past, but lately? I'm not sure what I believe anymore."

"Well, from what you've told me, it sounds like Conner behaved decently before his coma, yes?"

"Right."

"So let's rule out the punishment theory. And have you ever considered that Nate's ability to read your mind is actually a gift from God?"

I gave a shaky laugh. "More like a curse. Would *you* want a guy around who could read your mind whenever he was within a two-mile radius?"

She shrugged. "Could have some benefits."

"Well, I'd like it much better if I could read his mind instead. Besides, I'm sure hearing my thoughts totally sucks for Nate."

"Why is that?"

"Because I spend a lot of time worrying about Conner."

"But you are interested in Nate. You said you were going on a date tomorrow night."

I shrugged. "Yes. I mean, he's hot and nice and caring and funny. Outside of reading my mind, there's nothing annoying about him." Leaning forward, I posed a hypothetical question. "Do you think you can be in love with two people at once?"

She scooted her rolling chair forward. "Maybe."

I crossed my arms over my chest, frustrated over the fact that therapists seemed to enjoy giving one-word answers and withholding their opinions. "Do you think we can have soul mates in nonromantic ways, who are our friends?"

Her lips slightly parted. "I guess you'll have to answer that question for yourself. Do you think both Nate and Conner are your soul mates?"

Holding my breath in for a moment, I thought about her question. "I don't know. My definition of a soul mate probably doesn't have the same connotation as it does to lots of other people, given my faith and my recent experiences. I mean, it's so bizarre Nate can read my thoughts. That ties him to my soul in inexplicable ways. Maybe God ordains certain attachments to our souls to help us in our lives, people he knows will love us unconditionally no matter what, who will be there with us for the long haul. Who will stand by you, even if distance separates you. That's the kind of soul mate I want, whether romance is involved or not. Maybe that's why I can't forget about Conner, either, even when I want to. I don't think it's a coincidence I met him the first day of kindergarten. He was meant to be my best friend, and I, his. So, yeah, I do think Nate and Conner are both my soul mates in a sense."

My statement was decisive, like I knew the fact without thinking about it.

Dr. Judy's expression relaxed, her butterscotch hair framing her heart-shaped face. "Well, it sounds like you're discovering the answers on your own. So, why not try to embrace this turn of events in your life? Like you said, there are no coincidences. Maybe God imparted this knowledge to Nate for a reason."

My mouth opened and closed as I tried to keep up with my own thoughts. "So I should try to find out what that reason is? Keep

117

meditating with him so more visions will come and try to make those visions come true?"

A look of pure horror flashed across Dr. Judy's face. "I'm saying some things can't be explained. I mean, do you understand how life began, the nature of time, whether there is free will or it's all destiny? Some things are so inherently complex that they will forever elude human understanding. No philosopher, scientist, or psychologist alive today has the foggiest notion of how the mind, time, or consciousness works. It's arrogant to suppose those things will *ever* be understood completely." She spoke the next words slowly, like she wanted each syllable to sink in. "I'd say forget the past and remember how to live."

My mouth tightened. "This just feels like something out of a movie, ya know?"

There was a moment of silence as she ran her petite fingers through her wavy hair. "But your life isn't a movie. This is real now. And you have another chance at happiness. I want you to get out there and live passionately. Sometimes the best thing you can do is shut off your thoughts and listen to your heart instead."

More clichés. The only thing that could make this hour complete was a "Reach For The Stars" poster with Oprah's picture on it.

Dr. Judy slid her rolling chair back from her desk, signaling our hour was up. I stood, blood thundering in my ears as she walked me to the door.

"Thanks for the talk."

She peered down at me, meeting my gaze. "You're welcome. I hope I helped you in some way. Make an appointment with my secretary to come again in two weeks. But if you feel like you need to come in any time before then, just call the office, and I'll squeeze you in. I don't want you to feel like you're all alone in this, but it sounds like you have a good support system with your friends already."

"Except Conner." I still had so many questions I wanted to ask her about him. "You think I should forget about trying to figure out what's wrong with him?"

Placing her hand on my shoulder, she said, "Not at all. I apologize if I gave you that impression. I just don't think you should spend so much of your energy focusing on his problems when you can't control what he does or doesn't do. The only person you can control is you." She tucked her notebook under her arm. "Have you ever thought about inviting him to church?"

I gave a dismissive wave of my hands. "He's never been interested in that sort of thing."

She nodded. "Doesn't mean you can't ask again."

Pushing my glasses up, I titled my head to the side. "I didn't know a shrink could talk so much about God."

Dr. Judy laughed, the sound angelic. "Some of my counseling is faith-based, if my patients request it. Your mom did. She said you'd be okay with that aspect."

"Oh. Well, I'll ask Conner, if you think church will help."

"It's helped you in your life, yes?" She watched me expectantly.

Crossing my arms over my abdomen, I nodded.

"Good. I'm here if you need me, Olga. Remember, listen to your heart."

With that last piece of advice, I shuffled down the sidewalks of Grand Haven on my way to work. One good thing about having a near-perfect photographic memory was being able to recall every little word she'd said to me. Now that I looked back at our hour together, I thought the strangest thing about the experience was when she said, "This is real now."

What the heck did that mean? And she told me to forget about the past, but I never told her my visions with Nate felt like memories. I thought again of my flashback in Dr. Judy's office. Simply, I'd assumed she wouldn't understand any of it. Now I had a distinctive feeling she knew a lot more than she let on.

CHAPTER TEN

"You should always leave loved ones with loving words."

—Nate's Thoughts

"Your jeans are way too tight on me," I told Tammy as I stepped out of my closet after changing. She'd met me at work to drive me home and help me get ready for my date. "Duh! That's how Latin jeans work. Too tight means they fit just right."

I grimaced. "Until I rip your fancy pants as soon as I try to sit down."

She shrugged. "Perfect. All the easier for Nate to get into them later."

I flung my hair tie at her. "Shut up! I'm only keeping this date because I promised. I don't have many friends and don't want to lose this one, that's all."

Laughing, she picked up my hair tie and placed it on my desk. "Whatever you need to tell yourself. Come sit. I'll flatiron your hair."

Plopping down in my swivel chair, I studied the sheer black top she let me borrow, paired with my gray cami underneath. "Ugh, look. These pants are so tight you can see fat rolls through this shirt when I sit down. I'm changing."

Tammy held my shoulders when I tried to stand. "One, no, you're not. Two, what fat rolls? You're making excuses. Just shut up and rest assured there's no way I'm letting you change. After I get done with your hair and makeup and you put on my black knee-high boots, every guy in Grand Haven will notice you tonight."

I blew an errant strand of hair out of my eyes. "Exactly what I don't need. I don't even know how to pick between two hot guys. And please go easy on the makeup."

"Relax. You barely need any. I'm just sticking to neutral tones to help highlight your beautiful face."

I opened my mouth, stunned to hear Tammy calling me beautiful. Suddenly, another faraway memory drifted into my mind. I was dressed in black boots stretching to my knees, to where a red plaid dress I wore ended. As I sat in front of a vanity, Tammy tried to perfect my nineties grunge look.

Taking a deep breath, I hesitated, unsure if I should say something.

"What is it?" Tammy asked, parting my hair.

"It's not just Nate I'm having visions about. I just had one about you helping me get ready for something, like we'd done this before."

"What do you mean? We have done this before. I helped you get ready the night before Kyle's party."

I knew I sounded crazy, but I wanted desperately for someone else to remember what I did. Maybe if I described the vision to her, something would trigger her subconscious. But after I told her the details, nothing seemed to register on her face. Remembering the "real" comment from Dr. Judy, I realized that maybe these things only happened to me during Limbo. *Limbo? Where did that come from?*

"Never mind. What are you doing tonight? Going out with Kyle?"

She picked up a narrow section of hair and applied pressure, straightening my frizzy curls like a pro. "Sorta. I told him I wanted to hold off on any solo dates. I think my life list for this year should include taking a break from guys. Do you realize I've never really been single since I was ten?"

"For real?"

Picking up another section of hair, she nodded. "Yep. So anyway, to answer your question, I'm going with Nic, Sean, Kyle, and Conner to Jumpin' Java tonight for a karaoke contest."

Trembling, I told myself it was stupid to be jealous. Tammy and Conner were over before they even started, and I had a date with Nate, and she liked Kyle now, I thought. But Tammy noticed the color draining from my face.

"Olga, don't worry," she said, adding some more hair serum before tackling the other side of my head. "I'll keep Conner out of trouble while you're not there."

I nodded, thankful she couldn't see my wretched heart. "I know. It's just the last vision Nate and I shared took place at that coffee house, and you were there with us."

Now she looked paler than I did. "Oh. Then you should come after you're done with your official date business."

I frowned at her in the mirror. "I don't know if hanging out with Conner while I'm on a date with Nate is the best idea."

"Hey," she interjected. "It's about time someone gave him a taste of his own medicine. Besides, don't you and Nate want to see if your vision goes down the same way in real life?"

Real life. There were those two haunting words again. "I guess. What time are you going?"

She glanced at her watch. "We're meeting in just over an hour."

"What time is it now?"

"Almost five, so I better hurry with this makeover. Nate should be here any minute. How long are your parents letting you stay out?"

"Same as always. Eleven."

Tammy rolled her eyes, setting the flatiron down and picking up a compact. "Jeez, they sure do keep a tight leash, don't they?"

I closed my eyes as she covered my lids in powder. "It'll change to midnight when I turn eighteen next month. How late are you guys staying at Jumpin' Java tonight?"

"Until they close at eleven. Then we were gonna maybe hang at someone's house."

I felt her brushing on eye shadow. "Okay. We'll try to make it there by ten."

She held one lid open to apply mascara. "Where's Mr. Hottie taking you tonight anyway?"

Wrinkling my nose, I said, "Your guess is as good as mine."

A few seconds later, the doorbell rang. Tammy hurriedly applied some peach-colored blush and lip balm.

"What do you think?"

I paused to examine my reflection in the mirror before bending down to slip on her boots. "I think I believe in miracles now. If you can make me look this good, then anything can happen."

Squealing, she clapped her hands. "I know! I mean, you are pretty, but I made you look smokin'! Come on. I want to see Nate's face when he sees you."

She pulled me down the hallway, barely giving me enough time to snatch my purse off my bedpost as we left the room.

Before I could catch my breath, there stood Nate in my doorway, stealing more of my breath away. He dressed in jeans, tan suede shoes, and a gray collared T-shirt that displayed his bulging biceps. His hair was crammed underneath a black fur trooper hat, and he looked adorable, holding out a bouquet of flowers for me.

He blushed, and I realized he heard how I saw him. A beat later, he grabbed my hand and kissed it. "You look amazing. Absolutely beautiful."

"So do you. And these flowers, they're gorgeous!"

"I grew them at school with the Interact Club. You should join us. We garden twice a month, clean up around campus once a month—"

Tammy giggled. "You're killing the mood here, Barca. Good thing Olga's parents aren't home from work yet. You can practically smell the lust in here." She pulled out her phone. "Let's get a picture of my favorite pair of goody two-shoes before you leave."

Nate shrugged on his denim trucker-style jacket and tugged me to his side. I tried not to melt as Tammy said, "Say, 'I love Olga.'" But when Nate actually obeyed and said the words, it was kind of hard not to.

"You ready, beautiful?"

I nodded. "Yep, but do we need Tammy to give us a ride somewhere? I just realized neither one of us can drive."

He slapped his forehead, shutting my front door behind him with his other hand. "Now why didn't I think of that?"

"You're mocking me, aren't you?"

"Maybe."

After we climbed the stairs to the front of my apartment building, I spotted the four-wheel bike outside that could seat two. "So we're roughing it tonight?"

Nate walked over to the bike and rang the bell. "Hey, I'll have you know this is a top of the line, three-speed Surrey I rented for this occasion."

Getting into her Lexus, Tammy laughed. "You kids have fun! And don't worry, Olga. I applied enough hairspray that no strand will even think about curling back up. See you later."

I hopped onto the seat next to him. "Okay, Mr. Adventure. Where are we heading?"

"Downtown to the C2C Gallery off Washington Avenue for an informal painting class."

Groaning, I admitted, "I've never been much of an artist."

Nate pedaled, checking both ways before taking us across the parking lot. "Most people aren't." He laughed at me biting my lip and paused at the stop sign. "Olga, stop worrying. This is for fun. You won't be graded on your canvas. Now, start pedaling or we'll be late." He tapped the backpack in the front basket. "And if you need some fuel, I have coffee in a thermos."

"You think of everything."

"I think everything of you." He took hold of my fingers on the handlebar.

Melting. "This bike is awesome. I like the red and white circus top design." I pointed my index finger above our heads, subtly sneaking my hand away. I didn't want to get his hopes up any higher than they already were.

"It's called a sunbrella. Learned some biker lingo today."

"When are you getting your license back?"

He shook his head. "Not until the end of the school year, but I don't even know if I want it. Grand Haven is a small enough town to get around by foot, bike, or skateboarding. Then I'll be off to college and living on campus. I kind of want to stay away from driving for as long as I can. When will you have your license?"

"I'm taking Driver's Ed at school right now, so I should have it by December when the class ends."

"Oh, right. Brittney told me at the football game last night how you hit that bird on your first test run yesterday. I'll remember to stay inside come Christmas break."

I slapped his arm, ignoring the pain of jealousy at the mention of Brittney. I'd seen them sitting together with a big crowd of people up in the stands while I cheered below, my heart not in my peppy words and motions at all. "For your information, Mr. Know It All, that bird hit me, not the other way around."

He flashed his perfect teeth in a smile. "How exactly does a bird willfully fly into an oncoming car?"

Scowling, I explained, "I wasn't even driving! I was at the stop sign, and he literally flew into my windshield."

"So what you're saying is, wildlife would rather willingly commit suicide than face you on the road."

Sliding my hand to his nape, I tugged on some stray hairs sticking out from his cap. "Are you done now?"

"Just getting started. Was it a two-way or four-way stop?"

I raked my gaze over him, wanting to slap and kiss him at the same time. "What does it matter?"

"I'm just trying to picture the whole scenario in my head, looking for any loopholes in your story. I don't know if I should be dating a girl with homicidal tendencies toward birds."

With a laugh, I said, "We're not dating. I agreed to one date. And you are so ridiculous. He didn't even die."

"You *saw* him fly away then?"

My shoulders drooped. "Well, no. We all got out of the car and looked around, but he was nowhere to be found."

"Why didn't you entice him with some birdseed?" His gaze penetrated me, holding me still for his interrogation.

"Where would I get birdseed exactly?"

"You don't carry any on you?"

"Nope."

"Well then, you should've sacrificed your lunch if you really cared about the bird."

"My lunch was back in the classroom!"

"See, that's why smart people always carry some birdseed."

"There is nothing smart about your logic or that bird." I ripped the hat off his head. "Now, you will stop this madness or the hat gets it."

The bike stopped abruptly. "The only one getting it is you."

He kissed me, all the bird talk forgotten.

My heart thudded in my ears. His kiss was a lot different than Conner's. Not bad, just different. And for some reason, familiar. A drowsy warmth washed over me, and another memory flooded my mind.

Conner kissed me, winding his hand into my hair, the other on my hip, pulling my chest to his. The intensity grew, our breaths ragged and swift, until Bo cleared his throat, reminding us we weren't alone. I felt my cheeks blush and twisted my hair back into a knot.

After a second, Nate pulled away. He frowned, then took the hat and settled it back on his head. "I'm guessing you saw that vision, too?"

"Hmm."

I resettled my body to start pedaling again. Why did I have visions of kissing Nate when I kissed Conner a few nights ago and then envision kissing Conner while kissing Nate now? "Here's the thing. You should have an apology coming, but I can't control these visions or memories or whatever they are from floating to the surface. I'm beginning to think the only reason you see the same thing as me is because you can read my mind. Do you think that's possible?"

Nate closed his eyes. "Bo was in your vision, though. How do you even know what he looks like?"

A particular melancholy revealed itself on Nate's face, and I wondered how I could've missed Bo being in my vision until now. "He was Conner's roommate in Juvie."

The words flew out of my mouth without any prompting.

Tears appeared in Nate's eyes without much prompting, either. "What does that mean?"

I shook my head. "No idea."

For the rest of the short ride, we were both quiet. I think the vision had stolen our breath and our words away.

When we pulled up to C2C Gallery, music blared from inside. Nate held my hand as he led me to the entrance, cold wind slapping my cheeks and bringing the strong scent of paint from the open doorway.

"Olga! Nate! Down here!" Thankful for the interruption, I peered down the sidewalk.

Kyle waved to us from the front of Jumpin' Java across the way, about a block up the street, Conner standing next to him and looking pissed. Clearly, Kyle had missed the memo that Nate and I were on a date.

Nate looked down at me through the thick shield of his dark lashes. "You want to join them?"

"You wouldn't mind?" I whispered.

He leaned back on his heels. "No. To be honest, I'm not really in the mood for romance anymore." His tone wasn't mean, just honest.

Every nerve in my body relaxed, thankful we were on the same page for once. "So, should we just leave the bike here?"

"After you, my lady." He gestured toward the coffee shop, and we started walking, decidedly not holding hands.

A wise decision because Conner looked more lonely than I'd ever seen him, even though he was surrounded by the Jedi Order as they sipped coffee from their cups at an outside table. He leaned his chair against the window, his ear turned toward the karaoke music blaring inside, but his gaze remained fixed on me with an aching look. Ugh, that look broke my heart. I longed to run to him, but I knew that wouldn't be fair to Nate.

"You really do attract birds," Nate said, brushing the side of my arm.

"Huh?"

"He's watching you like a hawk. Kind of freaking me out. He better not act like a jerk tonight."

I nodded, knowing that no matter how he acted, I couldn't stop the invisible force drawing me to him. Once we arrived, Nate mumbled something about getting me coffee and went inside, all our friends following him. Except Conner.

"Your hair is down."

"Tammy straightened it for me." I grinned, proud of myself for stringing together a coherent sentence with all the mixed emotion swirling inside me.

He tried to smile back, but the gesture fell short. "Looks like you're breaking free of all sorts of things tonight."

"Conner—"

"I'm gonna go, Olga. You deserve to be happy." His voice was barely audible over the girl inside murdering the Whitney Houston song, "I Will Always Love You." Her song choice fit, though, because what exactly was I doing by agreeing to this date tonight? I'd always love Conner, no matter how drawn I felt to Nate.

"What? No, don't go. I'll go."

He shook his head, giving me a quick once-over. "I'm not leaving because of you. I'm tired is all."

Liar. "Okay, well let me walk you to your car. Where are you parked?"

He jabbed his thumb behind him. "Just around the corner here."

I followed him to his Ford Escape Hybrid. He unlocked the door with the remote on his keychain but didn't climb in. Instead, he leaned against the cab and faced me, regarding me with an unfocused gaze, his eyes filling with tears, once again breaking my heart.

Even though I came here with someone else, I longed to comfort him, to kiss him. But wasn't I longing to kiss Nate just minutes ago? I felt so confused. My thoughts made me hesitate but didn't stop me from closing my arms around Conner, burying my head against his shoulder. We rocked together, unsure of who started the motion, unable to stop. Until finally, our eyes met, and the longing to kiss him overwhelmed me. I stepped away.

"Not here, Conner. I can't do this right now."

"When? I know I don't deserve you, but I still want to take you out on an official date, too. Even if it's just one time."

Now my eyes filled with tears, and I had a moment of absolute clarity. All this time I'd been waiting for my first date with Conner, but my subconscious knew I'd already had it. Only something prevented me from remembering the experience. And it totally sucked.

"Tomorrow then. Meet me in the parking lot of Saint Patrick's Church for ten o'clock Mass. We can go out afterward."

Conner's eyes flared. "Mass? How about after? Ten is early for me."

I shook my head. "Then come to the 11:45 service. This is my stipulation. You can take me out only if you come to church with me. Even if it's just one time."

He nodded. "I hope you can feel how much I want you."

I gulped. "I do."

"Good. That's why I'm saying yes to this stupid plan of yours. Just out of curiosity, did Nate's offer to take you out come with any stipulations?"

Every organ in my body felt like it was on fire under his gaze. "That's how I got him to leave your house Monday night, remember? And anyway, we're not really even on a date anymore."

"Oh, yeah." He gently put his hand on my shoulder, sweeping my hair back. "I'm actually surprised you're out at all. Your mom didn't freak out about you spending the night with me?"

Nodding, I said, "Dad actually lied to her about it and said I was at Nic's. He said he'll repent for it at confession next time he goes."

"Good." He brushed his thumb across my cheek, then leaned in to kiss me there. "Until tomorrow." After watching him pull away, I had to figure out how to move my legs one in front of the other and join my friends inside. The rich, stimulating rush of brewing coffee drew me in, brushing off the uncomfortable and thrilling encounter with Conner. My gaze bounced from couples leaning toward each other at the bistro tables to the laughing groups of people my own age crowding the booths. Finally, I spotted my friends at a booth all the way in the back. Nate waved me over. If he'd heard my thoughts when I was with Conner, he didn't show it.

"Here you go."

"Hmm, thanks, Barca. You are a gift from the gods, truly."

For one split second, we just stared at each other, like looking into a crystal ball.

Tammy's voice broke through our shared memory of the vision, completing it. "You two are so cute together. You'll make adorable, dorky babies someday. That is, if the date went well. Which I'm assuming it did since Conner's not here."

I heard Nicole kick her under the table.

"Ouch! What'd ya do that for?"

My hand jittered as I sipped the chocolate-drizzled, Snickers-flavored mocha with whipped topping. The gesture wasn't lost on Nate. "You probably drink enough coffee to make a rhino's heart explode."

"So?"

He flashed me a lazy grin. "Just saying."

A few songs later, we watched as Sean got crowned third place winner in the karaoke contest, a prize that came with a twenty-five-dollar gift card to the coffee house. Then we laughed as he hopped onto the stage and lifted his shirt, mimicking the Truffle Shuffle from *The Goonies* movie.

Nate motioned toward the wall clock. "It's ten thirty. We should peddle home before you're late."

We were quiet for most of the way until he finally brought up the subject I'd been dreading.

"Do you want to tell me why you're going out with someone else tomorrow?"

I stared up at the stars, praying for a shooting one, thinking I could really use a wish right now. "I think it has to do with how much history there is between Conner and me. He wants to take me out on at least one proper date, and I need to let him."

Nate winced, like my explanation caused him physical pain. "You're right. I just wish you two would've figured out you're not right for each other before I met you. Would save us a lot of time. You love me, even if you don't know it yet."

"The thing is, I think I do know it. I just don't feel it yet. My mind is having a hard time keeping up with what my heart already instinctively knows these days."

At my admission, my heart raced wildly as he steered us into the parking lot of my apartment complex. Like a gentleman, he came around to my side of the bike and helped me down, not letting go of my hand.

He held my hand to his mouth and kissed the top.

"You really do have a way of making me want you," he whispered, before our lips met.

He backed me against the freestanding garage next to my apartment building so our bodies matched. Just as I raked my fingers through his dark, shaggy hair, my mind flashed to Conner's pained expression earlier tonight.

I jerked away from Nate, holding one hand to my chest and one hand to my sweaty forehead. "I'm sorry. I don't mean to torture you."

He released his grip on my waist. His face held its own look of apology, and his was beautiful. "There's nothing to be sorry for. This situation is really confusing. We just need to get to know each other more, see if we remember. What do you say to sneaking out tonight?"

I didn't answer, so he made up my mind for me.

"Meet me outside your window in an hour."

He peddled away. Taking in a deep breath, I tried to hold myself together, wondering what kind of girl would want to kiss a guy who read her mind and gave her visions? What kind of girl would simultaneously want to make out with her best friend after he slept with another one of her best friends? The kind of girl that had lost her mind, that's who.

CHAPTER ELEVEN

*"Second star to the right
and straight on till morning."*

—J.M. Barrie, *Peter Pan*

So, when's the last time you went through a whole day without a cup of coffee?" Nate asked me. We were lying on an oversize beach towel at the top of a sand dune overlooking Lake Michigan. I'd swapped out Tammy's Latin-style jeans and sheer shirt for a more comfortable outfit: my Grand Haven High Buccaneers sweatshirt and sweatpants. I'd also swept my hair into a bun and washed off all the makeup Tammy applied earlier. No reason for Nate to think we were on a second date already.

"I can't remember. Why?"

He picked up an antique handheld telescope he'd brought from home and squinted into the eyepiece. "I don't know. I want to be around you for a day when you don't drink coffee."

"So your type is moody, irritable, and fatigued?"

He passed the telescope to me. "You're my type. I just want to know every side of you."

Swoon. "You're sweet, but Dad started giving me coffee at a very early age, so unless you add time travel to your list of supernatural abilities, don't hold your breath for that wish to happen."

He laughed. "Okay. Your turn."

"My turn for what?"

"We're playing twenty questions. Question two, go."

"Oh. Have you ever been in love?"

He got up on one elbow and peered over at me. "Have I not made my feelings for you clear enough?"

The black sky threatened to swallow me like an abyss at the honesty of his admission I so wasn't ready for. "Okay, wow. Yeah. I guess I mean before me."

He draped another towel over us as the wind picked up. "I thought I was with my last girlfriend."

"How long ago did that end?"

After several minutes of him staring into the starry night sky without responding, I glanced at him.

"The day I got into my accident."

Sitting up, I hugged my knees to my chest. "What do you mean?"

Gathering a handful of sand, he made a pile. "Well, I actually dated a girl for the last three years. That's part of the reason why I was so upset when my dad got his new job here. We were going to try the long-distance thing, knowing it would be hard. Then she decided to break up with me the last day of school, said she didn't think it'd work out."

I nodded, like what he said made sense, even though it didn't. How could he date someone for three years and not tell me about it yet? Three years is a really long time, especially in high school.

"Olga, my feelings for you were immediate. As soon as I *saw* you, I knew Lindsey made the right decision for both of us." He smiled but not his usual carefree grin. This smile held vulnerability.

"Have you talked to Lindsey since you called things off?"

"Nope. Now, you just asked about five questions. My turn again. When did you know you were interested in becoming a writer?"

I could tell he desperately wanted to change the subject.

"For as long as I can remember. Mom would always read me a bedtime story until I deemed myself too old for that sort of thing at age ten, and then I always fought for more solo reading time at night. Mom wasn't big on gifts, but she did buy me all these classics, like *A Christmas Carol* and *The Swiss Family Robinson*. Reading is like a religion to me, ya know? Words are so emotional, the way they help us communicate with one another. There's such beauty in them. My love of reading birthed my love of writing. I wanted to be part of that magic. So I filled journal after journal with my own stories. Then when I took Journalism freshman year and joined the *The Bucs' Blade*, I realized the power of seeing your words in print. Actually, the *Grand Haven Tribune* just hired me to be their teen correspondent. Once a week, I'll be giving my opinion on the latest happenings in the world from a young adult's perspective, so I'm pretty excited about that. What about you? When did you know you were interested in music?"

He smoothed his sand pile down until it flattened. "I guess when I was five. That's when Dad put me in guitar lessons. School ended about an hour before my mom could pick me up, but he felt like letting me sit in afterschool care was a waste of money. As fate would have it, there was a music store across the street from my school, so the crossing guard helped me walk there every day for a lesson, Monday through Friday."

"So, what's your plan after high school? You mentioned college before. You don't want to pursue a music career?"

"Nah. I'm not massively concerned about making it big as a musician. I mean, it'd be sweet and all, but I'm completely content doing music as a hobby. Probably sounds like a stupid thing to say to someone who's so passionate about their art."

"Not at all. I like how you're not deluded into thinking you can easily become a rock star. Lots of guys at school seem to think they're going to be the next big thing at whatever sport or hobby they're involved in. So you get kudos in my book for not being disillusioned. What do you want to major in?"

"Philosophy."

I snorted. "Okay, I take my kudos back."

"I know, I know. Being a big thinker hardly translates into a solid career path. Still, I like to picture myself leading lectures at a university."

"What does one do with a philosophy degree until they can achieve that status?"

Nate shrugged. "Lots of things, actually. I'm thinking I'll maybe go into counseling. Help screwed-up adolescents like me. The whole experience with killing Bo and hearing your thoughts has taught me a lot about the human condition." He nudged me with his toe. "Maybe I'll even go into journalism. Follow you and your stories around the world."

The way he pronounced things so openly excited me. Unlike other boys, his words held conviction. It was something that drew me in, and then I realized that maybe he spoke with such declaration because he'd already followed me to all those places we didn't quite remember.

"So, Mr. Philosopher, pick a word that best describes you and tell me why."

"It'll be hard to pick just one. I'm a very complicated person." He winked at me before holding up his finger. "Adventurous. Every summer, until this past summer, my whole extended family would rent a houseboat to travel across the four Great Lakes around Michigan, and my cousins and I would spend the month of July water-skiing, knee boarding, and tubing. When we docked, we'd find cliffs to jump off and rocks to climb. There were usually places to zip-line during our vacations, too. My parents even let me firewalk with them last summer."

"Firewalking sounds awesome!"

Before Conner's accident, I'd never understood why anyone would want to do that. These days, I found myself craving adventure, though. Of course I hadn't done anything remotely adventurous yet, but I definitely wanted to. I guess near-death experiences tended to have that effect on people.

"It is, makes you feel so alive! Like you can take on the world. You should try it with me some time."

"I would love to. Anything else I should know about you?"

"I maintain a huge garden at my house. Actually, I might minor in herbology. I'd love to teach people how to live off the land. I also try to do yoga and meditate as often as possible, and don't hate me, but I actually prefer tea to coffee."

"Shut up!"

He covered his face with his hands and groaned. "I've ruined it now, haven't I? Tea is a deal breaker."

"No, it's just, I can't believe you do yoga! I mean, I knew you were different from other guys, but not that different!"

Peeking at me through a gap in his fingers, he said, "Hey, how do you think I maintain my six-pack abs? Yoga is the most grueling cardio workout I do seven days a week! Come over one morning. I'll show you."

"I'll take your word for it."

"Too bad. There are lots of fun poses we could work on together." He wiggled his eyebrows at me. "Just think about it. All right, my turn. Tell me about your ideal guy. This should be easy since all you have to do is point to me."

"Okay, first quality. He must be super humble."

"Dammit."

I laughed. "Honestly, I don't really know. I haven't had much experience with guys, so I'm not sure what my ideal qualities are."

"What have you seen in Conner all these years?"

He asked the question with such tenderness it made my chest ache. "I guess his loyalty. He hasn't cared that I'm this big nerd, a girl who never wears makeup, whose hair is too puffy, who never has stylish clothes. He accepts me for me, all of the Jedi Order does. Plus, he helps me lighten up, since I'm way too serious most of the time."

With red cheeks, Nate stared at the ground and brushed his hand over a pile of sand.

"He may not be the right guy for me. Only time will tell. But he is my best friend, my rock. He'll always be a part of my life. So if you're still interested in spending time with me, you're gonna have to deal with that. Can you?"

Nate took a deep breath and hesitated, like maybe he debated ending our game of twenty questions now. "There's this memory I have. I remember flashing lights, lots of people running around, the sad, scared faces of those I loved, and more tears than I ever wanted to see any parent cry. I was a wreck lying in the hospital, thinking about Bo's funeral and wishing I could be there. Thankful at the same time I couldn't be. Not sure if I could walk up to his parents and speak, offer my condolences. But when I *saw* you for the first time, a strange, peaceful feeling came over me. A sort of clarity. A deep connection to life I'd never felt before with anyone. Olga, being with you is like this experience that's allowed me to step out of my big ego and connect to something bigger than just having fun. My accident and Bo's death already laid the groundwork to make me humble, but it also killed me inside. Meeting you was my wake-up call, and

I've never felt more alive. Not even while doing all those crazy stunts. So, the answer is yes. I can live with anything, as long as you're in my life."

So. Dang. Swoonworthy!

As he slid onto his back, hair still crammed under his fur hat, I noticed the beginning of a mustache and shadow-beard forming and found it irresistible. I traced my finger over the thin line above his lip down to his chin. He tugged on my hand, and I could tell he wanted to kiss me again, but instead I rested my head on his shoulder.

Sighing, he asked, "What's your most irrational fear?"

"Why?"

"So I can scare you on Halloween."

"Jerk. That's my birthday, ya know. A little over a month and I'm legal."

Nate cleared his throat, like he was trying to hide a laugh. "Lucky. I missed having a birthday/holiday combo by one day."

"When's your birthday?"

"February fifteenth. Maybe that's why I'm such a romantic, being born so close to Valentine's Day and all. Love was in the air."

"So I'm three and a half months older than you?"

"Hot, right? You little cougar."

I rolled my eyes. "Now I know this will never work. I'm too mature for you."

He pulled me closer to him. "It's funny. I spent my whole life in a hurry to grow up. A lot of the adrenaline junkie things, like skydiving, you usually have to wait to be eighteen for. But now that I've met you, I just want to freeze time."

Melting. I needed to focus on his question before I let him kiss me again. "Drowning in poop."

"What?"

"That's my irrational fear." In a shaky voice, I recounted the experience with Conner daring me to jump into a ruptured septic tank, but Nate didn't seem to comprehend my trauma because all he could do by the end of my story was crack up.

"I'm sorry," he said between laughs.

"Shut up. I don't believe you." I pinched his arm. "What's your most irrational fear anyway?"

"Someone stabbing me."

"Okaaay." I drew out the word. "Elaborate, *por favor.*"

He kissed the top of my forehead. "I don't know. I've been to a lot of rock concerts over the past few years. There are always big crowds, and I just began to think someone could very easily stab me. Nobody would ever know who did it."

"You are a mystery, Barca."

Twirling my Morticia Addams ring, he asked, "What's this silly ring about? You never take it off."

"Conner gave it to me on my sixteenth birthday. Actually, it was a regift from five years earlier when I gave it to him one summer."

His smile faded. "So you like rings. Good to know. Do you want to get married?"

"Are you proposing to me already?"

"Not yet. I'm saving that for our third date."

"Just checking. And I'm not sure. I mean, you can read my mind, so you probably know I've always envisioned marrying Conner one day. Now though... I wonder if I'm too selfish to ever get married."

"Why do you think you're selfish?"

I glanced toward the lifeguard tower, the flag there flapping in the wind. "For starters, I'm an only child, so I'm used to getting my way. Plus, I'm realizing something lately. I keep thinking of how Tammy should stay single because she's always had a boyfriend since forever. But even though I haven't had much guy experience, I've been guy obsessed my whole life, even if it was one guy in particular. Kind of makes me crave some freedom and independence, like maybe I shouldn't worry about picking you or Conner. But that also sounds absurd to me because you're both so wonderful. How could I refuse both of you?"

We were silent for a moment.

"Barca, I do like you. You know this. You can read my thoughts. But please understand, I don't want you to get hurt. I'm worried I'm using you as some emotional crutch. My heart is so confused right now it's probably better we just stay friends."

A glimmer of hope remained in his eyes. "But what about our connection... I mean, don't you think we owe it to ourselves to see where this takes us?"

Pushing my finger to his lips, I meant to quiet him. Debating this right now would do no good because I'd just end up more confused. But then the feel of his supersoft lips against my finger distracted me and all I wanted to do was kiss him, to forget about everything else for a moment. I knew it was a shallow thought, especially after I claimed I wanted my independence not thirty seconds ago. But before I could pull back, he took my face in his hands and kissed me. My breath hitched, and we locked eyes for a moment, his gaze seeming to ask if this was okay. I remembered I didn't have to *say* anything. Relaxing into the kiss, I closed my eyes and titled my head to the side. It felt like we'd done this many times before, so comfortable was our kiss. For the first time, I felt loved unconditionally. Just like God, Nate could hear all my wretched thoughts, yet he still wanted me. I didn't need to keep myself covered up with him. It made me bold. My hand flew to his chest, my heart crashed into my sides, my breathing came fast. He slipped his tongue in my mouth, and I gasped, then…

We trace our names in the sand, and then he snaps a picture of us next to our designs. We lay on our backs, staring at the cumulus clouds in the light of the moon and look for pictures in the piles of puffy cotton. "I know this probably sounds strange since I just snuck out for the first time, but I've never felt more at peace than this moment," I tell him. Fireflies flit past us.

"I know what you mean," Nate murmurs, the moon full and bright behind him.

I sat up in a cold sweat. Beside me, Nate did, too, shaking his head.

So far our vision of the house party and coffee house came true. Did we make them come true? But then, why did they feel like memories? And we didn't have this vision of the beach until we were already here, so it wasn't a premonition. Then there were the other memories, the ones with Tammy and the ones with an angel talking to me, the dream Conner had of being in a prison when he received his first shock therapy. Add on Nate reading my mind and Conner waking up from his coma acting strangely, and all of this had to be connected. The knowledge of it came from deep down and hovered at the surface. I could see it right in front of me, but I couldn't break through. Couldn't figure out how these things fit together. It made me terrified and more determined. There'd never been a puzzle I couldn't solve. I wasn't going to give up until I cracked the code. But somewhere in the back of my mind, I possessed the odd knowledge that this was the easy part. Darker roads lay ahead.

"I agree," Nate said, hearing me work out my thoughts. "It's definitely all connected."

"Yeah?" I couldn't tell whether he actually believed we were all connected somehow or just grabbed on to the thought so it'd help keep me near him a little while longer.

He lay down next to me and reaching across, took my hand in his and laced our fingers together. "I'm telling you the truth. You can trust me."

I was too tired to argue. Exhausted, I fell fast asleep.

"You're grounded, young lady!" Dad yelled, jabbing a finger toward me as Nate and I peddled through the parking lot of my apartment complex.

We hadn't woken up until 7:39 a.m., and with the three-mile bike ride back, it was past eight now. My parents already had all the neighbors up and looking for me.

"I'm sorry, sir," Nate said, hopping off the bike and hanging his head low. "This is all my fault. It was my idea."

Dad ignored him. "Get inside right now!" He pointed to the front door. He pointed a lot when he was angry, which wasn't very often. Usually Mom did the yelling.

Both my parents followed me inside, Dad the last one in, slamming the door in Nate's face with full force. "I don't even know what to say right now. This behavior isn't like you. We raised you better than this. Just… go get ready for Mass. We leave in an hour."

Anxiety pulsed through me as I remembered my plans for the day. "But Conner was going to meet me for 11:45 service."

"Really?" Mom asked, her tone saturated with surprise. "Well, call him with the change of plans. Then you're grounded, from your phone and from all social activities. Outside of church, school, and work, you're home. Understand?"

"Yes, ma'am. For how long?"

"How long do you think you should be grounded?"

I frowned. She'd never asked me that before, but I guess I didn't usually do things to get grounded, either. "Two weeks?" A girl could try, right?

Mom's cackled response startled me. "Try two months!"

My heart froze. "Mom, that would mean being grounded on my birthday. You're seriously going to hold me hostage even after I'm a legal adult?"

"She has a point, Elizabeth," Dad interjected, his face less red now.

Mom took a deep breath. "Fine. You're grounded until your birthday. Go take a shower, Olga. I don't want to see your face until we're leaving for church."

Quickly, I did the mental math. Forty-four days. That was longer than Jesus spent in the desert! But I didn't think now was a good time to argue my sentence.

"Yes, ma'am."

I knew I should call Conner and fess up about not being able to make our date, but the thought made me want to puke, and I wanted him to come to church. Sending a text to meet at ten instead, I got in the shower and washed off the sand. I wished washing away my guilt were just as easy.

"Why the change in plans?" Conner asked with a yawn, stretching. Bags under his eyes dominated his face, his shaggy, surfer-style blond hair pushed away from his forehead by a pair of Ray Ban sunglasses. He dressed in gray swim trunks and a black T-shirt, hardly church attire, but I guessed I should just be thankful he came. Seeming to notice my ogling, he said, "What? I came dressed for our date afterward to make things easier. I hope you remembered your swimsuit underneath that flowery sundress of yours. You got my text, right?"

I still didn't have the guts to tell him the truth. "It's too cold for swimming."

"That's why we're sailing. We can't stay off the water together forever. I already missed joining the sailing team this year. Don't worry, I already checked the weather forecast. Nothing but clear skies ahead."

Clutching my purse, I almost breathed a sigh of relief because fear over sailing with him again could give me a way out of my date without telling him about last night. But then I remembered he doesn't give up so easily. Time to come clean.

"So, guess what I did last night?" Ugh, I was trying to keep my tone light, but I realized too late it sounded like taunting.

"Cried yourself to sleep over picking Nate for your first date instead of me."

I eyed the cross above the entrance to the church, praying for a little help.

Conner seemed to notice my anxiety and was quick to try to end it. "Hey, joking. You said to guess, so I did. What's up?"

"I got myself grounded."

The ache on his face was palpable. "How?"

"I snuck out."

His relaxed posture stiffened, and he knew.

Our eyes held, frozen, the color of his irises turning black—an eerie contrast against the blue sky. Staring at him, I felt like I was spiraling down into a bottomless chasm. He stumbled forward, like someone pushed him from behind, except nobody was there. The bell rung, signaling the start of service, but the sound seemed like a million miles away. I couldn't tear my gaze away from Conner, couldn't form words. The face I saw before me was a monster, unrecognizable. Simultaneously, it was as if Conner noticed me for the first time. He bared his teeth, then kicked my feet from under me, my back landing with a heavy thud on the grass.

"Enough Mr. Nice Guy." He hoisted me up and threw me over his shoulder, heading for the parking lot toward his Ford.

Screams desperately clung to the inside of my throat, but I couldn't force them to my mouth. I couldn't understand what happened. Was he kidnapping me?

He threw me into the passenger side of his hybrid, then ran to the other side and hopped in. I tried leaving, but he yanked me back when I was halfway out the door, then kept my head down with a heavy hand. "Don't worry. I'll show you how a real man operates," he said, turning the key in the ignition. "You'll forget all about that little punk, Nate."

Suddenly, there was a hand grabbing Conner, shoving him outside the vehicle. Another hand punching him repeatedly, screaming, "Did you really think you could get away with this? I'll kill you and go to jail forever before I let you hurt her."

Nate. Either he stalked me or could hear my thoughts. I didn't care how he knew I needed help; I was just happy to see him. But then Conner threw a punch and hit his face so hard that he flew backward. I rushed to Nate's side, and Conner took the opportunity to flee the scene, wheels squealing as he drove out of sight.

I bent over Nate. "Are you okay?"

"I'll live," he said quietly. "But I can't promise the same for your best friend if I ever see his face again."

Tears streamed down my face as I shook my head. "Whoever that was, that wasn't my best friend."

CHAPTER TWELVE

"Maturity has more to do with what you've learned from the past than your age."

—Nate's Thoughts

I'd been taunted by nightmares ever since Conner disappeared that day in the church parking lot, exactly forty-four days ago. In my dreams, his teeth were bared in a grimace, lips shrunken back. Empty eye sockets peered down at me before the feeling of his cold, hard fingers flinging me over his shoulder came. He'd bring me to a dungeon, where he revealed his true self. Flashing a smile of black decay, he'd tell me, "We're all reduced to this eventually anyway."

Then I'd wake up, sweating profusely and in a fit of anxiety. I didn't understand any of it. Part of me wondered if a demon had possessed him, and I wanted to ask a priest about it. But were demons even real? I'd never heard Father Jamie talk about them. I'd been reading a book on spiritual warfare we stocked at the Bookman, but for some reason, even though I always believed in angels, I thought demons were the inventions of Hollywood. Now I wasn't sure. Now I was pretty sure demons weren't only real, but that I'd even caused one to take notice of me at one point and put Conner in danger. I knew this because of the journal.

I didn't know where the Daily Meditation Guide came from, only that on the day Conner disappeared it wasn't on the desk in my room, and the next day it was. Funny thing, there were journal entries written in my handwriting that I had zero recollection of writing. More curious, the entries were dated in the future, next June to be exact. One spoke of the vast empty hole in my heart exactly Conner Anderson shaped, how Nate didn't fill the void, and I'd never fully let go of Conner. A later one sounded like I was trying to talk myself into waiting longer, to be more patient for answers about Conner before I embarked on a mission concerning an Alpha File 120 so it wouldn't fall into the wrong hands. Plain as day, I just *knew* those wrong hands meant a demon. I just didn't know who to talk to about it. Of course, I told Nate; he'd hear about it in my thoughts anyway. But seeing as neither one of us had any new memories to share, we were road blocked.

My only solution was to protect myself as best I could, so I started carrying my pocket-sized mass book around with me and wearing my rosary beads wherever I went. Those kind of things did a lot to solidify my freak status at school, but I didn't care anymore. Praying every spare moment I had, I was so distracted that I practically knocked everything down I came into contact with. I knew I only saw the tip of the iceberg that was my problems, and God alone saw the big picture and he worked slowly, but I wished he would hurry up with some answers already.

The one silver lining was my parents released me from my grounding sentence after just two weeks. I'd done some research on my computer concerning how long teens should be punished, then presented my findings in an essay: Most experts agreed that longer than two weeks would not teach the child anything because consequences for poor choices only worked if the teen was able to get back the ability to make wise choices.

If Conner hadn't gone missing, I doubt they would've gone for it, but I got their sympathy vote. Not that I used my freedom for any more make out sessions with Nate. Instead, the Jedi Order accompanied me to all of Conner's most commonly visited haunts—the nearby music store, the beach, the coffee houses, the pizza parlors, the bowling alley—in search of him, hoping he'd show up eventually. But finding nothing, we'd each return to our homes feeling more miserable each day. The police weren't exactly out there looking for him very hard either, since Conner had turned eighteen in June. My parents helped Mr. and Mrs. Anderson search whenever they could, not that Conner was their favorite person these days after what he did to me. But they wanted the *real* Conner back, too.

In an effort to lift everyone's spirits, Nate suggested we all go firewalking for my eighteenth birthday. His idea was the only thing that'd made me smile since Conner left, even if it did mean another possible grounding sentence, since we were skipping classes. Nic picked me up for school as usual. No sleeping in so we wouldn't raise suspicions with my parents.

"Good morning, sunshine!"

A wave of hunger hit me. "Can we stop for some food on the way to the firewalking place?"

"Change of plans," Nic said, searching for something good on the radio. "When Nate looked online last night for the closest place to firewalk, he realized everyone would need parental consent, since we're not all legal like you, and that'd be kind of hard since we're skipping school today. Plus, not everyone has money to burn. Get it, burn?" She laughed at her own joke.

"Hahaha. Very punny."

She flipped the visor mirror down and reapplied some lipstick at the stoplight, ignoring my equally corny joke. "Anyway, we're heading to Sean's cabin in the woods for a barbeque. After they're done cooking the hamburgers, they'll scoop out the hot coals and make a path in the grass for us to walk on!"

"Please tell me this is the start to a 'You Know You're A Redneck If' joke."

She threw her head back in laughter. "Ha! Now that's funny."

"Thank you. But seriously, this has disaster written all over it."

Nic batted my concerns away. " Relax. Today is going to be a good day. I just know it."

I hoped she was right, but an hour later, we pulled down the dirt road to the cabin Sean's parents used as a tiny vacation getaway three miles into the woods and saw Conner's vehicle parked next to the house.

We sat in the car for several seconds, listening. Silence never seemed so loud. Nobody else had arrived yet. At least Tammy's car wasn't in sight. She was the one chauffeuring everyone, but they had to stop at the store for supplies along the way.

"Does your cell have service here? Mine doesn't."

Biting her lip, Nic checked and shook her head. "Nope. We're in a dead zone."

No kidding.

"Should we leave and come back? I mean, he could still be dangerous. We should wait to confront him until everyone is here."

Hands slamming on the trunk made us both jump and scream at the same time. Turning around, I spotted Conner through the back windshield, his expression as grotesque as ever.

"Nic, go!"

Launching a tsunami of curse words, she spun the wheel frantically like a DJ running turntables. Instead of getting out of the way like a normal person would, Conner leaped onto the hood, laughing at us like he was having the time of his life as Nic surged forward.

"Olga, what do I do?"

"No idea!" I withdrew the rosary from underneath my hoodie and started praying, praying God would give me some answers. When I looked up, I saw Tammy's Lexus barreling toward us on a dirt road only wide enough for one car. If this was a game of Chicken, Tammy won.

"What the frick!" Nic shrieked.

Thinking fast, I placed my hands on the wheel and jerked her Honda Civic out of the way, causing Conner to fly off into a tree.

Tammy rolled her window down and shook her fist. "Haha, suckers! We win!"

I threw myself out of the car and ran to Conner, who lay unconscious in the grass.

"Jesus! Is that Conner?" Sean shouted, rushing to my side. Apparently, they hadn't seen him through the thick cloud of dust churned up by the speeding cars.

"Conner!" I yelled, tears beading in my eyes.

He twisted in my arms, and I breathed a sigh of relief, thankful he was alive.

Sean, Kyle, and Nate all crouched around us.

"Olga, go wait in the car with the girls," Nate instructed.

Ignoring him, I watched Conner slowly pry his eyelids apart. His eyes were a pure blue. *My* Conner.

"Olga," he whispered.

"Hey." Relief made me shudder.

Nate lifted me up and set me aside. "Go in the house with Nic and Tammy. Now. We'll deal with this." He smoothed the hair off my forehead. "Trust me."

"Ha! You'll forgive me if I have a few reservations about trusting you with Conner after you threatened to kill him the last time you saw him."

"Exactly. If he hurts you now, I won't be able to stop myself. So please go inside. I promise not to hurt him." He made an *x* over his heart as a way of demonstrating the seriousness of his oath to me.

"No way. I'm staying out here with Conner."

Nate threw his hands in the air. "Fine. But at least stand back while we inspect him for injuries then."

I nodded, then watched wearily as Kyle and Sean made sure Conner was okay before proceeding to ask him some questions about how he got here. Nic and Tammy flanked each side of me, holding up my trembling body. A black cat appeared out of nowhere and flicked her tail at us just once before vanishing in the woods.

"This place is creepy as hell," Tammy muttered. "Who's idea was it to come here?"

Nic raised her hand. "Sorry. It seemed like a good idea last night. Sean and I have been talking about coming up here anyway to…" She paused, struggling for breath.

Patting her shoulder, I said, "Well, you know what they say. The road to hell is paved with good intentions."

"Agreed," Tammy said, then took out a cigarette as I sighed. "I know you hate it, but I need a smoke to calm down."

As soon as she said the words, the scene around me disappeared and merged into a new one, Tammy still beside me but overlooking a lake instead.

"Why do you smoke so much?" I ask her, holding up my hands. "I'm not judging, just curious. It's your life, and I respect that." Shaking my head, I continue, "I can't believe I spent most of high school stereotyping you as a single-minded, snobby, backstabbing cheerleader."

147

Tammy takes one last drag, then stomps out her cigarette on the ground. "Girl, neither can I. I mean I only stole your prom date, threatened to light you on fire, and slapped you in the face."

Blinking, I realized I was sandwiched between Nic and Tammy in the woods and Tammy still smoking her cigarette.

"Where did you just go?" Tammy asked me.

I stepped away from them, shaking. "You've never thought about lighting me on fire, have you?"

She straightened to full height. "Another vision?"

I nodded.

"No, not that I remember anyway."

"That's comforting." Although it wasn't really.

For the next half hour, I paced around Conner, praying and rubbing my rosary. Finally, the boys let him stand, and I rushed to his side to help him walk toward the cabin.

He flashed me a grateful smile. "Hey."

"How could you disappear like that?" I knew I should be angry with him for our last encounter. But the boy who threw me into his Ford wasn't the same one before me.

"Believe me, I'm wondering the same thing," he replied, rubbing the back of his neck and wincing.

"Are you hurt?"

His steps faltered. "A little."

I supported him as we climbed the front steps, deciding my interrogation could wait. From all the supplies lying around the cabin, it was obvious Conner had been hiding out here for the better part of the six weeks he'd been missing.

"We'll get you some ice and Tylenol," Nate said, ushering me into the kitchen with him as Conner lay on the couch.

From a drawer, I retrieved a Ziploc baggie and filled it with ice as Nate filled a glass with tap water. He pursed his lips in worry, searching the cupboards for what I assumed was pain medicine.

"Conner claims he doesn't remember attacking you or anything from the last six weeks. Says the last thing he knew he was going to sleep after seeing us at the coffee shop."

"I know. I heard. Do you believe him?"

"Well, he should win an Oscar if his story's an act. He was pretty convincing when we grilled him outside."

"So now he's suffering from amnesia in addition to Post-Traumatic Stress Syndrome and a bipolar disorder?" *And a possible demon possession.* "Things just keep getting better and better. What do we do now?"

Nate shrugged. "Obviously, we all have a lot to figure out. But for now, everyone's hungry, and it seems like fate has brought us here together for a reason today."

"So we stick with the plan."

Nodding his head, he said, "Yep. We'll have ourselves a barbeque and a firewalk."

I bit my lip, nervous. "Okay."

He gave my shoulder a quick squeeze. "Here, take this to Conner. I'm gonna help Sean get the stuff out of the car. Kyle will stay in here with you girls in case anything funny happens with Conner."

"Oh, I don't think he's in the mood to tell any jokes."

Nate chuckled, kissing my forehead before he strode out of the kitchen.

As I headed back to the living room, tears sprung to my eyes as the events of the past months caught up to me. I sucked in a breath and told myself to grow a pair. All this crying was really getting on my nerves.

"Here. A double dose of pills should help with the pain." I grabbed two throw pillows off the love seat and propped them behind Conner's head. Immediately, he popped the four pills into his mouth, like relief couldn't come fast enough. Then I lifted the glass of water to him and placed the straw on his lips. "Drink."

He drained the entire glass.

"I'll get you some more."

He grabbed my hand, then pulled me into a hug. "I hate that I'm the cause of your tears."

"You've caused a lot more than that, buddy," Tammy said from across the room.

Glowering at her, I said, "Don't take that tone with him. Whatever's happening to him isn't his fault."

"Who's to blame then?" Conner asked, taking the glass out of my hand and placing it on the coffee table.

"Me," I answered flatly, soaking in all the guilt like a sponge.

He scrubbed his fingers through his already disheveled hair that was in desperate need of a trim. "What are you talking about?"

I shrugged. "I just can't ease my conscience that this is all my fault." I went on to tell him about the mysterious journal that showed up at my house while he was gone.

Conner laughed, the sound startling me.

"What's so funny?" I asked without any trace of humor.

"Sorry. It's just, this sounds worse than a plot we'd see on a Spanish soap opera or something."

"Oh, yeah, I can't wait until Mrs. Garcia plays the next episode in class," Kyle yelled. "I hope Jaime and Carlos finally hook up."

We all laughed for a minute before he continued, more serious this time.

"Can I give you your birthday present while we wait?" He slipped his hand in his pocket and pulled out a small angel pin. "This used to be my grandma's before she passed. I don't think she'd be opposed to you having it. It'll get a lot more use from you, even has your birthstone since Grams was born in October, too."

Holding out my hand, I studied the shiny opal twinkling in the light. "Kyle, this is beautiful. Are you sure your parents won't mind you giving it to me?"

He smiled. "On one condition. You stop wearing those rosary beads as a necklace all the time. No offense, but you've turned into one of those spooky religious people."

Tammy laughed. "Yeah, on that note. You should probably open my gift."

She handed me a wrapped box, and inside I found a small plastic container that said "Our Daily Bread" on the front. Inside were tons of index-sized scripture cards.

"I found those at a little gift shop downtown with the same idea Kyle had in mind, apparently. I'm hoping you just put a card or two in your pocket instead of carrying around that mass book. Seriously, you look ridiculous."

Even though she delivered an insult, her tone was meant to soothe. I knew she and Kyle both had good intentions, so I thanked them and figured they were probably right.

After Nic gave me a prayer box she made, decorated with pictures of the Jedi Order, beads, lace, and little crosses, Nate sent me a text telling me the food was cooked and to come outside. Sure enough, hamburgers and hotdogs were on the picnic table, while a ten-foot path of coals fresh off the grill lined the grass nearby.

"We're seriously still doing this?" Tammy asked.

"You don't have to, but it's something Olga and I need to do," Nate explained cryptically. Turning to me, he said, "Ready to roll? We don't want the coals to cool down too much."

I gulped several times. "Yeah, what a waste that would be. You really think this will work?"

Nate picked up the plate of hamburgers. "I'd bet my lunch on it."

"That's all this is worth to you?"

"Hey, I take my meat very seriously. Now listen, I'll go first so you can see it in action. When you go, the best tip I can give you is to keep your gaze ahead of you, repeating the words 'cool grass' over and over until you're across. Don't look down and don't let your mind think about the heat. Mind over matter."

I nodded stiffly. "Sounds easy enough."

Nate practically glided across the coals, but that didn't stop me from having a full-blown panic attack when it was my turn. This caused Sean, Kyle, Tammy, and Nic to go before me, demonstrating how easy walking on fire was even for first timers. The Jedi Order lined the path: Kyle, Sean, and Conner standing on one side, Tammy and Nic on the other, and Nate waiting at the end. I backpedaled a moment, then increased my speed, muttering, "Cool grass," as instructed while swiping the air in front of me as if the action would cause me to go faster. Finally, Nate wrapped me in a hug at the end, stumbling a bit to the side since I'd apparently jumped on him.

Panting, the stinging anticipation returned. We locked eyes, and I heard a distant voice whispering in my mind that what the mind could conceive, it could achieve, when screams of agony came from behind us. Conner had decided to firewalk, too, but he only trekked halfway across. Something terrible burned inside him. We could all see it, like he'd swallowed the sun and it lay decomposing within him.

Sean and Kyle pulled at his arm from the side, but he wouldn't budge. Whatever lived inside him had rooted him to the spot.

Rubbing my new angel pin, praying for help, I remembered the vial of Holy Water in the pendant around my neck. Something prompted me to buy the necklace at the bookstore during my shift on Monday and fill it with Holy Water during my confession yesterday afternoon. Stepping forward, I dabbed the water on my finger and made the sign of the cross on Conner's forehead, his face close to blistering as he gritted his teeth.

Nothing.

I placed my rosary around his neck and threw the entire contents of the vial on his head, continually making the sign of the cross while reciting a prayer from the mass book I'd memorized. "Saint Michael the Archangel, defend us in this battle. Be our protection against the wickedness and snares of the devil. Rebuke him, we humbly pray, and do so through the Prince of the Heavenly Hosts. By the power of God, cast into hell any evil spirit who prowls about, seeking the ruin of our souls."

Two seconds later, he rested his head on my shoulder, finally free from the coals. I wiped the sweat dotting his cheek and took comfort in the beat of his heart thudding against my chest. Glancing up at the unblemished blue sky, I saw a flash of white wings and muttered an amen, knowing I didn't carry this burden alone. One other thing I knew irrevocably. Demons not only existed, but one was definitely responsible for trying to destroy my best friend. I just didn't know why.

CHAPTER THIRTEEN

"The unleashed power of the atom has changed everything save our modes of thinking and we thus drift toward unparalleled catastrophe."

—Albert Einstein

Nate sat with me in the backseat of Nic's car as she drove us toward my house, Sean riding shotgun. Kyle had gone with Tammy to take Conner to North Ottawa Hospital to be treated for the burns on his feet, already a mess of massive blisters. I'd sent his parents a text telling them to meet Conner there, too, exhausted to actually call and explain things. Worst of all, I needed to find a way to tell my parents what happened while convincing them I wasn't crazy.

The dusk faded into darkness as Nic exited the highway and made her way along the familiar roads. My tired mind clicked off the landmarks: Meijer's Grocery Store, Walgreens Pharmacy, the post office, the cemetery, my church. Thank God some things stayed the same. As Nicole made the right-hand turn into the parking lot, the streetlights surrounding my apartment complex were just coming on. Even though I'd only left this morning, it seemed like so long since I'd been home.

Sean and Nic muttered their goodbyes as Nate helped me out of the car and walked me to the front door.

"You want me to come inside with you? Assure your parents you aren't bearing false testimony?"

"Nah, I doubt the Pope could even help me now."

"All right. Happy birthday." With a quick kiss on my cheek that made me feel all warm inside despite the cold, he turned on his heel and made his way back to Nic's car.

Sighing, I gathered my courage for the confrontation with my parents. I really didn't want to relive the events of the day, would've much rather gone to bed instead. But the Jedi Order needed help. The police would never believe what we saw, and out of everyone's parents, mine were by far the most spiritual. Did my parents believe in demons and angels? I wasn't sure. None of my friends did until today. My parents definitely believed in the saints and their power to help us though.

I entered the apartment, yelling for my parents. They stepped inside from the back porch, Dad carrying a plate of hamburgers. "There's our girl! Just in time for your birthday dinner," Dad exclaimed as I slumped at the sight of his choice of meat, all the memories of the day flooding my insides.

"I think I'm gonna puke."

"Oh no. What's wrong? You catch a bug at school today?" Mom inquired, digging through a drawer for the thermometer.

Guess they hadn't received the automatic voice mail my school sent out for absences yet. A pang of guilt shot through me as I realized they'd figured I'd been at one of my extracurricular activities this whole time. They trusted that I'd never rebel against them, even on the birthday that made me a legal adult. Well, it was time to start acting like one.

"I didn't go to school."

It took a while to explain everything from the beginning, such as how Nate could hear my thoughts and how I had visions that seemed to display the future but in memory form. How, after Conner ran away, I discovered a mysterious journal in my room and was drawn to a book on spiritual warfare that I'd stocked on the shelves at the Bookman. That I started to worry Conner was somehow being possessed by a demon, how the reading gave me nightmares but prompted me to wear my rosary and carry around my mass book and even a vial of holy water. And finally, how I really only half believed until I saw something inside Conner and a flash of wings with my own eyes earlier today.

Mom gasped throughout the story, twisting her hands in her apron. When I finished, she came over and gently touched my shoulder. "Sounds like you've been through quite a lot since Conner woke up. I wish you would've told us all of this sooner."

I pulled away. "Yeah, well, sometimes you're not the easiest people to talk to."

"Hold on, Elizabeth," Dad said. "Can I talk to you in the bedroom for a moment, please?"

My mom nodded, then followed Dad down the hall. He closed the door behind them, but that didn't stop me from listening outside.

"Are we actually believing this crazy story?" he whispered.

"She saw it with her own eyes, John. Why would she make up such a scenario?" Mom answered, suddenly my champion.

Dad sighed heavily. "I don't know. Maybe she's trying to get attention or trying to get out of trouble. Maybe she's, you know…"

"Crazy?" my mom finished for him.

I slumped against the wall, defeated, knowing this was exactly the response I could expect from telling anyone about today. Still, I needed to at least try to make them believe.

"She doesn't seem insane, though," Mom continued.

"Well, I don't know how you expect me to believe this tale." Hearing the bedsprings creak, I knew Dad had stood.

"Where are you going?" Mom asked impatiently.

"To search her room for drugs." He jumped when he found me right outside the door.

My gaze darted between them. "Think what you want, but I'm not crazy and I'm not on crack or anything. Take me for a drug test right now. I'll prove it."

Mom stood up and grabbed her purse from the hook by the door. "Come on."

"Are we going to the hospital?"

"No, we're going to see the priest."

A few minutes later, the parking lot of St. Patrick's came into view, packed for the annual All Saints Day celebration. Mom pulled her

Camaro into the last empty space, her front bumper sagging from overuse since she bought the car the year I was born. In an odd way, I found myself relating to the tired state of the car, my mouth hanging open in exhaustion, wishing I could pass on my responsibilities to someone else. I was sure Mom wanted a new car, too.

"And you don't think Nate has anything to do with Conner's... possession?" Mom verified for the umpteenth time.

"Nope. He's been the one trying to help me figure out this whole mess the most."

She brushed a curl out of her face with her wrinkled hand. "You're certain you trust him, one hundred percent?"

"Yes, Mom. You'll see he's trustworthy after you get to know him."

She held out her hand, and I placed my palm in hers and let her lead the way into the church. "Are you in love with him?"

I looked up, studying the stars, gulping in the cold October air. The moonlight didn't penetrate the shadows like the evening Nate and I sneaked out, but it was comforting to know a little light could always be found even on the darkest of nights. "I don't think so, Mom. My feelings are strong, but I don't think I've known him long enough to tell if it's love yet."

Mom looked at me, determined to get a straight answer. "Like you've known Conner, like you *know* you love him."

I nodded. "The old Conner, at least."

"Honey, I've been a fly on the wall in your friendship with him for twelve years now. You two have been inseparable, and I've watched your relationship grow more intense over the past year. If you're confused, then tread lightly, or someone will get hurt, possibly all three of you. I know it's hard to let go of our childhood attachments, but you're an adult now. It may be time to do so if your feelings are strong for Nate." She opened the oiled wooden door to the church.

Shaking my head as we stepped inside, I said, "Mom, I thought you loved Conner like a son."

She grinned. "I do, honey. But that doesn't mean I think you two are right for each other. But if *you* love Conner, you owe it to him to give him one hundred percent of your heart to see if there's a chance for romance there. Above all, to thine own self be true. I've never once

156

questioned you as to why you didn't have a boyfriend or told you being with someone would make life easier or more complete, and I never will. We all have our own path to follow in life. I've raised you to be independent and intelligent, but some decisions can only be made by listening to your heart."

Finally, a piece of advice from my mother that I understood. For all her faults, she really did raise me right. "Thanks, Mom."

A moment later, the white-robed figure of Father Jamie waved a hand toward us from the front of the church, and we made our way through the crowd of children and parents to see him. "Olga"—he greeted me with a firm handshake—"I see the grace of our Lord is with you this Halloween evening. I'm delighted you decided to come volunteer again this year. When I didn't see you here at first, I supposed you were getting too old for this sort of thing."

Mom didn't waste any time explaining the real reason we showed up at the church tonight. Anxiously, I chewed my lip, awaiting his response.

Father Jamie glanced around the room when she finished, seemingly in shock. I didn't take his expression as a good sign of faith. Then all he said in response was, "I see."

"Well, what should we do?" I blurted out.

"There's not much that can be done tonight," he explained. "But bring him by my office tomorrow after school. I'll need to do some research in the morning to gather some ideas."

Mom looked as puzzled as I was. Weren't priests supposed to have all the answers?

Seeming to read my thoughts just as easily as Nate, he added, "I'm sorry, Olga. I'm not God, only God's servant."

"But aren't you supposed to be a miracle worker?"

He smiled. "I'll try my best."

I nodded, accepting that answer would have to do for now.

Mom and I made our way to the exit, making the sign of the cross as we left.

Stomping on the welcome mat just inside the church lobby, I dislodged what I could of the mud crusting my boots. It'd been raining nonstop all day, adding to my already dreary mood. Conner's feet were wrapped in bandages, and his sandals made slow scuffs against the thin carpet as we made our way to Father Jamie's office. The steady click of my wristwatch reminded me of how much time our short walk was taking, the quiet of the sanctuary amplifying the sound. Sandals weren't the best choice of shoes for today's weather, but Conner said his blisters hurt too much for anything else. I was actually surprised to see him at school today, but he reminded me he'd missed too much already. So much that his parents had to reenroll him this morning to attend his classes since the school automatically dropped you after two weeks of unexcused absences. He had a lot of making up to do, but I assured him I'd help him get through his workload so he could graduate on time. Right now, though, there were more pressing matters.

The church bells rang outside as I knocked on the door, letting us know it was exactly three o'clock, and the signal felt like a death knell.

"Come in," Father Jamie called in a voice that seemed to hold a smile, his usual tone.

Inside, books covered the entire surface of his desk. Behind him, volumes crammed his shelves, wooden soldiers guarding impenetrable secrets I'd never understand, but I hoped Father Jamie could at least enlighten us.

"This must be Conner," he greeted, extending a hand before gesturing for us to take a seat across the desk. "How are you feeling today, son?"

Anyone could tell from the way Conner's arms squeezed his chest that he didn't trust the priest. We had gotten into an argument at lunch when I told him we were going to my church after school, but in the end, he agreed we had no other options left.

"Okay," he answered, curling his fingers around the edge of his chair.

"Well, I understand you're desperate for answers. Why don't you tell me your story."

Conner sighed loudly. "I thought Olga already filled you in."

Father Jamie nodded. "She did, briefly. But I'd still like to hear it from your perspective to make sure we're all on the same page."

"Well, okay then. Her stalker Nate moved in as my hospital roommate—"

Holding up my hand, I interjected, "Not my stalker."

Conner ignored me. "Her stalker moved into my room and about a month later, I woke up. But I didn't feel like me anymore. It's like this thing possessed me, and I couldn't stop it. Sometimes I'd feel like myself again, but most of the time, I was just a passenger along for the ride. I remembered everything, well mostly, unless it was a night of heavy drinking and drugs."

Father Jamie frowned.

"I didn't want to! I was powerless to stop. Then six weeks ago, I apparently attacked Olga and ran away. Hid out in a friend's cabin in the woods, but that time is lost to me. Then all my friends showed up at the cabin yesterday, including Nate. I swear he's somehow responsible for my destroyed life."

"You're responsible for your life, no one else," Father Jamie said, shuffling some books into a pile. "Although it's possible demon possession is at play here, your actions have opened up the possibility. Have you been seeing things? Hearing voices?"

"No. And I don't care what you say; I know Nate is linked into this somehow."

"Linked, maybe, but probably not responsible. There's a difference."

"Okay, Father. Why do you think this is all happening to me then?"

"I'm not sure. I wish I had all the answers, but I'm just a man like you. But I would like to baptize you right away. I assume you've never received this sacrament before?"

Conner's gaze shifted to me, then back to Father Jamie. "No. But what would be the purpose of baptizing me?"

"Baptism has six primary purposes, which are all supernatural effects, something you've become quite familiar with over the past few months." Father Jamie picked up the stack of books and filed them back onto the shelves behind him as he spoke. "First, the removal of guilt of both Original Sin, meaning the sin imparted to all mankind by the Fall of Adam and Eve in the Garden of Eden and personal sin, the sins we have committed ourselves. Second, the remission of all punishment we deserve due to sin, both of this world and in purgatory, and eternal, the punishment we would suffer in hell. Third, the infusion of sanctifying grace, the life of God within us, the seven gifts of the Holy Spirit, and the three theological virtues."

"Huh?" Conner asked, his voice cracking.

Father Jamie turned and nodded toward me before taking his seat again. "Olga can explain this to you in more detail later, or if she's unable to, then perhaps her parents can. Really, I could go on and on about all the purposes for baptism, but I think we should do this as quickly as possible. Delaying baptism until you fully understand the sacrament may put your soul in danger. The most important thing is for you to align yourself with the mystical body of Christ on Earth instead of the devil. Even if you don't believe all these things, I think baptism will still help safeguard you. Of course, I can shove religion down your throat all day, but if you don't draw closer to God, ask his forgiveness for your sins, and pray, then baptism can only carry you so far."

Conner nodded.

"Now, we can do this one of two ways: the pouring of water over your head or the immersion of your whole body in water. Which would you prefer?"

Conner looked at me, his chin trembling, and I realized how scared he was. Placing my hand over his, I repeated a piece of advice he quoted to me often. "Somebody used to always tell me, go big or go home."

A small laugh escaped his lips. "That somebody used to be pretty wise."

I squeezed his fingers. "Still is. He just lost his way a little."

He pulled me into a hug, then gave Father Jamie a small nod. "Immersion it is."

Father Jamie's smile grew wide. "Good choice. There are some white robes you can change into in the room to the left of my office. Meet me by the stage in five."

As I stalked to the door behind Conner, Father Jamie cleared his throat. "Olga, may I have a word alone with you for a moment?"

Conner looked me over, questioning. I shrugged, ushering him out the door before returning to my seat.

"What is it?" I peered up at Father Jamie through my spectacles.

"I just wanted you to understand that I don't think we should discuss these events with anyone else. No need to cause alarm in our community. I'm more than obliged to help, of course, but I've never seen anything like this, only heard about such things. Here's my business card with my personal cell number in case the demon shows up again." He leaned forward over the top of his desk to hand it to me.

"Also, I must be adamant in my belief that you stay away from this Nate. We don't know if the two of them are connected, but the timing of his arrival to our town and Conner's possession and reading your mind does seem strange. Until we know what we're dealing with, well, I can't forbid you, of course. But I do hope you'll adhere to spiritual instruction and respect my wishes."

Wonderful. A few moments passed in silence as I thought about what he said.

"Olga?" Father Jamie raised one of his brows into an arch. "Do you trust me?"

I nodded stiffly, biting my lip until I tasted blood.

"Good. Then it's settled. Promise me you'll stay away from Nate as much as possible. Of course, you should still pray for him daily, as will I."

A knock at the door startled me as I nodded.

"I'm ready, Father Jamie."

Several minutes later, I looked on as he baptized Conner. "In the name of the Father, and of the Son, and of the Holy Spirit, you are now a new creation in Christ. The old has passed away, and the new has come."

Dripping wet, Conner smiled at me like he really believed he might have a chance at a new life. I smiled back, even though a part of mine was over before it ever got a chance to begin. Ironic that I'd finally gained my precious independence by following someone else's orders.

CHAPTER FOURTEEN

"Should Old Acquaintance be forgot,
and never thought upon;
The flames of Love extinguished,
and fully past and gone."

—Robert Burns

Conner and I made it through the end of the semester without any more incidents. To keep my thoughts off Nate, I stayed true to my promise to help Conner study, as well as tutoring Tammy so she could hopefully get a college scholarship. But, first, I made her give up smoking. She still smoked the occasional cig but not religiously like she used to. Mainly she smoked one at parties and concerts. We'd been going to quite a few of the latter in the past two months. Since Conner seemed back to normal, the Cantankerous Monkey Squad booked gigs all over the county. I felt bad that that left Nate as the odd man out, but even after Sean and Kyle convinced Conner they should let Nate stay on as a fourth member, Nate declined their invitation.

After telling Nate about my promise to Father Jamie, he fought me a little on my decision to end things between us. He agreed that he and Conner were connected, but that was the key, not the problem. But in the end, Nate said he cared about me enough to respect my wishes. Conner told me that proved Nate didn't care about me enough because he'd never let me go, no matter who told him to stay away. Maybe he had a point, but that also meant I didn't care about Nate too much, either, and I knew that wasn't true.

These days, Nate hung out with this guy from school named Adam all the time. I didn't know much about him except he seemed like a fellow adrenaline junkie. I saw them doing tricks on their skateboards by the boardwalk sometimes, and I hoped Nate wasn't doing anything too risky. But, mostly, I tried not to think about him at all. I'd made a promise to a priest before God, and I didn't think I should take any chances by breaking it. My senior year had already gotten off to a rough start.

Now my life felt like it'd returned to the normal of last year. Going to school, hanging out with the Jedi Order, working, Conner picking me up from the Bookman every night so we could study together. It's what I'd been wishing for since Conner woke up from his coma, so why did I feel a giant void inside me? That's the nagging question I tried to ignore while closing up the store on New Year's Eve.

"What's he doing here?" Nic asked from beside me, nodding toward the bench outside the bookstore.

I halted my vacuuming and studied the figure, then clicked the handle into an upright position. "Nate." I gasped. "I don't know, but I'll go find out. Can you finish for me?"

"Of course. Leave. You're still picking me up for the concert tonight at five, right?"

"Yep," I said with a distracted nod.

I retrieved my purse from the back room, then stepped outside and drank in the sight of him. He looked ruggedly handsome, sporting an unshaven face and wearing a pair of faded jeans, a blue and white plaid shirt with an unzipped gray hoodie, and a gray wool cap covering his shaggy, medium-length hair.

"Hey," was all I could manage.

He looked at me and through me at the same time, like he could see down to the depths of my soul. "Nice to finally hear your actual voice again. I've missed the sound."

"Nate, what are you doing here?"

My heart beat way faster than it should, but before I heard his answer, my mind illuminated with a wild memory.

I plunge deeper in the water, swimming softly toward the glow. As soon as I reach the wormhole, a whiplash current catches me, sending me spinning like a tornado into an abyss until I arrive at the base of a waterfall. Before I can take in my surroundings, a pair of hands grip my shoulders from behind.

"You're all right?" Nate's voice is low and soft. "I've been sick with worry."

I feel a burst of love for him. "Nate, what are you doing here? I thought you…"

When it ended, I understood in my head what my heart told me all along. I could trust Nate. He'd been there for me before, and he wouldn't let me down.

He patted the space next to him on the bench, his face more certain than it looked a moment ago.

"How are you?" The question came out sounding too formal, too polite for what we'd been through, even if we couldn't remember it all.

"I've been better. Hoping the new year is a lot better than this one. Though I guess I can't complain too much since I did meet you." He tugged at his cap. "I got you a Christmas present." Smiling, he handed me a box.

"But Christmas already passed."

He shrugged. "I was on a skiing trip with my family. Just got back. In fact, my parents wanted to stay a few more days, but I was adamant about coming home today."

My eyes widened. "Why?"

"Because I wanted to ring in the new year with you. Go ahead, open your gift."

I peeled away the plain green paper and lifted the lid on the tiny box. Inside awaited a Magic 8-Ball wrapped in tissue paper with a note that said, "Ask my ball if we should attend the concert together tonight. Here's hoping the outlook is good."

I snorted. "Was that supposed to be funny?"

He shrugged again. "I tried. Go ahead, shake my ball."

Our gazes remained locked as I shook the plastic ball for a good ten seconds before peeking at the transparent window on the bottom of the ball for my answer. "As I see it, yes."

Nate stood and reached for my hand, making me shiver, giving me all kinds of good chills. "Well, there you have it."

"So we're putting all our trust into a toy used for fortune-telling now?"

"Got any better ideas?"

"You gave me one of these toys before, remember?"

I found myself wondering how I knew that. I confused myself now. Could I really be so sure?

His expression looked tortured. "Is that so?"

Dropping my chin to my chest, I said, "Yeah. I mean, I don't know. I think so."

"Olga, if we don't solve this mystery between us, I'm gonna lose my mind. I've already been losing my mind, missing you like crazy. At school, I've been taking notes on your thoughts instead of what the teachers are saying."

Okay, that's creepy.

"I know, but I just want to know you completely, every side of you, and you aren't giving me the chance. Your thoughts are all I have left now. I feel so lost without you, like I don't have a purpose for living."

I paced the sidewalk in front of him. "We can't keep doing this. It only makes things worse."

He grabbed my waist and held me in place. "Stop what? Being apart? I agree."

"No!" I yanked away from his grasp and slammed my hands on his hard chest. "Being friends that kiss or whatever. It's too confusing."

"Exactly. We need to be more than friends who kiss. Because I'm so in love with you, Olga. Please, I know you miss me, too. I can hear it. I just need you to start being honest with yourself."

I met his gaze, panting. "I do have feelings for you. But I also know from these memories and the journal that I've unwittingly hurt you and Conner and possibly others in the past and caused great upset. I'd been impatient. So now I'm trying to choose the right things to do in order to set this situation right again, to rectify the wrongs I've done. The angel in my vision said we've been given a second chance. And this time around, I'm not going to let my ego or my fears or my doubts cloud my choices."

"All you've been doing is letting fear and doubt cloud your choices! You're all talk, Olga." Never before had he spoken so sternly with me, and several moments passed in awkward silence before I could respond.

"I'm sorry you feel that way, Nate. The last thing on earth I want to do is hurt you. But I could end up hurting you so much more if I jump into this. It's not about my path anymore. It's about the path God laid out for me. He's locked things away in us to be of service, to do good things in this world, maybe even great, but I don't know where to begin yet. I have to wait upon him to show me. Don't you see that?"

"So it's not because of Conner?"

"Ugh, no! It's never been about Conner, not really. It's been about finding the strength deep down inside ourselves to move on, to do the right things even when it's hard. And it's about being there for a friend."

With a tired face, he said, "Which is what I'm trying to do! But oh, I forgot. Everyone who doesn't agree with your plan is stupid. Freaky genius girl always knows best. Because even though God created all men equal, he made you better. Want me to raise that pedestal for you?"

"Huh? That's not what I'm saying. Why does it feel like you don't trust me to do the job right myself?"

"You obviously can't." After a pause writhing with tension, he added, "There's a difference between being independent and being smart enough to accept help when you need it."

I could hear the pain in his honesty. "Fine. I'll stop shutting you out if you promise to give me some space and not rush in to save me all the time. The Jedi Order only has a few months left together. If I suck at this as much as you say I do, then I'm going to need some practice being independent before I'm on my own."

His nose wrinkled, like he inhaled a foul odor. "You're twisting my words, but I don't want to argue anymore. That's not why I came here. I. Just. Want. To. Help. You."

Frowning, I nodded. "Why don't you come home with me? We can celebrate New Year's together if you still want to. I have to change for the concert tonight before I pick up Nicole and Tammy, unless you'd rather walk. If I remember correctly, you had some concerns about my driving."

He looked over at my dad's old Ford truck parked in front of the store and smiled. "I think you're worth risking my life over."

Pulsating music throbbed in my ears and shook the ground. People bounced and bobbed to the beat as Kyle nailed his long drum solo for their finale song. Nate and I didn't talk much during the outdoor concert. We'd have to shout over the blaring speakers to do so. Actually, it was somewhat nice not to make small talk after the three-hour car ride to Traverse City with Nate, Tammy, and Nicole. I sneaked a glimpse at my watch. An hour until midnight. A headache formed, and stupidly I missed my old curfew of eleven. I hoped there was a bottle of Tylenol with my name on it at Grandma's. Since my grandparents lived in Traverse City and had a big house, we were all crashing there to avoid a long drive back home with all the drunks on the road. I wished I would've thought this out better, though. How would Conner and Nate staying under the same roof for the night work?

I peered out from behind a cluster of girls lifting their hands and swaying them to the music. Instantly, Conner's gaze pinned me to my spot. No doubt, seeing Nate here with me jarred him. I'd contemplated texting before the show to give Conner a heads-up, but I didn't want to upset him before he went on stage. Shoving my freezing hands into the pockets of my jacket, I tried to act cool, though my stomach churned with anxiety. When the song ended, Conner hopped down from the stage and weaved through the crowd, heading straight for us. I smoothed down my hair.

Stupid, stupid girl. This was a bad idea. I tried to spot Tammy or Nic, to signal them for help, but I'd lost them in the crowd a few songs ago when they snaked their way to the front to be closer to the stage.

Nate tugged on my sleeve. "I'm going to get a drink." He pointed to the outer edges of the crowd where the food and beverage trucks were set up. "Want anything?"

"Hot chocolate, please."

He took off before I even answered, already knowing.

Conner came to a halt about a foot in front of me. "Where's he going?"

I blinked. So not the question I expected him to ask. "To get a drink."

"Are you guys here together? Like together together?"

Ah, there it is. Not knowing how to answer that question, I scanned the crowd. "You know, we have this thing with the visions? The last one we shared was of him helping me, and I just thought maybe he could help again..."

Awkwardness filled the air around us, and I cleared my throat.

Conner sucked in a breath and blew the air out of his cheeks. "These last two months have been so good. I thought maybe it was the beginning of something new between us. I thought maybe you'd found a way to forgive all the horrible things I did to you earlier this year."

Tears burned at the back of my eyes. "I have."

"But do you... I mean, don't you think we're closer than just friends?"

"We are closer than friends. We've been through too much together not to be." I took a step forward and lifted a hand to hold his.

"Well," he said, an uneasy look on his face. "What does that mean then?"

I looked down, unable to meet his gaze. "I'm not sure. But I am sure that we'll always be there for each other, no matter what."

Conner ran a hand down the edge of my cheek and cupped my chin. "I've been holding back on asking you out again because I've been too distracted getting my life straight, and I didn't want to rush things before I had stuff figured out and mess us all up again. But now I'm looking at you with him tonight and thinking I'm so stupid. When I woke up that night before school started, the night when it was really me, I realized what I'd almost let slip by. I don't want to make that mistake again."

I set my jaw in determination, summoning the courage to spit the words out honestly. "Conner, I love you. You know I do. But there's also this feeling of vulnerability, fear, jealousy... sort of haunting me."

"Jealous of who?"

"Of all the girls you were with when you weren't you. And the truth is, even though I love you with all my heart and always will, I'm ninety percent sure we wouldn't work right now... There's just too much going on. I'm not ready. You're not ready."

He flinched back slightly, then sighed. "All righty then. I'll hold on to that ten percent until you change your mind. I'm gonna get myself a drink."

After our confrontation, I stood on the outskirts of the crowd with Nate, nursing my hot chocolate, second-guessing what I told Conner. The headlining band's thrashing sound was one of a kind, but I couldn't enjoy any of it.

"Do you like what you hear?" Nate shouted next to me.

Nodding a yes, I watched with envy as Tammy dragged Kyle to the center of the crowd, dancing tight against him, the music and colorful lights turning her body into fluid rhythm. Every male around them had their sights on Tammy, the platinum blonde with big boobs in a long-sleeved slinky, short gold dress despite the cold. Black tights covered her model-perfect legs, paired with furry leopard-print boots. The predatory gleam in her eyes wasn't for any of them, though; the look was for the boy standing right in front of her. No amount of smoky eye shadow could hide her longing. Even if she was staying single right now, she still made the boy thing look so easy.

"Thank you," I said to Nate, who sipped a hot chocolate of his own.

"For what?"

"For the drink. For putting up with this drama. For not giving up on me even though I deserve it."

He looked at me over the rim of his Styrofoam cup. "No need to thank me. I'm here for you, Olga. I always will be. Even if you decide you want to be with Conner. If you ever need me, even if it's just to talk to someone, about anything, I want you to come to me."

An intense feeling of déjà vu washed over me, forcing me to squeeze my eyes shut. I forced them wide open, looking at Nate as he hitched up the collar of his jean jacket against the icy wind. He peered down at me.

"What?"

"You didn't feel that?"

He made a face, sipping his hot chocolate again. "Maybe."

"Maybe?"

He rocked back on his heels. "Olga, it's hard for me to separate your thoughts from mine sometimes. But yes to that déjà vu thing."

"Sorry."

He shook his head. "For what?"

"For taking over your mind."

Chuckling, he said, "I rather like the invasion. Most of the time."

I didn't know what to say. He was so incredibly sweet that staying away from him seemed like the worst idea on the planet.

"Do you want to dance?" Nate nodded toward our friends and held out his hand in an offer.

By now, Sean and Nicole were drawing an audience with their spectacular booty shaking while Conner innocently danced with a young fan who looked about twelve.

Once I said yes, Nate threw our cups away and lightly wringed my wrist with his fingers. We fought our way through a gauntlet of rough bodies, stale beer breath, and New Year's Eve fanfare. Halfway to our friends, a collective shout went up with the chorus, and someone's drink christened the top of my head. *Gak! Why did I ever agree to this?*

Nate made an impatient noise and wiped the liquid off with the sleeve of his jacket. "Come here." He drew me to him, curling his arms around my back.

The clouds dropped snow right when the song ended, just before midnight, the perfect weather to epitomize a new beginning. Tilting my head up, I caught the cold drops on my tongue. Near the front of the stage, Traverse City's own version of Times Square hung high above a twinkling Christmas tree. A giant lit cherry began to drop, a symbol of the Traverse City region since seventy-five percent of the nation's cherry crop grew here. Nate and I joined the countdown at ten. At zero, we turned toward each other, and I began sinking in a sea of images flooding my mind.

"I Don't Want to Miss a Thing" by Aerosmith blaring over loudspeakers.

Everyone dancing.

The disco ball rotating steadily, illuminating the room.

Me, pressing my body against Nate's.

Him, leaning down, his hand on my cheek.

Both of us, kissing.

Then Conner was there, slamming into Nate and tackling him to the ground.

"Conner! No!" I screamed.

But it was too late. Conner, his eyes widened into dark circles, punched Nate square in the jaw. *Crap! Not again!*

I put my hand over my heart, wondering if it'd burst from anxiety. "Where's Kyle and Sean?" I screamed toward Tammy and Nic. "They have to stop this!"

Too shocked and afraid to move, I watched Nate take Conner by the front of his shirt with one hand and punch him in the throat with the other. The hit didn't deter Conner one bit. He took Nate's face in both hands and slammed his head against the asphalt. Sean and Kyle were there a split second later, throwing him off Nate, but it was too late. Nate lay on the ground, out cold. And *my* Conner had already left, a monster in his place once again. I couldn't even imagine the dark times that lay ahead in the new year.

The plate of just-baked chocolate chip cookies lay untouched on the spotless counter in Nate's kitchen. Mom tried to make small talk with Mrs. Barca, who mostly remained silent and stiff as we waited. She'd probably decided we were all crazy. I'd told her about the demon possession; there was no way not to when Mom called in Father Jamie.

I took a sip from my mug of coffee and smiled at Mom, signaling I appreciated her efforts. On the stove, a pot of boiling soup threatened to spew everywhere. I knew the feeling, forcing down the urge to throw up. Quietly, I reached over from my stool next to the island and turned the dial to low heat just as Father Jamie came in.

I jumped up. "Can I see him yet?"

He had been in Nate's room for about an hour, along with several area bishops, assessing "the situation."

Father Jamie hesitated. "I suppose it will be all right for you to see him. As far as we can tell"—he motioned toward the bishops standing behind him—"there's no evil spirit in him."

Duh!

"Whatever's happening to Conner, and between you, Nate doesn't seem to be the *cause* of it. Although I would advise you two to be vigilant. From the stories you've told me, it seems seeing you and Nate together brings out Conner's dark side. He may come after you again."

It seemed that the power of my and Nate's vision last night caused us to act it out without even realizing what we were doing. When Conner saw us kissing, he went nuts.

Rubbing my angel pin, I thought of Conner, out there all alone somewhere again. How long would he stay away this time? "Father Jamie, why did the d-d-demon come back? I thought Conner was safe after you baptized him." I still had trouble wrapping my mind around the fact that my best friend was possessed.

Father Jamie shook his head. "I hoped he would be. But whatever spirit is possessing him must be strong. Some are more easily deterred than others. That's not to say we should give up. Greater is He that is in us than he who lurks in the world, seeking to destroy it. Hold on to faith that good will triumph in the end, Olga."

Mom stood, clutching her purse. "Thank you for your help, Father Jamie. I'll walk you and your friends out."

Father Jamie nodded. "Peace be with you," he said to Mrs. Barca and me, speaking with finality, like he wanted to wash his hands of this whole situation.

I whirled around to face Mrs. Barca, my eyes pleading, afraid she'd prevent me from ever seeing her son again.

Her chin trembled, but she nodded her head.

Running down the hall, I didn't stop until I stood at Nate's door. I tiptoed in, afraid he might've already fallen back to sleep. He suffered a concussion when Conner knocked him out last night, so we had spent three hours in the hospital with him until Mr. and Mrs. Barca arrived. Conner was nowhere to be found, but Nate's parents were pressing charges, so now there was a warrant out for his arrest. The rest of the Jedi Order crashed with me at my grandparents' house for a few hours, unusually quiet, before getting up at eight to make the long drive home. When I finally walked through the front door of my apartment, I was crying. Mom held me, and Dad brought me a cup of coffee. I curled up on the couch and told them about Conner hitting Nate and then running away. Dad stroked my hair as Mom got up to call Father Jamie, who decided a house call was in order.

Now Nate laid back on his black futon, his head propped up by two pillows. He wore Star Wars pajama pants and a brown T-shirt fraying at the edges. He looked up as I approached him but said nothing.

"Hey, Happy New Year." My heart pounded. *Does he blame me for what happened?*

Smelling freshly showered, he tucked a piece of wet hair behind his ear before scooting over and patting the space next to him.

I sat, sliding my glasses off and setting them on his nightstand before wiping the water from my eyes. "I owe you an apology."

His splotchy face held a look of solemnity. "Don't. I know how guilty you feel. I can read your thoughts."

Holding up a hand, I told him, "Just let me *say* the words." I paused for a deep breath, willing myself to keep a steady voice. "I put you in danger by going out with you last night. Father Jamie was right. I should've stayed away from you."

Nate gave me an incredulous look. "Let me get this straight. Conner attacks me, and *you're* to blame? I'm confused."

I sighed. "You're an innocent in this whole thing, and Conner could've killed you last night because you were with me."

"Look, I don't need you to protect me. I'm a big boy. And I'd rather die than not be part of your life." He ran a hand through his hair. "I almost killed myself when you wouldn't talk to me. Not like trying to, but I kept doing these crazy tricks on my board out at the boardwalk, on the edge of the pier. All these show-off tricks that Evel Knievel probably wouldn't even do. Adam kept telling me I had a death wish."

"You shouldn't do that," I scolded. "Promise me you won't try any crazy stunts again."

His gaze seemed to drink me in. "I was just frustrated, trying to feel alive. Bo's death still wears on me, you know. I know it may not make sense, but being with you is the only thing that takes my mind off the accident. Like you're the reason I lived. If I don't have you in my life, then it feels empty. I just want to be around you, Olga. Please don't shut me out."

I leaned in closer, whispering an okay against his cheek, breathing in the smell of his hair and body wash, a smoky vanilla with a hint of musk. I'd looked in his shower when I used his bathroom earlier.

"Now who's creepy?"

"Shut up."

My crazy heart swelled at the smile he gave me. I thought about Mom telling me I owed Conner one hundred percent of my heart to see if any romance existed between us, but sometimes a girl didn't need romance and passion. Sometimes she needed stability. Conner was gone again, and didn't Nate deserve one hundred percent of my heart to see if there could be something between us, too?

It seemed like I watched myself having this conversation from very far away. From here, even though I sensed I'd been through all of this before, I couldn't tell what the ultimate outcome would be. Yes, I had to have the courage to wait for answers. But waiting for the other pieces of the puzzle to be revealed didn't mean I had to pack up my life and put it on hold until then. All I had now was what clearly lay in front of me at this very minute. No matter what'd happened between Nate and me before, this existence in the now was what we owned. Too much waiting for the future to happen meant I didn't live today. And I wanted to own each second now could give.

Wasn't living what second chances were all about? Maybe I'd fall in love with Nate and get hurt. Maybe I'd hurt him. Putting it off until I had all the answers didn't mean a guarantee we'd work out. The only way we'd know was to give it all we had, regardless of what had been or what would be. It meant we took a chance on love because love was worth the pain. It meant we had enough faith to try. Enough faith to know if we didn't end up together in the end, that didn't mean it was all for nothing. Enough faith to know everything happened for a reason, and all would be right in the end. Triumphs *and* failures make us who we are. And I wasn't the same me as I was back then, wherever we'd been before. Now, I was finally strong enough to fail, finally strong enough to live.

Nate pulled me close. "There's a quote I read. 'How vain it is to sit down to write when you have not stood up to live.' Thoreau said it."

I interlaced all his fingers with mine. "How long have you been waiting to use that one on me?"

"I've been waiting for the right time." He looked over at me and smiled. "Now, will you please go on another date with me?"

CHAPTER FIFTEEN

*"You shouldn't be so eager to find out a secret;
it could change your life forever."*

—Nate's Thoughts

I aimed my flashlight at the fake rock Hide A Key. Quietly, I unlocked the front door and turned the knob, the flashlight barely piercing the blackness inside. This had been my idea, but suddenly I froze with terror. Part of me knew I was insane for technically breaking into Sean's cabin, but the other part of me knew I needed to be brave. It'd been nearly six weeks since New Year's Eve, and without any leads, I knew the time had come to conduct my own investigation. The tricky part was convincing Nate. He didn't think either one of us should come, or that we shouldn't bring the whole Jedi Order if we did. But I argued we needed to protect them. All the paranormal happenings seemed to revolve around Nate, Conner, and me. I thought keeping things between our smaller inner circle was best, for now at least, until we knew more about what we were dealing with.

Actually, it took a lot for me to involve even Nate in my plans. Mom had taught me to be independent, tough, sacrificial. But I had the sensation that I'd wandered down the road of self-sufficiency before, a little too far, and that it had snowballed out of control. Maybe that's why Nate could read my mind. It was hard to be too self-sufficient when someone heard my every thought. His gift was my curse and my blessing.

My heart pounded faster as I fumbled for the light switch inside the cabin. Breathing a sigh of relief that Sean's parents kept up payment on the electric bill for this place, I dropped my backpack to the floor and tucked the flashlight in its front pocket.

After about twenty minutes that felt like two hours of looking around, Nate turned to me. "We can't put it off any longer."

The only place we hadn't looked was Sean's parents' bedroom, all alone in the back of the cabin. The floorboards creaked as we made our way to the closed door. On the handle hung one of those *Privacy, Please Keep Out* signs people used at hotels. With every fiber of my being, I wished I could do just that. But nothing could keep me from entering now. Unless I heard a strange noise. Then I'd probably break the record for world's fastest sprint.

Pausing, I prayed silently that nothing but answers greeted me beyond the door. Then after a final deep breath and a quick look over my shoulder at Nate, I flung the door open. Coldness and dust greeted us as we entered. I gritted my teeth, forcing away the urge to run. A sliver of light shone from the moon in the curtainless window, but there wasn't a lamp anywhere in sight. Nate stretched his arm back and flicked on the hallway light, giving the bedroom a feeble brightness, but I still found myself wishing I hadn't set down my flashlight earlier. The thought of going back for it crossed my mind, but I didn't think my stomach could handle the walk back to this room again, and I didn't want Nate to leave my side, either. Thankfully, there weren't many places to search. The bedroom was small, just green-painted walls, an open closet, *praise God*, a bed, and a nightstand. Then my gaze landed on a wooden statue standing on top of a trunk in the far corner. It was in the shadows, just barely out of the reach of the light coming from the hallway.

I'd never noticed any witchcraft-like items around Sean's cabin or his house before. I crept closer, the hairs on my arms rising as my fingers brushed against the cold wall in the dark. For a moment, I couldn't muster the courage to pick up the statue. His sadistic smile made me uneasy, like the doll knew what I was looking for even if I didn't necessarily know myself.

"Looks like an African Voodoo doll," Nate said from beside me.

The statue had brown skin stretched around a small head with empty eye sockets. His hands were posed in prayer, but as I ran my own trembling fingers across its rigid surface, I didn't think it was God who he expected to answer.

"You can't hurt me," I told the statue, even as I fought the impulse to hurl it across the room, afraid it might. The whole experience was getting to me, the room feeling like an echo of something dark.

"Come on, Olga. There's nothing here. Let's go."

I nodded, but when I went to set the statue back down, I noticed it'd been standing on top of some file folders. Breathing in deeply, I tasted fear on my tongue as I opened the first one.

I gasped. Inside the folder was an autopsy report for Conner, as if he were already dead. I scanned the page, reading the report with horror.

"Aside from the medical jargon being all Greek to me, none of this report makes sense, right?" Nate asked, rubbing the back of my neck.

"Right." I swallowed a vast amount of saliva. "Conner never died; he'd lapsed into a coma for eighty days."

I picked up the other two folders, then slowly made my way back down the hallway. Nate followed silently, turning off the light as we passed. I stubbed my toe, immersed in rereading Conner's report instead of looking where I walked. But the pain was distant compared to the real migraine forming as my mind played the what if game… What if Conner did really die? A yoke of heaviness choked off my air supply as Nate and I sat down at the kitchen table to look at the second file. I froze. My breath tucked itself away in my chest, refusing to come out, refusing to believe. The autopsy report claimed I died a week after Conner on April ninth from a drug overdose in an apparent suicide.

"What the heck?" Nate looked like everything around him was suddenly unfamiliar.

My eyes crossed from trying to comprehend it all. Taking a deep breath, I forced myself to read the last file, not surprised this time to see Nate's name at the top. His date of death was May 18, 2012, from a car crash.

"No autopsy this time, though, just my death certificate. Why?"

I tried to think about things logically. "Well, death from a car crash wouldn't need an autopsy report. But Conner could've died from the lightning strike or drowning or hypothermia, any number of things, and his parents would want confirmation. And if I committed suicide, my parents would want closure on how I did it, too, I guess."

Could all of that really have happened?

Then I noticed words scrawled very lightly in pencil at the bottom left-hand side of each report. On Conner's, the word *Juvie/Camp Fusion/Leo*. On mine and Nate's, *Limbo/Grand Haven/Judith Newton*.

My stomach clenched with the distinct feeling of needing to throw up.

"Dr. Judy's last name is Newton." Nate's voice seemed to be coming from very far away. He stared into space rather than at me.

I nodded slowly. Even though I never called her by her last name, I remembered seeing it on her door.

"Why would her name be on your autopsy report and my death certificate? And what's Limbo?"

Limbo. I turned the word over in my mind. "Actually, I had a memory. I didn't know what it meant, but the word floated to the front of my subconscious after my first counseling session with Dr. Judy."

Suddenly, I felt teary and more unsure than I had before coming to the cabin. I didn't understand any of it. The only thing I did know was I needed to get out of this place. Swallowing hard, I spun back toward the front door with the files in hand.

"Let's go."

I hitched my backpack over my shoulder and in a trancelike state, watched Nate flick off the light switch, lock the door, and replace the key in its fake rock. We ran down the porch steps to Dad's Ford in record time. Like banshees hunting a graveyard, the wind shrieked, grabbing at my hair and trying to ensnare me. I pulled my jacket closer, burying my face in the fuzzy collar as I threw my stuff in the cab and hopped in. The darkness was beyond imagining while we drove down the dirt road stretching three miles before reaching the highway. Even then, home seemed impossibly far away.

"So, why did you want to see me together today, Nate and Olga?" Dr. Judy leaned back in her chair, a pad of yellow paper on her lap. She wore a silver blouse with navy pants, her hair up in a tiny bun.

I hadn't seen her since my follow-up appointment in September, so I decided to come right out and say it. "I found my autopsy report last night."

"What?" she exclaimed, aghast. "How would you have an autopsy report if you're alive?"

"That's the million-dollar question, isn't it?"

She crossed a leg over her knee. "I'm afraid I don't understand what you're saying."

"Really?" Nate's usual carefulness was gone. "Because we figured you'd know something about it since your name was on her file, not to mention my death certificate."

"Me?" she asked soberly, trying to wave us off. "There must be some mistake. First of all, you're not dead—"

"No. We're. Not." I emphasized each word. "So why don't you tell us exactly what's going on here?"

Dr. Judy looked from my face to Nate's, her usual warm expression on edge.

"I don't know who you are." I looked her up and down with a cold stare. "But I'm going to find out. You counseling me, Conner, and Nate was no accident, was it?"

Her face turned ashen, pallid.

"Yeah," Nate interjected. "It's not like you're the only therapist in this town. How'd we all end up with you?"

She shrugged. "Not to sound presumptuous, but I come highly recommended. It's called word of mouth."

But I didn't buy her contrived explanation. Her voice rang with alarm.

There was a long pause, me looking at her quizzically while Dr. Judy undid the top button of her blouse.

Finally, she broke the silence. "Olga, Nate, I don't know what to say. Maybe someone is playing a joke on you or trying to turn you against me. Can you tell me where you found this curious report?"

I smiled. Everyone thought I was so naïve. And maybe I had been. After all, I once jumped into a pile of poop because Conner told me to. But that girl was gone, and the new girl in her place would lie and cheat to get answers if she had to. Desperate times called for desperate measures. "You know, before Conner left on New Year's, the spirit inside him told me the most interesting story." Conner had continued to see Dr. Judy when he was himself, so his parents had informed her about his newest disappearing act. "He told me Conner had died the night of the lightning strike. I died of a pill overdose a week later. And Nate died in a car crash on the last day of school. He told me about Juvie and Leo.

More importantly, he told me about Limbo and you." The thought Dr. Judy could somehow be behind all we'd experienced made me shiver.

Dr. Judy leaped out of her seat, slamming her notebook on the desk in front of her. "I think you two should leave."

"Why did you become a therapist, Dr. Judy?" I squelched the desire to grab her by the shoulders and shake her.

She froze. "I wanted to help others, of course."

"That's what I thought. But what I want to know is how can you expect to help people when you withhold information they need to know? *Conner* is *missing*."

"I know," she whispered. "But I don't know how to find him. I can't answer any of the questions you have."

"But you do know the answers to our questions, don't you?" Nate dug his fingernails into the arm of his chair, waiting, hoping.

She shook her head. "I honestly don't know what's going on right now. But I will say I don't think you're crazy. There are evil spirits at work on a daily basis. I see them getting inside the mind of my patients all the time. Clearly, one is targeting you. But I am not the enemy. Whoever's living inside Conner, whoever's sending you on a wild goose chase, that's your enemy."

I forced myself to remain calm. "So what you're saying is we're on the same side."

"Yes, exactly." She grinned, as if to reassure us.

Nate let out a long breath. "But you still won't tell us anything."

She sighed. "I'll tell you that you're right in thinking that me being your therapist along with Conner is no coincidence. Do you believe in angels and demons?"

The standoff was starting, and I didn't like it. "I didn't use to, at least the demon part. But how can I not? Not after everything that's happened, after everything I've seen with my own eyes."

"Okay, then." Dr. Judy pushed a pen around her desk. "Do you also believe in divine intervention?"

I didn't understand why she asked me this. "Yes."

"Wait." Nate clenched his teeth, then unclenched them. "Is that like when God uses a miracle to stop someone from getting hurt?"

Dr. Judy walked to the one window in her office and stood there, looking down at the street. At least, I hoped it was the street. I began to sense unseen spirits in this room, and it creeped me out. "Divine intervention is so much more than that. People are always shaking their fist at the sky, asking why God doesn't intervene. But the truth is, he does. He places people like you and me in the right place at the right time to be a catalyst for someone in need, for each other. Many times, we aren't even aware we're taking part in a divine plan."

"Are you saying you believe God put you here for us?" Nate finally asked.

"It's a humbling thought, isn't it? To think there are seven billion people in this world and the God of the whole universe has thought of you and what you need in a particular moment."

I recognized the beginnings of an admission in there somewhere. "Does God ever change his mind?"

Her whole body tensed. "Why do you ask?"

Hesitating, I wound my long red hair into a bun like hers. "What if Conner, Nate, and I really did die? But the results were so catastrophic that nothing but an act of God could change the situation for better, so he changed his mind. I mean, God isn't limited by time and space, right? He could turn back the hand of time."

Dr. Judy pinched the bridge of her nose. "You really are a smart girl, Olga. I suppose if you get Genesis One, where God created the Heavens and the Earth, then you understand anything is possible."

My eyes lit up. "So you agree that's the best possible hypothesis. And now an evil spirit... a demon, is possessing Conner because someone is mad about the whole thing. Maybe Conner was sent to hell, and the demons feel robbed or something." I hesitated, noting how insane this sounded. "Do you have anything to add?"

"No," she muttered.

I scoffed. "You know, Mom and Dad always told me not telling the whole truth was still a lie."

Crossing her arms over her chest, she tucked in her bottom lip. "Please, Olga, trust me on this. No matter what you believe, I do have your best interest at heart."

"Trust you? I barely even know you!" My gaze bounced from her to the framed picture of the pier behind her. "Or do I?" Adjusting my glasses, I waited for a confirmation she would never give.

Nate squinted at her. "Come on, Dr. Judy. Your name was on my and Olga's files."

She waved a hand. "Someone obviously wants to confuse you. And it's not God. He is not the author of confusion. The best thing you can do is let this go."

"That's your response? My best friend is missing and being possessed by a demon! I need some real answers!"

"Please, Olga. I wish there was more I could do, but that's the only answer I can give."

I took a breath, but I was beyond calm now. "Oh, okay then. I guess I'll just skip out of your office and continue my parade of unicorns and rainbows because, ya know, let go and let God, right? Divine intervention means everything happens for a reason and everything will turn out for the better. No need to worry. I'll just keep on YOLOing."

Dr. Judy's eyes snatched at mine with fury, with unspeakable truths. "This conversation is getting us nowhere. Perhaps we should reschedule for another time."

For a moment, we all sat in silent helplessness. The drone of the wall clock measuring time seemed to make the seconds move slower.

"Time isn't what we think, is it?" I asked her. "It's confusing. So many clocks running at once, it's hard to tell which one is the *real* time. But the pendulum always swings back, and we return to the place we were before."

I knew my thoughts had taken another weird turn, but I had this feeling that what I said actually made sense to Dr. Judy.

She nodded. "You have no idea."

I looked at Nate, then tucked my hair behind my ears. "That's right. I don't. And whose fault is that?"

Shaking her head vigorously, she said, "Like I said, this conversation was a mistake. You need to leave now, both of you."

I stood, gathering my book bag before heading to the door. Just as Nate turned the knob, Dr. Judy spoke.

"Olga, if that thing inside Conner contacts you or Nate—"

"You'll be the last person we call." I cleared my throat, nodding for Nate to open the door.

And with those parting words, I closed the door behind me.

CHAPTER SIXTEEN

"To me, the thing that is worse than death is betrayal.
You see, I could conceive death,
but I could not conceive betrayal."

—Malcolm X

The next night, I lay awake in bed and thought about Conner. I'd just returned home from a celebratory dinner with my parents. Earlier today, I received my letter from the University of Michigan. The acceptance didn't come as a surprise, but the statement Dad showed me at dinner was. Turns out he started an investment for me the day they found out Mom was pregnant and I had $67,980 for college! All this time, I thought we were poor, but really, Dad was just the cheapest man on Earth.

I debated telling them I applied to Harvard, too. But I didn't know if they'd exactly be happy I went behind their back. The University of Michigan had always been the goal we worked toward together, and my scholarship was contingent on going to an in-state school. Getting into Harvard was a long shot anyway, but one I felt compelled to take when sending out my college applications in the fall. For now, though, I'd keep my mouth shut. Too many things were up in the air, like Conner missing again.

I picked up the Daily Meditation Guide off my nightstand, wondering if the mysterious journal had any new words of wisdom to offer me tonight. But none of the verses, prayers, or profound thoughts grabbed hold of me. I felt lost. I knew God didn't will trouble, but why wasn't he sending more answers my way to help Conner?

Reaching over to return the journal to its place, I jumped. A girl sat on my floor, only I could see through her. She was pale, even for a ghost, and she wore a blue sundress, her long locks in a messy bun on the top of her head. If I didn't recognize her from my vision, I would've trembled in fear. Instead, my face broke into a smile at the memory of her as I scrambled out of bed.

"Grace?" I crouched down next to her on the carpet. "What are you doing here?"

"I came to help you," she said seriously. "I planted your old journal in your room a few months back in hopes it'd help you remember enough, but it hasn't. But never mind that. We haven't got much time."

My whole body relaxed at once. Finally, I was going to get some answers. "I'm so glad you're here. I keep having all these memory flashes and—"

"I know," she said with a relish.

"You know? How?"

"Well, I'm dead. So were you, Nate, and Conner once. But none of you ever went to heaven. That's where I am now. Did you know there's a huge football arena in heaven? We have these passes we use to get in."

"You watch football in heaven?"

"No, not football. We watch the ones we left behind. Our passes keep track of our hours. Each newbie gets three hundred sixty-five hours a year, one hour a day, but we can use the hours however we want. We have a tiny screen in front of our seat when we sit down. We type in who we want to see, slip on a special pair of glasses, and voila, we see the game of life being played on the field. Each person sees something different, our own friends and family members, but we're all there to cheer them on, to pray for them."

"I thought everyone would just be worshipping God in heaven."

"Oh, that's definitely the focus. I mean, it's so glorious, you want to just fall down on your knees and sing all the time. But you don't forget about everyone you've left behind, especially at the beginning of your afterlife. You still want to see them until they move on with you, but your viewing time decreases a little bit each year."

"That makes sense." Sort of. None of this really made sense.

"Yeah, and our passes expire after seventy-five years because really, most of the people we cared about will be gone by then."

"So, you care about me? Were we friends when I was dead?"

"Not really, no. Nate was more my friend than you, but you're the one whose best friend is being possessed by a demon. And it's just so frustrating watching all of you not remember the predicament that landed you here in the first place and watching my mom keep everything from you. I'm just so sick of all the secrets, so I'm here to give them away."

"Your mom is Dr. Judy." My voice was hushed but certain.

Grace nodded.

"How exactly did you come here, though? The dead can just visit Earth whenever they fancy a visit?"

"They can if they're half archangel." Her face shone with the admission. "But I still don't have much time."

A second later, she launched herself into telling a hurried story about how in the past, Conner *did* die from the lightning strike, how I swallowed an entire bottle of pain pills after his funeral and it caused my accidental suicide, how Nate died in his car crash drag racing Bo, and I spent a year in Limbo with him after our deaths, how her mom had been our counselor in Limbo, too, how Dr. Judy learned about Grace's suicide the day Nate and I told her we wanted to become spirit guides instead of moving on to Heaven, how we trained with angels named Riel and Ash as they mentored our work with Grace, but how I couldn't concentrate on the assignment because suddenly, I knew I was dead and that meant I could possibly find Conner in the Underworld. My worry for him caused me to regress from the state of joy and peace I'd achieved with Nate during Limbo and sent me on a rogue mission of my own, where I conspired with a demon named Sam to visit Conner in Juvie in exchange for stealing a file from Spirit Guide Headquarters.

"I'm such a jerk," I said, feeling feverish.

I'd let Grace tell the whole story without interruption, partly out of worry she'd disappear before having enough time to explain everything, partly because I tried desperately to recall it all. Hearing the truth didn't make me remember, but it did make me feel sick to my stomach.

"I screwed everything up."

Grace looked at me, her eyebrows drawn together in concern, her hands clasped together as if she prayed. "Partly, but your heart was in the right place, and that made all the difference. In the end, your actions bought you, Nate, and Conner another chance of life. But not without making some enemies first. That's what I'm really here for, to warn you."

"What do you mean?" Surely there couldn't be anything worse coming than what she'd just described to me.

"Sam," said Grace, looking vaguely toward the clock hanging on my wall. "He got kicked out of the Underworld for what he did, and the demon in charge there wasn't too pleased about that."

"Who I'm guessing was Satan?"

"Right. Sam's memory was wiped clean, too, but Satan found a way to get those files to him, the same ones you and Nate discovered at the cabin yesterday. That made Sam curious enough to pay a visit to Grand Haven, and when he discovered Conner in a coma, he took advantage of the situation."

"What? That's why Conner woke up."

"Yes, but now Sam remembers who he is. He's been staying with a Satanic priest who called on greater demons to get some answers. He'll be coming after you soon."

"For what?" I asked slowly, my brain struggling to absorb yet another piece of shocking information. "Just to mess with me?"

"He wants revenge for getting kicked out of the Underworld." She chewed her lip. "How he'll get it, I can't tell you."

My eyes bulged as I clutched my arms. "But I thought you came here to *tell* me things."

Her stance was unmoving, her hands still folded neatly in her lap. "Oh, I did. I can't tell you because I don't know. But I'm certain his revenge will revolve around you. He's obsessed with you."

"Should I be flattered?" I grinned bleakly.

"I wonder..." Grace spoke into the air rather than at me, her posture straightening. "But that can't be his plan. It'd never work on Earth, would it?"

"What? What are you talking about?"

But in that moment, Grace held up a hand to silence me. "I have to be very careful what I say. There are demons here now, listening. I don't want to give them any ideas with my theories. Plus, I'm causing a disturbance. Your guardian angel is having a fit over your shoulder. He thinks I'm compromising your soul by telling you all of this, but I think I'm giving you the chance to fight."

My heart would surely burst, it pounded so fast. "There are demons in my room right now?"

"Yes. Okay, I'm going," she whispered, looking over my shoulder. "Be careful, Olga! I won't be able to come back. I've already used all my observation hours watching this unfold, so I won't know what's going on to help you anyway. My hours will renew at the end of May, and I'll check on you as soon as I can, but hopefully this will all be over by then. Good luck."

With a faint pop, she vanished from my room before I could even scold her for not saving some hours. I guess I should be thankful for what little information I got, though.

Too terrified of demons in my room, I decided to sleep on the couch. I knew the vile creatures could probably follow, but the sound of the TV softly playing the global evangelism channel comforted me. My rosary lay on our coffee table shaped like the state of Michigan, and I slipped the necklace on, then clutched our family Bible as I stayed wide awake into the early hours of morning, wondering what to do next.

CHAPTER SEVENTEEN

*"You can do something in an instant
that will give you heartache for life."*

—Nate's Thoughts

After school the next day, I shuffled slowly through the hospital entrance, down the corridors, even taking the stairs to the third floor instead of the elevator, trying to think of the right words to say.

The waiting room stood empty, the secretary gone from her desk. I assumed Valentine's Day wouldn't be a busy day for counseling, and it looked like I was right. So I let myself in the first door and walked down the small hallway leading to Dr. Judy's office. Today I came alone. Actually, I hadn't even gotten the chance to tell Nate about Grace. He sent me a text in the morning saying he wouldn't be at school, that he was on his way back to his hometown to visit Bo's grave. It was something he wanted to do before his eighteenth birthday tomorrow, to help him move on with his life. Now he was too far away to hear my thoughts, and I didn't think it fair of me to burden him with more stuff. I could wait to tell him when he got back.

Just when I was about to knock on Dr. Judy's door, I heard a male's voice inside.

"Ash and I appreciate you volunteering to come back to help with this, Judy, but I think you should leave. We'll find a replacement for your position here."

"Are you firing me, Riel?" Dr. Judy's voice was pinched tight.

"You know we have to be careful about interfering in their lives. Besides, she doesn't trust you anymore."

My heart sped up. Riel, my angel boss, was here! And he sounded exasperated.

I pressed my ear to the door.

"She wants answers. Can you blame her?" I heard Dr. Judy say.

"What do you suggest I do?"

"Show her your angel wings. She'll trust that."

Angels really have wings? Suddenly, my heart flipped at a memory of flying with him and loving it. Was that where my newfound love of adventure had come from?

I heard Riel exhale dramatically. "Maybe I should just alleviate Conner. Never liked him in the first place."

Gah! What? I whipped out my cell phone, ready to dial 9-1-1, when I realized how ridiculous my story would sound.

"Riel, be serious. You know what that did to Olga the last time."

My mind flashed to the autopsy reports, and I clutched the cross around my neck.

After a popping noise, I heard his voice again. "Look, I'll have a guardian keep close tabs on her and Nate to report any suspicious activity back to me promptly. All the recon we did New Year's Day points to Sam as the most likely culprit possessing Conner. So assuming it is Sam, how much time do you think he's spent ruling Conner?"

"By my estimates, close to twenty-four weeks altogether over the course of the past eight months. You know that only gives us about two weeks to work with. If Sam is able to hold on for more than half a year within the first 365 days, then Conner could be lost for good, and we can't allow that to happen."

Every muscle in my body tightened, my breath bursting in and out. *Okay, calm down, Olga. Calm down. Be patient.*

"Time is running out then, but we're bound to spiritual law. We can't *tell* her." His voice dripped emotion I didn't understand.

"I know. At least she believes in angels and demons now, so there's a possibility her spirit will be awakened to the spiritual plane unseen by most."

"Let's hope so," he answered quietly. "I'll be in touch soon. In the meantime, you'll need to report to headquarters for a new assignment tomorrow morning."

I gulped, not wanting to be caught in my first act as a spy. Squatting, I hid myself behind a water cooler. Not the best concealment, but the quickest solution. But even though I didn't hear the male's voice anymore, he never left the room.

Of all the reasons I could think of for how he performed this disappearing act, the only one that made sense was the most unbelievable of all.

An angel had been in Dr. Judy's office, and he just disapparated to his headquarters in the Underworld, a place where I used to work with Nate.

Holy headlines, Batman!

Maybe the thought of an angel meddling in my affairs should've brought me some comfort, but I froze, horrified. The three of us, Conner, Nate, and me, were at the center of much bigger events than I ever suspected. Events I didn't think we had any hope of controlling. I sucked in deep breaths, still squatting against the wall with my head in my shaking hands, trying hard not to faint. Grabbing a tiny cup, I stood, then pushed the blue button on the cooler, not caring if anyone heard me. I needed water, needed to curb the nausea overwhelming me. In a daze, I drifted out of the office, forgetting about Grace and why I came in the first place. It wasn't like Dr. Judy ever gave me the answers I wanted anyway. And I'd already heard the awful truth: they wanted me to remember, but they couldn't help me do it. I was on my own.

CHAPTER EIGHTEEN

"People are like stained glass windows;
they sparkle and shine when the sun is out,
but when the darkness sets in,
their true identity is revealed only if there is light within."

—Elizabeth Kubler-Ross

I slipped on my knee-length red strapless dress, then paired it with a white sweater and pumps. Dresses weren't my thing, but I figured Nate's birthday deserved an exception. I sat down in front of the mirror and combed my hair, giving myself a chance to unwind for a few moments, to think back on everything I overheard in Dr. Judy's office yesterday. Keeping my thoughts to myself about my spy work would be difficult tonight, but I wanted Nate to enjoy his eighteenth birthday, so I was waiting until the end of our date to tell him what I learned. Needless to say, I was extremely grateful for the distraction of celebrating his birthday when he returned to school today. Plus, the trip back to his hometown had been emotionally draining on him. I think his own thoughts occupied his mind so much today that he didn't pay attention to mine.

Nate reading my mind had to be connected to all this. Should we keep investigating or just wait it out? Truthfully, I wanted to give up because my body trembled at the thought of what I could find if I awakened myself to this so-called spiritual plane. But I also couldn't forget about my best friend. I also had to think of Nate and tread lightly. We were together now. But even if Nate had stolen my heart, I still owed Conner my loyalty. Choosing one over the other proved impossible. Even here, about to go on a Valentine's date with my first boyfriend, when I should feel elated about not being alone, I felt guilty, like I'd abandoned Conner. Looking in the mirror, with all my red hair down and lips painted hot pink, I looked wild. At least my look matched exactly how I felt inside.

When I came out a few minutes later, I found Nate debating theories on the afterlife with Dad, apparently because of some religious special report playing on the news before a commercial break. I took the opportunity to drink in the sight of Nate. He looked sleek in charcoal-colored suit pants with a matching tie and a white button-down shirt, his black leather jacket channeling a young-looking Tom Cruise. I wasn't in the mood for a deep convo, especially about the afterlife. For once, I was in the mood for romance, so I quickly whisked Nate away.

With a warm smile, Nate helped me into Dad's truck, then climbed into the passenger's side. I took a minute to adjust the seat and mirrors before backing out of the garage. "So, where am I taking us for our first Valentine's Day/birthday celebration?"

"Don't forget we're celebrating your early admission to UM, too." Nate reached over, brushing my hair from my face. "Head toward the waterfront downtown. And don't forget, you promised me you'd have fun tonight. And it's my birthday, so you have to give me what I want."

"What do you want, exactly?" I tried to make my voice sound sexy, but instead my words came out unsteady.

Nate chuckled. "Oh, I'll get what I really, really want later. I'm a man now, so you can take full advantage of me."

My smile tightened into a hard line. "Turning eighteen doesn't make you a man."

"To the law it does. But according to my levels of extreme masculinity, I'm actually twenty-two." He flipped through the radio stations until he landed on "Can't Hold Us" by Macklemore, and he sang along to the chorus about this being our moment while banging on the roof of the cab.

I rolled my eyes. "Why twenty-two? Why not twenty-eight or forty-seven?"

He shrugged. "Twenty-two is the age I picture getting married. You know, once I'm out of college. But I'm so in love with you, I feel like I could marry you tonight."

I looked out the windshield, surveying the town as I tried to process his comment. The moonlight streaked across the sky, transforming the ground into snow-crusted treasure. "Twenty-two is still really young to get married."

"You think so?"

My breath hitched in my throat as I thought about it, about marrying him. I knew I could one day, knew he would do anything for me. He'd sacrificed so much for me already. But was sacrifice love? I'd been in love before, but my feelings for Conner felt so different. I didn't ever feel like Conner needed me, but Nate did. Was that a good thing? I guessed it was good to need the ones we loved, but I also thought about what it could do to you if your whole existence was wrapped inside one person. Thinking about my accidental suicide after Conner's death, I shuddered. I had so many more reasons to live now. So many possibilities I found myself imagining. But doing big things didn't mean I needed to let Nate go, did it? I didn't even want to entertain the thought, especially when he was close enough to listen.

"Here, open your present." From my purse, I pulled out the oversize envelope containing his card and personalized CD. "Happy birthday."

"Wow, first the coffee candle and chocolate chip cupcakes at lunch, and now this?" He leaned over and kissed my cheek.

"The candle was a selfish gift on my part because I'm tired of smelling those incense in your room; plus I wanted to give you something that reminded you of me. And the cupcakes were my mom's idea on our way home from dinner the other night. I think she felt bad about never bonding with me in the kitchen and realized she didn't have much time left with me going away to college soon."

"Well, I'm glad I got to reap the benefits of your mom's guilt. I ate another two when I got home. What was her special ingredient?"

"She adds a little package of fancy grated German Chocolate to the mix."

"It was excellent. I liked how you guys sprinkled the powdered sugar on top instead of doing frosting, too." He peered at the CD in his hands and read the words scrawled in marker on its surface. "Nate's Life Playlist Part I. You did not make me my own personalized CD!"

I nodded. "One hit song from each year you've been alive. All of them are from top-ten lists. I tried to pick songs you'd actually like or reminded me of you in some way."

"This is the most awesome present anyone has ever given me. You need to park so I can thank you properly."

I laughed, relieved he didn't think my gift was too hokey. "You need to tell me where to park first."

"Right at the curb here. I thought we'd enjoy some Victorian charm."

"Harbor House Inn?" My heart pounded in a near panic attack.

"Hey, relax. I didn't book us a room or anything. I wanted to do one last reckless thing to celebrate the end of my youth, so I thought we could crash a wedding."

Raising my eyebrows, I said, "Really? Isn't that kind of a douche bag thing to do?"

"What? No, it'll be fun."

"Whatever. How'd you find out about it anyway?" My voice sounded sharp, and I regretted the tone. If this was what he wanted to do for his birthday, then I should go along with it.

"I checked online to see if I could find any weddings taking place in Grand Haven tonight. Figured my odds were good with the holiday. Sure enough, there's a destination wedding and reception at the inn this evening. That means nobody will recognize us at the party since they're out-of-towners."

I sighed in relief. "You know, most couples celebrate their first Valentine's Day with dinner and a romantic movie."

"Well, I can read your mind. We aren't like everyone else."

"Fine. But we go in, dance to one song, then leave. No funny business."

"Absolutely not. I'm highly trained for this sort of thing. I watched *Wedding Crashers* last night and gathered some tips. One of the rules is to not use real names. I saw this game people were playing online called *What is Your Star Wars Name?* Mine is Barna Regow. Yours is Worol Wegra. So those will be our aliases."

"What? How did we end up with those names?"

"Don't ask questions. Just go with it. Also, another tip is to blend in while standing out. So I get why you want to leave after one dance, but we gotta make it a big dance number. Go big or go home."

"That's what she said."

"Now you're feeling me."

"What about the Chicken Dance...? Is that big enough?"

He shook his head. "No Chicken Dance. No exceptions."

"Okaaay. Then how about the YMCA or the Macarena? Because outside of the standard party songs, I'm not much of a dancer."

"That's okay. Just follow my lead."

"What if we get caught?"

"Break something and use the distraction to run."

"I'm not destroying property."

"Fine, pretend to speak another language."

"I do speak another language. I speak Russian."

"Really? How?"

"Have you ever paid attention to my name? I'm named after my Russian grandmother. She makes me speak in Russian every time I visit her in Traverse City. I guess you missed that part when you were in the hospital on New Year's."

"Is that why you're the president of the Multicultural Club at school?"

I laughed. "Don't know if that's why I'm the president, but yes, that's why I'm a member. It's for students who can speak another language or want to learn about other cultures."

"Huh, I always wondered why you were part of that club. Well, good, that could come in handy. Also, please talk dirty to me in Russian later. That's all I want for my birthday besides crashing a wedding with you."

"I still don't know. I have a bad feeling about this," I said, quoting my favorite line from Star Wars as I took the key out of the ignition.

Nate hopped out and jogged around the truck to open my door. "Come on, this will put your journalism skills to work. You can write a story for the next issue of the *Bucs' Blade* titled 'Top 5 Ways to Crash a Wedding.'"

He pocketed the card and CD inside his jacket while I basked in the landscape, taking in my hometown with new appreciative eyes, nostalgia winning out as the dominant feeling with the thought of leaving for college in a few months. Arm in arm, Nate and I walked up the steps to the wraparound veranda extending the full length of the inn.

He squeezed my hand. "Ready?"

"Ready as I'll ever be."

Once inside, we followed the arrow pointing us toward the *Morales/Coka* wedding reception. Even without the sign, the cheers and applause following the announcement of the bride and groom when they entered the room as husband and wife would've led us straight to the party.

"Good thing this wedding party took over the whole inn," a maid whispered to a waitress as we passed them in the hallway. "Looks like they're a wild bunch."

Terror seized my heart, worried they'd ask to see our invitation, but they didn't even notice us.

We waited until we heard the music for their first dance, and then Nate opened the door to the reception area, and I closed my eyes, breathing in the fresh scent of roses. When I popped my eyes open, Nate flashed me a flirty smile I quickly returned. There was something to be said for bonding over new adventures like this together. I'd never felt so close to anyone besides Conner, but I'd known him since kindergarten.

We scanned the perimeter. There were five long tables on each side of the room with a dance area in the middle. Strobe lights coming from the DJ's corner worked the crowd into a dancing frenzy as a Latin number blared from the speakers, definitely not the typical first dance.

I elbowed Nate in the ribs. "You want to change your mind about the Macarena? We could mimic those moves pretty easily to this tune and be out of here in five."

"Chill, girl. Come on. I'll get you a drink."

After a slight hesitation, I followed him over to the makeshift bar in the corner of the room. We were only going to grab some waters, but then the bartender handed us each a mixed drink.

"It's on the house," he told us with a wink.

"From who?" I asked, sniffing the glass.

"From me. I've done enough weddings to know when someone's crashing."

I hit Nate on the arm. "I told you we'd be caught!"

"Relax." The bartender wiped up a spilled drink on the counter. "I'm the only one who knows, and I won't tell anyone. Go have some fun. But the second drink you pay for."

"Awesome. Thanks." Nate clanked his glass against mine. "Cheers!" He jerked his head back and downed the whole thing at once.

I took a tentative sip of mine, not wanting to feel rude toward the bartender who didn't rat us out. Luckily, the DJ announced everybody could join the newlyweds on the dance floor, so Nate set my drink down to whisk me away to the center of the room.

"Mambo madness, here we come!" He stopped and pulled me close. "Listen to my count, follow my lead, and try not to step on my feet too hard in those heels. One, two, three, four. One, two, three, four. One, two, three, four. You step in the two and three, pause in the one and four."

When I didn't get the hang of the Mambo after a minute, he improvised. Spinning me left and right, hugging me close to his hips before twirling me away from him, snapping his fingers in the air. By the time the song ended, I panted for breath and felt like I couldn't get enough. Laughing, he dipped me backward and kissed me.

After we broke apart, I ducked from under his grip.

"Where are you going?" he asked as I pushed past him.

"To get a drink. I'm thirsty."

He put an arm around my shoulder. "My kisses make you hot, huh?"

I blushed, but before I could answer with a clever retort, I spotted Conner standing at the drink table, not a trace of blue left in his eyes. His head bowed, his gaze fixed on me. He wore an untucked long-sleeved black shirt with khaki pants. His blond hair was a mess, long overdue for a cut just like the last time he'd disappeared.

"What the hell?" Nate whispered beside me.

My heart hitched in my chest. "Act cool. Let's see what's going on."

Nate yanked my arm. "Olga, no. Don't go over there."

"I have to," I whispered. I had to see if any part of *my* Conner was left.

Nate shook his head. "Fine, but I'm calling the police." He patted his pants before cursing silently. "I left my cell in the truck. Do you have yours?"

I shook my head. "No, mine's in the truck, too."

"Maybe the bartender has one I can borrow."

I struggled to make my next words come out, but no matter how spooked I was, I knew I needed a moment alone with Conner. "No—here—take my keys—I'll be fine in here for a moment—there's too many people around for him to try anything."

Fishing the keys out of my purse, I handed them over.

Nate sighed and squeezed my hand as he took the keys. "I'll be right back. Do not leave this room. Yell in your head if you need my help. You'll be all right."

I opened my mouth to assure him I would be, but Nate had already turned away, running from the room. When I looked at Conner again, he beckoned me forward with his index finger. Long gone was the good, obedient girl who did everything Conner told her to. And fake Conner was the last person I wanted to speak with, but I owed it to *my* Conner to learn all the information I could about the demon possessing him.

"Fancy meeting you here." He stood with his back pressed against the wall.

My lips and chin trembled, but I forced my voice to remain calm. "Yes, it is." I gazed into his black eyes, searching for a connection to *my* Conner, a binding feeling that would reassure me he was beyond whatever facade stood in front of me. I felt the tiniest hint of something and prayed the real Conner felt it, too, to have at least a little piece of him here with me. "You've been away for a while."

His nostrils flared. "Didn't have a choice. I knew I'd be thrown in jail if I stayed. Or worse, that priest of yours would've found a way to get rid of me for good."

Sweeping a hand over my forehead, I wiped off beads of sweat. "I thought he already had."

He shoved off the wall and drew closer. "Nearly did. The fire and baptism was disconcerting, for sure. I grew small, almost imperceptible. But every bad deed the real Conner did made me grow stronger again. I knew he felt me, was terrified of me. But his pride kept him from saying anything. Soon I'd grown big again, waiting for my moment to take over, knowing my time would come. You're to thank for that. Conner feels this ownership over you. Seeing you with Nate again finally let me loose."

I shrank back. Why was he suddenly telling me everything and being truthful? It could only mean he was here because he needed something from me. "Is he still in there somewhere?"

"Yes. I'm not strong enough to make him completely dormant like I did last time. I feel him whimpering and writhing. Quite annoying actually."

I wanted to spit on him. "How do I get him back?"

"Yes, I'm doing fine." He raised his voice a little, annoyed. "Thanks for asking."

We stared at each other in critical silence for a moment. Obviously, he wasn't going to answer my last question, but I had to try for something more. This was the first opportunity I actually had to talk to *him* since figuring out the truth.

Biting my lip, I blurted out the next question that came to me. "How did you find me tonight?"

"I've been tracking you since yesterday. Couldn't let that little punk get you all to himself on the most holiest of pagan holidays." Even though Valentine's Day was yesterday, we waited to celebrate tonight because of Nate's birthday; Nate had been out of town until late last night anyway.

I pressed my elbows into my sides, wishing I could disappear. "What do you want from me?"

"Come on. They're serving dinner. Let's not be rude, darling."

"I'm not hungry." *Nate, where are you? Hurry up!*

"That hardly matters."

As Conner pulled me to the nearest seat, I cringed. He pulled my chair out for me with the courteousness of a perfect gentleman. Others sat down at the table, too, but they weren't within earshot and hardly seemed interested in introductions. Candles flickered around the rose centerpiece, the light dimming in the room as waiters delivered Caesar salads and dinner rolls. I took a sip of water, wishing I had that drink from earlier. I scanned the room for Nate but didn't see him anywhere. *What's taking you so long?*

"Looking for your boyfriend?"

I glared at him. "What did you do?"

He turned his chair to face me. "I paid the bartender to give you those drinks, but first I spiked Nate's with a little concoction of my own creation."

Tears sprung into my eyes, and I tried to sprint from my seat, but Conner was faster. He yanked my arm and pulled me back down.

"Relax, sweetheart. The effects were almost immediate, probably the minute he stepped out of this building, but he'll be okay. On the other hand, you won't be if you try any funny business." He pulled up his shirt to reveal a gun stashed in the waistband of his pants.

I swallowed hard before unfolding my napkin and placing the cloth in my lap, keeping up the show. "Fine. Where is Nate now?"

"How should I know? Effects include slurred speech, inability to concentrate, poor coordination, dizzy feelings, lack of inhibition, and amnesia. He's probably wandering around like the babbling idiot he is. But don't worry, he'll come around in thirty minutes or less when it wears off. Though I doubt he had the presence of mind to make that 9-1-1 call. Pity. But that gives us just enough time to plot our next move."

Raising my eyebrows, I stared him down with a fierce intensity. "And what if I had drank the spiked cup instead?"

He shrugged. "I would've found another way. Once we begin our work together, you'll discover I don't give up easily."

I leaned forward, my anger fueling some courage. "Together? I'll never work with you. I'd sooner kill you first."

He tangled a hand in my hair. "You silly girl. I can help you discover everything you want to know if you'll come with me."

My body went rigid. "To?"

"My house of worship."

An involuntary shudder passed over me. "Which I assume is some sort of satanic cult?"

"Dingdingdingding! Yes, I believe Lucifer will answer all our questions if we call upon him directly. You see, the truth is, I'd been having trouble even remembering who I was before possessing this body."

I paused, debating whether I should tell him what I'd found in the cabin. Closing my eyes, I wished Nate were here for me to talk to him telepathically. But Nate was gone for the moment, and I hadn't even clued him into everything yet. "I found what you left in the cabin."

"You've been reading my diary."

My hands fidgeted, turning over the butter knife on the table. I wondered if I could stab him with the knife and wrestle the gun away without hurting anyone. *Unlikely.* "No, the autopsy reports. You keep a diary?"

He shrugged. "Maybe. Those reports are quite curious, aren't they? When I arrived on Earth, I had nothing. No memories. Just the knowledge that I'd fallen and needed to possess bodies in order to stay alive. I was all the way in L.A., so I picked an actor to possess for a while. Great fun. But then I got an anonymous envelope in the mail with those three reports in them. Intrigued, I made my way to Michigan to investigate, possessing different people for the journey, never staying in one body for long so I wouldn't raise too much suspicion. When I finally arrived in Grand Haven, you can imagine my surprise at seeing the three of you alive. Since Conner was unconscious, he seemed like the easy target for me to possess. Plus, Nate and you were already believers, very difficult to control for me. As they say, ignorance is bliss."

I scoffed. If the past months taught me anything, it was that ignorance *was not* bliss.

Conner patted my hand, and I had to fight the need to break out the sanitizer from my purse. "You and I are in the same predicament. We both have memories missing. But I need a solid link back to Conner's life for the priest to perform the ritual to summon a greater demon from the Underworld to give us the answers we seek."

My breath caught. Grace told me he'd already summoned a greater demon to remember who he was. Why did he lie? *Um, because he's a demon!* I didn't think I should rat Grace out, though, so I played dumb.

"Are you kidding? Demons are destructive beings! How do we know the demon won't just kill us and a bunch of other innocent people if he's unleashed into the world?"

Conner snorted. "Demons have already taken over the world; humans are just too arrogant to notice. The truth is, when those people you see on the news go on killing sprees in the mall or drown their babies or drive their cars off bridges and tell the police the devil made them do it, they're telling the truth. But humans don't like to think about what they don't understand, so they ignore the occurrences and chalk it up to crazy talk."

"So you're not afraid of this ceremony you want to do at all?" I asked heavily.

He shook his head. "Why be afraid of the truth? Doesn't the truth set you free? Besides, my priest has ways to keep us safe."

I thought about calling him by his name to see what happened but decided against it. The less he knew about what I knew, the better. "Your *satanic* priest has ways to keep us safe?"

"Yes. I've been staying in a storage room in his church over in Battle Creek. He's been like a father to me. Much more than that God of yours has ever been to Conner."

"Don't pretend to know Conner just because you're possessing his body at the moment."

He rested an arm on the back of my chair. "Just so you know, I'm the one giving the orders."

"But you can't make me go." This was a guess, but I figured if he could, he would've used the gun to kidnap me already.

"That's correct. For the spell to work, my priest said the blood of the anchored soul linked to Conner must have free will intact."

"Blood? Meaning you'll need some of mine?"

"Only a little cut on the hand. Don't sound so afraid. Fear is weakness."

Fear is the path that leads to the dark side. Never had Yoda's words of wisdom seemed more true. "I'm not afraid," I lied. "I'm just having trouble understanding the rules of the supernatural going on here. Are you saying Conner's soul isn't anchored to Earth but to me? And if so, how do you know this if you don't know us? You don't even know yourself."

From the corner of my eye, I saw the bride and groom making their way around the tables, greeting everyone. I'd forgotten that we were even at a wedding reception. At least we were far away from the happy couple, far enough away from everyone else at our table for them not to hear us as they happily chatted away with one another.

He looked at me for a moment like he actually felt pity for my cluelessness. "I may not know who I am, but after possessing Conner for so long, rest assured I do know him quite well, and I know what makes him tick. And what makes him tick is you, my dear. I can sense the powerful recognition and exchange of energy that takes place every time you're around him. You two are like a magnet with two polarities, one positive and the other negative, but the magnet is whole within itself."

"And if I don't come?" I felt like crying, but I knew I needed to hold myself together. I could cry later.

"Well, that would suck for me, since God designed all these soul things to begin with a free will choice, and there's no way to change that. But unless you have any ideas on how to save Conner yourself, then I'd say you're stuck with me."

I sighed, looking at Conner. His eyes were flat, unreadable, and I realized even though a small part of Conner writhed inside of this body, the best friend I'd known since childhood was gone. And time was running out. I really only had one chance to save him. "Yes, I am stuck with you, but I do have another way of saving Conner. Possess me instead. I won't fight you. I'll freely invite you in. And then we can find our answers together."

Conner's face twisted. "You really do love him, more than yourself?"

Nodding, I said, "I already watched him almost die once." Memories flooded my thoughts, of holding Conner on our tiny sailboat, his face the color of death. I remembered the elation I felt at hearing he was awake after being in a coma for so long. Sam had brought him back to life the first time, but now it was my turn. Between Conner and Nate, they'd find a way to rescue me before Sam could permanently possess me. I was buying us some time. I only wished I would've told Nate about Grace's visit and Dr. Judy's conversation with Riel earlier.

Sam smiled and studied my face for a long time, and I studied his, realizing I didn't even think of this person in front of me as Conner anymore. Whatever Sam was testing me for, I seemed to have passed because he held out his hand. "You promise you won't fight me on this? Because if you do, I'll go right back into Conner."

I took a deep breath. "Go ahead. Take my body. I promise I won't fight as long as you promise to leave Conner alone."

His whole body shifted toward me. "Open your purse so I can drop the gun in. We may need a weapon at some point."

I did as instructed, fighting back tears.

Sam grabbed my wrists with both hands, his dark eyes focusing on me. Something in the space between us shifted, and then I gasped. The moment he entered felt like a kick in the gut and made me double over. Looking up, I saw *my* Conner's eyes again, confused and conflicted. Then my head involuntarily jerked backward.

"Olga," Conner whispered. "Nononono. What have you done? Sam, get back in me right now."

"Too late." The words sounded like my voice, but I had no control over the movement of my mouth. The little comfort I felt was that Conner knew the demon's name was Sam, too. My head throbbed, and I felt light-headed as I stood, clutching my purse.

Conner stood, too, taking a step toward me. "I mean it. Get out of her now, or I will—"

"You'll do what, lover boy?" I threw my head back and laughed. "Honestly, you don't know when to quit, do you? So I'll spell it out for you. You're quitting now. Otherwise, I'll shoot you in the head, and even if someone does discover how to rid Olga of me, it won't matter because she'll be sent to prison for life. We already went over the whole bit about humans not believing in demon possession. I do hope you paid attention."

Conner's hands clenched into fists at his side, and his whole body shook like he might explode, but he gave a slight nod of understanding.

"Good boy. Now you'll wait ten minutes before leaving the reception, or I'll fire." I lifted my hand and brushed a piece of hair off his forehead, then pressed my lips to his.

Something sounding like a strangled sob escaped him, and when I pulled away, his eyes shone with tears. "Olga, I wish you wouldn't have done that."

At first, I thought he meant the kiss, and I wanted to tell him that Sam did it, not me. But as I walked away, I realized he meant letting Sam possess me in the first place.

PART TWO

"That is love,
to give away every single thing,
to sacrifice everything,
without the slightest desire to get anything in return."

—Albert Camus

CHAPTER NINETEEN

*"The solution to a problem
changes the nature of the problem."*

—John Peers

Conner

After five minutes were up, I bolted from the reception area, unable to wait any longer. I couldn't believe what Olga had done. Did she really think inviting Sam in to possess her would be better for me than being a prisoner in my own body? Every good memory I had was tied to her existence. I couldn't live without her. I wouldn't.

My fists slammed against the inn's door, and I stepped into the cold night. From the elevated porch, I searched for that punk Nate. Olga's Dad's truck wasn't parked across the street anymore. Since Sam didn't take my keys, it stood to reason I still had my car here. The car I couldn't care less about. It's Olga I wanted back. I looked toward the harbor. The lake's surface looked like shards of broken mirror catching the moon's glow. Awesome. Matched my breaking heart perfectly.

The stomping of feet from behind distracted me from my thoughts, and I turned to see Nate racing toward me. His fists were clenched, ready for battle. I put out my hands to stop him, but the combo of the wind and adjusting to being in control of my own body knocked me off-balance. His kick to the ribs is what knocked me into the railing, though.

"I don't want to hurt you. I just want Olga." He stood over me, his hands held in surrender.

I laughed deliriously, the crazy past ten months catching up with me. "Yeah, me and you both, *hombre*."

He stared at me like he didn't know what he was looking at. "Conner?"

"Yep, it's me. Olga is gone."

Nate held out his hand to help me up. "Did I just knock that... thing... out of you?"

Rubbing both hands over my back, I tried to ease the intense throbbing there. "Nope. Olga invited him in to herself to save my sorry butt, then he, she, whatever, took off."

He shook his head. "And you just let them?"

I kicked the railing. "There was nothing I could do to stop it all! She took the gun I had and ordered me to wait ten minutes or she'd shoot. Whether she meant herself or me, I wasn't sure. Doesn't matter for Sam. He can just jump bodies, right?"

Nate glanced up and down the quiet street. "Where do you think she would go, now that Sam...? That's his name? The demon?"

I nodded. "Yeah, and he knows it now, too. I'm not sure why he kept up the dumb act for Olga back there, claiming he didn't know who he was."

"But he's possessing her?"

Leaning against the railing, I still struggled to catch my breath. "Yep."

Nate buried his face into his hands, his next words coming out all muffled. "Where would he go?"

"No idea." I dug around in my pockets, looking for clues. Nothing. My memories were always fuzzy when Sam was in my head. He shut me out as much as he could. "But we need to do something, and fast."

"We should check her house first and warn her parents about what's going on," Nate said.

Driving was the last thing I wanted to do with a pounding headache, but we ran to my car anyway. "Don't you have Olga's keys? How'd she leave?"

"I had just gotten the door unlocked when I passed out. When I woke up, I was lying on the sidewalk. She must've moved me there before taking off."

Too bad Sam didn't just run him over. I glanced at Nate as I started my car, thankful at least that he couldn't hear my thoughts. After a minute of driving, I felt him studying me. "What?"

"Just trying to figure out why Olga keeps risking her life for you."

The heat from the air vents tossed the pine-scented air freshener hanging from the rearview mirror, but that's not what made me sweat. "I don't know. She definitely shouldn't. I'm not worth it."

He picked up my *Christmas in the Stars* CD sitting between us on the drink console. "There's a Star Wars Christmas album?"

I nodded. "Olga got it for me. Said she found it on Black Friday at Best Buy for $1.96."

Nate smirked. "What a freakin' bargain."

Squinting hard as I approached a stop sign, I said, "Seriously. 'What Can You Get a Wookiee for Christmas When he Already Owns a Comb' is classic. I don't care if I die in December or not, I'm instructing Olga to play that at my funeral while serving Wookiee cookies."

"I can arrange that to happen sooner than later if you'd like."

I let loose a quick, disgusted snort. "I'd like to see you try. Oh wait, that's right, you've been trying to get rid of me ever since you got to Grand Haven. But guess what, I'm not going away."

He threw the CD back down. "Look, you'll always have a special place in my heart as my first archrival and everything, but I think we need to put all of that behind us now and be civil. We need to work together to find Olga, and she'd want us to be friends anyway."

My stomach squeezed in on itself. I wasn't sure if it was his kick from earlier making me want to puke, or how he always claimed to know what Olga wanted. "I don't know, man. Everyone has to have an enemy. Harry Potter has Voldemort, Spider Man has Green Goblin, Luke Skywalker has Darth Vader, and I have you. We bring balance to the force."

His cell alerted him to a text message, and he pulled his phone out of his pocket.

"Olga?"

"No, just an old friend I ran into last week."

He slid the phone back into his pants, but not before I saw a girl's name on the screen. "Who's Lindsey?"

Nate grunted. "That's only something I'd tell a *friend.* Now, are you ready to talk to me like a normal human being, or are we gonna sit around discussing superheroes and villains all night while our girl is missing?"

I faux laughed. "*My* girl, and you can't talk to a psycho like a normal human being."

He took a deep breath. "Yeah, well, normalcy isn't really our thing. So I doubt you'll have trouble believing what I have to tell you."

Pulling up to Olga's apartment building, I killed the headlights. "What do you have to tell me?"

Nate's hands shook in his lap, putting me on edge. "You might want to keep the car on for the heat. This may take a while."

Everything in me, my body parts and my insides, felt cold as I listened to Nate telling me about him and Olga breaking into Sean's cabin and finding some mysterious files. I rubbed my hands along my arms and swallowed hard. "I don't understand. If the three of us died, how are we here now? Did we come back to life after spending time in another dimension without remembering it? Do our parents know we died on the table?"

Nate stretched the cuff of his black leather jacket over his palm, like he was desperate for warmth too. "I don't think I have enough information to answer any of those questions. It was really confusing to us, too, and Dr. Judy didn't offer any answers when we visited her the next day. She told us to let it go. The thing is, it would make sense that maybe you and I died after our accidents without remembering. I've heard of weird stuff like that happening before. But what about Olga? She never swallowed a whole bottle of pills a week after your accident. And it seems like our parents would've mentioned something about us dying on the table, unless the doctors didn't tell them. I don't know. Nothing makes sense."

"Let's go see if Olga's inside. We can brainstorm this later."

Nate nodded, and I slid the key out of the ignition. Over the past eighteen years, my worship of everything Star Wars had been the only religion I'd known. But as I walked up to Olga's door, I found myself praying hard.

CHAPTER TWENTY

"We are responsible for what we do,
no matter how we feel."

—Nate's Thoughts

Olga

My skin tingled as I sat on my bed, shaking uncontrollably. Strangely, I could still feel my body. I just wasn't in charge of it anymore. I had no idea how or when I'd gotten home. This was what Conner had explained to me. Patches of time go missing without any hope of getting them back. All I knew was Sam's presence vibrated and hummed underneath my skin. I walked to the bathroom, splashed my face with cold water, then studied my reflection in the mirror.

Sucking in a deep breath, I said, "Olga?"

The flash of darkness around my corneas told me my own personal demon was talking to me. I'd known weird this past year, but this moment took the cake.

"Consider yourself lucky," my reflection told me. "Unlike Conner, I'm going to communicate with you so we remain on the same page. We are going to lay low for a while. Your parents and friends won't notice anything is off. I'll make them think you were strong enough to kick me out, and I went away for good. I can access your mind to keep up your grades for school. Is that all right with you?" I heard the sound of my giggle, but nothing in my spirit wanted to laugh. "Oh, that's right. You don't have a choice."

An icy chill raced down my spine, and a memory flashed in my mind, a memory of me from another perspective.

Sandals clack across the tile, and I look up to see a young girl approaching the bed, black-framed glasses covering beautiful blue eyes. Her long, red curls are frizzy, and she's a petite little thing, a couple inches over five feet maybe. She wears slim white pants that end at her ankles and an unzipped gray hoodie over a T-shirt featuring a Shakespeare quote. Despite her fidgeting hands, she looks excited. I recognize her picture from the file. Conner instantly responds to her, jumping around inside like a dog greeting a human at the door.

"Took you long enough." I make my tone flirty, seductive.

"I know! I'm so sorry! Phone was off." She rushes to his bedside and gently wraps her arms around his neck.

She smells fresh, and on the spot, I want to lick her milky-white skin, but I resist the urge for now. "You can squeeze me harder, Olga. I'm not going to break."

She laughs, giving him a little squeeze, then carefully sits next to him on the bed. A few faint freckles decorate her skin underneath her eyes and across the bridge of her nose.

I can feel how desperately Conner wants to touch her, so I let his hand come up and cup her face. A palpable zing—unexpected and almost like lightning bolts of energy— causes me to suck in a breath of surprise. I have to have her. I shove his hands in her hair and pull her toward me with a fierce longing. She goes limp as his lips attack her, perhaps too shocked to respond. I decide to wake her up, too. When I shove his tongue in her mouth, she pushes her arms against his chest and shoves him backward.

The rush of adrenaline deflates, but I keep my gaze on her. "What's wrong? I thought this is what you wanted."

"I do. But, Conner, you just woke up, and I don't know. It just isn't how I imagined my first kiss."

I chuckle internally. "Your first kiss? Well, that explains why you were so bad at it."

Her cheeks flush red as I laugh aloud. Her chest rises and falls with rapid breaths, her taut nipples teasing me through her shirt. Possessing her would definitely be my body of choice, so much innocence to ruin. But first I'll have to find a way to get her to invite me in. I bet Conner could help with that part.

Seeing the memory from Sam's point of view was unbearable. A flood of rage rushed through the parts of me I could still call my own.

"Do you see now, love? This has been my plan all along. You're the one I wanted. And now that I have you, I'm never letting go."

A knock sounded on the bathroom door. "Olga? Nate and… Conner… are here to see you."

The spirit smiled at me with an ugliness no mirror could truly capture. I realized then what a conundrum I'd gotten myself into. The spirit within me didn't possess one trace of humanity but was also an intelligent being, probably smarter than me, and a thousand times more powerful.

My hand turned the knob.

Mom rubbed her temple. "What's going on? You come home early from your date with Nate acting all weird, now he's here, with Conner. And Conner says he's back to his old self. Do his folks even know he's in town again? Isn't there a warrant out for his arrest?"

"I'm not sure." It was my voice, but the sound pushed from my lips seemed foreign. "He date crashed us earlier, and we had a fight, so I left and came home. I didn't want to talk about it, still don't."

She narrowed her eyes at me. "You just left Nate alone with him? On his birthday no less! Olga, at the very least, you need to come out of this bathroom and apologize to Nate."

"Okay." Again, the voice belonged to me, but I had no control over the words.

"Good. Your father and I will be in our room phoning Conner's parents. We'll leave the door open, so yell if you need anything." She angled her body away from the door so I could walk past her.

Conner and Nate stood side by side in my living room. Nate leaned toward me, studying my eyes. *Nate, I'm here! I can't control my body, but I'm still here. Please hear me! Sam is gonna try to hide in me so nobody thinks I'm possessed.*

Nate took my hand. "Are you okay, Olga?"

I nodded, feeling buzzed like I had after those two drinks at Kyle's house party in September. "I was too strong for Sam to hold on. He didn't come back to Conner?"

Don't listen to him, Nate! I'm here! I'm here!

Conner's arms were tight over his chest. "I'm just fine and dandy. Why don't we move this conversation to your back porch?"

I let Nate lead me outside, my ability to move my legs without my brain's command a mystery. The three of us sat on the lush bank of the pond behind my building, our shoes dangling above the motionless water. A deer briefly lifted its head near a patch of duckweed across the way, eying us curiously before disappearing into the night. Ever since I'd moved into this apartment when I was eleven, Conner and I would come out here to talk, knowing our conversations could remain hidden here among the tall cedars.

Conner gently took my left hand while Nate still held my right one on the other side of me. Conner's rough fingers felt warm against mine, dainty by comparison. An obvious vibration hummed inside me at his touch, something I didn't feel when Nate touched me. It made me feel free, even though I wasn't. Conner's wrinkled brow, his flushed cheeks, and his concerned smile made me love him all over again.

"What do we do now that Sam is gone? Did he give you any clues as to where he was going?"

He's right here in me! Every cell in my body cried the truth, but there was no way to force the words to my lips. I thought maybe they'd at least see something different in my eyes, though I hadn't always seen the change in Conner's eyes… only when Sam got really angry. And for now, he was playing it cool.

"A spirit came to my aid. Said Sam was condemned back to hell forever. He won't bother us again."

Liar!

Conner nodded, smiling.

"Well, that's extremely lucky for all of us," Nate said.

"Luck has nothing to do with it. Olga is strong, too strong and too pure to be possessed." Conner's words gushed like tears. "And although what you did for me was brave, it was incredibly stupid. I thought I'd lost you."

He brought his arms around me, holding me, but Nate refused to let go of my hand.

"Conner." Mom's voice reached through the darkness from the porch. "Your parents are here to take you home."

"Crap. I'll call you later, okay?" Conner's whispered promise in my ear made me greedy for more of him.

I didn't know if my personal demon's lust made me crave his touch or if a stronger connection to his soul existed when I was really only in spirit form now. Or maybe there was a stronger connection because we shared the same demon. *Ugh.*

Conner patted my leg, kissing my forehead before standing. "Take care of *my* girl tonight," he told Nate. "And thanks for your help," he added in a low rumble that sounded sexy as hell.

Nate and I sat in silence for a while. A breeze winnowed along the water's edge and through trees, filling the air with the scent of wood smoke. Soon, I heard a car start and back out of the lot, and I figured that was Conner leaving with his parents. I watched my fingers skim the surface like water striders, creating ripples that carried my touch across the pond. I just wished my thoughts could still carry to Nate's mind. I'd tell him all about the conversation I had with that young girl in my room, and about the one I overheard in Dr. Judy's office yesterday with the angel. Wait, what was his name? That was weird; I could barely keep myself from thinking about him all day, and now the name eluded me. Riel! Yes, that was it. I wondered if he could help me. If only I would've told Nate about it earlier. Oh well. I might as well have some fun while I could. I lifted my wet hand and trailed it down Nate's cheek, neck, and underneath the collar of his shirt to his shoulder.

His eyes lit up, but he gently took my hand away and held it firmly in his. "There will be time for that later. It's been a busy day. I think you should rest, don't you?"

I nodded, the need to shout any more thoughts at him disappearing as he began to hum—a soft, smooth tune mingling with the flutter of a sole bird overhead. A smile on my lips, I closed my eyes and let the rolling lullaby sing me to sleep, the invisible force keeping me trapped inside my own skin.

CHAPTER TWENTY-ONE

*"Not until we are lost
do we begin to understand ourselves."*

—Henry David Thoreau

Nate

When my alarm clock went off Tuesday morning, I tried not to panic. Since Friday night, I'd slept a total of six hours at best. School was the last place I wanted to be today. I needed to conduct more research. I'd had an extra day of investigating with President's Day giving us a long weekend, but my research was turning up nothing but dead ends, and I needed to go to school to keep an eye on Olga.

My iPod lay on top of my sticker-encrusted desk, and I grabbed it, along with my laptop, and cleared away a pile of twisted blankets from my black futon before sitting. My ear buds blared "Hopeless Wanderer" by Mumford & Sons, fittingly singing about a heavy heart and clouded mind as I brought up the Internet. At the Google prompt, I typed more searches, trying different combinations in hope of some answers. Juvie. Camp Fusion. Leo. Dr. Judith Newton. Limbo. Real.

I laughed when the definition popped up for that last word: actually existing or happening, not imaginary. Because none of this could really be happening.

After Olga fell asleep Friday night, I carried her to her room and took the files she'd stolen from Sean's cabin. She'd told me she hid them in her underwear drawer, figuring nobody ever looked there. I debated telling her parents about the possession before I left, but I didn't want them to start acting differently and tip Sam off. The last thing I wanted was for him to disappear like he did with Conner. If Sam knew about my mind-reading trick, it was clear he didn't think I could still hear Olga's thoughts now that he'd taken over, but I could. The thoughts were faint, like an echo you hear far away, but still there.

All weekend, I devoured every article I could find on demon possession, searching for a way to get Olga back. When I returned from my day trip back home last Friday, I could tell she kept something from me, something having to do with Dr. Judy and somebody named Grace and another person named Real. But I could also tell she was keeping it from me because she wanted me to have a normal birthday, so I left the subject alone, figuring she'd tell me later that night or the next day at the very least.

Yeah, well, the best-laid plans.

But for whatever reason, Sam seemed bent on acting normal inside Olga. She showed up for work on Saturday, then spent that evening catching Conner up on some schoolwork. I guess even possessed Olga preferred his presence to mine if he was around, but I wasn't giving up. All day and night, I scoured websites, looking for anything that would help me rectify the situation. I even went to the hospital, hoping to speak to Dr. Judy, only to learn she'd left town for another position. Another dead end. At this point, I came to expect those.

On Sunday, I made Conner go see Father Jamie with me. He prayed over Conner and gave the all clear that Conner was free from evil spirits. Then I told both of them about hearing Olga's thoughts within her possessed body.

"You can't cast a demon out of someone who has invited the evil spirit into them freely," Father Jamie had explained.

"So there's nothing we can do to help?" Conner asked. To his credit, he actually puked when I told him I could hear her trapped thoughts. The guy was as sick over this as me.

"I'm afraid that even as a man of the cloth, I'm ill-prepared to offer any answers in this particular area."

Still, I went on to tell him about the files we discovered in Sean's cabin, figuring he was our best chance at receiving any help, but he didn't know how to interpret those, either.

"Stick to what you do know to help you. We know from Conner that demons can read the minds of the ones they possess, can acquire the knowledge and manors of their hosts. Imitate them. We know that the holy water and baptism only made the demon recede a little, not fully leave Conner. It didn't leave until he had another place to go. In this instance, Olga's body. Not all demons have a body, and that's what we seem to be dealing with. In the Bible, Jesus once cast a demonic spirit into a herd of pigs."

"But you said we can't cast the demon out of Olga if she willingly invited it in," I reminded Father Jamie.

"That's correct. So use what else you know. You know you can read her mind. You know you shared waking visions with her when you meditated, which she once explained to me seemed like memories. Maybe those memories happened in a spirit realm you were together in called Limbo. Maybe Conner spent time in a realm called Camp Fusion. Could Leo and Real be the angels or demons in charge of the realms? Could they work with angels that walk among us? Dr. Judy, perhaps?"

That was forty hours ago. And forty hours after leaving Father Jamie's office, the one thing I knew was I knew nothing. I stared at the computer screen, wondering what I'd missed, wondering if Father Jamie had been right about Real being an angel. For a good hour after I got home yesterday, I contemplated meditation to call upon him or Leo, but not knowing for sure what I was dealing with stopped me. No way was I willingly calling what could very well be demon spirits into my home.

A soft knock interrupted my thoughts.

"Nate?" Mom's voice. "Are you going to get ready for school?"

With nothing else left to do, I shut my laptop and hopped off my futon. "Be right out."

A half hour later, the bell blared. My Adidas scuffed against the hard floor of the classroom as I made my way to an empty chair. I sighed heavily, slumping into the cold seat, then stashed my book bag between my feet as someone approached and passed me a handout. Looked like we had a substitute today. Awesome. Maybe I could get away with sleeping through class.

The sub clapped his hands together twice, calling the class to attention. "Good morning! Your teacher is running a little late today, so I'm filling in until she arrives. My name is Riel Taanach." He pointed to the board behind him. "That's spelled R-i-e-l, but pronounced Real as in, can this professor possibly be so freakishly young and good looking? To which the answer is, for real, which is my cheap trick of making you laugh by using an idiom that will hopefully make me seem younger than I am."

My head jerked back. This had to be the same guy. It wasn't a common name. At least, he was the first "person" I'd met named Riel. For one moment, I stared with bulging eyes toward the board, disbelieving. Had I wandered into some freaky episode of *The Twilight Zone?*

"Now the question I want to postulate today is this: if you only had one day to live, what would you do?"

Riel's question jolted me, causing me to sit up straighter.

"Whether you like it or not," Riel continued, "you're all just a pawn in this chess game called life. Today we'll be discussing the novel you've been reading for class, *Through the Looking Glass* by Lewis Carroll. Then you'll write a personal essay, answering that question about what you'd do with one day left to live."

Is this guy for real? Well, yeah, I guess he is. But this is really kicking my butt. Good or bad, here's the guy with all the answers to my questions, and he's come to lecture me on Alice?

"Alice ponders what life would be like on the other side of the mirror. Have you ever stopped to think about that? What lies on the other side of this life when it's all done? Alice thought if she poked just behind the wall-hung mirror above the fireplace, there would be an almost real house filled with beautiful things. To her astonishment, she was right. She finds her alternative universe. There she meets Tweedledee and Tweedledum."

A.K.A. Conner and me? Is this some sort of analogy he wants me to understand?

"They tease her that she's only an imaginary figure who will cease to exist the moment the King wakes up. Many would connect the Biblical parallel Lewis, who served as an Anglican deacon, tried to make. The King is much like God, and we can be taken from this world whenever he decides. But no matter, Alice proceeds. She wants to get to the top of the hill so she can see the garden better. There's a path leading straight to it—at least it looks that way, but no, it doesn't at all—but she supposes it will at last. But how curiously it twists, more like a corkscrew than a path. Another path goes straight back to the house. Still, she keeps trying, keeps holding on to faith. Eventually, she must walk backward to get where she needs to go."

He hopped on the desk, smirking. I wasn't sure why, but even though it was an inappropriate time to have that completely asinine smile on his face, I felt like I could completely trust him.

"Now she meets the Red Queen, who asks two of the most important questions one can ever be asked. One, where did you come from? Two, where are you going? Think of all the things you've accomplished to get you to this point. High school will soon be a distant memory for you seniors."

Heat tore through my chest at the thought. I wondered if I'd manage to hold on to Olga when our time here was up.

"As you think of where you came from, and move on to the place you are going, you'd be wise to remember life is meant to be lived in the past, present, and future at the same time. You're no longer children. But we must be like Alice, willing to chase that white rabbit down the hole with childlike faith. To be brave enough to step through the mirror into the unknown and then take part in it. To believe in six impossible things before breakfast." Riel glided over to me, standing directly in front of my seat. "If you can, then your life can be a wonderful adventure, no matter what stage you're in. You have forty-five minutes to complete your essay. Turn them in before the end of class."

The door flew open, and our regular teacher stepped in, surveying the classroom with a confused expression.

"Ah, Mrs. Lory, just in time. The students were just getting started on their assignment."

With that, Riel left. My hands shook as I gripped the pencil. Then I jumped up, letting Mrs. Lory know I had to use the bathroom. But Riel was nowhere to be found in the halls. No tinkling of bells, no flash of light, no trace he was ever here left behind. He had simply vanished. *What was the point of all that?* I guessed some answers could only be found when you were brave enough to search for them on your own. And I was ready.

CHAPTER TWENTY-TWO

"God grant me the serenity
To accept the things I cannot change
The courage to change the things I can,
And the wisdom to know the difference."

—Serenity Prayer

Conner

There was nothing worse than wasting another afternoon spending time with Nate. Well, I guess I could think of a few things I hated more. Being possessed by a demon and then having the girl I love sacrifice herself to that demon to save my sorry butt definitely topped the list. Which was why I found myself at Nate's house after school today.

I pulled my hair into a mini ponytail. With all the crap going on this year, haircuts were the last thing on my mind. "So to recap, you're saying Riel, the same person you heard mentioned in Olga's thoughts, showed up to sub for half your English class this morning and gave you a lecture about Alice in Wonderland?"

Nate nodded. "That's correct."

I snorted. "What the hell does that even mean?"

He twisted a cord bracelet on his wrist and looked down at his laptop. "I don't know. But he seemed legit, like he was one of the good guys. I'm leaning more toward angel than demon."

"Oh yes, I can see how you'd be so certain after one little confusing lecture."

Ignoring my jab, he scrolled through research on the Web, trying to decipher Riel's cryptic lecture. Some people thought Lewis Carroll was trippin' on drugs when he wrote his stories about Alice, but others theorized he had a near-death experience he pulled from when writing. Maybe that's what those autopsy reports meant; Olga, Nate, and I all died, but then we were brought back to life.

"Man, when did life become pure fantasy?" I rubbed my forehead, fighting a headache.

"We can discuss that later. Right now we need to figure out what Riel was trying to tell me."

"No dip, Sherlock." I groaned. "I just have no clue how to do that. Olga's the smart one."

Nate leaned back in his computer chair. "When Olga and I meditated, we shared those visions. Father Jamie thought that was a clue, and I agree. This article says we can leave the physical realm to enter the spirit realm. Maybe those visions were like a bread crumb trail God gave us. We're supposed to use meditation as a vehicle to enter the spirit realm and get some answers. Riel was there today to help push me along."

Shaking my head, I walked over to the magnetic dart board on his wall, took a few steps back, then tossed one of them. Bull's-eye. "Holy crap, man! Did you see that? I hardly ever even hit the board."

"I think that was a sign we're on the right track."

Laughing, I said, "Or maybe this is all, and I quote Han Solo, a lot of simple tricks and nonsense."

"Maybe I'm just hoping out loud. But it's all I have to hold on to right now."

After throwing two more darts, both landing just outside the actual circle, I went back to lingering over Nate's shoulder. "So what now?"

He clicked on the mouse. "Google stuff about entering the spiritual plane."

After reading over some more crap for an hour, Nate pushed out of his chair and paced his room. "Seems like all the research generally agrees on one principle: the spirit realm is here with us, anchored to

Earth, but not usually seen by humans, although angels and demons there always see us."

"The whole concept seems totally absurd." My voice cracked, every inch of me falling apart trying to figure this out. "I mean, this whole time, I've been surrounded by angels and demons and never gave it another thought. But I guess, given the last year, nothing else makes more sense. Man, it's just so crazy."

Nate stopped pacing. "If I had a dollar for every time I thought that this year, I wouldn't ever have to work a day in my life. Question is, are you man enough to try meditation with me?"

I had to hand it to him. He knew how to get to me. On the last site we were on, it said the first step to entering the spirit realm was to achieve a state of total meditation and prayer to achieve an expansion of consciousness that would let us in. Once we achieved the state of consciousness needed, we could ask for angel help. Angels were always there, wanting to help, but with free will intact, they had to actually wait for us to ask. So, we assumed Riel would be there somewhere, waiting.

Scrubbing a hand over my face, I wondered how people ever solved problems before the Internet was invented. "I'm definitely man enough, but this is serious stuff. We're not talking about light meditation."

He dropped down on the floor. "Don't you want to get rid of this evil spirit once and for all, though?"

"I'm just trying to make sure this is the best way before we do anything stupid."

Nate rolled his eyes. "You have any better ideas? Because I'd love to hear 'em."

That would be a hell no. "Fine, then let's hold hands and get this party started."

He laughed. "We won't need to hold hands. At least, I hope not. Just sit across from me and take your shoes off."

"Shoes off?"

"Just do it. It helps you to become centered for deep meditation."

Now I fought the urge to roll my eyes as I slipped off my Vans. "Groovy. What else do I need to do, hippie? Don't tell me I need to get naked."

His mouth twitched; whether it was from irritation or fighting a smile at my little jabs I couldn't tell. "Shut up, close your eyes, and start to inhale deep breaths. Find your happy place to help you relax."

I forgot all about giving him crap and did as he said, ready to get down to business. Putting my palms on my knees, I searched for a happy place and quickly found one with Olga. I imagined I walked with her along the beach, the blue sky and colorful rays from the sun soothing me. She wore this strapless sundress that barely reached the end of her fingertips, and I admired her smooth, creamy skin. I wished she'd show a little more flesh sometimes. Then...

Nate is there. He leads us to a patch of sea grass concealing a small sailboat. "You ready?"

I help Olga into the boat, then shove off shore before hopping on. The three of us float on glittering waves, letting ourselves relax as schools of neon blue fish dance in the current. Seagulls swoop through the sky. Boats drift across the water in the sunset. I don't feel anything except a sense of lightness and serenity. I fill myself with the smell of the fresh air, the sound of the water gently slapping against the boat, and the sight of Olga's beautiful curls blowing across her bare shoulders in the wind. I look back at Nate and notice he's admiring Olga, too.

"It won't be long now," he says.

The sun disappears behind the horizon, and a moment later, moonlight flickers against the water and a shooting star shoots across the sky. My heart aches for more of Olga, but when I think about kissing her, she points to a bottle bobbing in the water. Stretching my arms past the boat, I grab it and take out the tiny piece of paper inside.

"Faith is as simple as taking a breath," Nate reads over my shoulder. "Commit your cause to the Lord; let him deliver—let him rescue the one in need."

Our eyes flew open, my breathing anything but relaxed.

"Wow," Nate said, looking about ten shades of white. "That vision was intense."

"My body feels all tingly. Does your body feel tingly?" I leaned back, examining my hands.

"Here, have something to drink." He reached for a water on his desk and then handed the bottle to me.

After I took a few long swigs, I felt a little more normal. "So, did you see everything I saw? You were on the beach and on the boat with Olga and me the whole time?"

Nate nodded. "The vision felt real again to me, like the distorted form

223

of a memory, except distorted because you were there. Being with Olga on the beach is your happy place, too? I guess I should've thought about that before we started."

I slid my shoes back on. "Yeah, what's up with that? You two have never even gone to the beach together, have you?"

"I thought you knew… about us sneaking out together?" He wouldn't even look me in the eye.

My gut clinched. "Right. Moving on." *How could she think she's better off with him?* "I noticed we didn't even make contact with Riel or any angels. How do we move from visions to entering the spirit realm?"

He sighed and sank back on the plush carpet. "Not sure. That paper in the bottle said it will take faith. We didn't pray before starting. We should probably pray next time."

Jumping up, I went over to the corner where my book bag was stashed and slung it over my shoulder. "Olga told me that sometimes, at her church, Father Jamie asks them to fast because some things can only be accomplished through prayer *and* fasting. Something about spiritual discipline being indispensable for accessing God's power. I think that should be our next step."

He reached back and grabbed a pack of gum off his desk before popping a piece in his mouth. "Fasting… You mean you don't think we should eat?"

I checked the time on my phone. "It's almost eight. I told Olga I'd give her a ride home from work." Nate's eyes bugged out of his head for a moment, and I knew my announcement bothered him, which to be honest, is sort of why I mentioned it. "But, yeah, you can fast one meal or not eat until we do this again tomorrow. It's up to you. I've seen Olga do it for twenty-four hours before, and she was fine. Drank plenty of water, obviously. I can give you a lift home again tomorrow, and we'll give it another try."

"Can't wait."

I'd have to be an idiot to miss the sarcasm in his voice. "Cool. Don't forget to say your prayers tonight like a good boy."

CHAPTER TWENTY-THREE

"Life is made of ever so many
pairings wielded together."

—Charles Dickens

Nate

Heat ripped through my body. I knew I was being a moron. Knew a demon possessed Olga. Could hear her faint thoughts of apology to me inside her somewhere. But seeing her legs draped across Conner's lap, her arm around his neck, drove me crazy.

I narrowed my eyes at Conner, assigning the blame to him. He knew we started dating while he was gone. So he should respect some boundaries, but instead, he took full advantage of the situation. Pissed me off. But I also couldn't do anything. I wasn't going to play into the demon's hands and risk Olga's soul by causing a scene. Deep down inside, part of me knew Conner probably thought the same thing. That playing along was best for Olga. So I bit my tongue from across the lunch table to prevent myself from saying anything stupid and imagined my fist connecting with Conner's face multiple times when this was all over.

When the bell rang a few hours later, I actually shouted, "Thank God!"

Earned me some quizzical stares, laughs, and a scolding look from my teacher, but I didn't care. Never had a school day felt so long. The whole lunch experience from earlier in the day created a complete buzzkill between Conner and me on the drive to my house. Not that we ever had great chemistry, except we loved to hate each other. Add that to the fact neither one of us ate during lunch so we could fast, and you got two very grumpy teen boys trying to enter the spirit realm today. Not ideal conditions, which Conner seemed to realize as I pulled into my driveway.

"You gonna keep up the silent treatment all afternoon?"

I got out and slammed the door. "Please, you deserve way more than that. I'm letting you off easy in the interest of Olga."

Conner shoved the hair out of his eyes as we stepped inside my house. "Guess I'm an idiot for complaining about you not talking to me, but I have this strange compulsion to explain myself to you. You realize Olga and I have loved each other since the first day of kindergarten, right? This isn't really a new thing. You and her are the new thing."

Now I slammed the door to my bedroom. "You're really cracked if you think demon-possessed Olga picking you over me is how a good relationship works."

"That's not what I'm saying. What I'm saying is now you know what it feels like being on the other side, and you've known Olga for less than a year. Imagine knowing her for practically your whole life, waking up from a coma finally ready to tell her you love her, only to lose her to the new kid in town because you're being possessed by a demon and hurting her all the time. Hurt something fierce, man. So excuse me if I'm enjoying giving you a little taste of your own medicine."

I pulled the string attached to the light/fan combo on my ceiling and plopped down on the carpet. "Whatever. I hope you realize I can take you with my eyes closed, and I will after this is all over."

He waved his hand in front of his face as he sat across from me, like we'd said enough. "I just hope you can channel some of that cockiness today and be bold enough to get us into the spirit realm and demand an audience with a freakin' angel."

I gave him a little nod. "I can. But you'll have to control your thoughts. If you listen only with your mind, then fear and disbelief will probably make their way into your subconscious. But if you listen with your feelings, then you can tap into your concern for Olga's soul and soften the lines between the realms."

He twisted the cap off a Mountain Dew he brought with him and took a swig. "Right. Exactly what I was thinking."

Douche. "Let's get this over with. Close your eyes, take a deep breath, and just listen. Give full attention to your intentions with Olga, and don't forget to pray this time like a good little boy."

He smirked at my use of his joke, then closed his eyes, and I used the sudden quiet to forget about him and follow my own instructions. I listened to the sounds around me, to my slowing breaths, to my heartbeat, to the howl of the wind outside, to the cars going by on the nearby road, to the laughter of kids playing in the neighbor's yard. I kept taking those long, slow breaths, just listening, as I focused on my intentions for Olga, to rescue her soul. I allowed the listening to expand beyond my mind, beyond my own breath, my intention. I focused intensely until I became oblivious to my physical surroundings, and then I muttered a prayer.

The moment I opened my eyes I felt it: a swirling air brushing my cheek. I stiffened. A coldness starting in my chest spread through my veins like a doctor injected it with a needle. As the feeling crystallized my insides, I swallowed my fear and reminded myself of positive thoughts. *I will receive exactly what I need. Angels are nearby. I am safe here.*

A feeling of vertigo washed over me as I hesitantly looked around. This meditative state wasn't like the one Olga and I ventured into previous times, where we visited new places together. Instead, Conner and I stayed in my bedroom, except my room didn't exist in the same manner in the spirit realm. Images were disproportionate, like reflections stretched in a carnival mirror. And rather than being lit by my lamp shining in the human plane, an omnipresent white glow illuminated the atmosphere, similar to the way beams of light streamed from a stadium in the distance.

Supernatural movement, a fleeting form I could see through, floated just outside my window. I squinted into the haze and made out a few dark shapes near the fish pond in my backyard, and I remembered in that moment I needed to pray. Across from me, Conner nodded, like he had the same exact thought.

By some divine intervention, I felt the words forming on my lips with no effort, despite my fear. A moment later, an angel popped in front of us. His arms and legs resembled polished gold, his face lightning. Radiating light bounced off his wings until he landed on the carpet, and the wings folded into themselves, the brightness disappearing with them so I could actually see his more human face. It took me a minute to realize the angel was actually Riel, and I almost had the inclination to throw myself at this feet, elated we were finally about to get some answers.

"Is this the right guy?" Conner whispered. "I was expecting to see a tiny cherub like we studied in art class."

Riel narrowed his eyes at him. "Just for the record, I never really liked you."

I sucked in a breath, pushing to my feet so I could speak with him, man to man, but he still towered over me. "So you do know us? Are you my... I mean... our... guardian angel?"

He squinted at me. "I'm much more powerful than your typical guardian. Usually, this sort of visit is out of my jurisdiction."

"Right." I raised my eyebrows. "Why did you come then?"

Riel smirked. "Olga may have slightly distracted me from my normal duties. It's important for me to tell you how to get rid of that pesky little demon permanently."

I nodded and shoved my hands in my jeans pockets, thinking of what to say next, but Conner beat me to the punch.

"So you know all about the three of us. Are you the one causing Nate's mind reading, the visions, the memory flashbacks? Did you send those files they found in Sean's cabin?"

Riel rubbed a hand over his face. "The bottom line is I'm bound by spiritual law, prohibiting me from giving many answers. Fabricated or not, you were never supposed to see those reports. I certainly didn't send them." Glancing at my alarm clock, he pursed his lips. "The thing you must understand is you're living a life where past, present, and future are fused together in timeless unity. Nate hearing Olga's thoughts is indeed a result of that fusion."

I wanted to bang my head on the wall at his vague explanations. "Okay, so our visions feel more like memories because of this fusion then, from a time in the past we don't remember?"

Riel took a deep breath. "It's your consciousness and her consciousness coming together, recognizing your souls are linked together from a past experience. It's like your human psyche is trying to work out the puzzle, piece by piece."

I looked at him, trying to process his explanation. "So we'll always have these visions? I'll always be able to hear Olga's thoughts?"

"No. The Man upstairs put an expiration date on your ability to read her thoughts. That little side effect will end a year from the day you met this past May, in this present time. As for the visions, I believe those will cease after the fusion of your past and present experiences are complete."

The levelheaded side of me felt relieved. I knew Olga hated that I could read her mind, but I would miss her thoughts and our visions. "Great. So how many things did we do together?"

Looking me over, Riel laughed. "Well, she had a task of eighteen things, but you didn't do all of them together."

"And you said the Man upstairs gave me this ability? As in, God? Why?"

He crossed his huge biceps in front of his chest. "Even after all my years of working with our Creator, he is more of a mystery to me every single day. I do not pretend to understand the mind of God, but I do know he always has your best interest at heart."

Conner pushed to his feet. "How do I factor into all this?"

Riel narrowed his eyes at him. "You were out of my jurisdiction, so I wasn't concerned about you. However, our girl Olga desperately wanted to find you in the Underworld and went on a rogue mission to find you at Juvie."

Conner dropped his Mountain Dew in surprise, spilling the green pop all over my carpet. "So I was dead? We all were? But how? We don't remember any of it. Our parents sure as hell don't remember us dying."

"Mr. Anderson, watch your language. And, please, stay seated."

Riel pointed his finger at Conner, and he flew backward and landed on my futon. I did a double take when I noticed Riel now held the soda bottle in his hand, the wet mess on the carpet already gone.

I could tell Conner wanted to take a swing at Riel, but even he wasn't dumb enough to get into a fist fight with an angel, so instead he asked another question. "How do you expect me to chill right now? You have answers. You can easily explain everything to us right here, right now, but instead you deny us the truth."

Riel ran a hand through his surfer hair. "Wrong again. Not easy. Very complicated. Furthermore, I believe the pair of you summoned me here today for some help with a demon, not a round of twenty questions. Is the correct, Mr. Barca?"

"Huh?" Too overwhelmed to think, I'd completely forgotten my true purpose of entering the spirit realm. "I'm sorry. Yes, please tell us what we can do to help Olga."

Riel threw the Mountain Dew back to Conner, then rubbed his hands together. "What Conner experienced with the possession, and what Olga now experiences, is also a result of the fusion binding you all together in this. The scum who sent those reports to the demon, Sam, was someone very upset about a… situation you three were involved in. Satan wanted revenge, and Sam has been an instrument of that retribution. Demons like Sam are tied to the spiritual realm, but they can break the barrier through possession. They usually don't because they know they will be Judged the most severely when their time is up. But if they can possess the physical body for more than half a year, spiritual law dictates they can make the attachment permanent. There would be little hope of ever getting Conner back after that, which is why Olga invited Sam in. She had overheard a conversation between me and Dr. Judy a day earlier. Of course, we didn't know she'd listened outside the door at the time."

Tilting my head to the side, I decided the time for polite chitchat was over. "Why would God even allow demon possession to happen?"

"He allows it because man's free will can invite evil in. He doesn't like it, of course. Every person has a guardian angel to help prevent these things from happening, but sometimes they do."

His lips parted, as if he wanted to say more but held back. Conner whipped his head between Riel and me. I trembled under the angel's gaze until he finally spoke again. "You will need to get Olga to ask the demon to leave, and then you'll need to give him a place to go."

I rubbed my neck. "One, how do we do that? Two, where? I wouldn't even offer up my worst enemy to be possessed by that thing."

Riel laughed. "It wouldn't exactly be angelic for me to suggest such an act, either. I meant you need to send him back to the Underworld. The angels will take him into custody from there. In order to do so, you'll need to create an environment for Olga that will enable her to kick Sam out." He nodded toward Conner. "You, whip out your phone and type up some notes for this. I don't have time to be summoned twice."

For once, Conner did as told.

"There's a portal in every city leading to the Underworld. In Grand Haven, that portal is located in Duncan Woods."

Every radar in my body went off. "The woods bordering Lake Forest Cemetery?" I had visited the graveyard a few times since moving here, imagining what my headstone would say if I would've died like I should've in my car accident.

Conner nodded. "Those are the ones. Nice little forest nestled right in the middle of our town. Olga and I used to go sledding there all the time when we were kids. Creepy as heck at night, though. One summer, Olga and I spent the whole day biking around town and somehow ended up in the woods at night. She swore up and down she saw some moving shadows near this big boulder about one hundred, maybe two hundred, yards from the border of the cemetery."

"That would be the portal. The boulder marks it," Riel explained. "In fact, if you touch it now, even in the dead of winter, the rock will feel hot."

I dropped into my desk chair, hitting my scalp on the headrest. "Whoa. So how do we open the portal?"

Riel didn't miss a beat. "Blood is the easiest way. I suggest you or Conner offering yourselves up as a sacrifice."

"What?" I shrieked.

A quarter appeared in Riel's hands. "We'll solve this the old-fashioned way. Heads or tails?"

"Are you serious?" Conner asked, his voice breaking.

Riel laughed. "No, but you should've seen the look on your faces. Priceless." He flicked the quarter in my direction, then launched right into a very complicated scenario. "Obviously, the boulder is too big for you to move. You'll need to call on the angel Synoro, the gatekeeper, to open and close it for you.

"Go to the woods at midnight when there's a full moon and make a square three feet by three feet, to symbolize the trinity. Pour olive oil along the perimeter of the square. Then set a blessed candle on each side of the square to represent the north, south, east, and west. Mix some sage, frankincense, and myrrh oils together and spray the air with it, the boulder, even yourselves. All of this will help protect you against evil spirits."

My whole body stiffened as I listened to his instructions. "Where are we supposed to get all this stuff?"

Riel shrugged. "Any whole foods market will have the pure oils. Candles you can get anywhere. To bless them, just say a prayer over them. It's two other items that might prove difficult to find."

My nails bit into my hands, my fists clenched tight as I waited for him to continue.

"Both you and Conner will need to meditate and go to the spirit realms of the Underworld you were once a part of. That means Nate will be traveling to Spirit Guide Headquarters on the Limbo plane, and, Conner, you'll visit Camp Fusion in Juvie, alone. The leaders there will only permit one of you to come and only for a few hours. Once there, you will have to follow your intuition to guide you to an item to bring back. Something that signifies your journey. I can't tell you what that item is; only you will know when you find it. Once found, you'll use it to mark your territory."

I didn't need the light that naturally radiated from Riel to see how confused Conner was, and for once, we were on the same page.

"Say what now?" he asked, halting the typing on his phone.

Riel turned toward Conner. "Here's how it works: after you get everything and go to the spot in the woods, you find a way to draw Olga there. Rest assured Sam will see what you're trying to do when she arrives. Evil spirits seldom give up without a fight. He will take action against the two of you, and he'll call on other evil spirits to help him stop you. Ignore them. Only speak directly to Olga's spirit. Talking to demons only gives them more power. Hopefully Olga will be strong enough to kick Sam out, but you can't kill him, only make him go away. After she commands Sam to return to the Underworld, ask the angel to open the portal immediately and then to close it. If you don't ask specifically for both, Synoro won't do anything but stand there. Give me your phone."

Conner shrugged and handed over his cell.

"I'm typing in the words you'll need to say. They're in Hebrew, so you'll need to look up how to say them. I assume you two are familiar with Google?"

He stared us down, and at first I didn't think he was serious. But I guess he wasn't playing around because, after a minute, he handed the phone back to Conner and continued.

"After Synoro closes the portal, blow out the candles and put them in a box, along with the items you found at Juvie and Limbo, and lock it. Dig a three foot hole where you set up the square and bury everything there. Make sure you spray the box with the sage, frankincense, and myrrh mixture. After you close the hole, pour more of the blessed olive oil on top of the soil. That's how you mark your territory."

I groaned. I was glad we didn't have to urinate on the grass to mark our territory or anything, but this sounded like a lot of work for something I didn't even begin to understand. "What does marking our territory do, though?"

Riel crossed his arms. "It's a covenant with God. It will help keep the three of you safe from paranormal activity for the rest of your lives, unless someone removes the box. This is why you can't tell another living soul about this. You can ask your friends to pray for you, and in fact, you should, because intercession is a very powerful thing. But nobody besides the pair of you is to know the specifics. Any questions?"

Conner and I looked at each other, then back to Riel. "But is three feet enough?" Conner asked, seeming to read my mind. "Seems easy enough for someone to discover the box at that depth."

"I'll come and put my own seal of protection over the spot after you finish. Unless someone knows about it who happens to become the demonic prince of Grand Haven, the box will be very difficult to discover."

A chill rippled through my arms, raising goose bumps. "A demonic prince? What's that?"

Riel pinched the bridge of his pointed nose and squeezed his eyes tight. "An evil person can, at times, become a demon prince put in charge of a city that has fallen into a great deal of sin. Grand Haven is a good town, so hopefully you won't have to worry about that ever happening."

We lapsed into silence, only nodding in response.

"You have your instructions. Follow them perfectly because I don't have the time or inclination to babysit you. May God's grace shine upon you." He popped his wings out, and the light threatened to blind me again. "Catch you on the flipside."

My heart sank as he disappeared and everything in the room returned to normal. Even though he had been the most awesome creature I'd ever seen, I hoped the flipside was still a long way off in a galaxy far, far away.

CHAPTER TWENTY-FOUR

"He who controls others may be powerful, but he who has mastered himself is more mightier still."

—Tao Tzu

Conner

Entering the spirit realm happened the same as before, except I was alone in my room tonight. Mom and Dad were fast asleep upstairs, and hopefully they stayed that way. After our visit with Riel last night, I offered to go first and tell Nate about my experience before he ventured to Limbo. Didn't want him getting too cocky, thinking he was better than me at all this spirit stuff.

The realm remained dark and okay, I'll admit, a little scary, until I called out for angel help. I watched pinpricks of light stabbing down from my ceiling. Gradually, my vision lightened as the foggy filter draping over the entire realm lifted. Before I knew it, my dresser, my bed, and the carpet I sat on were suddenly more vibrant, like someone had opened a stopper at the base of a rainbow and released all the color. There was no other way to describe it. The angel appearing in my room was like an eight-foot-tall, living, breathing rainbow, his colors spilling over everything and warming me in his presence, despite the freezing temperature outside. He didn't speak at all but held the most soothing existence of anything I'd ever encountered. Then I realized he was waiting for me to speak, and I didn't want to keep him from more important matters. But really, what could be more important than my girl Olga?

"Conner Anderson," I said, thinking not introducing myself would be rude. "I come humbly before you to ask your help in taking me to the spirit realm of Juvie. Camp Fusion to be exact."

He bent down and held out his hands. The hair lifted on my nape and on my arms, but the time to doubt had come and gone. The only way through this was by faith. As soon as I touched the angel's hand, a shock went through me, illuminating my skin until I wore a multicolored coat like the celestial being standing before me. The angel looked down upon me with warm eyes. *Do not be afraid; I am here to help you,* they seemed to say.

"I will take you to Leo." The angel's voice reminded me of the gong sounds coming from Coast Guard ships when docking in the channel downtown. "A word of warning, though: the longer humans stay in the Underworld, the weaker your physical body becomes. You can lose yourself in such a place. Work quickly."

In an instant, the light around us intensified, and the cold air returned, whipping around us like a tornado. I tucked my head into my chest as the angel continued to hold on to my hands. The wind slowly faded until only a gentle breeze remained, and I looked up. The angel had disappeared, and now I stood across from another angel who looked like he was made of fire and brimstone. It seemed I was dropped off in a school office. A desk sat in the center of the room, the edge lined with framed photos of a bunch of kids, a few looking vaguely familiar. There were also a couple of padded chairs, an aquarium in the wall, a potted plant in the corner, and a smudged plate-glass window looking into a school hallway. My ears ached, my head pounded, and my eyes leaked tears as I took in my surroundings. *What the heck? Tears? When did I become such as wuss?*

Suddenly, the new angel loomed over me like an angry wave who'd like to swallow me whole. "I thought I told you to stay out of trouble."

He gestured for me to take a seat, and I did, obviously. "You're Leo."

He nodded, then pointed to me. "And you're Conner Anderson. Now that we've gotten that straightened out, why don't you tell me why you're back at my camp?"

I started babbling about everything that happened since April first. The more I talked, the more ashamed I felt at my douche behavior, although most of it was out of my control. Still, if I'd been a better person, if I'd put just a little faith into God rather than myself, then Sam wouldn't have been able to possess me in the first place.

Leo's lips curled into a smile after I finished my story. "Trouble sure does follow you, kid. You should probably check the tree house or the island in the middle of the lake. That's where you spent most of your time hanging out when you were here, besides your tent. But you wouldn't be able to go in there without disrupting Bo, and you need to avoid contact with everyone while you're here. Shouldn't be too hard since it's after the midnight curfew. Everyone is in their tents right now."

Am I imagining things, or did he say it's after midnight? "I started meditating at nine sharp. Did my traveling take three hours? Because I swear it felt like three minutes."

He ran a hand through his messy hair, which looked about as coarse as a horse's tail. "You're in a different time zone, that's all. We're actually almost a full day behind Earth time, in case you get held up here. I assume Raphael warned you to work quickly, though? Your body will get weak. Plus, things won't look as clear to you here, since you're not a resident anymore."

I gave him a small smile. "Yes, sir." *Sir? Where did that come from? This realm is already changing me after a few minutes.* "Um, how big is this place? Can I have a tour guide or something to find the tree house and lake?"

He walked over to a filing cabinet in the corner, and when he stood over me again a moment later, he held out a map. "This feels like déjà vu. You're here." He pointed to Camp Fusion High. "Use the front door and follow the brick path. Check the lake first, since it's right across the way. You can use one of the sailboats docked there to reach the island. I'll let the guards know you have clearance to be here for a few hours."

I stood and held out my hand. "Thank you for your help, sir." *Again with the sir? Being here must make you automatically more obedient or something.*

"Godspeed to you, kid."

With that, I stepped out of his office into the school hallway. There was a cafeteria with picnic tables to the left and a bunch of announcements tacked to an overly large bulletin board on the far right wall. Curious, I walked over to the colorful fliers. One in particular caught my eye. Free guitar lessons from Bo Reyes every Thursday night from six to seven at campsite number one. Leo mentioned someone named Bo, the guy who took over my tent when I left or my roomie while I was here? The name seemed vaguely familiar, just like the faces in that picture in Leo's office. Shrugging, I made my way to the front doors and pushed them open, hot air rushing in.

A deep breath escaped my lungs. The shock of heat in February caused an immediate outbreak of sweat as I tiptoed down the stairs. Quickly, I passed two guards who simply nodded at me. A gray haze caused me to squint as I studied the layout of the map and then my surroundings. I could see through the fog, yet it tainted everything my terrified gaze landed on, as if the entire camp had been draped in a translucent cloud of smoke. And something moved on the edge of my vision, drawing my eyes in its direction. I wanted to go back and ask Leo if demons were here, too. This was the Underworld. But I fought the being a wuss thing and shrugged off my paranoia, walking in the direction of the pristine lake.

A few minutes later, I untied a sailboat from the dock, and my gaze followed an eerie burst of motion, but the thing was too fast for me to get a good look. I spun in the opposite direction, squinting into the ghostly gloom as I tracked another movement. That's when I spotted him.

In the distance, I saw a demon watching me, wrapped in an almost solid sheet of ominous shadow. He was disfigured, sort of like Tolkien's depiction of evil personified in the character Gollum from The Lord of the Rings trilogy. I wondered if this is what all demons looked like in their true forms. I almost asked what it wanted, but then I remembered Riel cautioning us about speaking to demons. Talking to them only gave them more power. Without knowing what else to do, I ignored the little beastling and shoved off shore in the boat.

She was a nice fifteen footer, and in my head, I named her *Gollum*. I wished I would've brought a flashlight. Moonlight flickered against the water, but it did little to penetrate through my hazy vision. Remembering the navigation light, I flipped it on so I could see in the darkness, then went about setting a course, avoiding the jagged rocks along the shore and the floating dock. Fireflies blinked in the breeze that was nauseatingly warm, and I slapped my neck as a mosquito bit me.

"What the hell is this place?"

A loud pop reverberated through the atmosphere, and the demon materialized in the boat, causing me to yelp in surprise. I eyed the dark creature, his red eyes never leaving mine. There was nothing, nada, remotely human about him. Not wanting to speak to it, and not knowing what else to do, I somehow managed to focus enough to steer the boat toward the tip of a narrow island. As quickly as I could, I jumped out of the boat and secured the line to a post in the sand. The demon didn't follow me. Maybe he wasn't allowed to.

Cattails nodded in the breeze, pointing toward the center of the small island where a single oak tree loomed. I shuffled my bare feet through the sand. My legs shook a little. I didn't know if it was from my body becoming weaker already or from fear over the demon possibly popping in front of me again. As I neared the tree, I felt a charge in the air around me. Breathing became more labored. I focused on taking deep breaths, but the task was difficult in this humidity. With each step I took, it felt like my feet became ten pounds heavier, sharp shells digging into the soles of them and making me wince. I stumbled on my last step and leaned against the tree. My shoulders shook. I was barely keeping my crap together, and then I saw the carving. CA+OW=TLF.

"Conner Anderson plus Olga Worontzoff equals True Love Forever?"

Suddenly, this tree wasn't only vaguely familiar like some of the other things in this realm, and the mist lifted at our initials. I knew this was what I needed to bring back to mark my territory. Obviously, I couldn't bring the whole tree, so I had to peel away the bark with our carving. After picking up a sharp shell, I chipped away at the task. I felt a sharp pain underneath the nail on my left pointer finger as I finished up.

"Bloody hell!" Red leaked from the gash where the edge of the shell sliced me open, but I had my piece of bark. I slipped it into the back pocket of my jeans, then steeled myself for the walk back to the boat when I heard a familiar pop. After turning around, I froze, my eyes hot and stinging as I stared into the scarlet eyes of the demon.

He lurched forward and snatched the bark out of my pocket with his creepy skeletal fingers, cackling. I half expected him to start mumbling, *"My precious,"* but instead, he turned and ran toward the boat.

"Riel? Leo? Raphael? A little help here?" I croaked out, my broken words sounding like they came from someone else. *Wuss.*

Then I remembered Riel's words about having childlike faith, about not being afraid. Everything looked so dark. I couldn't even see the demon anymore. My vision faded fast, so I closed my eyes. I forced myself to breathe in and out through my nose like Nate instructed me to when we meditated. I pictured the fear leaving me, Olga's freedom on the horizon. Then I shouted a prayer so fierce my voice felt hoarse afterward. When I opened my eyes, my sight had returned. I started forward in the direction of the boat and tripped over a dark form. The demon. He was awake but immobilized for the time being. I used the opportunity to seize the tree bark from his hands.

"I'm ready to leave, Raphael."

The glorious colors of a beautiful rainbow enveloped me again. My hand breached the gap, grabbing on to the angel's as a cord of energy pulled us through the spirit realm, the scene fading around me before I could even process what happened. Then the whole atmosphere seemed to shift, as if recalibrated, and I thought of the article Nate found comparing travel to spirit realms like changing radio stations. Just because you switched channels sometimes, it didn't mean the other station ceased to exist.

When I opened my eyes, I was back on the floor in my bedroom, watching the light fade until the only illumination left came from my lamp, so insubstantial in the wake of an angel.

CHAPTER TWENTY-FIVE

*"People you expect to kick you when you're down
are the ones to help you get back up."*

—Nate's Thoughts

Nate

ll day, I was like a can of soda, shaken and ready to spew. I met up with Conner before school so he could tell me all about traveling to the Underworld for our assignment. An angered heat burned through me when showed me the bark he tore off with his and Olga's initials carved into it. Since Olga and I were both part of Limbo and shared those visions, I thought we had been together *together* in the Underworld. I might as well have been that stupid tree, my heart the bark that he'd cut into.

I waited for Mom and Dad to go to bed for my meditation session. Since Dad always stayed up to watch the news at eleven, I waited till midnight to start. After locking the door, I took a seat on the floor, wearing my flannel pajama pants. There was nothing like a good pair of flannel pajama pants for a successful meditation session. With deep breaths, I focused on happy thoughts, but neither brought me into the Limbo plane, a spirit realm, or even visions. Mastering myself again, I tried some yoga poses to relax before starting over. Didn't help. So I got up and put on soft music and lit a few candles. Nothing again. *Crap. How bad does this suck?*

Manning up, I sent Conner a text, asking him how he did it the night before.

Exactly how u showd me—not workn 4 u?

I sent him a no, and after another hour of trying, gave up and went to bed. Expecting Conner to be cocky about him getting in without any problems, I was surprised when he tried troubleshooting the situation with me instead. But that still got us nowhere.

During the next three days, I read over my research again. Scrolled through Conner's notes on his phone. Prayed, even fasted some more. But the weekend didn't bring any improvements. I was starving myself now, not able to fall asleep, and becoming light-headed when I tried to do any little task. When Monday came around, I skipped school, determined to make something happen. Tonight was the full moon. If I couldn't gain access today, Conner and I would have to wait another month before we could complete the mandate Riel gave us. Another month of Olga being possessed. Another month of her spending time with Conner and ignoring her boyfriend. Sam was keeping up the good girl act while he possessed Olga for now, but my intuition told me that wouldn't stick for long.

And now I knew how to stop all of it, but I didn't have the faintest idea of why I couldn't get to Limbo, and there was nobody else to help me except Conner, the last person I wanted to call on. My whole life felt like a lie with a huge chunk missing. I didn't even know who I was anymore. Some days it felt like I never would.

What's wrong with me? Why can Conner get into the Underworld and I can't?

Yeah, that's a complaint I thought I would never have. I let out a deep breath, discouragement overwhelming me like a dark cloud. The sound of the doorbell a little after four o'clock interrupted my self-loathing. My insides tingled with hatred when I opened the door to Conner's face. I knew why he didn't come straight over after school ended at 2:37 p.m. He would've taken Olga home to change and to eat something before dropping her off for her shift at the Bookman. And then he'd get to pick her up at eight and take her back home. Even though I knew he offered the rides to keep close tabs on her, I couldn't help resenting him.

With a sense of foreboding I'd never get Olga back again, I shoved Conner off my front stoop and slammed the door. I walked into the kitchen to get a glass of water, trying to calm down, but I couldn't. Had he kissed Olga? Done more? Her voice was so faint now I couldn't hear her thoughts unless I was right next to her, and she usually didn't let me get that close anymore. I wanted to believe the part of her still present inside her body wouldn't cheat on me, but I knew even if she did, I couldn't hold her responsible with Sam controlling things. Sick images swarmed my mind, and I tried to push them away. If I couldn't enter Limbo, there'd be nothing I could do for her. Steeling myself to try again, I shuffled back to my room, only to find Conner sitting on my futon.

His pupils were wide as he held up his hands in surrender. "Nate... listen."

Something about the way he said it made me take another deep breath instead of punching him for crawling through my unlocked window.

"We're not going to solve anything by fighting. Like it or not, we're in this together. Can we at least resign to be frenemies?" He cracked a smile.

Even though I didn't feel it, I returned his joke. "Well, you know what they say. Keep your friends close, but your frenemies closer."

"Exactly." He held out his hand for a fist bump.

I tapped my knuckles against his. "Just don't expect me to braid your hair any time soon. You ever gonna cut that rug?"

He shook his head. "I'm not cutting it until this whole thing is over."

Taking a seat in my computer chair, I couldn't stop my leg from bouncing. That's what living off coffee for three days did to you. Olga would laugh at that. "What are you, superstitious?"

"How can you *not* be superstitious after everything that's happened?"

"I guess."

Conner looked over at me, quiet for a minute, a first for him. Boy loved to run his mouth. "So what do you think is going on? You got cold feet about venturing into the Underworld? Because that's totally understandable."

There was no teasing in his words. It made me want to jump out of the window he had sneaked into.

I pushed to my feet, feeling not just the weight of my iPod and cell phone in the pockets of my baggy shorts but the weight of the world as I paced around my room. "Don't get all psychiatry on me. That big head of yours might explode. I'm the thinker. I'll figure this out."

"First of all, it's okay to be cocky if you're the shiznit."

"I've got no problem pimp slapping the shiznit out of you to cure that problem. And by the way, that word is played out. About time you update your vocabulary."

"And second," he continued without missing a beat. "This is serious. The full moon is tonight. We need to be ready to go at midnight. I already went and bought all the stuff we need except the candles for the... ceremony? I don't know, whatever you want to call it. I got it all this weekend. Said prayers over the oils and everything."

"Perfect. Then you should go. You can't come with me to Limbo. I'll meet you at Duncan Woods at eleven thirty p.m. so we can set up. Just think of a way to get Olga there."

The look on his face told me he wasn't agreeing to that plan even before he opened his mouth. "Well, that doesn't make sense. Me inviting her to the woods at midnight already seems weird. Weird is more your thing than mine."

I could tell he was trying to lighten the mood, but it wouldn't work this time.

"And if you're not ready to go, I'll have to think of an excuse to invite her there again on March twenty-seventh for the next full moon. Sam isn't stupid... He'll know something is up."

I plopped back into my chair and groaned. "Whatever. Just leave me alone. I'll text you after I get back from Limbo."

Conner shook his head. "Call me if you need *anything*." He held out his fist, and I grudgingly hit it with mine. "You got this, man."

I watched him leave through the window again and spent the rest of the evening trying everything I could think of. Took a hot shower to relax. Stood upside down, thinking maybe increased blood flow to my brain would help. Took a run to clear my head. Took another shower. Ate dinner even though I wasn't hungry. Let myself sleep for an hour, hoping some rest would cure the problem. Woke up to my alarm with a pounding headache, my body aching for more z's.

Why wasn't anything working? Did Conner know something he wasn't telling me? I screamed into my pillow and punched my futon. Deep down, I knew Conner was a good guy and wouldn't do anything to jeopardize Olga's soul.

Why hadn't Riel explained more? Had he thought gaining access to the realms would be easy? He seemed to care a great deal about Olga, so I didn't think he'd leave out information on purpose, either. Maybe this was a situation the angel never encountered before and therefore, didn't have all the answers for like I'd hoped. If so... Had he been wrong? But Conner did get into Juvie.

My cell alerted me to a text just after nine.

Any luck? Im w/Olga-need 2 know if I shud invite her 2 woods 2nit

His words hit me like a sucker punch to the gut. I typed out a no, then cried myself to sleep, feeling powerless to do anything else.

CHAPTER TWENTY-SIX

"You can keep going long after you think you can't."

—Nate's Thoughts

Olga

Something was up. Sam, eager to get rid of Conner, practically pushed him out the door just after nine when my parents announced they were turning in for the night. But instead of keeping my old routine like he usually did, Sam didn't change into pajamas. He took off my glasses, then stared into the tiny mirror hanging in my bedroom.

"You know, I've come to love you a little bit, Olga."

You don't know what love is!

He looked to the window. "I may be a demon, but I do know what love is," he muttered impatiently, turning his gaze to the sky. "Angels and demons aren't as black and white as portrayed in Hollywood, you know. Demons aren't always bad. In fact, we were angels once, cast out of heaven for daring to question God's authority." He clucked his tongue, *my* tongue. "And the angels that remained in God's good graces, well, let's just say they're not always good, either. What do you say to that?"

I groaned but withheld my thoughts, wanting to shut him up.

"Speechless? That's a first. At any rate, you better be nice to me. There are worse ways to do what I'm doing tonight. Even if I do have a soft spot for you, do not underestimate how cruel I can be when prompted."

What are we doing tonight?

"Oh, dear one, haven't you wondered why I've been taking such good care of you? Why I've been pumping your body full of vitamins?"

His tone sounded excited, giddy.

"I was delighted when I took possession of your body that night on February fifteenth and discovered you were in the midst of your cycle. Meant I didn't have to wait long at all to implement our plan. It's a bit of a guessing game, but today should mark the first day of your fertility window. Given the full moon, the priest and I agreed there was no time like the present."

What priest? Father Jamie?

He chuckled, but there was no humor in the gesture. "Oh, that would be quite the plot twist, wouldn't it? But, no, I'm afraid Father Jamie has not come to the Dark Side. I'm talking about the priest I mentioned to you that fateful night we became one… the satanic priest I stayed with in Battle Creek. He'll be here any minute to pick us up."

Why?

"I just love children, don't you? So innocent, so easily manipulated. I've always wanted one of my own, and now I'll have one with you."

You're going to let… that priest… take advantage of me?

He reached up and ran his, *my*, fingers over my chest and down my abdomen. "No, Olga. I want you pure. The priest has donated his chauffer services, and I've already stored my donation of… genes, and tonight the priest is taking us to a doctor we found about an hour away who is willing to perform the procedure."

Artificial insemination?

"Precisely. You see, I owe you a bit of an apology. I wasn't as clueless as I first claimed to be. My mandate from my father, after I finally discovered who he was a few weeks ago, was always to possess you, but we knew you'd have to invite me in to do so. We figured continuing to possess Conner was the best course of action since Daddy Dearest knew you'd given up everything for him before. You see, my father has desired an army of half breeds for a long time now, but he had been going about it all wrong. Since all demons are male, he always sent them to Earth disguised as the best-looking men of this world to impregnate the women here, but their bodies could never take the change and they died, along with the half-demon fetus. But with me inside you to play host, your body should be strong enough to handle the change. I don't know why Father didn't think of this sooner."

Because he's stupid. All demons are. My anger caused my body to quiver.

Sam laughed. "My father isn't just any demon. He is Satan himself."

You're kidding.

"I kid you not." He applied some lipstick in the mirror. "Anyway, don't fret, darling. Once you give birth to our little experiment, I won't have any use for you. If we're successful, the priest will take the baby to raise him or her as his own, and I'll leave you to impregnate our next target. I can't stay with you forever, sweetheart. I know you're disappointed, as am I, but we'd raise too many suspicions if I stayed around much longer."

And if you fail?

He slammed his, *my*, fists down on my desk.

"I will not fail!" Taking a deep breath, he smoothed down my dress.

Wearing a dress should've been the first clue to Conner something was off tonight.

"Failure would mean your death, and neither one of us desires that outcome. But even your death won't mean the end of me. I'll just possess someone else. So don't get any funny ideas about trying to swim to the surface to take your own life to save humanity. I've covered all the bases. The only hard part will be keeping the pregnancy from your parents and friends. But even that shouldn't prove too difficult. Gaining thirty pounds from emotional eating will be understandable after the year you've had. It will be interesting to see if Conner and Nate still want you when you're a fat cow."

A text let Sam know our ride had arrived. He turned out the light and left through the front door, my parents already sound asleep. Once on the open road, the priest stepped on the gas, going way past the speed limit. When we got out of the truck after what felt like the longest ride of my life, the wind howled at our back. Sam pulled the coat around us tighter, but it made no difference. I hadn't felt warm in weeks. The back alley where we parked smelled like a thousand cats had defecated there. It was a black hole into which every piece of trash, every sinister sound, every dead end had been sucked. Not exactly a prime location for a refutable clinic. After a sweeping look, the priest knocked on a back door, and a man wearing scrubs answered.

"Right on time. Come in. Hurry up."

As he spoke into my face, I couldn't help but notice his breath smelled no better than the alley. Walking through the tiny space to the examination room, not bumping into a counter or cardboard boxes or bloody wastebaskets proved difficult. The whole place smelled like vomit, blood, and sweat. A lot of equipment appeared to be held together by duct tape alone. After Sam flicked on the light, he wasted no time in disrobing.

Show a little respect and shut the door!

Sam chuckled. "But I like showing off my new body. You should flaunt it while you got it, love," he said, shutting the door. Within the span of a minute, he donned a papery thin gown opening in the back. There was no operating table, only a gurney covered by a disposable sheet where we sat waiting. "Ready, doc!"

The man in scrubs entered and shut the door again, thankfully wearing a mask pressed over his mouth and nose. At least I wouldn't have to smell his foul breath again, which was really the least of my worries. The priest must've waited outside, which was another small relief.

"Lay back, please." He adjusted the overhead light, put on a pair of blue latex gloves, then picked up an instrument from a green cloth-lined tray before starting. "Be still and this will only take a minute."

Sweat dripped down my forehead and neck as he completed the procedure. Sam may have been in control of my body, but that didn't mean he controlled how I felt. My breaths were rattled as tears streamed down my face, my stomach contracting with severe cramps.

"Almost done down there, doc?" Sam asked through my heavy breaths.

I felt the cold swipe of an antiseptic being applied, then heard a loud snap of the gurney as it tilted so that I lay with my hips higher than my head.

"This is to facilitate the deposit in the cervix to enter the uterus. Stay like this for ten minutes. I'll come back in to check on you then."

His chair scraped the floor as he got up, and I listened to water running in the sink and the squeak of rubber soles leaving before I spoke to Sam.

Mark my words. I will destroy you if it's the last thing I ever do, even if I have to die trying.

Sam wiped the sweat off my forehead with a flourish and laughed. "You'll have to catch me first."

CHAPTER TWENTY-SEVEN

"Either you control your attitude,
or it controls you."

—Nate's Thoughts

Nate

Today marked a month since Riel visited Conner and me in the spirit realm. When I woke up this morning, I expected the first day of spring would bring me a renewed hope. Even better, I hoped the last few weeks had been a terrible nightmare. But that was childish thinking. With a sigh, I walked through the front door of Grand Haven High. The Jedi Order stood huddled together near the stairwell and wished me good morning on my way to class. I didn't return their sentiments. They still tried to include me in their weekend plans, but I always declined, feeling unworthy of their kindness. Their best friend was wasting away inside her own body, but Conner and I couldn't tell them about any of it. Everything inside me went cold and tight at the thought. There were days I didn't know whether I hated myself or Conner more. *I can't get into the Underworld no matter how hard I try... Why is everything so easy for him?*

I couldn't hide my hatred from Conner, either. Every time he tried to help, I lashed out, leaving me with no one to talk to about the situation. Hopelessness overwhelmed me. Trying anything else seemed futile. I knew nothing, had no new ideas, and remained painfully aware Olga would be lost for good if I couldn't break through to the other side. I spent every evening in pure silence, meditating to the point of being light-headed. Out of despair, I called Lindsey last night, just wanting to hear the voice of someone who actually liked me. Twisting the cord bracelet she gave me when I visited my hometown last month, I thought of the words she said when handing me the gift.

"So you'll never forget me. I know I'll never forget you. You never forget your first love."

The thing is, Lindsey was special, one of the most beautiful and sweetest girls I knew. But she wasn't my first love. I had thought I knew what love was… until I met Olga. And that's why I wore the bracelet, as a reminder of what I was fighting for. I had to get my girl back.

When I walked into my first period English class, I wished I could transform into the light feather I dreamed about during meditation because Mrs. Lory, who was also the drama teacher, announced we'd be moving to the auditorium to watch the dress rehearsal for the spring musical this morning, so the drama students could have an actual audience for their last practice.

But somewhere in the middle of watching *Joseph and the Amazing Technicolor Dream Coat* I had an epiphany. Here was Joseph, who went from being a slave to a king overnight. He went through hell, but in the end, being sold into slavery at the hand of his brothers was worth it because the experience led him to the place God had for him. That's why Joseph wasn't mad when he saw his brothers years later. Joseph told them what they meant for evil, God meant for good. I finally understood those words. This whole time, I'd been coveting what someone else had, just like Joseph's brothers did with the coat. They weren't really jealous of the coat, but of how their father treated Joseph, like he was the favorite son. The relationship Conner had with Olga is what I coveted. I thought back to the phone conversation I had with her a few nights before Sam took over. She told me about Father Jamie's message during the midweek Mass. He had said you could never drag anger or bitterness to the place God has for you. I needed to release that crap I'd been holding on to about Conner and not just seek the place I was trying to get to but seek God.

"I'm sorry." I raised my voice to be heard over the loud blasts and gunfire belching out from the zombie game Conner attacked like the undead really were trying to take over the world.

"What for?"

I leaned against the video game. Around us, neon lights flashed, and the sounds of pins being knocked over sounded from the bowling lanes behind us. I'd asked him to come hang out with me in the arcade of Starlite Lanes after school today, hoping I could at least beat him at a video game while I apologized. But Conner was in the zone. Should've made me mad again. The truth was, though, as I watched him, the way he tackled each zombie coming through the doorway with his fake shotgun, I not only didn't feel angry anymore, I felt bad for the guy. The way Conner leaned in too close to the screen, blue light bathing his untamed face, made me think of all those times when he was being possessed by a demon, trapped inside like a zombie. Must've sucked.

"For..." I didn't know how to put my feelings into words. Talking about serious stuff was way easier with girls. Definitely easier to pretend I wasn't jealous of him. "For hating you. I've been feeling so depressed over losing Olga, then jealous that you got into Juvie so easily, envious she only wants to spend time with you, even if she isn't herself. Every time I see you two together at school, I'm reminded of the history between you. I miss her so much, and I don't even know if she'd be with me anyway, since you're back. Everything just makes it so hard not to hate you, to wish you were gone like before. And I know that's wrong, and I think it may be why I'm blocked from getting into Limbo. So I asked you here today to ask for your forgiveness."

Conner groaned. "Man, I feel like crap for making you feel like crap, even if I didn't like you before. Of course I forgive you. I'm the one who should be asking for your forgiveness for everything that's happened since last summer."

Laughter escaped from my lips in a snort.

"What?"

I shook my head. "It's just... you said, even if I didn't like you before, like you've changed your mind. Are we... friends?"

He stepped away from the zombie game. "Yep. And let's agree to keep our bromance simple. No more crazy complications like love triangles and demon possessions."

"Sounds good to me, as long as you let me have Olga." I realized too late how my words might make me sound like a douche instead of the lightness I aimed for. That's why I almost had a heart attack when Conner pulled me in for a hug instead of flipping me off.

"If that's what she wants when all of this is over, I promise I won't stand in your way."

When I returned home from the bowling alley, I wasn't in a rush to meditate like usual. Instead, I ate dinner with my parents for the first time in a month. Then I dusted off my Bible and read through the story of Joseph and spent time praying. For once, I wasn't anxious. I knew I'd get to Limbo tonight.

After a few minutes of meditation, I felt the shift in the air, a dull coldness. Wincing, I formed my eyes into slits. Just like when Riel visited, I remained in my room, everything clothed in shadows. Immediately, I called upon angel help like Conner had. The same rainbow-colored being came to me. I had to admit, I was a little disappointed there weren't any unicorns to take me to my destination. The angel did not speak, only stared down at me on the floor. After I explained why I needed his help, there was suffocating darkness for a moment before a blinding light came, like a rapid sunrise. Heart pounding, I opened my eyes. I sat in a metal chair in an unfamiliar room with gray carpet, white plaster walls, and extreme fluorescent lights.

I looked around for someone to talk to, but the room remained empty. There were no windows, only one door with a number eight on it. Sweeping my hand through my hair, I called out a hello, but nobody answered. For a moment, I freaked out. I had no idea what Limbo was, how long I'd once lived here, what to do now. My and Olga's files said Dr. Judy on it… Would I find her here somewhere?

Guess there's only one way to find out.

Swallowing back my fear, I took a deep breath, slowly made my way to the door, then opened it. I padded down a wildly long, vaulted-ceilinged hallway lined with numbered doors until something slapped me on the back. I jerked forward.

"Took you long enough."

After catching my balance, I turned around. "Riel? What are you doing here?"

"I live here."

I sucked in a surprised breath. "Why didn't you just take me to Limbo when you left the first time?"

He ruffled my hair and laughed. "You had to let go of some things you were holding on to first."

I stood there, looking at him for a few minutes.

"Disappointed? Were you expecting someone else?"

I shook my head, then nodded. "Dr. Judy's name was on my file."

Riel shrugged. "She did counsel you during your Limbo timeline, but I'm the one who orchestrated your experience. And when your time was up, you came here to my headquarters to help others in the Limbo plane. Come on."

He nodded toward the door at the end of the hallway, and I followed behind him. "Do you often bring people to your headquarters to live when their… time is up?"

Waving a dismissive hand, he admitted, "Not usually."

Of course, no real answers out of him still.

"Ah, here we are." He opened the door to sunshine, green grass, flowers everywhere, and a fresh breeze. "Welcome to my home. I do believe you may find what you're looking for over that way."

Before I could follow the direction of his finger, he caught me up by the waist in one swift motion and took to the sky, his wings spread wide.

"What are you doing?" I yelled.

"Oh, come on, pretty boy. Don't tell me you're afraid of heights?"

For the first time in forever, I might've laughed. "Yeah, right. You just caught me by surprise. This is kind of… weird."

"I'm sure you meant to say totally awesome or whatever the kids are saying these days." He nodded down below to illustrate.

Surveying the scene beneath me, I saw brick courtyards with fountains, plants of all descriptions tumbling in green profusion, a veranda shaded with movable awnings, picnic tables, hammocks, wicker rocking chairs, plastic lounges, poplar trees like the ones I had planted for Mom in our yard, trees bearing apples and lemons and oranges and avocados, tomato and pepper plants, chrysanthemums and tulips and geraniums, ferns, rose arbors, pine trees, cinder paths shaded by tall oaks circling the entire property. It was paradise.

"Yep, totally awesome."

"Exactly, pretty boy."

"Is this where the Garden of Eden was?"

Riel sighed. "I wish. You can't even imagine that kind of beauty. But unfortunately, you humans have a way of screwing everything up. I do admire your green thumb, though. Not typical for a boy your age."

"How do you know I like to garden?"

He dumped me unceremoniously onto a dock. "Are you seriously going to question my vast amount of knowledge after everything that's happened?"

"Sorry," I said, standing up and dusting myself off. "Us humans are a little slow." I winked at him.

"Don't wink. People will think you're up to no good." He gestured to the lake and surrounding beach with his hands. "You had a special... moment here. I'll give you some time to walk around and find something to mark your territory." Pushing his robe to the side with a flourish, he sat on the dock and dipped his feet into the pond as his wings folded in on his back.

Sunlight sparkled against the water as I shuffled to the small patch of sand to the left of the dock, warmth radiating up through my feet. People... or angels... were busy splashing and dunking each other in the lake, filling the air with shrieks. I crossed my arms over my chest, thinking how unreal all of this was. Instead of stressing over my lost sense of time, I filled myself with the smell of the fresh air and the peacefulness of this place. It was the closest I'd ever been to Zen. Already shoeless, I shuffled into the water. A net of slimy weeds snagged at my legs as the waves gently slapped against the shore, spraying my cargo shorts. Studying the bottom of the lake, I bent down and picked up a few white rocks near my feet. My heartbeat sped up. I watched as one pebble I threw skipped over the surface once, twice, three times before blurting out, "Found it!"

Riel flew to where I stood and stared at my hand clutching the pebbles. "A rock?"

I cleared my throat. "Is that an acceptable item to mark my territory?" Crossing my fingers, I prayed he said yes. I was so tired of screwing up. Apparently, I said those last words aloud without realizing it.

Riel grinned. "Resist the temptation of being troubled. Make yourself vulnerable. Only then do you become strong. Just look how easy everything was today."

Shaking my head, I told him, "You know that goes against every worldly wisdom out there, right?"

"Trust me. I haven't let you down so far, have I?"

His eyes glittered with the mischief of knowing things I didn't, but before I could answer, he called for the angel to take me home.

CHAPTER TWENTY-EIGHT

"After all, what's a life, anyway?
We're born, we live a little while, we die."

—E.B. White, *Charlotte's Web*

Olga

I couldn't remember when I'd felt so tired. All I wanted to do was sleep, which would be understandable. It was my only way of escaping everything happening to me. But my breasts were swollen, and I craved vegetables. *Vegetables!* I never craved healthy foods before. The procedure that sleazy doctor performed on me exactly thirty days ago was stuck on repeat in my head, in Sam's too. So after school today, he asked Nic to stop at the Meijer's store on the way home.

She nudged my side with her elbow. "Sure. You need something for your hot date with Conner tonight?"

At lunch today, he'd asked me to a romantic picnic in Duncan Woods at midnight. If I were me, I would've told him he was being creepy as hell. But I wasn't me, and the thought of sneaking out and meeting Conner there excited Sam, so he accepted the weird invite.

"Yeah."

He turned to look at her. A piece of her black hair flew in the slight breeze coming in from the cracked windows in her car. I felt Sam's desire to kiss her, and I fought it with all my might, knowing I couldn't make him do anything. Especially now. I was so darn tired.

Sam chuckled on the inside as Nicole pulled into a parking spot up front meant for expectant mothers. My pulse sped up, wondering if Nic had somehow already discovered my deepest, darkest secret.

"You'll be quick, right? This special parking is so dumb anyway." She brought out her "now hear this," pissed-off voice. "Let's push feminism back a hundred years and declare you can't walk when you're preggo! We are so not using these spaces when we actually do get pregnant, a very long time from now, of course. We're better than those losers who get knocked up during high school."

Sam let a snort escape my lips. "I know, right? I'll be right back. You need anything?"

His seductive gaze moved down the length of her legs, clothed in black fishnet stockings today.

Nic cleared her throat, seeming to notice. "Um, I'm good."

"Yeah, you are."

Her eyes bulged. "Are you okay?"

Laughing, Sam got out and headed straight to the feminine hygiene department. He glanced around to make sure nobody was looking and shoved an early pregnancy test in my purse.

"Don't want any of the outstanding citizens of our small town blabbing about their high school valedictorian getting knocked up," he mumbled under his breath to me.

"Olga?"

Sam jumped. "Conner? What are you doing here?"

He gestured to the shopping cart that contained four candles. "Just gathering some things for our date tonight. How about you?"

Acting as if nothing was unusual, Sam turned and grabbed the largest box of condoms on the nearby shelf. "Same."

Conner's eyes went wide, and it took a minute before he could speak again. "Oh."

"Yeah." Sam slipped an arm around Conner's back, then dropped the box into his cart. "I'll let you take care of these. See you soon." Sam kissed Conner's cheek, then patted him on the butt before leaving.

After Nic dropped us off, Sam went straight to the bathroom and locked the door. He pulled out the box. Opened it. Read the instructions. Took out the strip. Removed the cap. Tried to pee but couldn't. Sighing, he shoved everything back into my purse and walked to the kitchen.

"It's super annoying you don't have that frequent urination thing yet. What do you want to drink, darling?"

Coffee. It's a natural diuretic, after all.

Plodding to the kitchen, Sam pulled a bag of Starbucks Caramel from the canister and measured out two tablespoons of the ground coffee. A minute later, the stimulating rush of brewing drew me out, brushing off the stress of the moment. Unusually kind, Sam even coated my Harry Potter mug with caramel syrup before pouring in the coffee, then topped it off with whipped cream and more caramel drizzle.

"Cheers, love. We'll have something to celebrate with Conner tonight. And this way, if someone does discover the pregnancy, you'll have someone to blame."

I almost chuckled as I remembered the words on the coffee cup, "I solemnly swear that I am up to no good." For Conner's sixteenth birthday, he'd asked his parents to take me and him to the opening of the Wizarding World of Harry Potter at Universal Orlando. He gave me the cup as a way of announcing our summer trip. I knew he didn't even care about being there for opening day, but he knew I'd never have the money to go on my own. He always had my best interest at heart.

He won't let you seduce him.

"No, not me. But he'll let you. He's wanted nothing more than your hot little body ever since I've known him." He ran my finger around the rim of the mug, then took a sip of the sweet goodness, and I groaned. "Oh, you like what Daddy gives, don't you?"

He was on his third gulp when something felt off, sending him rushing back to the bathroom. After vomiting into the toilet, he smiled at me in the mirror as he wiped my mouth with a washcloth. "I don't think we need this little test to confirm things, but let's take it anyway, just for kicks."

After urinating, he laid the strip on the counter, then sat down on the edge of the bathtub, scrolling through my and Conner's old text messages on my phone while we waited the five minutes. It was the longest five minutes of my life, and given everything that happened this past year, that really said something. When time was finally up, Sam jumped up to look at the stick, which now had two stripes. Again, he looked at the directions, letting out a whoop at the confirmation two stripes meant positive.

Inside, I shrank smaller and smaller, suffocating, feeling like I was being sucked into an oblivion I could never return from. I couldn't think of any way to fight back. My prayers went unanswered these days. What would happen to my soul if Sam managed to hold on to my body for more than half a year? Would I be sent to heaven or hell? Maybe I was already damned for inviting him in on my own.

Twisting and turning, I tried to break free, but I felt so drained. Heaven, hell, or simply vanishing from the face of the planet would be better than this anyway.

CHAPTER TWENTY-NINE

*"Even when you think you have no more to give,
you will find the strength to help a friend."*

—Nate's Thoughts

Conner

Gulping the cold air, I tried to slow my breathing to listen for any strange sounds as I lit the fourth candle. Nate walked around the tiny square with catlike grace, and I thought again how I would've figured he was gay if I didn't know better.

Wishful thinking.

The air smelled of matches, olive oil, sage, frankincense, and myrrh. I pulled out my phone and used the flashlight app to examine the lay of the land, but Nate waved it away.

"We don't want to call any more attention to us being here than needed."

Surveying the area in darkness, I couldn't help but notice how the moss slowly swaying in the chilly breeze looked like dead bodies hanging from the skeletal tree branches. The clouds parted and revealed the full moon, but the added light did nothing to quell the anxiety churning in my stomach. A gush of wind blew hard, and I held on to my Nike toboggan so it wouldn't fly off my head. I thought my hat's slogan, *Just Do It*, was appropriate for tonight. But then the breeze carried the sound of howling that sent chills down my spine, and I wanted to sprint in my Nike shoes to get the heck out of here instead.

"Please tell me there are wolves in these woods," Nate whispered, checking his watch.

"Because you want to get mauled to death?"

He shrugged. "If you ask me, sounds better than what we're about to do."

Turning my face away from the bitter wind, I was about to respond with a comeback when I figured, *What's the point?* He was right, and he could probably hear how hard my heart pounded anyway, so playing cool wouldn't work this time.

A minute later, I tensed when I heard a loud thump. I turned my head just in time to see Nate's body crumple to the ground, Olga standing over him with the shovel I'd brought. For a moment, we stood looking at each other, and then she narrowed her eyes, now black instead of blue, to the square with the lit candles around me. There was little sound in the forest, only our breathing fogging in the air and the wind sliding through trees.

Olga jerked her head toward the square. "This is your idea of a romantic picnic? Bringing my ex to watch? I like it. Very voyeuristic of you."

I rolled up my shirtsleeves, knowing there was no use in pretending any longer. "You always did have a good vocabulary."

She smiled, a disarming grin edged with darkness. "Wait until you hear what I have to say next."

Using words I never heard before and didn't understand, she called out, sounding like a hissing snake.

I assumed this was the part where Sam called upon evil spirits to help, and my suspicions were confirmed a minute later. Behind Olga, larger shapes lumbered, and though I couldn't see them clearly, I knew they watched me. I reached out, my fingers trembling as I began to speak to Olga's spirit.

"Olga, I know you're in there. Please fight the darkness and come back to me."

She growled in response.

On the periphery of my vision, I saw more things rushing through the darkness from the cemetery. Things that were large, dark, and fast and seemed to weigh me down with their presence. My heart thumped painfully. A spike of adrenaline tightened in my chest as I vowed to protect Olga at all costs. My gaze darted to follow the odd forms, measuring them up to see what it'd take to defeat them. They walked with the lopsided grace of a hunchback and had too many limbs to be human. I gulped.

Olga paced back and forth in front of my square, her red hair still bright in the darkness.

I met her gaze, focusing on my love for her. "Olga, I'm here. Nate is here. We found a way to save you, but you have to kick the demon out yourself. We can't cast him out for you, since you invited him in. Fight, Olga. I know you can do this. Come home before it's too late."

The dark shapes in the distance moved closer, until they lined the entire perimeter of my small square. I didn't need to look down to know my whole body trembled as the dark figures murmured along with Sam, making my eardrums thunder. A figure, one of the peculiar ones with too many limbs, stepped to the line, threw his head back, and growled. His face, hallow and scathed, assured me the threat of danger was real. Clearly, he'd been in a few fights during his lifetime. But true to Riel's word, I remained protected; the demons seemed unable to cross the line.

Unsure of what to do next, I prayed aloud. Just simple words from my heart because it was all I had now that Nate remained out cold. He was supposed to be inside the square, helping me, and the truth that I stood alone in this hit me like a million pinpricks all over my body. Except the figure stepped back from the line and yelped, as if my words actually burned him. The other figures whipped their heads about, but no words spewed from their mouths anymore. And I knew the angels must be at work doing warfare, too, even though I couldn't see them. It was now or never.

"Olga, I love you. You haven't lost yet. You're not alone in this. I'm right here. Don't surrender. Please, Olga. Fight back. Focus on all the good things in your life, on my belief in you, even if you doubt yourself. Use the good to push out the evil."

Olga inhaled sharply, and then her body flung onto the ground as if shoved from within. For a moment, she lay so still I thought she was dead. When I was almost ready to leave the safety of my square and go to her, she turned her head toward mine, her eyes shimmering with blue even though the rest of her body remained still and cloaked in shadows.

"Conner," she said through a clenched jaw, as if speaking brought her great pain.

My heart filled with emotion at seeing my best friend lying face down on the cold ground, shivering as though she'd fallen into the freezing waters of Lake Michigan, fighting for her life because of me once more.

Her head lifted higher, and she inched her body closer to me before something within her chuckled, and her eyes turned black again. "You think you can save yourself? For what? A life of continued suffering. I can give you fame, success, wealth, and power beyond your wildest dreams. I can make you a *New York Times* bestseller, a Pulitzer prize winner, anything you desire and more."

I shook my head violently. "Olga, if there's one thing I've learned this past year, it is a person who lives only for himself destroys himself. He's pure evil, trying to lead you down the road of worldly prizes, and none of it will last, Olga. We know that now more than ever. I visited the Underworld while you've been away. I met angels. I saw how vast and wide this universe is. I know it's hard, but fight back. We only suffer here a little while, and then there's a whole other world God has waiting for us."

Olga gagged and coughed, fighting, but her eyes remained black as Sam spoke. "A lifespan of sixty to eighty more years is still a long time to suffer."

Her body jerked on the ground again, her eyes turning blue once more as she found the strength to stand. "Conner, I've never been more scared. I feel so tired and small. I don't know how much more I can take. And now I'm…"

I looked directly into her eyes and stretched my arms forward, willing all the love I had for her to be felt in the deepest part of her soul.

She placed a hand protectively over her stomach. "I'm afraid. Sam impregnated me with a demon. If I kick him out, my body won't be able to take the changes. I'm dead either way. Just save yourself before you or Nate gets killed."

Nate stirred at the mention of his name, but he didn't get up. I wondered if he could hear her confession.

"What?" The tightness in my throat barely let me get the word out.

"I'm pregnant," she whispered.

Her two little words weighed me down, and I couldn't think of what to say in response. Something flipped in my stomach, and I thought I'd puke. I wanted to reach across the olive oil line and choke Sam out of her, but that wasn't possible. My throat ached with contained sobs and screams, but I forced out a calm response. One of us had to think straight. "You've been through too much to die now. There has to be a reason we survived all these things. Why we died and came back. You must be significant. Your best days are ahead, the worst behind you. I just know it. Nate was telling me about the story of Joseph, how God can bring good out of the worst evils. Don't you owe it to yourself to see what all the fuss was about? I have faith God won't let you die after everything you've been through. We'll figure something out."

Olga's eyes burned, turning back to black once again. She bowed her head toward me. "I hate to tell you this, but the horrific human condition encountered by God in the Garden of Eden still exists and has multiplied. There are wars, drugs, crime, famine, homeless, families falling apart, the environment trashed. Don't you see your world is a place filled with trouble, suffering, loss, grief, anguish, death? I can erase your pain and suffering, Olga. You won't have to feel a thing, just sit back and enjoy the ride. This life isn't worth it. I alone can give you the life you deserve."

My shoulders tightened; my heartbeat slowed. Time ran out, but I could see all the demons around me standing still and silent and knew angels must still be working on our behalf. "You're right. Our world has suffering. But love eases that suffering. Olga, if you stay with Sam, if you don't find the strength to fight back, you'll lose that love. The Jedi Order, your parents, me... Nate, we all love you so much. We'd do anything for you. Let what you see around us be evidence to my words. I'd rather die than live without you, and I know you feel the same way about me or you wouldn't have allowed Sam in. That's a love worth fighting for. Whether we're ever together doesn't matter. You're my best friend. Come back to me."

Olga's body jerked back, fighting, but it was Sam who still spoke. "Why would you listen to someone who did nothing but hurt and ignore you for so long, Olga? You'll only be abandoned again and again in this life. It's the cycle of destruction that humans endure over and over. He has a temporary crush on you now, but he has a short attention span. He'll forget all about his precious life lessons and you as time goes on. Humans only want what they don't have."

No longer possessing the strength to stretch out my hands, my arms went limp against my side. A lack of balance caused me to weave in place. The presence of the demons must've affected me even though they couldn't cross the line. "He's right. I can't argue my track record. I can't change the past. But that's why God's promise to never leave us is so powerful." My voice sounded thick and toneless even to me, and I sucked in a wheezing breath, wondering if I could free Olga before I passed out. "We might get lost sometimes, but we can always be found again." The woods spun, and the desire to flee overwhelmed me, but my limbs felt too heavy to move anyway. "The real question you need to answer now, before it's too late, is are you willing to be found again?"

"To be found by who?" Sam snarled. "Look around, Olga? Where is this precious God? If he loved you, cared about you at all, then why did he not prevent this all from happening in the first place? You really think he will save you now, with a demon possessing you and another one growing inside you?"

Uncontrollable tears leaked from my burning eyes. I used to think real men shouldn't cry, but I couldn't care less about losing my masculinity right now. All I cared about was losing Olga, so I pressed on. "The existence of evil and its ugliness is a sign of God's love for us. It shows He trusts we will overcome evil and allows us free will to wrestle with our wretchedness so we can be strengthened when tested. He uses the prayers of people to direct the action of angels to help defeat demons like Sam. They are here, ready to help as soon as you say the words. Even the Jedi Order is at the church with Father Jamie right now, praying, because Nate and I asked them all to, even though we couldn't tell them why. That's how strong their devotion is. They're there for us unquestioningly."

My knees gave out, and I collapsed to the ground.

Sam laughed. "When did you become Mr. Spiritual?"

I couldn't help but laugh in return. "Being possessed by a demon will open your eyes to spiritual things real quick."

In that moment, Nate lunged for the inside of the square, inadvertently blowing out one of the candles, and the demons all around us stepped to the line, suddenly everywhere and snarling.

"Olga!" I shouted. "You need to cast him out before it's too late."

Nate leaned against me for support and began to pray with words much more eloquent than mine, and I immediately felt inadequate. I wished I had been knocked out instead of him. All of this would've probably been over by now.

"What should I do?" I shouted to him.

"Pray too," he yelled back before continuing his pleas to God and the angels.

I wanted to tell him I felt much more comfortable trying to physically kick some demon butt, but before I could open my mouth, the creatures around us started speaking in their own demonic tongue, their voices so loud I couldn't hear myself think. A big bang sounded, and a burst of energy came from the ground, sending both Nate and me flying. Miraculously, I landed on my feet like a cat, but Nate slammed into a tree before crashing to the ground on his left side.

I tried getting to him, but the air shifted. Suddenly, I felt like I was spinning on a merry-go-round. The ground vibrated, and the hair on my arms and the back of my neck lifted, a heightening awareness taking over like it did just before lightning struck me almost a year ago. We'd come full circle. I let out a raspy breath as superdark clouds, almost pitch black in color, raced across the overcast sky above me. Increased heat despite the winter defrosted my numb fingers and toes. The change in air pressure made my ears pop like I was on an airplane.

Debris scraped my skin, an unseen force stirring up the dirt and making the woods quiver. Trees broke in half in the shrieking wind, some ripped up by the roots, blocking my path to Nate, to Olga, to the protection of my square. Amazingly, only the one candle Nate had snuffed was out, the other three still blazing. The angels were still fighting then. As my toboggan blew off in the wind, I wondered distantly if all of

Grand Haven was under attack or just us. All of hell seemed to be fighting, and the vortex felt like it'd rip my hair right off my head, too, my long strands stinging my face.

I straightened to full height, and all six feet of me stared down the storm and the demons causing it. Supernatural strength I couldn't explain helped me rush against the wind and jump over fallen trees. Olga stood just outside the square, shivering in her puffy coat. She whipped her head toward me, her eyes wide and pleading but still the color of utter darkness.

"No one has more power in your life than you." I put my hand on her head. "We hold within ourselves the power of our destiny. Fight, Olga. Don't give up. We all have a little bit of Darth Vader and Anakin Skywalker in us. We just have to figure out who we're gonna listen to the most. Fear leads to the dark side. Fight back before it's too late."

The gray, misshapen demonic creatures pressed even closer, ogling me and muttering words I couldn't understand again. It felt like there was no air for my lungs, and I wondered if this was what Olga's asthma attacks were like.

She sucked in a deep breath that ended in a coughing fit. Her legs folded beneath her, and she collapsed to the ground, her face twisted, but her eyes were like a crystal sea of glass. "Get out of me now, Sam... I am a child of the Light... Leave me... and never come back again."

For a moment she seemed to be choking, and then black smoke burst from her mouth, filling the atmosphere with a thick haze. Using the memorized words Riel gave me, I called out to Synoro to come and open the portal, commanding him to throw Sam's spirit into the Underworld. A peal of thunder rumbled across the sky, and a beautiful ball of glowing light descended in a melodic breeze. The shining figure of a huge angel dressed in armor glistening like jasper hovered above us, sending great flashes of light toward the surrounding demons, scattering them back into the shadows while the black swirl of smoke drifted to the boulder, now cracked wide open.

Then there was a sudden calm. My heart beat faster as I pulled Olga into my arms and into the protection of the square. I smiled as her eyes fluttered open. "See, that's why you don't mess with a Jedi."

She shook violently in response but not from laughter. "De—" The words seemed to freeze in her throat, and she pointed to her abdomen.

I raised my eyebrows. "That... thing inside of you... It's hurting you?"

She sucked in a breath in response, and my heart thumped painfully from the knowledge I could still lose her.

Nate stepped into the square, holding his left arm. With his right hand, he slid a lighter out of his jean's pocket and lit the candle he'd blown out earlier. "She probably needs to cast the baby demon out of her, too, before you ask Synoro to close the portal."

A groan escaped Olga's lips. "My stomach... on... fire." Her eyes fluttered in pain.

I closed my hands around hers, clinging to her fading life. "Don't quit on me now, Olga." My chin and lips trembled, and I worried she didn't have any fight left in her. She looked like death warmed over. "What do we do?" I screamed at Nate.

For every second he thought, Olga grew worse, and a growl sounded from the inside of her stomach that I was one hundred percent sure wasn't from hunger.

Nate dropped to his knees and looked at Synoro floating in the air above our square. "Can you take it out of her? She didn't invite this one in."

The angel smiled. "I was waiting for you to ask."

Synoro sucked in a deep breath, drawing a long, thin stream of gray smoke from Olga's mouth.

My eyebrows raised, I looked at Nate and mouthed, *"Nice."*

"Olga," I whispered fiercely, my gaze on her closed eyes as the smoke continued to float steadily toward the angel's opened mouth. Sweat beaded her forehead, and I wiped the drops off with the sleeve of my jacket. My heart beat harder with every second her eyes didn't open. Suddenly, the air exploded with a bolt of electricity, and a golden light as bright as the sun slammed into her chest.

Finally, she whispered back. "Conner."

With relief, I sagged against her. The rush of joy pulsed through my blood and made me feel unsteady, like I was drunk. Noticing a pink blush spreading across her pale face, tears flowed freely, the blow of everything we'd been through reverberating throughout my weak body.

"Conner," she whispered again.

I pressed my palm over her heart, so thankful for its steady rhythm. "You're okay, Olga. I'm right here."

"I know. I can feel you crushing my hand."

I looked down and noticed I'd turned her fingers purple from clenching them so hard. "My bad."

She smiled, then swung her gaze over my shoulder to Nate. "Thank you."

Nate nodded. "Any time."

Then he collapsed, landing directly on his bad arm and blacking out again.

"No!" Olga screamed. She tried getting up but immediately fell down, much too weak. "Conner, help him!"

Crap. "Hang on!" Shock wound through my veins as I wondered what else could go wrong. I commanded Synoro to cast the baby demon he now held in his mouth into the Underworld and close the portal.

With a nod, he did so in a matter of seconds and disappeared. The only sign any supernatural beings were ever in the woods tonight was a path of destruction leading straight to the cemetery. That must've been where all the wind came from. Had Sam awoken the dead to fight for him?

"Conner!" Olga's eyes churned with worry. "Nate! Hurry!"

"Right! It's just that I have unfinished business here. I have to dig a three-foot hole and—"

"Come back and do that! Nate could be dying!" She heaved with sobs.

As I slung Nate over one shoulder and Olga over the other, my breath was visible in the freezing air, and I was glad Sam had kept up my workout regimen when he possessed me. Usually, the layout of the woods and cemetery was really hilly, with lots of turns and dark corners, easy to get lost in. But now I had one trail to follow straight to the road, thanks to Sam, and the clouds from earlier had vanished, the full moon lighting my way.

After placing Olga in the front seat of my hybrid, I slid Nate into the backseat. On our way to the hospital, I couldn't help but think of how Olga had tried to save me for so long and how I never could've saved her if it weren't for Nate. Guess it was about time we returned the favor for him. Because one thing this whole experience taught me was you reap what you sow.

PART THREE

"For I know the thoughts that I think toward you,
says the Lord,
thoughts of peace and not of evil,
to give you a future and a hope."

—Jeremiah 29:11

CHAPTER THIRTY

"Our circumstances may influence who we are,
but we are responsible for who we become."

—Nate's Thoughts

Olga

A fter submitting my idea to the Guinness Book of World
Records people a month ago, they approved our "cup
song" attempt for graduation. I'd gotten the idea at prom
when everyone rushed off the dance floor back to their
tables, causing a little impromptu song magic to fill the room as
everyone chugged their drinks and flipped over their plastic cups. I'd
clapped, tapped, and flipped my red Solo cup on the table with the rest
of the Jedi Order, an idea instantly forming in my mind. The last four
weeks included a mountain of paperwork and evidence to collect for
certification on my part, but I was up to the challenge. The student
body had been practicing everyday at lunch, pumped to set a world
record and leave our mark at Grand Haven High School before we left.
On Monday, the school even showed *Pitch Perfect* the last two hours
after the day's finals were all finished. As we watched, I kept thinking
back to the story Nate told me about Riel's guest lecturing in his
English class, about high school being a distant memory and how his
relayed speech inspired me to leave a legacy behind. At the time, I had

no idea how, but doing something as big as breaking a world record seemed like the perfect fit. I wanted to be like Alice, to believe in six impossible things before breakfast. Go big or go home, as Conner often told me.

"You excited?" Nate asked as I joined our group of friends in the school's field house.

"More like nervous." I undid the top button of my silky white sheath dress underneath my burgundy graduation gown and smoothed my dress over my flat stomach, thankful I didn't have a demon hybrid growing there anymore. To my surprise, tears sprang to my eyes. I knew I hadn't really lost a "baby," but I felt sad at the memory of the experience, and suddenly I had to grip onto Nate for support.

"Hey, you okay?" Nate asked.

"Um, no. I'm freaking out. I just hope all goes as planned." I patted my dress, making sure my cup was still hidden in one of the handy pockets.

"Well, you look beautiful." He squeezed my shoulders. "You can picture me naked as you're making your valedictorian speech if that helps."

I combed my curls with my fingers. "You're making me sweat more, actually."

"Just think about all the fun stuff you have to look forward to before you leave for Harvard in a month. Tomorrow the Jedi Order is going to Michigan's Adventure, where you'll get to ride your first roller coaster. Then we're all camping at Grand Haven State Park Saturday and Sunday, having the annual Memorial Day barbeque on Monday."

I moaned. "Stop. Now you're gonna make me cry."

It'd been almost two months since Conner had dropped Nate and me off at the hospital before returning to the woods to "mark his territory," which he had explained to me later. Trying to come up with a cover story for our parents as to why we were all out that night was difficult, and I thought they'd try to ground me for a couple of weeks. But then the next day, I'd gotten a letter in the mail saying I was on Harvard's waiting list. It didn't mean acceptance, but they did invite me to participate in a phone interview, which was a good sign. I think my parents were so shocked I'd applied, then too proud to even think about a punishment. Plus, they suspected demons had been at work after Father Jamie mentioned the Jedi Order coming to the church that same day after school and asking him to pray with them. If only I could explain, but Riel had made it clear to Conner and Nate that we should keep the details between us.

The weird thing was, after the angel took Sam out of me that night, I regained more memories of my time in the Underworld. Some of them were faint, but one of them was very clear. I'd met Bo once, the guy Nate had his accident with, who also happened to be Conner's roommate in Juvie. Being able to give Nate closure, to tell him with absolute certainty that Bo forgave him and didn't blame him at all for the car crash, was the best thing about being touched by an angel.

But nothing compared to earlier today, when I received my actual acceptance letter to Harvard when I checked my e-mail on my phone at Jumpin' Java. Conner had picked me up for lunch, and when I saw the letter, I practically choked on my chicken salad sandwich. Harvard hardly accepted anyone off their waiting list. Harvard hardly accepted anyone, period. But when I did my phone interview last week, the alumni conducting it said I nailed all my questions before we hung up, and she seemed really impressed by the world record attempt I was organizing, and she went on and on about how wonderfully written my essay was. The essay topic I chose was to describe a person who's had an influence on me. I picked Conner, so it was fitting he was there with me when I received my letter.

Good thing I had coffee to wash down my surprise, too. Coffee literally saves lives. Conner was so excited when I showed him my screen in explanation he stood on the table and announced the news to everyone in the packed coffee house. As all the customers and baristas clapped, I shook my head in disbelief, my cheeks flushed red with embarrassment. Then Conner grabbed a To Go box and rushed me out of the restaurant, straight to the marina, so I could tell my parents in person. We cried and hugged for a good twenty minutes. Even now, hours later, I got a little teary-eyed thinking about it, and I probably would for the rest of my life.

The only drawback to my acceptance was it hinged on me attending their summer session, so instead of spending time in Grand Haven with the Jedi Order as planned, I'd be in Cambridge from June twenty-third until August ninth.

"Crying?" Conner said, coming up behind us and putting an arm around my shoulder. "Why are you crying?"

"I don't know. This is all ending." I gestured to our classmates as the teachers tried to organize everyone into a line. It was like watching someone trying to herd cats.

"Nah. It's not the end, just the beginning of something new."

"Exactly," Tammy chimed in.

"Now, go take your place of honor." Nic shoved me forward, and I laughed at the thought of her bossiness keeping me in line since fourth grade.

The benefit of being valedictorian was sitting up front with the rest of the students speaking during the ceremony instead of all the way in the back, where my Worontzoff last name would have condemned me to. Commencement was held outside at Buccaneer Stadium. With a smile, I watched everyone file onto our school football field, screaming and laughing. Some I wished I'd gotten to know better, but I was thankful for the close group of friends keeping me sane all these years. Since Conner's last name was Anderson, he sat directly behind me, Nate Barca just a few seats down from him. Conner reached for my hand. The gesture felt comfortable, familiar, a show of solidarity between the oldest of friends. We'd been together since kindergarten. That fact blew my mind.

We'd endured thirteen grueling years of school together. Could any experience bind two people together more closely than that? Maybe marriage. I wondered if I would marry Conner or Nate one day. I couldn't imagine ever being closer to anyone else besides them. The possibility seemed light-years away, though. Maybe one day Nate and I would be ready for each other again. Maybe I'd end up marrying some random stranger I met at a coffee house instead. Maybe I'd finally get together with Conner ten years down the road. Or maybe, just maybe, I'd stay happy and single my whole life. Because I finally realized having love in your life didn't mean having a guy. The point was the future waited with arms wide open, and I had options. But I didn't want to think about the future too much. I wanted to stay in the present, and right now I thought it was proper to be with Conner. From our first formative years of finger painting and recess, to learning about the three Rs, then being introduced to foreign topics such as biology and sex education in middle school, to physics and calculus in high school, we'd stuck together. Perhaps that was a greater accomplishment than landing at the top of the academic race.

The wind grabbed at my hair, swirling all the happy and sad feelings about graduating into the air around me. But the sun warmed my face, the scoreboard displaying a temperature of sixty-eight degrees, reminding me the brightest days were still ahead.

All the pomp and circumstance seemed to drag on as sweat skated down my back and sides. I sat ramrod straight in my seat when Conner finally stepped on the stage to sing the national anthem, twisting the Morticia Addams ring on my left hand. But as he belted out the lyrics, the words washed over me, reminding me the only light we have to see by is the dawn's, the future. I couldn't remember a day when the past, present, and future felt so fused together. Most people couldn't see time for what it really was, couldn't perceive forever. All the pain of the past year had taught me that we were in fact infinite. There was a profound peace in that thought, beyond the noise of the stadium. My breath caught at the beauty of Conner's concluding words. *The land of the free and the home of the brave.*

I'd been set free this year, and now it was time to be brave. My gaze stayed on my red-painted toes peeking out from my two-inch-high heels, a far cry from the stilettos I wore at prom last month when I went with the Jedi Order, and I prayed I wouldn't trip while climbing the stairs to the stage for my speech.

I cleared my throat once I made it. "One of the hardest things to do is to hold on to faith during times of transitions. Transitions are difficult because you're letting go of everything you've held on to. It's a great feeling of vulnerability. Worry happens. But I'm here to tell you to resist the urge to worry." I looked at Nate and smiled. "That cliché our parents and teachers have told us all these years is true: everything does happen for a reason, and everything will be all right. Now's the time to dream big, to follow your heart, to live on the edge, to love with passion. Do hard things. Start a bucket list. None of us is promised tomorrow, and when it's my time to go, I want to drop dead of exhaustion. So write a novel. Watch the top one hundred movies. Read the top one hundred books. Visit the top one hundred places. And while you're at it, why not break a world record?"

The crowd erupted with thunderous applause and wild cheering as they took a knee on the grass and placed the red cup they'd been hiding under their gown on the metal chair they'd sat on a moment ago. Conner stepped back up to the microphone to sing the lyrics we'd written together for the cup song parody. The original music from "When I'm Gone" by Lulu and the Lampshades started blaring over the loudspeakers as everyone "played" their cups.

"We've got our admission to colleges/Minifridge and microwaves/And we sure would like a sweet fake I.D./To enter the beer pong tournament on Fridays/When we're there/When we're there/We're gonna love it when we're there/We're gonna love all the exploration/And all the fun flirtation/We're gonna love it when we're there.

We've got our admission to colleges/And started making our bucket lists/We've got protests/Football rivals/We've stockpiled coffee for survival/So we can be sure to pass all of our tests/Now we're done/Now we're done/We'll miss each other now that we're done/We're gonna miss our basement parties/And the lunch food that clogs arteries/Yeah, we'll miss each other now that we're done.

We've got our admission to colleges/Got to learn our alma matter songs/And we'll go to Florida for spring break/But nothing will top our senior pranks/Our legacy here will be bigger than King Kong/Now we're done/Now we're done/We'll miss each other now that we're done/We're gonna miss dancing at prom/And recalling memories like we were in Nom/Yeah, we'll miss each other now that we're done.

When we're there/When we're there/We're gonna love it when we're there/We're gonna pack our beaded curtain/And a lava lamp is certain/We're gonna love it when we're there."

He stepped away from the podium to the roar and screams of our classmates all rising from their seats, fists pumping the air. A huge grin split down Conner's face, and he wrapped his arms around me, swinging me in the biggest of hugs. The excitement crackling throughout the stadium hummed inside my chest as everyone bumped and shoved and cheered. In that moment, lightning strikes, angels and demons, freaky mind connections, visions, and traveling to other realms seemed like a distant memory. Spotting Nate in front of the stage, we both threw our graduation caps into the air, and for one infinite moment, I breathed in the exhilaration of a life lived on the edge and felt the freedom of letting go.

CHAPTER THIRTY-ONE

"It takes a long time to become the person we are meant to be."

—Nate's Thoughts

Olga

Summer stayed late this year. On the last Friday of August, the digital sign along Harbor Drive flashed a time of 7:40 a.m. and a temperature of seventy-seven degrees Fahrenheit. Few clouds streaked the perfect blue sky, a lofty mirror of the lake below. Rays from the sun reached into my soul and made me pause to enjoy the moment for the first time in weeks. The water had a way of lightening my mood, probably because it brought back so many fond childhood memories. I smiled and took a deep breath of the hot air, glad to have such beauty accompany me for my week home. Conner and I were heading out from the marina for our first sail together since his accident, and we'd invited the entire Jedi Order along. It helped to have a big enough boat to hold us all now. The manager for the Cantankerous Monkey Squad had rented a seventy-footer cruising sailboat for us this weekend.

While I'd been away at Harvard these past two months, Sean, Kyle, and Conner had been living out their dream as rock stars. Right after high school graduation, the guys hired a manager who organized a small tour for them. They played gigs all around Michigan, gaining momentum, recording in a studio. Cantankerous Monkey Squad, their debut self-titled album, quickly climbed the indie charts. It was so strange to hear them being played on the college station at Harvard, everyone's summer soundtrack. Just this week, they signed with a major record label and would head straight to the studio to record their second album very soon. When their manager asked them how they wanted to celebrate, the boys decided they wanted to come home and get together with the Jedi Order one last time before their lives got out-of-control crazy.

I couldn't be more proud of them, but I'd also had an unexpected summer. My college roommate was involved with a group called "To Write Love On Her Arms." The nonprofit helps people struggling with depression. I thought having an organization like that on campus would be the perfect way to use what I'd gone through to help someone else, so I created an outreach program called Jeremiah's Place my first week of school. Obviously, I thought healing and coffee went hand in hand, so I approached local businesses for donations and opened up a café in a room at the Harvard Student Union every Friday night where students could come and engage socially in a relaxed coffeehouse atmosphere. The Cantankerous Monkey Squad flew in to play at my grand opening, drawing a large gathering. Tables in the back held games like Monopoly, Trivial Pursuit, Scrabble, Chess, and Checkers for the quieter crowd. And there was an area of couches to the side of the room occupied by the campus ministry volunteers where people could get counseling and prayer. I named it Jeremiah's Place after my favorite verse in the Bible, Jeremiah 29:11: "For I know the thoughts that I think toward you, says the Lord, thoughts of peace and not of evil, to give you a future and a hope."

The whole thing was a huge success, and local bands called *me* after our debut event to volunteer free concerts. Already I was working with Harvard campus ministries and their alumni, local businesses, and churches to raise money for a building where we could house a permanent café, counseling center, and a book shop, too.

Starting the chapter on campus inspired me to write an article based on my interactions with the people I met titled "Everybody Has a Story to Tell" that ended up published in the literary magazine, *The Harvard Advocate*. *The Huffington Post* republished the feature on their news blog, and the *Cambridge News* liked my piece so much they offered me a weekly online column under the same title. I even got to intern at the paper all summer, which meant I didn't come back home except for this one week.

But the thing about the Jedi Order was, whenever we hung out, it felt like no time had passed between us, like nothing had changed. We lost ourselves to lingering, daydreaming, talking, playing, eating, laughing, and just *being* over the hours, forming a tight circle on the top deck of the boat.

"It's so weird we're all off to lead our separate lives in just three short days," Nic said, stretching her arms behind her head.

She was starting school at Muskegon Community College to obtain her Associates degree in Business so she could take over the Bookman from her parents one day. Her and Sean had broken up a week after graduation. All the time spent with the band proved too hard for their relationship, but so far they'd remained completely friendly. Plus, she was already crazy for some new guy. He was in the Coast Guard, and they'd met at the annual Grand Haven Coast Guard Festival about a month ago.

"Half of our group already has," Tammy said. "I mean, I counted on Olga to make me feel like a slacker, but not these three knuckleheads."

Tammy had gotten a cheerleading scholarship to attend Grand Valley State in nearby Allendale. She planned to keep up her modeling to pay for other expenses, which didn't include alcohol anymore. It had been three months since she had her last drink, and even better, her dad agreed to attend counseling with her.

"Aww, you can come be my groupie anytime," Kyle told her, winking.

She stuck her tongue out at him and threw a pillow at his head in response.

"See, that's what I'm talking about." Sean laughed. "No matter how big we get, we'll be able to count on ya'll to keep us real."

"And I think, no matter how successful everyone gets, we should promise to meet back in Grand Haven once a year," Adam suggested.

He would be rooming with Nate at Central Michigan University. On a whim, they had decided to backpack around Europe the past eight weeks, staying at youth hostels. I was glad Nate didn't sit around sulking after I left for Harvard. He had gotten a second chance at life, too, and he wasn't wasting it. And he didn't seem mad at me in the slightest for choosing the single life for now. He even brought back a souvenir from his trip, a ring he purchased at the Cambridge Shakespeare Festival where he saw *Hamlet* with Adam. The silver ring held an inscription: "To thine own self be true." He gave the gift to me tonight, and I knew I'd wear it all the time, along with Conner's Morticia Addams ring, reminders of how much love God had blessed me with.

"I'll drink to that." Nate lifted up his glass, and we all toasted with our White Sparkling Grape Juice. Much to my delight, everyone abstained from alcohol in support of Tammy's lifestyle change.

Pulling in a deep, cleansing breath, I took turns fixing my eyes on the Jedi Order. No matter where I went, they'd always be with me… in the whisper of the leaves in the fall, in the bold taste of a fresh cup of coffee, in the feel of the sand beneath my feet, in the clean smell of the rain as it lulled me to sleep. They lived inside everything I did. They were the place where I came from, my home. Nothing on Earth could ever separate us… not distance, not time, not even death. With every passing hour, I thought there couldn't be a more perfect ending to this day, for it'd been the ending to so many days of my life. I was heading into the sunset with my best friends by my side.

We watched as the sun descended behind the horizon, the spectrum of the sky changing to orange, pink, and red hues. Clouds appeared lit on fire with vibrant colors, mixing green, blue, and purple on the reflective water. Birds probably chirped overhead, boats probably whizzed by, but I heard none of it. In the fading daylight, I had my best friends to keep me company, and their presence warmed me better than the sun.

"You okay?" Conner whispered in my ear.

"Perfect."

Being gone from everyone while I went to Harvard proved difficult, but it was also easier in a way, to distance myself from all the weirdness that had happened the past year. The memory of Sam possessing me and impregnating me with his demon spawn was almost too much to bear at times. Not to mention fiercely missing Nate, even though I thought we did the right thing by not getting back together right now. That's why keeping busy was so helpful. I'd even started writing a novel. The young adult book was about a girl who ventured into various realms of the Underworld, looking for the best friend she had lost. Purely fantasy, of course, but I hoped to finish it and submit the manuscript to literary agents by the end of the year.

I'd told Nate about my story on the phone this past week. He'd called as soon as him and Adam returned from their trip. I felt a little nervous telling Nate about the novel, but of course he was one hundred percent supportive and said he wanted to be the first to read it. Tonight though, we shared no private conversations, maybe because we didn't trust ourselves to be alone together. But we did share many looks, which all seemed to say, *We're trusting what's meant to be will be in the end.*

Conner took my hand in his and pressed our palms together, spinning my Morticia Addams ring with his other hand. "I'm so, so sorry for everything, Olga."

Sometimes it was as if *he* could read my mind, although that trick of Nate's ended the day after graduation, the year anniversary of the day we met. "For the gazillionth time, stop apologizing. I forgave you a long time ago."

"I know, but I just think, for some things, you can never say you're sorry too much. This is one of them."

"You were being possessed by a *demon!*"

He shrugged. "So I could just do whatever I wanted and blame it all on Sam? How very Crucible of me."

His words didn't hold pride anymore. The experience had irrevocably humbled him, and me. In some weird way, I was almost thankful for all that had happened. We were almost too spoiled, too naïve, before our senior year.

I smiled. "Nice literary reference, rock star. Look, some things change you, for better or worse, and you're never the same again. But one thing that will never change is you're my best friend, always have been, and—"

"Always will be, as long as you'll let me."

In that moment, my mind flashed to moments of our lives together— playing volleyball on the beach, riding bikes downtown, bonfires in his backyard, watching the fireworks show from the roof of his car during the Coast Guard Festival, going sailing and holding his body tight, terrified I'd never get to hold him again. There was way too much history between us to ever be truly apart. Even this summer, while we both became crazy busy, we'd sent each other texts on a daily basis.

I cupped my other hand around his. "Forever, and then some."

A second later, the sun completely disappeared. I blinked, trying to decipher the hard line dividing water and sky and couldn't find it. I thought of the lessons we'd learned during high school, academically and socially, and how much more we'd learn in the next four years, how time and space were nothing more than wisps of smoke, an illusion. An eternity had already passed between us. Even though we'd each follow our own destinies from this point forward, we were together with the type of intricate connection that's infused into your soul. Our bond was everywhere: past, present, and future. Smiling, I stared up at the sky. And I could've sworn I saw the outline of a cloud shaped like an angel watching over us.

ABOUT THE AUTHOR

Jamie Ayres writes young adult paranormal love stories by night and teaches young adults as an English teacher by day.

When not at home on her laptop or at school, she can often be found at a local book store grabbing random children and reading to them. So far, she has not been arrested for this.

Although she spent her youthful summers around Lake Michigan, she now lives in Florida with her prince charming, two children (sometimes three based on how Mr. Ayres is acting), and a basset hound. She really does have grandmothers named Olga and Gay but unlike her heroine, she's thankfully not named after either one of them.

She loves lazy pajama days, the first page of a good book, stupid funny movies, and sharing stories with fantastic people like you. Her books include the three installments of her My So-Called Afterlife trilogy, *18 Things*, *18 Truths*, and *18 Thoughts*.

Visit her online via Twitter, Facebook, or at www.jamieayres.com.

Photo Credit: *Owl Sisters Photography*

ACKNOWLEDGMENTS

I'd like to give thanks to:

Jesus, for my salvation. Just typing that brings me to tears!! You begin our stories, set each one of us apart for a specific time and place. I thank you that you're a plotter, not a pantser like me. You give each of us our own pen. You allow us to write the stories of our own lives. How much easier would it be for you to script each scene? But you love us too much for that. Your ending was our new beginning, and I'm eternally grateful.

Five important people who gave their thoughts to this book in its early stages:

(1) Deana Barnhart, who reminded me I needed ONE main plot and goal to drive the story forward instead of a million (can we say squirrel syndrome?),

(2) J. Keller Ford, who helped bring more torture to my characters and a greater climax,

(3) my 14-year-old daughter, Kaylee Ayres, who gave me her unbiased, unapologetic, and rather gruff opinions, as well as helping me to write Nate's prologue (I still think we should've published this novel with your notes in the margins because they were just hilarious!),

(4) Mollie Melton Yonker, who posted a beautiful "I've Learned" poem on Facebook (even though she doesn't have any recollection of this, lol) that spawned the idea for the book title/cover & Nate's thoughts (I wish I could give credit to the original writer, but the author is unknown), and

(5) Krystal Wade, who provided her initial gut instinct of the first read, even though it made me cry... but in her editor's way of speaking from the heart, she made the final chapters to this trilogy so much better. The emotional breakdown of this book turned out to be a blessing in disguise to provide the perfect ending, even if it wasn't the one I planned all along. Thank you, awesome ladies that you are, for listening to my own convoluted thoughts and giving me your wise ones in return.

To Curiosity Quills Press, for giving me my first chance at publishing and supporting me along the way! Special shout out to Michelle Johnson for designing such awesome kick butt covers and to Nikki Tetreault for coming up with such innovative marketing ideas! And of course, the goats, who can forget the goats?!

To Amy Carver, Sarah Rutledge, Heidi Saidi, Lilly Carrasco, and Jessa Russo, for your unwavering allegiance. Few people have cheered me on with such genuine love and enthusiasm. You are the cream in my coffee.

To my besties, for our GNO evenings that provides a much needed escape from all the voices in my head.

To my pastors over the years, for showing me the light. God is not waiting with a lightning bolt every time I mess up (which is wonderful, since I screw things up quite a bit). Instead, he loves us unconditionally and never, ever gives up on us.

To my writerly support system, especially the Insecure Writer's Support Group and Writers Helping Writers, for offering savvy tidbits of wisdom. To everyone who attended UtopYA 2014, your inspiring talks helped me finish this third book. I'll never forget Sylvia Day's and Gennifer Albin's empowering advice. And to Janet Wallace, the founder of the UtopYA Con: I'm sorry your cup song attempt didn't work out, but I put it in this book as a tribute to your awesomeness! Thank you also to the librarians, teachers, book bloggers, fellow writers, and booksellers who have given priceless word-of-mouth advertising because they thought my stories were worth sharing. I am forever grateful.

To my mom, for teaching me to believe in God from an early age. And for always making sure I had enough books to read with Saturday trips to the public library. And to my dad, for spending the summers of my childhood in and around Grand Haven with me, inadvertently supplying the wonderful setting for this trilogy.

To my teachers, for your belief in me over the years that I. Am. A. Writer.

To my students, past and present, thank you for your excitement over Mrs. Ayres getting her books published! Books kept me sane during my adolescent years, and it's a humbling thought to hear you say the same about this trilogy and declare Olga your favorite female book heroine. And especially Adam Strongin, you were taken from us far too early, but your light shines on. It's in remembrance of you that I added Adam to this book because one of the last lessons you taught me was that books can and do make a difference at a time when I was somehow doubting that undeniable truth.

To my own children, you deserve far more thanks than I can fit in a few lines, but know that I love you with all that I have and appreciate you putting up with Neurotic Author Mom, who absently nods her head to everything you're saying while having another discussion with the voices that live in her head (wait, why did that come out in third person?). And hey, at least you know how to microwave your own meals and fold your own laundry now! You're welcome.

To Dan Ayres. A long time ago in a galaxy far, far away, I spotted you sitting in the back row of my third period Word Processing class on the first day of high school and heard a voice in my head whispering for the first time. *You're going to marry him someday.* And me being me, I wasn't frightened by this voice but instead, plopped myself down in the seat next to you. We may have taken a detour for four years after that fateful day, but everything happened for a reason. You're always asking me if you're Conner or Nate—and the answer is, you are both! You are the man I imagine in every love story I read (even if I do add on some Theo James biceps at times *wink, wink*). I love you more than the sum of allll my book boyfriends (which let's be honest, is a ridiculous amount). You are my BFF. You are my soul mate. You are the reason I know true love exists. You are too good for words.

To Starbucks, Hershey's, and Google… I could not have done this without you.

To everyone else that I love. There are too many of you to name, but you know who you are and you are awesomesauce! Thanks for being part of my crazy life.

And finally, to my readers. For the past three years, I've lived in the world of my characters. Through them I saw my own goals, dreams, truths, fears, and thoughts. I know you saw some of your own, too. Thank you so, so, sooo much for sticking with me through this three-part roller coaster ride, full of plot twists, cliff-hangers, first loves, lost loves, poignant moments, and teenage angst. Your letters give me all the feels, and you helped cross off the #1 item on my bucket list.

I'll say it one more time: Eighteen things can save a life. Ecclesiastes 3:1 said it best, "To every thing there is a season, and a time to every purpose under the heaven." Throughout all of life's seasons, there is no greater gift than being there for your friends. It's your turn now. Go do wild and crazy things together and don't worry if you have to come up with a Plan B for your life, or even a Plan Z. Because sometimes it takes a long time to become the person we're meant to be. You'll get there.

LITERATURE CIRCLE QUESTIONS

1. Discuss the prologue. Did you like hearing Nate's thoughts? What surprised you when seeing things from his point of view?

2. In the prologue, Nate says that he defines rich by counting all the things he has that money can't buy. List all the ways that you're 'rich.' Do you agree with Nate's philosophy, or would you trade everything on your list for a million dollars?

3. Olga says, "What I thought about most was how Conner broke my heart. I thought him waking up from his coma would be our second chance, but the truth was, we never even got our first chance." Do you agree? Why?

4. Fun Fact: Jamie Ayres met her husband the first day of high school when she was fourteen and heard the first of many voices in her head, whispering she'd marry him someday. In the meantime, she fell in love with someone else while her future husband became one of her best friends. How do you think that experience influenced the writing of this trilogy?

5. The series title is *My So-Called Afterlife*. Do you believe in life after death? If so, what do you think it's like?

6. How would you react if you found out someone could read your thoughts?

7. Do you think we control our thoughts or do our thoughts control us? Support your belief.

8. Do you agree with Nate's eighteen thoughts that are featured at the beginning of some chapters? If not, which ones do you disagree with and why? Which 'thought' was your favorite?

9. Has this novel changed the way you regard death? Grief? God? Why or why not?

10. In a therapy session, Dr. Judy tells Olga, "I'm saying some things can't be explained. I mean, do you understand how life began, the nature of time, whether there is free will or it's all destiny? Some things are so inherently complex that they will forever elude human understanding. No philosopher, scientist, or psychologist alive today has the foggiest notion of how the mind, time, or consciousness works. It's arrogant to suppose those things will *ever* be understood completely. I'd say forget the past and remember how to live." Do you agree? How does one forget a terrible event from the past and move on?

11. When Riel substituted in Nate's English class, he lectured on Alice in Wonderland and says the Red Queen asked two of the most important questions one can ever be asked. One, where did you come from? Two, where are you going? Do you agree they're the most important? Explain.

12. Where did you come from?

13. Where are you going?

14. Who is your favorite character from the series? Why? Do you know any people like the ones in the Jedi Order?

15. Knowing what you know now, do you think it was necessary for Conner, Olga, & Nate to die? Would you change the ending of *18 Thoughts*? If so, how?

16. If you had the chance to rewind your life and go back to the past, would you? Has there been a year you'd like a redo on? Was it

because that period of time was so much fun or because there's something you wish you could change?

17. Imagine the Jedi Order together at their ten year high school reunion. What do you think they're up to?

18. Make a list of your own thoughts, or beliefs, that represent how you view life and the world around you. Can you come up with eighteen?

THANK YOU
FOR READING

Please visit http://curiosityquills.com/reader-survey **to**
share your reading experience with the author of this book!

Caller 107, by Matthew Cox

When thirteen-year-old Natalie Rausch said she would die to meet DJ Crazy Todd, she did not mean to be literal.

Whenever WROK 107 ran contests, she would dive for the phone, getting only busy signals. At least, with her best friend, even losing was fun—before her parents ruined that too.

Her last desperate attempt to get their attention goes as wrong as possible. With no one to blame for her mess of a life but herself, karma comes full circle and gives her just a few hours to make up for two years' worth of mistakes—or be forever lost.

Catch Me When I Fall, by Vicki Leigh

Seventeen-year-old Daniel Graham has spent two-hundred years guarding humans from the Nightmares that feed off people's fears. Then he's given an assignment to watch over sixteen-year-old Kayla Bartlett, a patient in a psychiatric ward. When the Nightmares take an unprecedented interest in her, a vicious attack forces Daniel to whisk her away to Rome where others like him can keep her safe. But when the Protectors are betrayed and Kayla is kidnapped, Daniel will risk everything to save her—even his immortality.

Deadgirl, by B.C. Johnson

Lucy Day, 15 years old, is murdered on her very first date. Not one to take that kind of thing lying down, she awakens a day later with a seemingly human body and more than a little confusion. Lucy tries to return to her normal life, but the afterlife keeps getting in the way.

Lucy must put her mangled life back together, escape re-death, and learn to control her burgeoning powers while staying one step ahead of Abraham, the grim reaper out to put her back six feet under. But can she really sacrifice her loved ones to stay out of the grave?

Exacting Essence, by James Wymore

Megan's nightmares aren't normal; normal nightmares don't leave cuts and bruises on waking. Desperate, Megan's mother accepts a referral to a new therapist; a doctor dealing with the business of dreams—real dreams. The carnival of terrors that torments Megan nightly is all just a part of the Dreamworld, a separate reality experienced only by those aware enough to realize it. On her quest to destroy the Nightmares feeding from her fear, Megan encounters Intershroud, the governing entity of the Dreamworld, and must work with her new friends to stop the agency from continuing its evil agenda, and to destroy her own Nightmares for good.

CPSIA information can be obtained
at www.ICGtesting.com
Printed in the USA
FSOW01n1108100216
16784FS